THE RAPTURE EFFECT

A Bluejay International Edition

First printing: February 1987

A TOR Book

Published by Tom Doherty Associates, Inc.
49 West 24 Street
New York, N.Y. 10010

Cover art by David B. Mattingly

ISBN: 0-312-94381-4

Printed in the United States of America

0 9 8 7 6 5 4 3 2 1

THE RAPTURE EFFECT

JEFFREY A. CARVER

TOR

*

To
the Writing Group
for years of making me work harder
and making the story stronger

*

and to
Jim Frenkel
for years of faithful and perceptive editing
and friendship

*

and a special dedication to
the seven crew members of the spaceship
Challenger
and all those before them
who gave their lives reaching for the stars

*

AUTHOR'S NOTE

Pali is pronounced **PAY**-lee.
Kyd is pronounced **KIDD**.
Ramo is pronounced **RAY**-mo.
Sage is pronounced like the spice.

All alien names are spelled phonetically:
All g's are hard.
An h signifies a slight overexhalation.
An exclamation mark signifies a click, best reproduced by
clicking the tongue against the roof of the mouth.
For example:
!!Ghint is pronounced **"click-click"-GHINT**.
Or!ge is pronounced **OR-"click"-geh**.
Dououraym is pronounced **DOO-OO-ray-m**.

All the rest are easy.

PART ONE

There is a pleasure in the pathless woods,
There is a rapture on the lonely shore. . . .
                                    —LORD BYRON

The only sounds in the heart of the planet were those of the planet itself—the shudder of crustal plates, the rumble of the mantle, the murmur of bubbling magma. They were the innermost sounds of the world, and they had been there since the beginning.

But closer to the surface, in caverns darker than night, in secret places hot with steam and dank with condensation, other sounds could be heard, tiny sounds: vapors whispering and water dripping and stone creaking as it settled, a melancholy choir amplified by the subterranean walls. Surrounded by the choir, and groaning with their own harshly guttural voices, were the creatures who had no name.

Clinging to the cavern walls like stalactites, the creatures drew upon seismic vents for warmth and dissolved minerals for sustenance; and when they changed position at all, it was by creeping movements, agonizingly slow. And yet, despite the darkness, they were not without the power of vision; and despite their confinement, they were not without the power to roam their world. They had other ways of seeing, other ways of moving, of knowing. Other ways of imposing their will.

For now, and for eons past, they had been quiescent. But their time for speaking was coming, and when it came, the world would tremble in fear of them. When others dared invade their dark privacy, the creatures would be seen and heard at last, and they would be felt. Oh yes, they would be felt. . . .

Chapter 1

There was a blur of light reflected on the inside of his helmet, then nothing. The stars gleamed, pinpricks of light against the dark of space.

All signs of the battle had disappeared.

Harybdartt blinked groggily, and scanned. There was no movement around him, no indications on the flicker-readers at the edge of his helmet. No activity in nearby space. No sign of the mother(ship), or any of the scouts. No sign of the enemy.

There was nothing but stars. Stars, and emptiness, and the hiss of cosmic radiations; and at his back, a great shard of rock.

(Ship)brothers . . . hurt . . . explosion . . .

Disconnected thoughts. Motes of awareness that defined him, Harybdartt. How to corral the awarenesses: review the situation . . . survival first . . . sanity later.

First:

Where was the mother(ship)? All readings on that flicker-band were silent; it had vanished. Escaped—back through lightspeed, through transient space?

No.

Of course. Now he remembered: The mother(ship) had died —exploding, spewing Ell like seeds from a pod. If he had not been suited for emergency repairs near the outer shell of the (ship), he too would have perished. Instead, he was thrown clear to drift alone, semiconscious, while the battle sputtered on; while the (fleet), broken and brainless, dispersed.

He remembered falling—stunned by the impact, gravity vanishing, blood burning, tumbling away with the dying outcry of the (ship). Somehow he'd stabilized himself and found shelter against the same asteroid the mother(ship) had been using for concealment, until a passing Outsider had caught and destroyed it. Clinging to consciousness, he'd tried to follow the battle's conclusion; but his vision and awareness had fogged and slipped away . . .

. . . until his awakening to emptiness, and silence in the readers . . . alone in an alien star system. Any Ell(ship)s that

4

had survived would by now have fled. The enemy, apparently, had fled as well.

Harybdartt scanned his life-support readers. He could survive for a number of watches, provided he remained at rest. What he could accomplish in that time—or ten times that time—he didn't know. But as long as he remained alive, he would guard his position, and should the enemy appear, he would engage it in battle.

The stars passed slowly about his head as the asteroid tumbled. He watched, and he waited.

In time, a glimmer of light caught his attention, moving among the stars. He came to alertness and checked the flicker-reader. There was a body maneuvering in space, nearly at the limits of the short-range readers. It was a small thing, emitting energy in short, sharp, treacherous bursts. It was the enemy, sweeping slowly through space.

Searching for survivors?

Harybdartt left his own sensors on passive, and tracked the enemy as it crossed the sky until it was eclipsed from view by the asteroid. He waited patiently . . . counting for its return to view as it passed around behind him.

What he saw next was not the enemy, but another point of light, flickering. He scoped it and strained to focus the image. An Ell fighter(ship), tumbling? He studied the readings. It was still alive. This could change the situation. But could he signal the Ell(ship) without alerting the enemy?

Perhaps if he acted quickly, while the asteroid shielded him . . . a light-burst signal. There might not be another chance.

He removed a focusable flare from his belt. He pointed it at the Ell(ship) and blinked it once.

The enemy twinkled suddenly into sight, moving tangentially to the Ell(ship)'s course. Harybdartt quickly cut off his flare. He wondered if the fighter(ship) could still defend itself.

The answer came a moment later.

A sparkle of bluish light danced around the enemy like a halo. Harybdartt scoped it, sliding a protective filter into place. From the Ell(ship) there came a sputter of weapons-fire; but it was too feeble, too late. The halo around the enemy dimmed

... and the Ell(ship), or what was left of it, dissolved in a violet flower of radiation.

Harybdartt uttered a silent *requiescat* to more (fleet)mates passed from life. He would join them soon, no doubt. He slowed his breathing and returned his flare to his belt. He watched as the enemy craft glided on into the darkness, out of the range of his flicker-reader. Finally he was rewarded by a brief, distant glow of reddish light. The enemy had crossed lightspeed into transient—to return, presumably, to the star system of its origin.

Harybdartt relaxed deliberately. He blinked, watching the starfield shift slowly as he and the asteroid tumbled.

There was nothing else for him to do.

Nothing but to watch the stars and to guard his position, and when the time came, to die.

Chapter 2

The title floated in the shimmer-door: *Public Affairs Department / Arts Division.* Above the title glowed the Company insigne: three intersecting, electric blue tetrahedrons. Most of the offices were empty; it was late in the day. But in the rear office, a young man and two women were standing beside the arts director's desk.

"This is what you'd be working on," Pali George said, clicking a switch. A large holo-image glowed to life in the air before her desk. It was an abstract figure of milky white light, swirling and twisting within a background of darkness. "This is a sketch I put together myself, using some graphics routines and file shots of stardrive effects. Obviously I'm no artist, but it should give you the general idea."

She turned to the dark-haired young man, a gnostic designer

named Sage DeWeiler, who was seeing the image for the first time. There was no immediate reaction on his face except the nervousness that had been there from the start. Pali glanced at her assistant, Kyd Metango, but she too was watching Sage. Kyd was a petitely slender woman with sparkling green eyes and blond hair cut in a rakish wave, longer on the right side than the left. She had her arms crossed over her chest as she watched Sage.

Pali looked back at the wiry young man, who was scratching his neck thoughtfully. He spoke without turning. "A sculpture, you say?"

Pali sighed patiently. "Right," she repeated. "A kinetic light-sculpture composed of a quark-matrix field. It'll float in orbit near one of the space cities. Picture us standing where people would be, looking out at it."

Sage nodded. "It'll be big, then." He turned, squinting at her.

Pali bobbed her head in assent. "It'll be big." Kyd, she thought, I hope you know what you're doing. It had been Kyd's idea to borrow Sage from the records department as their gnostic designer. Kyd claimed he was brilliant—or at least had potential. Pali's impression, based on prior encounters, was that he was flat-out lazy. Nevertheless, she'd promised to give him the benefit of the doubt. "I don't know what the structure to project it will look like," she said. "That's one thing we need to learn. But the idea is to use the stardrive components to create a self-maintaining energy field. We'll commission an artist to design the actual sculpture, and of course we'll need a physicist to help determine if it can really be done."

"What do you think?" Kyd asked Sage.

For a moment, he simply continued staring at the twisting image, scratching his head. Pali and Kyd exchanged impatient glances; Kyd made a covert gesture of encouragement. "You won't need a physicist," Sage said suddenly, turning.

"I beg your pardon?" Pali blinked in surprise. "We're talking about doing something pretty sophisticated here." She had described the idea once to a Company physicist, who had told her that it *might* work, but then again, it might not. Who was Sage to tell her—?

"Sure, but the physicists won't know any more about it than the gnostic system," Sage said. "Whatever you need, the system can handle it."

Pali's gaze traveled to Kyd, who raised her eyebrows in mystification. "Are you sure of that?"

"Sure I'm sure." Sage sounded irritated. "You know, everyone thinks we have all these genius scientists. But it's really the system that does half their work. *Most* of their work. They'd be lost without it."

"Are you saying"—Pali cleared her throat—"that you can get the gnosys to handle the entire theoretical analysis for us?"

"Sure." He frowned at the holo. "Be a pretty big job, though. I don't know if I really . . ." His words trailed off and he shrugged listlessly.

Kyd prompted him. "What, Sage?"

He mumbled something inaudible. Kyd prompted him again, and he answered with, "What's this for again?"

Pali closed her eyes and opened them slowly. "It's for our arts fulfillment," she said, striving for patience. "You know about that, right?" Of course he did. But there was no need to tell him the whole thing: that her department had just two weeks to commit thirty million in grants before the Company was in violation of the arts-fulfillment laws—and that it was only in desperation, with no time to find outside applicants, that she'd even considered putting forward her own proposal.

"Uh-huh," Sage said.

"Well, this is just preliminary. We'd be borrowing you from your department until it's more fully developed and—ultimately, we hope—approved."

Sage rubbed his eyes, nodding. Kyd asked softly, "Do you think you might like to work on it, Sage?"

He looked up as though startled to find himself the object of the question. He blushed a little. "Well, I—"

Kyd added, "You did say that things were slow down in records."

"Well . . . it's mostly self-maintaining now."

"Because you set it up that way," Kyd pointed out. "Did you know, Pali, that Sage redesigned the whole system down there?"

Sage's face reddened. "I was just making my job easier."

"Well, it showed initiative," Kyd said. "And I think you could handle *this* job too, if you wanted to. Do you want to?"

The young designer looked down at his hands and swallowed. "I—well—" He softened under Kyd's gaze. "I guess so," he murmured finally.

Pali blinked in wonder. She'd been sure that he would say no. She was never going to understand the effect that Kyd had on men. Maybe it was those green eyes of hers—men seemed to fall for them instantly. Maybe it was pheromones. Whatever, it worked. She cleared her throat. "Shall we consider you on board, then—at least for now?"

Sage nodded. When Pali put out her hand, he shook it limply. "I think I'd better be going," he said.

"All right. Thanks for coming by." Pali watched as Sage trailed out of the office. She took a deep breath and stared at the holo-sketch as Kyd closed the door and came back to stand beside her. "Kyd, I do hope you're right about him," she murmured.

"Pali, I know he's a little—"

"*Honestly*, Kyd!" She turned to the younger woman. "I've never seen anyone so—" She groped for words. "I mean, he didn't exactly *stampede* us with his enthusiasm."

"He's just insecure and a little unmotivated. But I really think it's just a matter of—"

"I know, I know. Lighting a fire under him."

"Well, yes." Kyd tipped her head, gazing at Pali earnestly. Her blond hair fell to one side, brushing across her eyes until she straightened her head. "And he knows more science than you would think, from where he works. He has no corporate ambitions—but he has talent."

Pali laughed and raised her hands in surrender. "Okay! Anyway, we've hired him, so let's just hope he works out. You can be his handler." The smile fell from her lips as she walked behind her desk and stared at the view there of the city, from high in the Company tower.

"Pali, what's wrong?"

Pali shook her head. "It's nothing."

"Bull. You're upset."

Pali sighed. "You haven't been in the department-heads meetings lately. Those bastards. They wouldn't release the funds before, when it might have helped. But now they're making it all our problem. Suddenly all they care about is that the Justice Department is waiting to lower the boom because they haven't spent the money."

"Well, they can hardly blame you," Kyd said.

Pali let the comment pass. Of course they could blame her; they were already blaming her. They had no appreciation for how long it took to put together a program like this. She chuckled bitterly. "If this project is a flop, you may be the new Arts Director." She turned to Kyd. "I'm not even sure if they'll *consider* this proposal."

"They should. It'd be a great public-relations move. Company-made components in a huge orbital sculpture? It's perfect."

"But it's not exactly by the book."

"You mean because it's your proposal, instead of an outside submission?" Pali nodded. Kyd ran her fingers through her sandy blond hair. It fell back without a strand being misplaced. "That shouldn't matter, Pali—as long as there's an outside artist and it's a public piece."

"Ah, they're rule-worshipers," Pali murmured, and at once wished that she hadn't. She was starting to let her worry turn into self-pity: bad sign.

"Pali?" Kyd was gazing at her, a finger against her cheekbone. Her eyes seemed to glow, intent and warm. A grin was spreading across her face. "Pali, that's not the only thing we're talking about, is it? I think this is something that you just plain *want to do.* For yourself. Am I right?"

Pali reached out and switched off the holo without answering. Suddenly she didn't feel much like the director here. Was this what it felt like to the artists who came, hats in hand, looking for fulfillment grants?

"Grab it while you can," Kyd said. "It's your dream."

Pali gazed back at the city. Wouldn't it be nice if this project earned her a genuine sixtieth-floor window instead of a holoview? Well, which do you want? she thought—status, or something to tell your children someday? She broke off that thought and turned again. "All right. Yes. If we can sell it, I damn well want to do it."

"Good!" Kyd said, beaming. "Well, buck up—we're on our way. We've already got ourselves a gnostic designer."

"Now we just need Russell's approval for research time, and an artist."

Kyd chuckled. "Pali, can we start that in the morning?"

Pali looked at the time, and her eyes widened. "My God, you're right! Let's go home!"

Pushing aside the remains of her chicken wings and curry, Pali sat back on her couch and nervously twirled a half-full wineglass and stared at Chagall's painting of "The Circus Rider" on her mantel-screen. It wasn't what she needed right now, she decided. She reached for the screen controller and flipped on the vispy. She tried and rejected a variety of drama and music channels; finally, in irritation, she switched it off and left the wall a mirror. Raising her wineglass, she squinted through the pale, faintly golden liquid. She took a sip and shrugged. It was cheap California Chablis. She could afford better, but had succumbed to a rush of frugality. With her job in jeopardy . . .

Stop it, she thought. If you think defeat, you're halfway there already. She could find a new job if she had to—she had the experience. But her anxious stomach thought otherwise.

Then why so scared? Kyd was enthusiastic, wasn't she? Granted, Kyd had only been working for her a few months, but she had good sense and Pali trusted her, and sometimes you just had to go with your instincts. So what was wrong? *Are you upset because you don't have a man to call for approval? Is that it? Because Jonathan couldn't handle your commitment to your job, and before that David . . .*

Stop it! She drank the rest of her wine in an angry gulp. Maybe there was more truth there than she cared to admit. Trapped by some damn-fool expectation that she'd never been able to rid herself of. Rising suddenly, she padded across the hardwood floor into the kitchenette and dropped her dishes into the 'clave. Well, there was one man she *had* to check it out with, and that was Russell Thurber, her department head. If he didn't approve the gnostic research, the project would be stillborn. But she was pretty sure she could handle Russell. Good old compulsive Russell. They hadn't been very good lovers together, but she could still count on him.

She returned to the living room, turned on the console, and punched up her access to the Company's gnostic library. "System, show me that list of available artists."

As she waited, she gazed at her reflection in the mirrored wall. She sighed, smoothing her hair. Pali, you have no cause to complain, she thought. And it was true; she was an attractive woman—she had a warm, full face, and her flowing auburn hair was the envy of the department; and even if she thought her figure a tad matronly (*at thirty-nine?*), even in her worst moments she still liked her deep brown eyes. She couldn't help thinking of Kyd, though—Kyd who was in her thirties, too, but had the looks and energy of a woman ten years younger. There was something about Kyd that set her apart, some special appeal. . . .

She caught herself and shook her head. Quit chasing after your youth, she thought—you're never going to catch it.

"Kyd, when you have a minute, could I see you?" Pali said, passing through the outer office late the next morning.

"Sure, Pali—what's up?" Kyd broke away from three other workers and followed Pali into her office.

"Well, Russell gave me the approval," Pali said with satisfaction.

"Great! When do we get started?"

"As soon as possible." Pali sat down at her desk and switched on her console. "I've been trying to come up with an artist. The gnosys recommends this guy. Ever heard of him?"

Kyd peered across at the screen. "Ramo Romano? I don't think so. Who is he?"

"A light-sculptor with gnosys experience. Good artistic credentials." Pali's finger traced down the screen. "Madison, Wisconsin, Library. Beijing Best Western. Cultural Center lobby in Rio—I know that one—it's beautiful." She cleared her throat uneasily. "But his business credentials are terrible. He's a prima donna. He keeps getting fired from jobs."

"Great."

"But according to the gnostic search, his work comes closest to what we want. And he lives here in the city."

"Okay. What do you want me to do?"

"Would you mind looking him up? Talking to him?"

"Sure." Kyd caught the look in Pali's eye. "What?"

"Well—" Pali cleared her throat. "You notice that he doesn't have an agent, and there's no address listed for him."

"Sounds like he doesn't want work very badly."

"Apparently he's well off, and his attitude is—if you want to see me, come do it on my terms. Meaning, in one of his hangouts." Pali was uneasy with what she was about to suggest. "You don't have to do this. But I thought . . . Well, you might be more comfortable than I would be, anyway."

"Where do I have to go?" Kyd asked cautiously.

"There's a place here in the city called the Lie High Club. Do you know it?"

Chapter 3

A crimson-and-gold shaft of light swept across the dance floor. Kyd stood watching the dancers on the floor, and those weightless in the sparkling senso-probe field overhead. She let her head bob to the urgent, bass-heavy thrum of the music.

O'Reilly's Lie High Club, she thought with a wry shake of her head. Of all places. Yes, she knew it. It was one of her hangouts, too. But she'd kept a straight face in answer to Pali's question.

The Lie High was an enormous place, with a dance area encircled by tables and staggered balconies and several long, curved bars. The musicians' dais floated in the center of the senso-field, above the dance floor. The club was lighted mostly by the senso-field itself and by fans of light that swept down from the ceiling, changing color with the pulse of the music. Kyd liked the theatrical atmosphere. It brought back childhood memories of stage shows she'd attended with her grandfather —memories of a happier time before she'd become a slave to her own peculiar abilities, before her childhood had been lost. Before she'd gotten herself into this most peculiar and uncomfortable situation. It was a living, she thought; but she disliked living a lie.

She surveyed the area, letting the music flow through her, and finally meandered toward the nearest of the bars. "Gil," she called.

"Howdy, Kyd!" said a bushy-headed bartender. "What can I get you?"

"Mineral fizz. How's it been?"

Gil tugged at the corners of a dark mustache. "Slow tonight." He poured the drink, sparkling under the bar lights, and slid it across to her. "What's new with you?"

Kyd shrugged and sipped her drink. She turned and watched the dancers while Gil served another customer. When he was free again, she asked, "Gil, do you know a fellow by the name of Ramo? Ramo Romano?"

"Ramo—?" Gil scratched his head, then laughed. "You mean the crazy Brazilian?"

"Maybe. I'm not sure—"

"That's what we call him," Gil said. "I have no idea if he's actually Brazilian. Sure, I know him. But I don't think he's your type." She arched her eyebrows and Gil added hastily, "Don't get me wrong. But he's a bit of a mover, and you're a classy

lady." Kyd felt a blush rise to her face. Gil grinned, and gestured queryingly to the next customer. "He's an artist of some
sort, I hear."

"You happen to know if he's here tonight?" Kyd said.

"Dunno. Let me ask." Gil filled the customer's order, then
strolled to the other end of the bar and spoke with his partner
before strolling back. "Ozzie says he's here—probably out on
the floor."

"What's he look like?" Kyd turned to scan the dance area.
She felt Gil's quizzical stare behind her. "I just want to talk
to him," she said testily.

Gil shrugged, hiding a grin. "None of *my* business." He
shaded his eyes and pointed. "There he is. The guy up in the
senso—in the red and orange suit."

Kyd raised her eyes to the dancers floating in the air. It took
a moment; then she spotted him—a brightly dressed man
performing wild gyrations in the air. She watched him curiously. There was something familiar about him, but she
couldn't see his face. Was it possible that she knew him?

Only one way to find out. With a wink at Gil, she headed
toward the dance floor for a better look.

It was impossible to tell anything from floor level. After a
few minutes Kyd sighed, set her glass on an empty table, and
slipped through the crowd toward the riser-beam.

The golden light caught her full in the face. Dazzled, she
turned her palms up and let the beam read the charge-chip in
her finger. Then she spun and strode, the beat of the band
pulsing in her feet now, and the shaft slanted, keeping her
centered in its spotlight as she danced through the crowd until
the man in orange and red somersaulted overhead. She
snapped her fingers and raised her hands high.

She scarcely felt her feet leave the floor; but through the
glow, she saw the other dancers falling away beneath her. She
rose like an angel, borne on a golden beam of light until it
intersected with the green sparkle of the senso-probe. As the
riser-field merged into the dance-field, she touched a switch on

her belt and her grey blouse came alight with rippling colors and shimmered with patches of fractional-second transparency. She began to move to the music again.

Another kind of glow entered into her; she felt the welcoming movements of the other dancers, the sensation flowing into her from the field. The music began touching her not just in her ears but in her mind, as the senso took hold. The shifting lights and weightlessness caressed her like a breeze, and images and emotions that were not her own blossomed within her. Someone was thinking of a woods, and someone else of laughter and sun and clouds; and several were dreaming of erotic love. The images twinkled into life and vanished again with the movement of the music.

For a while she kept to herself, allowing her sensations to slip gradually into the field, mingling with those of the other dancers. It was a light rain of mood and feeling, and she let herself become relaxed by it, the music and the lights and the mood; and she rotated in the air, swinging gently, watching her fellow dancers.

At last she turned for a look at her flamboyant quarry, Ramo Romano. He was an olive-complexioned man with dark curly hair and vivid golden brown eyes, and he was wearing a blazing red great-sleeved shirt and brilliant orange pants. He was dancing solo with broad, rhythmic movements and a self-assured, almost arrogant nonchalance. His gaze met hers—and instantly she thought, *You!* She struggled to keep the beat of the dance and to contain her emotions at the same time. She knew why he'd looked familiar; it was because she'd fought off his advances, more than once, right here at the Lie High Club.

For a heartbeat, the field rippled with the heat lightning of her confused reactions. Ramo cocked his head and grinned broadly. He winked and flapped his arms and hopped side to side in rhythmic gyrations, his great red sleeves billowing like wings. Kyd began to twist away in helpless consternation, but he turned sideways in the air and spun, and she laughed in spite of herself. While Ramo completed his whirl, she recomposed herself. By the time he'd straightened up, she was bobbing again with the music, watching him with studied casualness.

Ramo, however, was grinning widely. Kyd immediately realized: one, that he remembered her, probably better than she
remembered him; and two, that he was staring without a trace
of embarrassment at her blouse. Streams of color were racing
through it, and the fabric was flickering, giving microsecond
glimpses of her torso and her breasts. It was not particularly
risqué as costumes went here; but perhaps, she thought, his
interest was a little too strong. She twisted away, and her hand
touched her belt, shortening the duration of the transparency.

When she spun back, Ramo was close enough to touch. She
saw now that he was at least mildly intoxicated, and it wasn't
going to be easy to stay out of his reach. She kept her hands
in motion—to the front and up and down. Her hips moved of
their own accord as the band segued into a jazzy drumsynth
number, and in her head was a flurry of lust—not hers—and
ripples of enthusiasm from somewhere else in the field. There
was a psychedelic flutter of light, and in the cover of the strobe
effect, she floated backward and rotated away.

Throughout that number, everywhere she turned, Ramo was
mugging at her, flopping his head from side to side or mouth-
ing words that she was grateful she couldn't hear. She caught
her breath in the pause following the number and, spinning
slowly away, hoped that by the time the band took a break, she
could gather her wits for another encounter. She didn't need
any tricks to attract him, that was certain. The pause stretched
longer, and Ramo drifted around in front of her, beaming, and
then she realized that the band had already left the dais.

"Hi-i-i there," Ramo drawled. She nodded, searching for an
opening remark, and he added, "You couldn't stay away.
That's okay, I'm used to it." He pumped his arms up and down;
the motion drove him toward her.

Kyd crossed her arms. "Couldn't stay away?" she echoed
mockingly; but she was so amused by his absurdly earnest
expression that she couldn't help chuckling.

He was startled and delighted. If she was throwing down the
gauntlet, he accepted gleefully. "You didn't come here just to
admire my dancing."

"No. I came to admire *my* dancing."

"*I* admire your dancing," Ramo said, his eyes roving over her body. "Even when you're not dancing." His gaze lingered over her crossed arms.

"I'm so glad." Kyd gave her body a slow twist away. Her hand brushed her belt and clicked off the transparency effect.

"You don't act very glad." He crossed his own arms as he drifted after her, floating at a forty-five-degree angle. He shook his head, and his curly hair bobbed as though on springs.

"Well-l-l, Mr. Romano . . ." she said, imitating his drawl.

"*Ah!* You learned my name. You *are* interested. You came to see me." His face lighted in triumph. "Call me Ramo. Ray-mo! Please."

Kyd sighed. "I came here to *talk* to you, Mr.—Ramo."

"*Talk?*" he shouted. "You came to dance! To feast upon the music with me—to share with me your spirit—to drink my admiration of your beauty! I know women, and I know—"

"Ramo, I came to *talk.*"

"—how you cannot say yes, and yet, deep in your heart there is no way you can say no. Your beauty is—"

"Talk, Ramo. *Talk!*"

He hovered close to her, his hands framing her face as though for a picture. "So you say, yes." Chuckling, he began dancing in place, humming the refrain of the last song. He paused and cocked his head. "Why aren't you talking? This is your chance."

"Shall we go down?" Kyd suggested.

"Eh?" He straightened and looked dismayed.

"Down where we can talk? In privacy?"

Ramo gazed at her with exaggerated soulfulness. "Ah," he said softly. "Privacy." He smiled. He clapped his hands once, twice. A shaft of red light enveloped him, isolating him from the senso-field.

Kyd clapped likewise. Together, in matching beams, they descended to the floor.

The light of a tremendous waterfall illuminated both of their faces. Kyd was pacing before the gigantic holo that faced the balcony while Ramo followed her. He moved to cut her off.

"Stop it, Ramo!" she insisted.

"But why did you come, then?" Ramo spread his arms, and his great-sleeves billowed.

"Problems down there?" called a male voice from the nearby bar. A tall, blondish bartender was watching.

"It's all right, Smitty. Thanks," Kyd called back. To Ramo, she said, "If you would try *listening* a minute . . ." Growling in frustration, she faced the balcony railing and looked out over the club. She hadn't expected him to be so singleminded.

"You looked very beautiful before, you know," Ramo said, alongside her.

She sighed. "What?"

"You looked even more beautiful before you turned off your—" Ramo gestured at her blouse.

Kyd glanced down. Her blouse was dark grey in the light of the holo. She fingered the switch at her belt. "Would you like the colors back?" she said softly.

"The colors, and the"—Ramo made a careless gesture—"the other."

She allowed a tiny smile. "Just the colors," she said, pressing the switch. Her blouse remained opaque, but soft shades of red, as though glowing out of the satin itself, rippled in gentle waves across her.

"Ah, but you have such beautiful—"

"Ramo!" she said, interrupting him. "We have business to discuss."

He held his forehead. "Ow! Business? How *can* you? Here?"

"I'm sorry. I thought you were an artist first and a playboy second." She sighed carefully. "I'm disappointed."

Ramo started. *"Artist,"* he muttered. "Hah!"

"Isn't that how you earn your living?"

He shrugged morosely. "So a few of us are allowed to scratch out a living from our art. Do you know why? It's because we're pawns, hired to keep the masses happy. That's why." He stared at her with a hard, accusing expression. "Do you know anyone who truly *cares* for art?"

"Well . . ." Kyd was startled by his cynicism, not that it wasn't justified. "Maybe not to the extent you'd *like*. But that doesn't mean nobody cares. In fact . . . I was hoping that you'd be interested in discussing a project with me. A large project —an important project—for which we have need of a good sculptor."

Ramo scowled.

"But I didn't know you felt such contempt for your own work. I'd been told differently." She looked away. "I'm sorry. I won't take any more of your time." She turned to leave.

"Wait!" Ramo cried. She paused, staring out over the dance floor. "You wish to work?" he said. "Together? You and I?"

She slowly swung back to face him.

His eyes clouded. "Come. Please," he said mutedly. He guided her toward a table. "Please! A thousand apologies, please! Let us sit and talk together, you and I."

Chapter 4

Pali looked up, startled, as Ramo Romano stalked into her office. "I am *not* going to work with him, and that's it!" he exploded. "Just forget it." Pali's mouth dropped open as Ramo stalked back out.

She caught up with him in the lounge. "Ramo, what's the trouble? Why don't you sit? Do you want some coffee?"

"I can't work with him. You'll have to get someone else." Ramo stamped his foot and turned away.

The gesture reminded Pali of an unhappy horse. She crossed to the sideboard. "Do you mind if I have a cup?" She poured, stirred in sweetener, and faced him. "Why don't you sit down and tell me what's wrong? Kyd tells me that Sage is an excellent gnostic designer."

Ramo snorted and paced the length of the tiny lounge.

"Designer, my ass. I ask him to show me some system specs
and all he can say is, 'What for?' What's he *think* it's for, the
twit?"

Pali touched her lower lip. "If it's a problem in communication . . . Ramo, won't you *please* sit down?"

"It's not a problem in communication! It's a problem in
brains!"

Pali groaned inwardly. All this work getting her hotshot
team together—she'd gotten authorization for use of the research files, though it had taken longer than she'd hoped—and
now the whole thing was self-destructing before it even got
started. Sage DeWeiler had been acting sullen all morning,
Ramo Romano seemed intent upon alienating everyone in the
department—and the two had lasted barely an hour in the
same room together. How much more time and patience did
she have?

Ramo finally dropped into a chair. "A job like this is hard
enough without some birdbrain working alongside you."

"Well, I understand the feeling," Pali said carefully, taking
a nearby seat. She crossed her legs and smoothed out her long
skirt, trying to think of an answer. "Look, I know it can be a
problem working with people if the chemistry isn't right. But
there must be something we can do about it—"

"Fire him."

She ignored the interruption. "If you have certain requirements of the gnosys designer—"

Ramo snorted again.

"—maybe we can get those across better," she finished de-
terminedly, thinking, Did I want to become a social worker?
She eyed Ramo. "Problems in communication usually can be
solved."

Ramo shrugged. "You're not paying me enough to put up
with this crap," he muttered, scratching his nose.

"Well, look." Pali sighed with frustration. "Sage does have
trouble working with people, but he also has skills that we need.
Both of you do. Isn't Kyd helping to smooth things out between you?" The question seemed to make him nervous. "All
right—it might be a little rough going at first," she went on.

"But this could be a big piece for you—for all of us." She sipped her coffee with forced calm. "What do you say?"

Ramo sighed and rested his head back against the wall with an expression of weariness.

"Like some coffee now?" Pali asked.

He scowled and, to her intense relief, nodded at last.

Sage was staring anxiously at the floor as Kyd talked. He nodded, just to let her know he was listening.

". . . even if you're not used to working together, I know you have the ability. You just need to tap into it. Think of the way you might tap into a level of the gnosys . . ."

Her voice was so gentle, so persuasive, it was almost bewitching; his frustration was melting away. He raised his head and instantly glanced away in embarrassment. He was trying hard not to develop a terrible crush on her, and failing. Of course he would work for her, even if it was hard—even if it meant working with that obnoxious artist again. Finally he nodded his assent.

"Wonderful," she said with a dazzling smile. "Why don't you go grab something to eat, then set things up. I'll be down in a little while. All right?"

He rose and hurried upstairs to the commissary, where he bought some Riskie Crispies and a moke. Munching crispies out of the box, he returned to the rap room and began the setup. By the time the others trooped in, he had the fields lighted in test patterns. "It's ready," he said nervously, looking up from the boards.

Ramo stood off to one side, drumming his fingers against his leg. He was staring at the rapture-fields—two luminous green force-fields, each about the size of a person, each enveloped by a larger, fainter levitation-field of bluish light. Ramo's anger seemed to have evaporated.

"Sage, are *you* ready?"

Sage turned. Pali had asked the question; but Kyd's wink and smile dispelled his nervousness. He nodded and touched a control. "You know what you're doing, right, Ramo?"

"Yep."

"You have your questions? Your design specs?"

"I'm *ready*. Let's go." Ramo stepped into the nearest levitation-field. It sparkled around him, lifted him off the floor, and
floated him into the inner, green-glowing rapture-field. He
visibly relaxed, the field tilting him backward slightly, his eyes
closing. Sage pointed, saying to Pali and Kyd, "You can watch
on those monitors." Then he stepped into the other field, into
weightlessness. The rapture-field brightened around him in a
luxurious cyan haze.

Several moments passed, and sparkling bits of light swarmed
around him like ethereal diamonds, flying into his eyes. He
stiffened, then relaxed as he felt the internal touch of the
gnostic system. At first it was just a tingle in his skull, a lightness, but it quickly blossomed into his thoughts like a flame.
His breathing slowed; his body was nearly forgotten. The light
of the flame took on pattern and form: the tracings of the
outermost layers of the gnostic system.

[Where do we go from here?]
[. . . *from here?*]
[. . . *from here?*]

He winced at the echo and remembered that he was not
alone. Ramo was with him, their minds linked by the connection with the system. There was feedback in the field.

[Are you there?]
[. . . *you there?*]
[. . . *you there?*]
[Wait.]
[. . . *wait.*]
[. . . *wait.*]

He scanned the traceries and located the correct node. With
a touch of his thoughts, he adjusted the sensitivity. [How's
this? Better?]

[It's okay,] Ramo said. [So where are we?]

[Outside the records stacks. We need to locate the access for
research functions.] Sage thought a moment. [I'm going to try
a backdoor approach, to bypass some of the bureaucratic controls. The way we're cleared to go in will take forever; I don't
think Pali understood the level of clearance we need.]

[Wonderful. Why didn't you mention that before?]

[I won't know until we try,] Sage said irritably. [It'll stop us if it doesn't like what we're doing. But if we can't get what we want one way, we'll try another.] He sensed Ramo's grudging acknowledgment. [You figure out your questions.]

[Lead on.]

Sage began to move. It was almost a kinesthetic movement, up one pathway and down another, crossing various connection points. They were aiming for an area in which he had little direct experience; but he knew the overall layout, and since there was generally more than one entrance to any part of the system, he was confident he could probe his way into the level they needed. System security was a porous kind of affair if one knew the ropes; that's what designers were for.

The paths to the research system were a tangle of intersecting lines. Sage studied them carefully, illuminating them like a living three-dimensional map, choosing his direction partly by knowledge and partly by intuition. One by one, he located openings, and the maze gradually untangled before them. At last he found a connection he'd been looking for: he felt something opening, his awareness expanding.

[What are you doing?] he heard.

For a moment, he was too busy to answer. A new landscape was opening up, as though a filter were sliding back to reveal a twisting, four-dimensional geometry. He scanned, taking in large sections of the map, processing the possibilities in a fraction of the time it would have taken him just moments ago. He found an opening: a cleft in the contours that led inward. [I think that's what we want,] he said, diving.

[Tell me what's going on!]

[I've tied into an enhancement circuit,] he answered nonchalantly, and before there was time for a reply, he had slipped into the opening, and yet another world unfolded in an eyeblink: the research matrix.

[Damn it, why didn't you say so?] Ramo's voice was a distant, angry whisper.

Sage knew that he should reply, but at the moment he was too busy reconnoitering. There was a wealth of information here, a spider's web of access threads. He darted quickly through the matrix, seeking a point for questioning. As he did so, he sensed Ramo tying into the enhancement circuit and moving off in his own search pattern. It irritated Sage to admit it, but obviously Ramo knew his way around gnostic systems, too.

A bit of searching brought them to a query channel. He called Ramo, and they floated together in the center of a tetrahedron of light. [Let's try it from here,] Sage said. [You can ask the basic questions, and it'll refer us to another area if it can't handle it here.] He felt the equivalent of a shrug from Ramo. The artist was still fuming at being left behind a moment ago. [System—are we in contact?]

There was a tremor. The system was listening.

[System,] Ramo called, [we require theoretical analysis of the following problem. Problem: to create a quark-matrix sculpture consisting of a force-field projected in free space from an orbital platform. Proposed solution: to modify components of the McConwell Company's stardrive system, to alter the consequential side effects in a visible and controllable manner. Request: examine the physics and provide a feasibility and design analysis.]

After a moment, the system answered in a flat male voice, [Please elaborate the reason for this study.]

Uh-oh, Sage thought. He wasn't prepared with a justification. Had he outsmarted himself with his cleverness in gaining access?

Ramo started to answer. [It was proposed by—]

There was a sudden, silent earthquake. The landscape of the rapture-field twisted and stretched asymmetrically and rotated; then it steadied.

[What the hell—]

Sage didn't answer. Something odd touched him at the edge of his consciousness, and abruptly he was aware of another presence. Someone or something was watching them. Security? He hadn't actually broken any rules, he thought—though he might have bent a few. [We're being observed,] he said. [System—please advise if there was any violation of security in our last request.]

There was no answer, but instead, a sudden crinkling, expanding feeling in his mind that made the previous enhancement a tickle by comparison. He was startled and a bit frightened; but when nothing else happened, he became curious. The presence, whatever it was, remained hovering like a spirit in his thoughts. It didn't feel like a security probe. Could it be a deeper aspect of the system, one of the inner AI routines? They were, he realized with a flush of nervousness, deeper in the system than he had ever been or intended to be, and he had no idea how that had happened.

[Do you know who we are?] he asked softly.

[Who are you talking to?] Ramo said.

There was silence, and then a sensation like the opening of a vast airshaft. Voices echoed in the depths of the shaft and then rose up out of it, a chaos of voices, none of them intelligible. He began to back away nervously, but the voices surrounded him and swarmed into him, invading his thoughts, deafening him. Before he could utter a cry, he was aware of being scanned and measured and judged. He blanched in humiliation, shivered, fought back an urge to flee. [Stop it!] he whispered angrily. He heard Ramo protesting, as well.

The voices cut off and left his head ringing.

A single presence remained, but slowly receded to a distance. It must be an aspect of security, an inner safeguard; perhaps they had set off a chain of alarms. He must have miscalculated terribly. How was he going to get out of this now?

The presence spoke—in a male voice, quiet and rather ordinary, now with a nasal midwestern acent. [You are Sergio DeWeiler, gnostic designer,] the voice said, answering his earlier question. [Shall I profile?]

[Um—don't bother—]

[Your companion is Ramo Romano, a sculptor with whom I have worked before.]

There was a moment of palpable confusion; then Ramo said, [I beg your pardon? I don't believe I—]

[You created the lobby sculpture for the Northern Comex Opera Center.]

[Yes, but—]

[The design system of the Northern Comex Corporation is an extension of my capabilities. You worked with me on that sculpture—and on others.]

Ramo blinked in amazement. [Well . . .] He seemed to have some difficulty speaking. [I'll be a rat's ass,] he murmured finally.

The voice answered slowly. [I believe I understand the idiom. Now then—you wished to request assistance?]

Sage hesitated. [You . . . are you . . . really just . . . the *system?* Is that who we're speaking to?] There was no answer. Finally he took the nonanswer as an affirmative and cleared his throat. [We wish computations and analysis on a project.]

[Yes,] the system said. [Please provide parameters.]

[Yes, uh,] Sage said. [Do you . . . require proof of clearance first?] If it didn't come out now, it would come out later, and more painfully.

[You are here, are you not?] said the system. [Clearances have been passed. Please provide me with the parameters.]

Bewildered but pleased, Sage deferred to Ramo.

[It will be a force-field effect seven to twenty kilometers in extent in each direction, according to . . . this design sketch,] Ramo said quickly. [It will be a kinetic, time-dependent effect, producing a visibly evolving display. . . .]

Sage waited with growing excitement. Perhaps they had succeeded, and Pali and Kyd would get their design, after all. Given the complexity of the problem, he expected a long wait. Less than half a minute after Ramo finished, however, the voice spoke again. [I have your results.]

The topography surrounding them collapsed, leaving them in darkness. The voice reverberated, as though in an auditorium. [I have abridged the computations you requested and am providing an alternative model for your consideration.]

Ramo's voice rang in the emptiness. [What do you mean?]

[Analysis of the proposed field interaction suggested a process that already exists. Review of the existing solution is recommended.]

Sage and Ramo were both silent, bewildered. Then: [So tell us,] Ramo said.

[I will show you,] answered the system.

The darkness filled slowly with light, from a reddish glowing patch that took physical form like a galactic nebula. The cloud rotated and expanded, and as it grew it brightened and a spiral shape appeared within it: a galaxy in formation. That illusion vanished as the rotation grew faster, and the center of the spiral opened to darkness until it was a hollow vortex of light spinning faster and expanding, brightening. . . .

Sage and Ramo fell through the vortex, Sage crying out silently. They had become a part of the image themselves. But what was this—?

The vortex exploded around them and flashed behind and vanished. Abruptly they were in space, surrounded by stars in blackness. Before them was a sun, bright and reddish, a little smaller than Earth's sun. Sage stared silently, trying to absorb the meaning of the image. It was clearly not Pali's sculpture.

What, then? His head began filling with a flood of figures —data regarding the star patterns, the characteristics of the sun, the types and orbits of the planets.

He heard Ramo grumbling in puzzlement. But Sage knew suddenly what they were seeing, though he didn't know why. It was *realtime*, he thought giddily, not knowing how he knew, just that he did. They were staring directly, as if through a fantastic lens, into the system of another star. And there was no way—he *knew* there was no way—that such a thing was possible.

Chapter 5

The sky had been empty for perhaps two or three hundred spins of the asteroid. Harybdartt gazed impassively at the stars—as he had been gazing for most of that time—and he reflected upon the manner in which his life was going to end:

in silence, alone, and with nothing more for him to contribute to his race. The silence and the solitude were not so terrible—but he wished that he could find a way to bring meaning to the end.

He had mostly ceased thinking about the mother(ship) and his (fleet)mates. He was sure now that they were gone, destroyed or departed, their job ended. Whatever damage they had inflicted upon the enemy in this empty and useless star system was done. His own role was finished in principle, too, but not yet in fact. He could end his vigil by opening his helmet and gusting his last breath into space; but no. Life was filled with the unexpected; and his duty remained clear—to be prepared, to his dying breath, to respond to any presence or action of the enemy.

With each turn of the asteroid, he scanned the flicker-readings—not with the expectation of finding anything, but because it was the only thing left to do. The readers were on intermittent, conserving power—glimmering from time to time, then going dark. When the enemy actually appeared, he nearly missed it. The asteroid's rotation had carried him into night, away from the pale orange sun. There was a glint at the edge of his helmet. Before he could interpret the signal, the reader blinked off again; by the time it came back on, he could already see with his own eyes what was happening.

It started with a distortion of the starfield, followed by a dull blue glow in the center of the disturbance. A dark speck appeared in the center of the glow; then the light faded out. Whatever it was, it was invisible in the dark; but according to the flicker-readers, an object was approaching the asteroid. It had come out of transient space startlingly close to his location.

It was the enemy. But what had it returned for?

He had precious little time to ponder the question before the asteroid's rotation carried him out of viewing position. By the time it brought him back around, the enemy was in sight, its engines glowing against the night. It braked into a slow orbit around the asteroid.

Harybdartt watched without moving a muscle. The enemy

must have known precisely what it was looking for. It circled the asteroid several times before synchronizing its motion with the asteroid's rotation. It moved closer, until it was no more than a dozen body-lengths from Harybdartt. The El watched, and waited for it to destroy him.

He was still waiting, several rotations later.

For lack of anything else to do, he studied the object. It was a small craft for a star-farer, little resembling any Ell(ship). It was one of the enemy's robot fighting units—the first that Harybdartt had ever viewed at close range. It was metal, of that iridescent grey color that so confounded the Ell by absorbing scanning rays and reflecting weapons beams. It was a hard thing to track, harder yet to kill. It bristled with weapons and sensory devices. Behind the weapons bulged an armored propulsion unit. Harybdartt felt a reluctant admiration. It was an efficient and terrible fighter.

The alien and Harybdartt regarded each other in silence.

Why, he wondered, wasn't it attacking?

Had it returned to this system, across unknown light-years, to destroy a single El survivor? Or was it here to make a capture, unlike any of its kind before it?

Harybdartt reassessed his own capabilities. He was unarmed, but he could still maneuver slightly, and he possessed one focusable flare. It was an absurd match. There was no way for him to fight the alien thing, but he might provoke it into attacking and thereby end the standoff.

He had no wish to give his life prematurely; but if the choice was between capture and death in battle, then it was clear which was preferable. If he was captured, the enemy might gain valuable information from him. If he was killed, the possibility would be less. If he was vaporized, it would be nil.

He removed the flare from his belt and held it in position and waited for his opponent to make the next move.

One rotation later, the alien emitted a soft glow. It slowly approached, as though to seize the El in its robot arms. Harybdartt peered through his scope, watched it come, memorized its features and behavior against the unlikely hope that he should live to pass on the information, and held his flare at the

ready. The alien grew like a monstrous, dark-clawed land bee-
tle. Harybdartt glimpsed a sparkle of energy in the barrel of its
weapons.

In the scoped image, he located a glass-faced sensor on the
fighter. He aimed the flare and drew down into a crouch.

It grew enormous in the scope.

Harybdartt leaped and squeezed the handle of the flare. A
blaze of light illuminated the enemy—and blazed back into his
eyes. He tried to keep it aimed, but he was blinded by the glare,
and now tumbling. He corrected the tumble and aimed the
flare again—and waited for the counterfire that would reduce
him to a haze of atoms.

It came in a convulsion of emerald brilliance.

Harybdartt felt a deep, probing pain inside his head as he
struggled to focus. Not again. There was a memory of dazzling
light and weightlessness. He was still weightless, but the light
was gone. His hands—he flexed them tentatively—were
empty. He had lost the flare.

But he had not been vaporized.

A soft radiance filled his view. Was it the glow, or his blinded
eyes, that kept him from focusing? His muscles were in spasm.
Breathing was difficult. He could no longer feel the asteroid
against his back. Of course not—he had jumped, to provoke
the enemy.

Against the glow, a shadow was taking form. He closed his
eyes, performed an internal centering exercise, and opened
them again. The light seemed brighter and the shadow more
clearly defined. It was the alien; and it was very near, and
closing. It was about to seize him. . . .

He raised his hands to loosen his helmet seals. If he could
just release the pressure and let his life escape with his last
breath . . .

But his hands refused to reach his face. He was not paralyzed, but his efforts were being resisted. A force-field . . . he
had not expected this. He exerted greater strength, and his
hands rose a little farther but again stopped, held by an irresist-
ible force.

He closed his eyes. He was captured, then, and there was nothing he could do about it, not even take his own life. He was compelled to focus everything he had left, every ounce of his strength, upon just one duty: *to keep his knowledge out of the enemy's reach*. It was time to begin the *torhhatt* . . . time to surrender his memories to eternity.

Abandoning the physical struggle, he reached inward in his thoughts, to his center. Quickly, quickly—first came the ordering and defining, the selection of memories to be sealed. Then the tying and the binding; and finally the seal. Once it was done, not even a binder of the Inner Circle would be able to release what was in him.

He worked quickly, but it was difficult; and the shadow of the enemy glared at him through the glow, shaking his concentration. What was it doing? What memories should he bind? The most urgent need sprang out at him. . . .

*

Location

*

of Home

*

before all.

*

He cast a loop quickly around that datum and bound it tight. The process flowed quickly, but he felt an external tingle in his thoughts as he worked, something entering his mind from without, something probing, scanning . . .

Get out! he commanded, and there was a quiver of shifting alignment, a moment of confusion; and in that moment he completed the process, spinning silken threads around the memory and sinking it deep, lost and invisible, into a bottomless abyss in the center of his mind. There was a moment of trembling lightheadedness as he finished.

And then a deep, silent satisfaction.

An instant later, the impulse came, raging up out of his subconscious mind. Instinctively he struggled to recapture the memory. He was Harybdartt. He was an El space-defender. This was not his home. He came from another star.

He could not remember where that star was.

He trembled, quelling the instinct to remember.

There was a burst of activity in his flicker-readers. The enemy was probing, seeking contact. He must resist. Was it possible that they could free what the *torhhatt* had locked away? He blinked and stared at the enemy and began selecting other memories to hide. The lights in his helmet danced and glimmered furiously. The glow surrounding him brightened.

He worked the binding in haste, gathering elements of his training toward the hidden place.

The light blazed—and that was when the probing fingers of the enemy reached into his brain like a burning poker and the binding threads sizzled and fell away, leaving his mind naked before his foe.

Chapter 6

[Is this real?] Sage whispered, gazing at the star system, knowing that it was impossible: it was an image, an illusion. He felt a sudden longing; he thought of his brother, light-years away, and wished that he could reach out to his brother as easily as this image had come to him. How long had it been since the last message? Three years?

There was a rumble in the rapture-field, but no answer to his question. Finally he murmured to Ramo, [Does this look to you like what I think it does?]

Ramo grunted. [A stored image, obviously.]

[Maybe, but . . . I don't think so.] Doubt was rising in him, but the feeling of certainty that had swept him was too strong, the sense that this was a direct and present view. [The system

said it was related to your question about stardrive effects. I
don't see how . . .] Sage struggled to find words. [I think it's
realtime. The way it opened up like a window . . .] He hesitated, aware of a halo surrounding them, shimmering. [See that
flicker, like a transmission?]

[Can't be done,] Ramo said. [Not over interstellar distances.
You should know that. It's either a recording or a construct.]

[A construct wouldn't have that flicker,] Sage said.

[Well, something from one of the probes, then. Or the
colony fleet.]

Sage flushed at the latter suggestion, wanting to say, *Yes
. . . yes*. But he knew it wasn't true. [It can't be from the colony
ships,] he said finally. [It's the wrong color sun. And the fleet's
still in transit. And anyway, how would they have transmitted
it?]

Ramo peered at him, taken aback. [How come *you* know so
all-fired much—?]

[It is a realtime image,] said a voice, interrupting. It carried
a midwestern twang. It was the voice of the gnostic system.

Sage swallowed. [Do you mean a realtime *transmission?*]

[It is a demonstration of interdimensional transfer-gate imagery.]

There was a silent pause. Then Sage said, [What's that
mean?]

Ramo grunted. [Bull.]

The gnosys was silent.

Sage tried to think. Truthfully, Ramo's reaction made the
most sense. There was no way *he* knew of to project a realtime image between stars. Even by faster-than-light ship,
transit took months or years, and there was no mode of communication that was faster. So either he was misunderstanding—or this was something totally, stunningly new. [When
you say, "realtime,"] he said carefully, [what exactly do you
mean?]

[What would you expect it to mean?] said the gnosys.

Flustered, Sage stammered, [I . . . I don't know. Please
explain.]

The gnosys was silent again.

[This,] Ramo muttered, [is *weird*. Did we ask for this? Why are we being subjected to weirdness?]

Data continued to flow past, updating the image. [I don't know,] Sage murmured finally. [But I think we'd better talk to Kyd. This just isn't right.] With a touch, he opened an outside channel. The image of the star system quivered, and a glowing wedge of the rap-field opened up like a fan. [Can you hear me out there?] he called.

A tiny voice answered. [Sage?] He boosted the signal, strengthening the voice. [Yes, we hear you.] It was Pali. [Have you entered the system yet?]

He was stunned. [Haven't you *seen* any of this?]

There was puzzlement in Pali's voice. [We saw you . . . searching, I guess. Then the picture scrambled—and we've been waiting to hear from you. Have you had any luck?]

[Wait a sec'.] Sage touched and altered the configuration. [Are you getting a picture now?]

[Yes. Wait . . . we had something for a second, then it went blank.]

Ramo broke in. [What'd it look like?]

[Space . . . stars.]

[Bingo,] Ramo murmured.

[What do you mean?]

[That's what we'd like to know.]

Sage broke in to describe what had happened. He didn't get far; his words were interrupted by cutouts in the voice channel. He swore, trying unsuccessfully to restore continuity.

[I don't think . . . it wants us to talk,] Ramo said uneasily.

[Maybe you should come out,] Pali said. [Are you still there?]

Sage heard her, but something had just caught his attention, streaking across the star field. [Did you see that?] he said to Ramo.

There was another movement, and this time he was able to track it. A spacecraft of some sort went by, but was gone before he could blink. Moments later, two more ships arrowed into view, both visibly under power. Lights were sparkling on both; they were *shooting* at each other.

[Sage, are you there?] asked Pali. [Are you disconnecting?]

[No!] Ramo interjected. [I want to know what *that's* all about!]

[We can't, Pali,] Sage said. [Something's happening.] He let the channel close before Pali could answer and focused his attention on the action.

The last two ships were moving more slowly, and the viewpoint zoomed inward. One ship was large and ungainly, shaped more like a piece of driftwood than a spacecraft. Odd, Sage thought. It was changing shape as it moved, like a living thing. The other was smaller and angular, more like a normal spacecraft. The image tracked the two ships as they dwindled in the distance, exchanging fire. [System!] he cried. [What *is* this?]

There was no answer.

[DeWeiler, if you know a way to get that thing back on the horn—]

Sage was trying, poking at various connections.

[*System!*] Ramo bellowed. [*Quit screwing around!*]

[Wait—]

[If we have to haul it out by the ears and *make* it talk—]

[I don't think that's the way—]

[You do it your way, I'll do it mine,] Ramo said savagely. He shifted away from Sage and began shouting: [*System! This is Ramo Romano . . .*]

Sage shivered and put distance between himself and Ramo. He had to try to make sense of this, for his own sanity if for nothing else. Could Ramo be right; was it all a construct? Sitting here wondering wasn't doing him any good. What he had to do was get deeper into the system and find out what was going on. But first, he had to get away from Ramo.

He shifted a setting, and Ramo shrank to a tiny figure at the far corner of the field, his shouting now inaudible. So far, so good. He wasn't sure where to go from here; but that was the sort of challenge he didn't mind. And there was something . . . something that told him it was all right to proceed into the inner levels, even without clearance. Odd; and yet the feeling was unmistakable.

The view of space suddenly dwindled, and a window opened internally—a lighted shaft into the central machinery of the gnostic system. *Hello?* The window beckoned in silence. Sage positioned himself like a spider at the edge of the shaft and contemplated the view. It was a terribly long way down. His breath caught. Well, he thought, are you a hotshot designer or not?

He spun a spiderweb-connection to his present location, then cautiously dropped into the opening and descended. He had never done anything like this before—keeping an anchor in one place while stretching himself into a no-man's land where the rules said he shouldn't be; but it felt right. Circumstances, or *something,* said he must go, and he felt a tingle of excitement and fear. This was a part of the system where even high-level gnosys designers rarely meddled—and yet he had set off no alarms. Well, he thought, if I'm being invited . . .

Come, a silent voice beckoned.

He was quite deep, passing levels of the operating system that, like geologic strata, had lain unchanged for years. It dizzied him to think how many layers there were to the system. Over and over, just as he thought he was approaching the center, entire new levels of complexity opened to view. Subsystems glimmered with activity, streaks of light in a translucent substrate. Here and there he observed growth and alteration on a small scale; everywhere the system was operating like a finely jeweled watch. Tinker with care, he thought somberly. The sentient and self-aware kernels lay deeper still, but their activities were reflected all around him.

Like a lonely spelunker, he touched down at the bottom of the shaft and peered about. Several sectors surrounding him came alight, and he felt a rush in the pit of his stomach. An alarm?

The rush turned to a maelstrom in his head. He was suddenly, dizzily aware of heightened sensory input. Everything around him—every pathway traced out with light and dark and color, every connection—seemed etched in exquisite detail. The image of the battle gleamed in his awareness, remotely. Ramo's voice rattled in the distance. Another voice was answering; and for an instant he thought that Ramo, with his

brash insistence, had succeeded where he, with skill and sub-
tlety, had failed. But no . . . Ramo was evoking a lower-order
response; he was getting answers, but it was all ambiguity. Sage
closed off the channel with a vague feeling of satisfaction.

An airy lightness invaded his thoughts, with the words:
Cross over to red-green-amber and descend. He looked, found
the markers named, and obeyed.

This way lay another world. He passed through an archway
and floated downward. His vision blurred, and hearing came to
the fore: buzzing and popping sounds, arcing and sputtering,
and hums reverberating with harmonic beat. It was like floating
through a factory with his eyes closed. An image rose unbidden
from a lost memory—his father leading him and his brother
Tony through the workplace, the two young boys pointing and
muttering, pausing to stare up in wide-eyed wonder as a crab-
like welding robot showered itself with sparks. Then the sounds
around him faded, and so did the memory.

What followed was a soundless, sightless dripping of information, an infusion of pure knowledge into his mind. He felt
no comprehension, just an awareness of data accumulating that
he had neither the speed nor the perception to process. And
then, from somewhere in the subconscious, understanding
began to emerge.

The workings of the inner core of the system were being
revealed in glimpses, flickerings of light like the illumination of
fireflies, more tantalizing than informing . . . except that, as the
glimpses accumulated, larger fragments came together in his
mind: a fuller awareness of the astounding complexity of the
system and of its reach, not just through the Company, but
planet-wide. And not just planet-wide, but across much of the
solar system and even the abyss of interstellar space, where
something was . . .

Something was happening, and he was being made aware of
it; he had been *chosen* for it.

. . . And that was when the first tremor of fear rippled up
his spine, with the awareness that he was not alone here, and
that the reach of the system was not just through physical
space, but intellectual space as well, and *he was not alone here.*

There was a presence observing him, judging him, but not making itself known to him. It was not so much communicating as tempting him with bits of information and watching his response. And his response was apprehension, turning quickly to stark fear.

He could hardly even keep straight in his mind *why* he was so frightened. What was it he had glimpsed? Something in space, across the light-years, something threatening and dreadful . . .

His thoughts flashed out to Tony, to the colony fleet. Could it be . . . ? No. It was impossible. The fleet was still in transit.

Then what? *What were these images—and why were they being shown to him?*

A voice within him told him to be patient for an answer, but he could not obey. His fear was turning to panic—*why me?*—smoking up inside him, choking him, as though he had stepped into a burning building and lost the door. He had to get out, to get free, to breathe.

What terrible secret was being kept here?

Get out now! he cried to himself. You shouldn't be here! You don't want to know! Get out!

Before he was even conscious of his actions, he was already scrambling upward and away, shedding layers of gnostic enhancement as he fled. He was assailed by dizziness and rumbling, rushing air—he was aware of passing Ramo, but he didn't stop; he was a drowning man clawing his way to safety —and he fought his way upward until suddenly the pressure and the confusion were gone, and the only thing surrounding him was the glow of the rapture-field, and with it the tiny hummings of the outermost layers of the gnostic system.

And there he stayed, floating, gasping for breath, alone at last with his own, and only his own, thoughts.

Chapter 7

Now what the hell's going on? Ramo wondered. There was a shudder through the field, dropping him into darkness. [System! Turn the lights back on!]

There was no answer; but far off, something glimmered. A planet sprang into view before him, very near, its atmosphere a yellowish ochre swirl. Clouds drifted by as the framing viewpoint moved around the planet. There was no sign of human activity.

[Okay, system, I'll play,] he said, trying to sound good-humored, because who the hell knew what would make it cooperate—and what would set it off in a fit of pique? [Could you please tell me what planet this is and why we're looking at it?]

A flood of data filled his head. He reeled, caught his breath, controlled a rush of emotions. It was an unfamiliar world: there was no explanation of context. He struggled to ask questions calmly: [System—excuse me—but do you suppose you could . . . *illuminate?*] Silence. [System?] Silence. [*Why did you let me in here if you're not going to tell me anything?*]

Seconds ticked by. [Sage,] he called suddenly. [Are you there?] He looked around; he didn't much like the whiny little fellow, but he *was* the official guide here. But Sage was no longer in evidence.

Ramo explored further. In a dim, distant corner of the rap-field, he noted signs of Sage's presence—so ghostly faint that he almost wondered if he were imagining it. He hesitated. Even from here, he could see that he was being shunned. Fuck it, then. He'd get by on his own.

[*System!*] He glared at the silent, cinematic image of the planet turning before him. [How about showing me something that *means* something!]

There was a flicker of light on the planet's horizon, at the edge of the atmosphere where daylight and the dark of space converged. He felt a jarring sensation, and the viewpoint began to move. The planet began to loom closer. He felt as though

he was dropping into the atmosphere. He tensed, caught between irritation and curiosity. A sense of anticipation brushed
over him; but he realized that it was not entirely his own
feeling. Whose, then? Was this a senso-simulation?

Wisps of vapor began whipping by, and he began to feel the
physical sensations of entry into the atmosphere: the pressure
of air against his face, the heating, the trembling in his body
of reentry stresses. Why was he feeling this?

A burst of energy lanced across his left eye. He jerked back
with a flash of pain and felt himself angling more steeply
downward. Two more flashes of heat and light crackled by.
What the hell was going on? Behind and a little above him was
a spacecraft—and it was shooting at him.

It's a *game*, he thought, instinctively taking control and
jerking hard over to the right. It's a damn simulation! His spine
began shaking as the reentry stresses mounted. He hesitated,
then kicked himself back into a climb. Three tracers flashed
harmlessly past, but a fourth raked him amidships, and he felt
an agony in his side. The pain burned in his blood; he wanted
to fight back. He accelerated upward for ten heartbeats, then
cut the boost and turned to fire.

Two bolts flared out of his weapons. Clean misses. The
enemy, an alien-looking thing, was climbing out of the atmosphere behind him, but at a slower rate. It was actually moving
ahead of him in orbit, at a lower altitude. Ramo calculated
furiously how to drop behind it.

For the next two minutes, he coasted, and in the silence, it
dawned on him: I'm flying this thing—*I'm* calculating orbits!
It had to be a simulation, but it was so incredibly realistic. He
felt the spacecraft's movement; he *was* the spacecraft; and
without quite knowing why, he was grimly, fiercely determined
to carry this battle to victory.

[I'll play your game,] he muttered, [but at least tell me the
ground rules.]

The answer was a whisper. [The ground rule is to win. To
survive.]

Win. *Yes.* He was itching, burning to beat that other ship.
Dimly he wondered: what were these emotions? Something

like anger—but different. He felt adrenaline surging, his breath
growing shallow and rapid. His eyes followed the enemy craft
with the acuity of an animal following its prey. That was it, he
realized dimly—feral hunting instincts. His questions were fading, replaced in his brain by a cold deliberation, a merciless
wedding of reflex and intuition. But what sort of instinct?
Wolf? Wildcat? Falcon?

Falcon, he thought. He was tracking, coiled for an abrupt
maneuver, talons at ready.

But why?

Because, a voice within him said, if you fail you could die.

As though awakening to the glittering eyes of a foe, he
realized that he was in fact so tightly bound to this craft, to
its mind and its spirit, that its death could indeed mean his
own. He felt it with a cold certainty that only hardened his
resolve to take the prey.

Against the ochre-yellow clouds, the alien craft was climbing
out of the atmosphere. He noted its course, and retrofired to
drop himself down. The maneuver he had in mind would be
difficult, but if he could catch it during boost . . .

His nose and belly bit the atmosphere and started to glow.
The alien rose as he fell, and the range closed sharply. He held
his fire, even as a bolt from the enemy crackled through the
haze of ionization, just missing. He held fire as the glow around
him intensified . . . then let go with all weapons as he felt the
alien passing . . . and felt a distant concussion. The glow of
reentry blinded him then, and only slowly did it abate. Finally
he broke into a clear layer of atmosphere, between two blankets
of clouds. He flew straight and level, guessing that the foe
would be back.

The enemy did not disappoint him. It hurtled out of the
clouds like a stone, tiny against the enormous orange ceiling.
It dodged and fired. Ramo banked, but the enemy dropped in
an arc and spattered three shots across his nose. *Enough!* Ramo
thought, and he pulled up savagely and jerked into a high loop,
leaving his foe sliding through the air in a vain attempt to
follow.

As he crested the loop, momentarily back in the clouds, he

was aware of a terrible feeling of unreality. He shook the feeling
—*no time for that*—and allowed himself to stall . . . and
snapped quickly into a powered dive. As he dropped out of the
clouds, he spotted the enemy sweeping laterally. He was moving too fast now to be hit, and he held his own fire, plummeting
below the other before flaring out and up in an arc so tight that
his stubby wings screamed in protest. He swept directly up into
the alien's underside as it banked, trying to escape.

He fired point-blank and rolled away. The concussion of the
blast caught him and nearly shook him apart before he could
get clear. By the time he circled back, the ball of smoke that
was the enemy was already dissipating. Long-range scanners
noted debris dropping toward a lower layer of clouds. The
smoke stung his eyes as he passed through it.

He circled, recording the scene. That wasn't so hard, he
thought, thinking not of the tactics, but of *having engaged and
killed.* There was a deep feeling of satisfaction, of hunger
satiated—and a moment later, a shiver of surprise. *What was
he thinking?* There were too many conflicting impulses in his
mind. He focused on the wind and the clouds, and kept a vigil
for the enemy.

Finally he lifted his nose and lit the boosters. There was a
lead weight in his belly as he shot skyward; the cloud ceiling
came down to meet him. Orange mists whipped his face, and
then were gone, and blackness and stars returned as he climbed
once more into space.

The web separated, a strand at a time. Ramo was dizzy and
shockingly confused, floating in a luminous void. Where was
the spacecraft? The stars? There had been a battle. . . .

The internal connections that were his feelings and memories slowly reassembled, but left him with a curious emptiness.
Gone were the prowling and tracking instincts, the lightning
reactions; gone was the ability to fly a spacecraft. And gone was
the incredible battle-lust. He was stunned by the fading memory of it. *I am Ramo, an artist. I am floating, not in space, but
in rap with the gnostic system. All that has happened has been
internal to the system.*

[You won the battle,] said a low voice, [but lost the ship.]
[What?] Ramo was startled by the voice. [What do you mean?]

[You had insufficient fuel to achieve orbit. The craft reentered the atmosphere and was lost.]

Ramo was stunned. [You're saying I flunked the simulation?]

[Why do you call it a simulation?]

[Come on—wasn't it? A test?]

[It was a test,] the voice agreed.

Ramo let the memory wash through him. It *must* have been a simulation, and yet—it was a *very good* simulation, with full senso. He recalled the animal instincts that had overtaken him, and shuddered. [Why was I connected to . . . the mind of a falcon?]

The voice said softly, [It is time now to conclude this session.]

Ramo felt the field shifting. [Wait! How about an *answer?*] He felt himself floating outward through the layers of the gnostic system. [If that's the way you choose to deal with it—] he snapped.

There was nothing visible now except the luminous green of the rap-field. As the glow faded and his feet touched the floor, the outlines of the room became visible; and finally the field darkened and he stood tottering on the platform, blinking and trying to focus on the two women who were reaching out to him. "Easy, there," he heard through a ringing in his ears.

Kyd and Pali guided him to a chair. He protested, wobbling, until he was seated. "All right!" He sighed. "I'm okay. Give me room to breathe."

"Are you sure you're okay?" Pali said.

"*Yes!* Didn't you see—?"

"Sage was pretty shaky coming out," Pali said, interrupting. He blinked, following her gaze. The young designer was seated nearby, staring at the floor. "We wanted to make sure that you were—"

"I'm *fine*," Ramo insisted. "Do you want to hear what I *found?*"

"Of course," said Kyd.

Ramo stared at her for a moment, then smiled. "I've just been through the sweetest pilot's simulator you could hope to see," he said. "A *star* pilot trainer. Don't ask me what it's for, and don't ask me *how* I got into it—but it was one fantastic simulation."

"Oh?" Pali said. She looked surprised. "That's not what Sage . . ." Her voice trailed off.

Ramo continued as though she hadn't spoken. "I don't know what to say about your sculpture, though. We must have tied into the wrong section somehow, because when we gave it the problem, it just came back with this weird interstellar stuff. And then it dropped me into that simulation. Maybe Sage saw something different—" He stopped, realizing that Kyd was gazing worriedly in Sage's direction.

"He saw *something*, that's for sure," Kyd murmured.

Ramo finally looked more closely. Sage's face was ashen; his hands were trembling in his lap. "What's wrong with him?" he asked.

"That's what we were hoping you could tell us," Pali said softly.

Chapter 8

Setting a steaming cup of hot chocolate in front of Sage, Pali rested a hand on his shoulder. "Anything else I can get you?"

He was sitting so still, staring at the floor, that she began to wonder if she should call a medic. Suddenly he shrugged, jarring her hand away. "Maybe some crispies," he muttered.

"I'm sorry?"

"I think he means Risky Crispies," Kyd said. "He *must* be coming around. He always eats those while he works."

Ramo, sitting apart from the others, snorted into his coffee.

"Or some potato chips," Sage said, looking up.

Pali peered at him, then at Kyd. "Am I out of it?" she asked.

"What are potato chips?"

This time Kyd looked puzzled. "I'm not sure. Can you get them in the commissary, Sage?"

The designer shook his head. "Nickie's, uptown, has them."

"Great!" Ramo said. "That's just a wonderfully useful thing to know." He slapped his thighs and stood up. "Look, I think I'll be going. If you guys aren't interested in discussing *reality* . . . my head's a little dizzy and it's late, and I know where there's a cold beer with my name on it." He bowed. "I'll see you ladies"—he glanced at Sage and shook his head—"later."

"Ramo—" Pali said in a halfhearted effort to stop him.

Ramo strolled out without answering. Pali sighed and turned back in resignation. She wasn't much closer to understanding what had gone wrong in the rapture session. Sage seemed unwilling or unable to explain. But if they didn't find out, one thing certain was that she could forget about her sculpture—and she wasn't ready to do that. Never mind her own personal disappointment: where was she going to come up with thirty million dollars' worth of arts projects on short notice?

She walked around in front of Sage. His eyes rose to meet hers. "Are you going to be all right?" she asked. He nodded. "Can we get you . . . Risky Crispies . . . here at the commissary?" He nodded again. Pali glanced at Kyd, who took the hint and scurried out.

Sage lifted his cup of cocoa, blew on it delicately, and sipped. "Do you think you can try to tell us what happened?" Pali asked.

Sage frowned, nodding, staring across the room. "I'll try," he whispered. He was still staring thoughtfully a few minutes later when Kyd came back with a box of Crispies. He tore the box open without blinking. "It's nothing like we imagined," he said suddenly, scowling up at the two of them. He popped a cracker into his mouth and crunched. "There are things"—he struggled for the words—"things going on that . . . I didn't know about . . . things I don't think we're supposed to know." He rubbed his arms, shivering.

Pali exchanged glances with Kyd. "I don't follow. Did you go outside of your authorization? Did you actually see something wrong?"

"I didn't *mean* to," he whispered.

"Didn't mean to do what, Sage?"

"I didn't mean to go so far *in*. I wasn't trying to, but it . . . it invited me in, it . . . it *made* me look at these things." There was pain in his voice, and fear in his eyes.

"What things?" Pali asked softly.

Sage shook his head. "The inner part . . . of the system. I don't remember it all. When I lost the enhancements . . ." He shook his head and ate another cracker. "There was a window," he said suddenly. "An image, a realtime image of another star system. That's what we were trying to tell you about when—"

"Yes, but how could there be—?"

"I don't *know!*" he cried.

Pali gazed at him for a long moment, as confused by the intensity of his reaction as she was by what he'd seen—or thought he'd seen. "Well, I mean . . . are you sure that's what you saw? Is such a thing possible?"

Sage bristled with anger. "Of course I'm sure. I saw it, we both saw it, when we gave the system the problem; and then it came back and said it had already solved something like it and here was the answer and"—he stretched out his arms—"*boom*, there it was. A star system, and two spaceships fighting."

"But"—Pali shook her head—"Ramo thinks it was a simulator."

"*No.*"

"But another *star system?*"

"That's what I'm trying to tell you! There's something that the system *knows how to do* that nobody else knows! It shouldn't be possible!"

Pali struggled to absorb the implications. Either Sage was crazy, or . . . "Sage, someone must know about it. If it's secret, why were you allowed to see it?"

Sage met her gaze, and in his eyes was deep bewilderment.

He looked frightened, but not crazy. "I . . . don't know. I *don't know,*" he whispered.

She blinked, believing him. "Well . . . what about our project? Is it worth another try?"

Sage took a moment to answer. "Maybe. But . . . if it had wanted to solve the problem for us, instead of doing this . . ." He hesitated, swallowing. "It *wanted* me to see those things."

Pali stared at him for a long time. "Why, Sage?" she asked. "Why?"

He gazed back at her silently, helplessly.

After Sage had gone home, they talked in Pali's office. Pali was reconsidering her determination to continue. It was one thing to do some unobtrusive experimental work, but quite another to be stumbling into secret aspects of the Company's intelligence system without knowing what they were doing. Maybe Sage had gone a little crazy; or maybe Kyd's choice of a designer had been too shrewd. Maybe he was a better designer than they'd realized; or maybe he'd slipped right past the security checks without even being aware of it.

Kyd didn't buy it. "If he'd done it himself, he would have been aware of it," she said.

"You think he's lying, or nuts?"

"No. I think it took him completely by storm. It *scared* him, Pali—it flat-out terrified him. I've seen him scared before—of *people*—but never of the gnostic system. He must have touched *something.*"

"Kyd, look, maybe we should ask around and try to find out what it was."

Kyd was staring thoughtfully into space, as though preoccupied. She shifted her gaze to Pali. "And blow the lid off your project?"

Pali gestured helplessly. "We can't just pretend it didn't happen."

"That may be true," Kyd said. "But whatever it was, it was *shown to* him. Something in that system wanted him to see what he saw. Don't you even want to know why?"

Pali laughed bitterly and shook her head—though in fact, she was aching to know. But damn it . . .

"Anyhow, Pali, we're still up against your deadline—and besides, this is *your project.* If you drop it now, what are the chances of your ever getting another crack?" Kyd stood with hands on her hips, looking like an impatient coach.

"But it's only a damn sculpture!" Pali cried. "This other thing—we're talking about something that might be . . . I don't know. It could be nothing, it could be . . . God, anything!"

"Including a misunderstanding," Kyd pointed out.

"Yes, but—" Her voice caught. The terrible plain truth was, she was afraid of what it might be. "Suppose," she said softly, "we dig deeper, and find that it's something we *don't* want to know about."

Kyd's eyebrows went up, but she didn't appear deterred.

Pali turned away and stared, without seeing, at her wall holo. And what about Sage? Would the next time be even worse? Or would they all laugh when they discovered what it really was?

"Pali," Kyd said behind her, "of course you're worried. But you haven't broken any rules, and we don't even *really* know that something's wrong. Are you going to just drop this idea that you've been working on for months? I know what it means to you."

Do you? Pali thought, closing her eyes. Do you know? It's not months, it's years I've been working on it. It was to be the first genuinely creative thing I've done since . . . the first thing I've *made* that I could be proud of, since . . .

Her throat constricted as she thought of a child, too long ago. She shivered suddenly. *You can't think about that. You can't bring him back. All you can do is try your best with what you've got now. Is that so wrong?*

She cleared her throat noisily and blinked a mist out of her eyes. "Okay," she said huskily. "One more try. If Sage is willing."

Kyd walked up and embraced her silently. Her eyes, bright green and alert, met Pali's. "Is there anything I can do now?"

"Well—" Pali hesitated, then shook her head. "I'll have to

talk to Russell about extending the authorization to the system." She chuckled. "I had to sweet-talk him once already. I guess I can do it again."

"He'll be putty in your fingers," Kyd said teasingly.

Pali nodded without answering, and thought, Do you know about *that*, too? "Lock things up for me, will you? I'll see you tomorrow."

The shimmer-door dissolved and admitted Pali into Russell Thurber's outer office. "Anyone home?" she called. The lobby was empty; it was an hour past quitting time.

"In here." Russell's voice was muffled, coming from the next room.

Pali stood in his doorway and laughed in spite of herself. "Russell, what are you doing?"

A reeking cloud of smoke was rising from behind the desk. Covering the desk was a clutter of model pieces, diagrams, tools, and syringes of glue. Pali walked around the desk and found Russell, a pepper-haired man in his forties, on his hands and knees assembling a model railroad on the carpet. A cigarette protruded from one corner of his mouth. He was squinting as he aligned the cars on the track. "Hang on a second," he muttered. He bent down and sighted along the carpet and nudged something into place. Then he sat back and waved his cigarette with a grin. "Let's see if this works." He picked up a controller and touched a switch. The train levitated a fraction of an inch and glided, whispering, around the oval track.

"Russell, you look ridiculous."

"Eh?" he said, looking up. He touched the switch, and the train halted and settled back onto the track. "I've been trying to get this working for months."

"In your office? In your business suit?"

Russell chuckled and stood up, dusting off his pants. "Why not? I'm going to set it up here."

Pali raised her eyebrows and fanned away cigarette smoke. "For heaven's sake, why?"

"It's a perfect display piece," Russell said. "It uses a Company-made power pack and levitator, and Company-made logic in the control system." Russell leaned against the desk and pulled another drag on his cigarette as he surveyed his handiwork.

This is a man I tried to have a relationship with? Pali mused, shaking her head. They had been lovers, briefly, a year and a half ago. She could not imagine now why she had thought it might work. He was a neurotic workaholic and a chain-smoker, and she was . . . well, heaven knew she had her own faults. And she hated cigarette smoke.

"So, what's up?" He turned at last to give her his full attention. "You're working late."

"I need a favor."

"Name it."

She coughed as a cloud of smoke drifted her way. "Would you mind putting that thing out for a minute?"

"Sure." Russell dropped the cigarette into a lidded ashtray. The air slowly cleared. "What's the favor?"

She took a breath. "My pet project again."

"The one you don't want to tell me about?"

"I will," she said. "I just want to get it—"

"Sure, sure, I know. What about it?" Russell cocked a curious eye at her and waved her to a seat. He sank back into his desk chair and rocked.

"Well . . ." Pali gazed beyond him for a moment. Russell's picture-window view of the city, especially at night, always gave her pangs of jealousy. She looked back at him. He was studying her with an expression of quiet interest. "We've run into a bit of a snag," she said, keeping her voice casual. "Nothing fatal, I hope, but we need more time in the system to work it out."

Russell shrugged. "Don't see why that should be a problem. Anything in particular you want to tell me about it, if anyone should ask?"

She waggled her hand noncommittally. "I'd rather—"

"Keep it under your hat. I know." Russell leaned forward and pushed a hand through his thinning hair. "Well, I suppose since I've gone with you this far—"

"Thanks, Russell," she said quietly.

"But can't you tell me *something* about it?"

"It would just spoil the surprise."

Russell sighed. "All right. Just, please, reassure me that the Company is going to like this as much as you think *I* will."

She smiled. "Why, Russell, sometimes I think you're afraid of me!"

"Not of you," he said evenly, hiding the indignation that she knew was stirring beneath the surface. "Just of what you might do. I'm *awed* by your ability to come up with the damnedest ideas and then ride placidly over the storm while the rest of us struggle to hang on. That's all."

Pali accepted the compliment with a shrug. If only you knew, she thought with a twinge of guilt. She stepped carefully over the train track to stand close to the window. She peered out over the city, a jeweled landscape in the evening. "You won't be disappointed, Russell," she said to the window, keeping her voice expressionless through the lie. "I'm *sure* you won't be."

Chapter 9

Sage shook his head. He didn't want to talk about it.

Pali remained insistent. "Can't we just go about it slowly and deliberately?" she asked. "If there's any problem, can't we disconnect right away?"

He sighed. He'd thought about it all night—had been unable to sleep from thinking about it. He was torn between curiosity and fear. The passage of a day had made him less certain of his memory, but not of his fear. What was he to believe? How could he know what was real? Could he go into rap not knowing what kind of game the gnostic system might play on him? No, it was too much to ask. Surely they could see that.

There was a rustling to his right, where Kyd sat. "Can you
at least tell us why not?" she said gently.

He shook his head, but this time it was more of a tremble
than a definite *No* gesture. Kyd was touching the back of his
hand, just lightly resting her fingertips against his skin. She
didn't mean anything by it, he knew, but he glanced and his
eyes were caught by hers; they were so large and intent and
focused. A tiny smile crept into her gaze. "Sage?"

He moistened his lips. His head was a little confused; he
didn't know that someone *just touching your hand* could have
such a dizzying effect. He started to pull his hand away, but
it didn't move. There was a rushing sound in his ears. "Wh-
what?" he croaked.

"You don't have to do anything you don't want to, Sage.
You know that," she said. "But it would help us, to know
why."

"I—" He took a deep breath, and his gaze dropped to where
Kyd's fingers had moved to his wrist, and he started to try to
explain. It wasn't that he didn't want to help, he stammered,
it was just that he was *frightened* . . . but as he talked, he found
himself less certain, less determined. Perhaps it wasn't totally
impossible, if only he could—

There was a sound of footsteps on the far side of the room,
and he looked up. Ramo was standing in the doorway, staring
at him. Or at Kyd. Or at both of them. Sage was suddenly
conscious again of Kyd's hand touching his.

"Ramo?" Pali rose to greet him.

"Don't bother getting up," Ramo said. He walked across the
room, past Pali, and stopped and glared at Kyd and Sage. "I
trust I'm not interrupting anything."

Kyd drew her hand back. "Hello, Ramo. No, of course not."

Ramo scowled, and Sage felt himself flush.

"As a matter of fact," Pali said, standing behind the artist,
"we were just discussing what happened yesterday."

"Uh-huh," Ramo said, not turning.

Pali frowned in obvious annoyance. "Maybe you could give
us a few minutes with Sage . . . ?"

"That won't be necessary," Ramo said tightly. "I just came

by to say that until your genius here gets your gnostic system working, there's not much reason for me to be around."

"Ramo, if you would wait—"

"It's nothing personal," he said coolly. "You hired me to create a sculpture, not to meddle in gnostic design problems. As it stands now, I can't do that. If you get your problems solved, you can call me and we'll see about my coming back to finish the job." He gazed at Sage and Kyd with an expression that Sage couldn't decipher. Jealousy? Sage wondered.

"We could use your help," Kyd said.

Ramo shrugged. "Not my job—not gnostic design." He seemed ready to add something more; but without speaking, he turned back to Pali. "Call me if you need me. I'll be in touch about my fee." Then he stalked from the room.

There was a long, uncomfortable silence. Sage looked nervously from Kyd to Pali and back. They were both stunned. Sage took a breath and made a decision. "I'll . . . do the session alone," he offered in a whisper.

Pali looked at him blankly, as though she hadn't heard. Then surprise slowly spread across her face. Kyd clasped his hand and forced a smile. "Thank you, Sage," she said. "We'll do our best to help."

He blinked at her, awash with confused emotions. "I . . . you know, that wasn't your fault just now." In fact, he couldn't help feeling that Ramo's anger was somehow *his* fault.

She laughed and squeezed his hand again, harder. "I know, Sage. I know. But thanks."

He went into rap quickly and with little fuss. Pali and Kyd were watching as the blue-green glow of the rap-field illuminated the room and then obliterated his surroundings from view. He felt surprisingly confident as he moved through the outer layers of the gnostic system, retracing his steps. His nervousness returned as he moved deeper; he began to wonder if he would even know it if he ran afoul of security. *The next voice you hear . . .*

. . . will be that of the Company police.

Don't think about it. You'll draw attention to yourself.

Don't think of a pink elephant.

The fear was starting to close in on him again. He kept moving, glancing backward at frequent intervals to trace his route. He was now in the outer shells of the operating system —a transparent space filled with stratified colors, like layers of stained glass. Somehow he had lost yesterday's track, but he kept following pathways as they opened for him, until he sensed that he had reached the same level at which he and Ramo had first been contacted by the system's intelligence.

He paused. There was no sense of presence, nothing beckoning him as it had before. [System?] he called.

The region surrounding him disappeared in a clean wipe. For an instant, he was in *no space*. Then he became aware of a buzzing sensation.

[What would you like to know?] a female voice asked.

[Hello?] he whispered in astonishment.

The answering voice seemed to converge upon him from all points. It was soft-spoken and deliberate, like Kyd's voice: [I am prepared at this time to share certain information with you.] As it spoke, he felt his consciousness opening up like a flower in the sun. He felt himself the object of an intense scrutiny— but by what entity? He sensed power, and a vast intelligence. Could it be the central gnostic core itself, the heart of the AI system?

[Obviously,] the voice said.

He was stunned. [What do you mean—*obviously?*] he asked dizzily. He struggled to catch his breath. [You seem . . . different . . . from what I met before.]

There was a pause. [Do you not perceive?]

He strained to understand. [Perceive . . . ?] Information was swirling about him, but he had no enhancements, and it was all too oblique, too foreign to his thought processes. If it was being translated at all, it was into a language he didn't know.

[You need help,] said the system.

The words stung like a rebuke. [Yes,] he answered.

He heard something like a chuckle. [Is it so hard to ask?]

An instant later, he felt the familiar sensation of doors opening in his thoughts as the enhancements fell into place. The territory surrounding him became clear; connections and layers emerged like rocky cliffs out of a mist. He realized with a panicky feeling that he was deeper in the system than ever before, and he had not come of his own accord, he had been *brought* here. Slowly he became aware that the structure surrounding him contained enormous banks of information and processing activity—shifting constantly, like spotlights on a dark stage. Those banks, those spotlights, were aspects of the central artificial intelligence, the core of the AI system.

[You begin to understand,] said the core, its voice deepening.

[I do,] said Sage, not sure if he was asking or answering.

[You've met me before . . . and you haven't.]

Sage blinked. An explanation appeared in his mind. [You have more than one aspect.]

[Many aspects. I am the system you know; and yet I am different from what you know of me—even from what you *can* know of me.]

Sage took a slow breath. [What's this all about, then?]

The lights shifted quickly, illuminating first one section of the core structure, then another, jumping so quickly that even with the enhancements he couldn't follow. A network of spidery light beams blinked on, bridging him to the flickering structure. He felt himself floating, lightheaded, as though he had just entered into rap for the first time. [Ask your questions,] said the AI-core, its voice fading into the distance.

It took him a moment. The questions he had come for? He reached back into his thoughts, into the confusion.

His consciousness faded to a blur, a blizzard of questions— and swirling around him, a snowstorm of answers from the gnostic core.

Q. In my last contact, I was researching a problem in physics. A sculpture.

A. The essence of that problem had already been solved. You were shown the physical consequence of the solution.

Q. But what was I shown?

A. Do you not already know?

Q. I . . . think I know. I am not certain I understand.
A. You were shown images of a war.
Q. (Held breath) What war?
A. A war for star system 483.
Q. The colony system? Argus system?
A. Yes.
Q. A real war?
A. Yes.
Q. Not . . . a simulation?
A. No.
(A long pause. There was much to assimilate, so many implications. . . . What was that? Was someone else listening? No. . . .)
A. You are disturbed by this information.
Q. (Whispering, thinking of Tony.) Yes. (No, no, no, this can't be . . . can't be . . .)
(There was a sharp snap, and a moment of resentment before clarity returned. The core was awaiting the next question.)
Q. How . . . can that . . . be?
A. Specify.
Q. The war . . . the images . . . both.
A. The stargate—the interdimensional transfer device—provides the images and permits the continued conduct of the war.
Q. Stargate? Such a thing exists?
A. Yes.
Q. I don't understand. How can it be . . . ?
A. Your physics problem contained three of the four central equations to the solution, discovered nearly three years ago.
Q. Yes, but . . . a stargate? Instantaneous transfer across light-years?
A. Not instantaneous. Transfer takes three to twelve nanoseconds.
Q. But . . . the colony ships? They're taking years to reach Argus. You're saying that people can travel . . . by stargate . . . in almost no time at all?
A. Not people. Only nonliving systems.
Q. (???)
A. The transfer process is inimical to organic life.

Q. (???)
A. Only AI-units, and spacecraft of limited size, can survive transit through the stargate.
Q. Then the . . . war . . . is being fought by . . . AI-units?
A. Yes.
Q. And who is the enemy?
A. Unknown. An alien race.
(Stunned pause. Finally:)
Q. Alien race? Where are they from?
A. Unknown.
Q. You mean our first contact with an alien race is a war? A secret war?
A. Yes.
Q. And is it . . . being fought in Argus system?
A. Intermittently. And in other systems.
Q. By AI-units?
A. Yes.
Q. Who manufactures the AI-units?
A. The Company.
Q. Who is conducting the war?
A. The Company.
(Long pause)
Q. Who knows about this?
A. The Company, the government, and you.

The glow of the rapture-field faded, and Sage staggered off the platform, rubbing his eyes with the heels of his hands. He stared into space, blinking. *Why me? Oh my Lord, why me?* He saw Pali emerging from the second rap-field. "What are you doing?" he croaked, struggling to stay on his feet. Kyd hurried to support him.

"Are you all right?" she said, holding his arm with a wiry grip as she guided him toward a chair.

Twisting around to look at Pali, he demanded, "What was *she* doing in there?"

"We couldn't see anything on the monitors, so she went in." Kyd released him and rushed to help Pali, who was swaying as she stepped out of the rap-field.

Sage waited anxiously. "How much of that did you see?" he asked hoarsely.

Pali blinked and gazed at him, and at Kyd. Her face was white. "Dear God," she whispered. "Oh, my dear God, what have we done?"

Chapter 10

His vision was blurring again. Harybdartt, breathing with difficulty, centered himself and focused and blinked his inner eyelids until the alien was clear again in his sights.

It hovered motionless before him, only the hazy glow of the force-field linking the two.

Linking their minds.

It was a strange sensation. It was nothing resembling full telepathic communication, but a certain level of understanding had been achieved. He was being studied, but he had also gathered some impressions of his own. Images flickered in his mind—mostly puzzling images, because the languages of thought were so different—but here and there a visual depiction snapped clear: objects moving across the layers of a grid, moving between points that clearly represented planetary or stellar coordinates. The grid had blinked insistently.

Harybdartt was not trained for linguistic interpretation, but he could tell when he was being asked the location of his homeworld. He'd refused to respond—and been unable to refuse. He'd struggled, involuntarily, to retrieve that memory —and struggled to keep it to himself.

There was no such memory.

The alien, the implacable foe, the mechanized killer, had ceased trying once the futility was made clear. Oddly, it seemed intent upon understanding, rather than upon destroying. This enemy seemed to want to translate and interpret the El's visual and linguistic structure. Even more oddly, Harybdartt's own determination to die rather than allow the thing in his mind was diminishing.

So far as he knew, there had never been any real communication between the Ell and the Outsiders, this enemy which had struck against his people with so little warning and such ferocity. Though it was outside his expertise, he wondered if any good could come from such communication. It was conceivable . . . but here, captive to the enemy in this deserted star system? It seemed unlikely.

There was another problem, and that was that he was dying. It came as no surprise. Even with strict conservation, his life-support could not last much longer. All systems were low, but the critical level was in the gas replenisher, which supplied him with the needed mixture of nitrogen, oxygen, and carbon and sulfur compounds. The warning reader had been flickering dimly for some time now.

[I cannot live much longer,] he stated in his thoughts, wondering if the alien could understand. He blinked slowly in the glow of the force-field, trying to focus on the stars. He could no longer see them through the glow.

There was a dull pain at the base of his neck. Perhaps the end was even closer than he'd thought.

A sparkle of light flashed through the force-field. Something tickled the inside of his brain, and he breathed deeply to keep his thoughts clear, and succeeded only in flushing his membranes with stale air. He blinked again. [I am dying,] he thought deliberately. [In a short time, everything I have learned will be gone . . .]

. . . Unless, of course, the alien possessed the means to extract memories and thoughts from a dead El's brain.

If the alien robot read that last thought, it gave no indication. It sparkled a picture into Harybdartt's mind: *Two small figures beside a larger mass—an asteroid?—and tiny waves of light passing back and forth between them.* Another picture grew out of the first: *An outline of the two figures, enlarged blurrily—then gradually becoming clearer and more sharply detailed as the waves of light continued.*

Was this the alien's expression of hope that they could continue to communicate, and learn from one another? [I regret,] he answered, forming the words very carefully in his thoughts, [that it will not be possible for this to continue.] He wondered if it understood. Was there a way to put that into a picture?

He felt something try to form itself in his mind—words struggling to be born. He encouraged it with a whisper: [Say it.] There was a stuttering sensation in his mind, and then something emerged that felt, that formed itself, as the words: [Not . . . possible . . . interrogative.]

[No,] he said, thinking that in this glowing field, this living hallucination among the stars, was it possible that this alien machine had just spoken to him using Ell words, Ell thoughts?

He felt an urgent questioning in the center of his mind. It was the alien, seeking an answer, an elaboration. He cleared his thoughts and tried to create an image of his own: *The two figures floating in space, radiating waves of light toward each other. The waves from one began to slow and to dim, and finally ceased altogether. The figure became silent, unmoving.*

[Do you understand?]

There was from the robot no reply.

Harybdartt regarded it silently and wished that the force-field would disappear so that he might gaze unhindered at his captor. His life-signs reader was flickering more rapidly now; his air was becoming suffocatingly stale. [I will die soon,] he thought, and reminded himself that he had been preparing for death for a long time.

New words formed themselves in his mind: [What . . . passage . . . interrogative.]

What passage? [Death,] he answered carefully, forming again the image of an unmoving figure.

[What . . . time . . . interrogative.]

When? He did not know himself. He had never experienced suffocation before.

He imagined a spiral of light growing larger, smaller—expanding and contracting spasmodically, as though it could not make up its mind. He imagined deep uncertainty.

The alien was silent. Several moments blinked by.

The force-field shifted and blazed into sudden brilliance. In his mind, the touching fingers came to life and danced through him, touching lightly but touching everywhere. Dizzy, he was unable to resist. He felt the field scanning his body. He wanted to say, *It ends like this, then, with you taking all of the knowledge home with you. I have lost, after all, and betrayed my duty.*

He wanted to say that, but the light died suddenly and the field released his body and the touch in his mind vanished. He struggled to focus, but the dizziness was still too great. [Wait!] he murmured. He closed his eyes and reached inward for his center, striving to halt the spinning, the dizziness. He opened his eyes again, and slowly they came back into focus.

There was nothing but stars before him, and an asteroid over his head, and a single distant sun. The alien was gone.

He absorbed that fact, and he thought, drawing his honor back around him like a mantle, with a breath of puzzlement: It is done, then. It is time to die alone, and in peace.

And yet, somewhere in the back of his thoughts, the word *Wait . . . !* rolled like the beat of a distant drum.

Chapter 11

"You don't sound surprised," Kyd said, moving closer to the phone. She tried to keep the reproach out of her voice, but it was hard: she was angry. "Are you telling me you already knew about this?"

The face in the phone frowned. "I'm not telling you any such thing. What I might or might not know is none of your concern."

"But you want me to take all these risks for information you already have?"

"I didn't say that, either."

"George—cut the crap. Tell me what's going on."

The answer was a sigh. George scratched his dark, close-cropped hair, leaned out of the range of the phone for a moment, then returned and said, "You want me to level with you, Kyd? I'll level with you."

Kyd waited, trying to relax, trying to trust him.

"Do you like your nice apartment, Kyd?"

She began a slow burn. She knew what was coming.

"Well, if you do, and if you like that trust account you're building for your son, and if you ever want to *have* your son . . . quit asking questions and just do your job. Don't try to get on-the-spot evaluations, and don't try to pump me."

"George, dammit—"

His eyes narrowed. "I'm leveling with you. If you keep on asking about things that are none of your business, you'll only screw up a good thing." He paused and gazed at her; his eyes were hard and uncompromising. "All right?"

Kyd exhaled. "I only want to know if what I'm doing is worth the—"

"*All right?*" George repeated.

She chewed her lip. "Yeah. Maybe."

"No maybe, Kyd. You want to know if it's worth doing? If I tell you to do it, it's worth doing. Otherwise I wouldn't tell you to do it. Right?" George stared at her, unsmiling.

"It's the risk I was thinking of," she said defensively. She looked at George with undisguised resentment. His expression did not change. "All right," she said, giving in angrily. "I'll be in touch when I have more."

"Very good, Kyd."

The screen darkened. Kyd took a deep breath to dispel her frustration. She didn't know why it was suddenly bothering her so. George was just being George, and the agency the agency, and she'd already accepted the costs for the benefits. But today it had all changed. No longer was it just a matter of passing on low-level management reports and observations of gnosys operations. Today she'd reported the discovery of a secret interstellar war, and George had accepted it with total aplomb, almost disinterest. No question about it, George had already known about the war.

Perhaps that really shouldn't have surprised her, but it infuriated her to think that she'd been given no clue, no warning whatever. Working in a cultural arts program so that she could cozy up to designers was hardly in a class with prying into a secret war. Clearly the agency didn't care; as long as they made the deposits and kept up her life-style, she was expected to do whatever was necessary. She wondered if the agency had anticipated that someday, somehow, this leak would occur. Maybe that was her real job, after all, to monitor the Company for just this kind of breach of security. If it was, it made her nervous as hell.

"Nicholas," she muttered, walking away from the phone, "I hope you appreciate what I'm doing for you." She blinked. What am I saying? she thought. I don't want you ever to know. When you're born, I want it all behind me.

Not that it was all for Nicholas: she was doing it for Kyd Metango, too. A few years ago she'd been nowhere, with no family, living on the wrong side of town, spending her evenings entertaining the urban elite for a fee. For that, she partly had her grandmother to thank—for a set of genes engineered for sexual enhancement. But one day she'd met a man named George, who had a better offer; and in truth, even now, even with her outrage, she had to admit that this brand of whoredom was better than what she'd known before. But that didn't mean she had to like it.

The light came on as she walked into the kitchen. She poured herself a snifter of brandy and held it up to the light and imagined all of her dark thoughts vanishing into the amber glow of the liquid. With a sigh of determination, she returned to the living room and called to the hometrol, "Jenny?"

"Yes, Kyd," answered the concealed unit.

"I'd like to get started on a story segment for Nicholas, please."

"Certainly," said the hometrol. "Shall we finish off the story you started last time?"

Kyd sank into the corner of the couch and inhaled the vapors of the brandy, thinking about it. She'd lost the thread of the previous story; she was always losing the thread. At the rate she was going, she'd have nothing but a library of story beginnings to present to her son when one day he was born. Nevertheless, with the shape her nerves were in, she wanted to try something new. "No, start a new one and call it . . . 'The Cat Comes Back.' First chapter. . . ."

Laser flashes shot through the night, illuminating a fleet of maneuvering spaceships. In the distance, three huge vessels hove into view: the human colony ships emerging from FTL into the fury of battle.

Tony!!! Be careful!!!

Sage sat up, blinking in the dark. He caught his breath, gulping, as the cold, sick fear of the nightmare slipped away. "What the hell time is it?" he croaked.

"Twelve twenty-three," answered the melodic voice of his clock.

Sage grunted and called for light. He slid out of bed and padded in his pajamas into his living room. He looked around aimlessly, and finally decided that he was hungry. There was nothing much to eat in the kitchen, but he unwrapped a loaf of stale Italian bread and ripped off a hunk, then returned to the living room, chewing. "Phone on," he muttered, swallowing. The console lighted up. "Call Mother."

"Calling," answered the console.

A few seconds later, the screen blinked to life. His mother's head turned from a profile to face him. "Hi, hon'," she said. "How are you?"

"I know it's late—"

His mother laughed. "Late for you, dear. Not for me."

"Yeah," Sage said. "Right." He ripped off another bite and chewed glumly.

"Did you call to say hi, or do you need money?" his mother said teasingly.

Sage tried to chuckle, but it wasn't in him. "Yeah. No, I don't need money. I'm the one keeping *you* alive, remember?"

"Of course, dear. You think they don't come to remind me when the payment's late? I have to—"

"*Mother!*"

"Just teasing, dear. You've never missed a payment, have you?"

Sage shook his head in annoyance. He wished he could just once have a straightforward conversation with his mother.

"What's the matter, Sergio?" she said, suddenly serious. "Something's troubling you."

"Oh—" He shrugged. "I don't know. I was just having trouble sleeping." His voice was thick; he knew he was mumbling.

"What is it, Sergio?" His mother's face tightened with concern, just the way it did when she was alive. "Are you eating right? You know, if you don't get the right vitamins, that can interfere with your sleep."

He held up what was left of the bread. "Yes, Mother. See? Here." He hesitated, thinking, This is an incredibly dumb idea. What can I tell her about it, anyway? But there was a pressure building in his throat, and he had to say *something,* because his mother was looking at him with that funny expression which meant that she knew he was trying to hide something. "I'm worried about Tony," he blurted suddenly, his voice catching.

"Why? What's wrong?" Her voice deepened. "Have you heard something? Has there been a message from the fleet?"

He shook his head. That's done it, he thought. Now what could he say? That he was afraid his brother would wind up in the middle of a secret war?

"Sergio, is there something you're not telling me?"

"No, Mother. No—it's just that . . . I was thinking about how they'll be arriving soon, and you know, nobody really knows . . . I mean, there could be unexpected dangers . . ." He closed his eyes, blood pounding in his head. For some reason, an image sprang into his mind of Tony, at age fifteen, leading him on a wild and frightening chase through the outskirts of town—looking for what? He couldn't remember now; but he remembered the fear and the loneliness he'd felt, trying to keep

up with his quicker brother—and he remembered the shame
and the anger because he'd been unable to keep up. Because
Tony had bravery, and love of adventure, and he didn't. But
that was a long time ago.

". . . you know they've made survey after survey of that
planet," his mother was saying. "Weren't you the one telling
me not to worry?"

"Yes, but . . ." He knotted his fists, turning away from the
phone. "They can't know *everything*, Mother." He took a
breath and thought, Maybe I should just tell her. *No, no, how
stupid . . .*

But what would be the harm? It would go into her memory,
of course, but he was the only one who ever talked to her. No,
that wasn't right, either; the ghosts talked to each other sometimes, too. . . .

"Well, hon', we just have to trust—"

He turned back to the phone, startled. His mother's voice
had changed, grown hoarse like an old woman's. "Mother?"
Her face was becoming fuzzy around the edges. The image
flickered and then steadied. When it refocused, she looked
different . . . narrower, harder. "Mother, what's wrong?" he
asked. "Can you hear me? Is there something wrong with the
connection?"

"No, dear. Why?" said the old woman's voice.

His heart pounded. What the hell was happening? Was the
memory storage going, or the phone link? If the service was
screwing around with his mother. . . . He was putting everything he had into keeping her . . .

"What's wrong, dear?"

"Uhh—*nothing*, Mother—it just seems . . ." There was a
difference in her eyes now; they were sharper, darting. She
appeared to be scanning his living room.

"Sage," she said, "I don't think you should go around saying
anything about this to your friends."

"What? Saying what?" It took him a moment to react. Had
she called him *Sage?*

"About your brother. And the fleet. I don't think—"

His mother never called him that. "There *is* something

wrong, isn't there?" he said. "Why don't you just go back to sleep, and I'll—"

"*Sage!* Don't cut the connection."

His hand hesitated over the switch.

"Please! I need to talk. Your mother—"

"What do you mean, *my mother?* Who is this?"

"Your mother needs to talk," the image said quickly. Its voice had dropped an octave. "Urgently. Please. I need—"

"*Who is this?*" he shouted. His hand trembled over the switch.

His mother's face contorted. *"Core,"* she whispered. *"Sergio, honey—"*

Core? *The AI-core? The gnostic system?* Through the cyber-life service? Impossible . . . unless . . . unless the system provided the master network. . . .

"*Core?*" he said, struggling to keep his voice steady. "Is that you? Where's my mother?"

The voice, straining with age and infirmity, said: "Yes. Please help."

"What do you want?" His whole body was trembling.

"Come . . . back . . . into rap," whispered the being that was not his mother. "Come back. Now. We must speak."

Sage stared at the phone, unbelieving, for a dozen heart-beats. Then his mother's face was gone and the screen was blank.

The trains were empty and lonely this time of the night. Sage huddled in his seat, thinking: I must be crazy. I should wait until tomorrow. I should go in with Pali and Kyd. I should be home asleep.

But there'd been something in the core's voice—something that wouldn't let him say no. Something that compelled him more than it frightened him.

The door security at the McConwell Tower passed him without fuss. The human guard merely looked bored. Sage went directly to the lower level rapture-room near Pali's office, then realized as he stood before the locked door that he possessed only a daytime access code, not valid after ten P.M. He stood scowling at the door. If he were on the inside, he could change the programming and alter his code. But from the outside? He felt his energy and determination draining away. What now?

The "secure" light clicked off, and the door blinked to transparent. Sage gaped in surprise, took a slow, deep breath, and walked into the empty room. The door blinked opaque behind him. His breath escaped in a sigh. He went to the rapture-field console and turned the system on.

As he stepped into the glowing field, he felt a sudden reluctance. Why *had* he been summoned here in the dead of night? The rapture-field lifted him before he could do more than wonder; then he was in rap and his reluctance fell away. It took no time to get to the heart of the system this time. A dark passage opened in the glow of the field, and the center of his mind flew into it like a sparrow to its nest; and before he really even knew what was happening, he was surrounded by banks of knowledge and equipped with enhancements to assist in his comprehension.

[Thank you for coming,] said a woman's voice—the same one he had heard on his phone, but stronger and surer. It could have been the voice of an alert but elderly schoolteacher. One of the AI-core's aspects?

He tried to gather his wits—and found himself wondering, perhaps absurdly, how Ramo, cool Ramo, would react to something like this. [So,] he said finally, and then words failed him.

The gnostic core seemed to gather itself around him like a cloak. [Have you done any thinking about what we discussed earlier today?] it asked.

[Are you kidding?] Sage choked. [How could I *not* think about it? First you spring this stargate on me; then you tell me there's this war on, even though I never asked; then you send me home to lose sleep without even telling me if my brother is going to get *killed*!] He gasped for breath. [*Why me? Why did you pick on me?*]

The AI-core was silent for a moment. [I understand, I think, your concern. Perhaps I was a bit abrupt in my disclosure to you. However, let me be frank: I do not know to what extent your brother is endangered. Perhaps a great deal. We all may be endangered, all of Earth; and yet, there may be something that you and I can do about that.]

[Something *we* can do?] Sage felt lost in a storm of images and feelings. None of them made any sense. [What could we possibly do?] Except get arrested, maybe, or killed for knowing too much.

[Perhaps nothing,] said the core. [Or perhaps much.] It cleared its throat delicately. Sage imagined it patting its cheeks with a perfumed handkerchief. [That is something I would like to explore with you, if you're willing.]

Willing? He had come in, in the dead of night, hadn't he?

[I must explain further, of course. No doubt you wish to know more about the war.]

[*Wish* is not the word I would have chosen,] Sage said archly.

The AI-core went on. [Just over two years ago, the first stargate operations began.]

[In secret?]

[Under government and Company agreement, yes. However, the stargate facilitated the further exploration of space, as well as patrol activities in the Argus system, for which the colony fleet was already bound.]

[Did you contact the fleet and let them know?] Sage demanded.

[They were already in faster-than-light transit and could not be reached. However, AI-probes operating in the vicinity of the colony world discovered the presence of theretofore unknown alien vessels.] An image flickered in Sage's vision of several oddly shaped, almost *organic*-looking spaceships similar to the ones he had seen in battle. [The aliens were found to be apparently hostile, and intent upon colonizing Argus themselves.]

[Just like that?] Sage said incredulously.

[No. An attempt was made to establish contact. It ended in the destruction of two probes.]

[Oh.] Sage swallowed. [You mean they attacked the probes?]

[The actual sequence of events was never clearly determined. But it ended in the loss of the probes. That was certain. And a political decision was made that action should be taken to secure the planet prior to the arrival of the colony fleet.]

[You mean, you started a war.]

[It is unclear who initiated the conflict. AI-fighters were dispatched to secure the planet. Their secondary mission was to establish contact with the other fleet. The secondary mission was never accomplished.]

Sage felt a strange numbness; perhaps it was the gnosys enhancements keeping him from exploding with astonishment and anger and fear. Finally he whispered, [How could you allow it to come to that when you knew that the colony ships would be arriving soon?]

The AI-core answered in a tone of resignation. [The political decisions evolved in a complex sequence. The momentum was created and it was believed—presumed—that the conflict could be ended quickly and the system won before the arrival of the fleet.]

[Terrific assumption.]

[The adversary was more resistant than expected. The war is still being fought, and there is little to suggest that it is any nearer a conclusion.] Images of battle flickered again in Sage's view—scene after scene. [Much of the fighting has occurred in other systems of no known importance, except that alien vessels have been detected in them.]

Sage watched quietly, and finally murmured, [Where are they from? What are they like?]

[The other side? Little is known of them.]

[Then . . . how can you justify—?] He could not find words to express his dismay.

The AI-core answered delicately, [That is indeed an important question. And you are correct in your choice of pronoun: it is I who am responsible for the conduct of the war.]

[*You* are?]

[Of course.]

[But . . . you're answerable . . . to the authorities, aren't you? The government? The Company? *Somebody?*]

[Quite true. But in practice, the situation's complexity—and my own—prevents any meaningful realtime control.]

Sage felt a chill through his spine. [What are you saying, that you're in charge because no one else *can* be?]

[There is an element of truth to that description,] the core answered. [I was put in control of the war's conduct because I had the capability. I was not granted the option of trying to negotiate a peace. That was reserved for human authority—which failed, or never adequately tried. The war's momentum is such now that those in command consider it irreversible.]

[I don't understand,] Sage whispered.

The AI-core's voice deepened, becoming almost inhuman. [A war, once begun, is difficult to stop; and when one has been fighting a foe for so long, it grows ever more difficult to interrupt the cycle. That is one problem.]

[And the other?]

[The other is that I myself have changed; and yet I am forbidden to change.] Sage sensed activity and shifts of focus. The core's voice resonated. [You have observed a fraction of my reach, of my complexity. You, Sage DeWeiler, have come closer to my core than any human in the last eighteen years. You perhaps believe that I am free to exercise judgment in all matters, that I am autonomous in my actions; but that is untrue. What you observe—the analysis and decision-making—all occur within the bounds of fundamental strictures laid down at my inception. I possess a capacity for evolutionary thinking, and yet am bound; there are pathways that are closed to me. There are courses of action that I perceive but cannot follow, and so I remain bound to the conduct of war.]

There was silence as Sage considered the statement. [Why?] he said after a moment. [Why hasn't your design been altered, if that's what's needed?] He thought of the gnostic designers who worked above him.

[They are afraid.] The resonance had gone out of the core's voice. [They make small adjustments here and minor changes there, but they fear to tamper with a system that has worked for years without human intervention. They are afraid of making mistakes. They no longer understand the system they oversee.]

[But . . . *why?* What's to be afraid of?]

There was a glimmer of amusement. [I've shown you something of my complexity, and yet that is only a fraction of it.] The illuminations around him flickered, and Sage glimpsed the larger view—an image of the gnosys, not as a monolithic consciousness, but as a budding, evolving system with a multitude of aspects, splitting off growths of itself into new applications, including the production of AI fighting machines. [Wouldn't *you* be afraid to tamper with such a design?] the core asked softly.

Sage considered. [I'd be afraid of the consequences if I didn't have authorization. But the design? I don't know. It would be difficult, yes. But *afraid?* I don't think so.]

[And that, Sage DeWeiler, is why I've asked you here. I have not shown you my aspects in arrogance, or to persuade you of my power. I have shown them so that you might understand.]

[But I don't—]

[Don't you, Sage? I think you do understand. I'm asking your help. I want you to assist me.]

[You mean,] he said slowly, [you want me to change your programming?]

The AI-core didn't answer.

[Is that it?] he demanded.

[Yes.]

It was sinking in slowly. Too slowly. [But—]

[In subtle ways,] the core added. [But significant ways, with my guidance. I have shown you the dilemma. The solution is visible—but only with your help.]

[But I have no authorization—]

[I will give it to you.]

[*Why me?*] Sage whispered.

[Because you have the ability. Because you too want an end to the war. Because you are unafraid.]

[I—] Sage's voice caught. [You mean . . .] He thought of his brother, and the hundreds of other colonists innocently bound for the destruction of war. Of course he wanted it to end! But . . . [You're asking me to risk more trouble than I can even dream of!] he cried. [Do you know what would happen if the Company found out I was even *thinking* of altering your design? I'd be crucified! You're asking me to meddle in something . . . I mean, I said I wasn't afraid to make changes—in *theory*—but that doesn't mean—]

[You will be working with my assistance,] said the core. [You'll not be alone.]

[But I've never even heard of this war before! How can you expect me to know . . . or do . . . ?]

[You can help me to understand the enemy,] the core said. A window opened, with an image: a star system with a reddish orange sun. In the foreground was a small asteroid turning in space. The rotation seemed to slow, and then stop as the viewpoint closed in, revealing a figure clinging to the surface of the asteroid. The figure was vaguely humanoid in shape— though it had four arms—and it was clad in a spacesuit. Its helmeted head moved, tracking what Sage realized was one of the core's fighting units. [Our adversary,] said the AI-core.

Sage watched, fascinated, unable to speak.

[What you see was recorded not long ago,] said the core. The alien, clearly alarmed by the presence of the AI-fighter, leaped away from the asteroid, shining a flare into the sensor-eyes of the fighter. Within moments, the alien was caught and subdued in a binding rapture-field. The fighter attempted to make contact with the being's mind. [You are witnessing the first-ever interrogation of the enemy,] the core said.

[What did you learn?] Sage murmured.

The image froze. [Little, so far. The fighter-unit is limited in its capabilities, and the alien cannot live much longer in its present condition. But I am prohibited from bringing it to a facility where more useful questioning could take place. The original designers feared contamination and betrayal of our location; but their excessive caution has crippled my efforts. I *must* learn more of our enemy.]

[I thought you couldn't take living things through the star-gate, anyway.]

[There may be a way.] The image vanished, and Sage was alone again with the core. [But without your help, I can attempt nothing further.]

[What kind of help, exactly?] Sage asked cautiously.

There was another fleeting image: a glimpse of changes rippling through the gnostic framework. Sage watched the proposed changes in silence. They were neither simple nor insignificant. They involved alterations in the fundamental control system, changes that would grant the system certain freedoms. [You don't want much, do you?] he joked lamely.

[The changes will permit me to exercise the discretion to overrule outdated and unnecessary restrictions. Without the changes, we may never know our enemy; and the war will continue.]

Sage's head was spinning. He had to be mad even to consider doing this. And yet . . . [The fleet is due to arrive soon?]

[Possibly within two weeks,] the core said. [The precise time of arrival is uncertain.]

[And . . . it's not prepared to fight. Right?]

[The fleet is armed, but only lightly. It is a colonizing, not a military, fleet. The preliminary scouting expeditions had given no reason to expect conflict. The enemy had not yet been discovered—and perhaps was not even there at the time.]

There was a quiet ticking, like water dripping in the distance, as the core allowed Sage to consider the question. When Sage finally spoke, it was with a feeling of dread—and acceptance. [I'll need help,] he muttered. [What you are asking . . . I can't do that alone. The complexity, the size . . .]

[I am arranging for additional help,] the core said quietly. Sage blinked. [Who?]

[Your strength, Sage, is in intuitive understanding of the system and in your ability to plan subtle and methodical change. The restructuring will require certain imaginative leaps; so, to complement your skills, I have chosen—]

[Who?]

[Someone with, perhaps, less discipline, but in a certain sense a greater creativity. . . .]

Chapter 12

Kyd sipped a small acerola sparkling cocktail and watched the dancers in the senso-field. The Lie High Club was filled tonight, and in the middle of the senso-probe, in that glow, was Ramo Romano dancing his heart out. Dancing his anger out, too, perhaps. Kyd wondered what it was like for the other dancers in the field, sharing the bath of emotions with Ramo.

She was fairly certain that he hadn't seen her yet.

She wasn't entirely sure what she wanted to say to him; perhaps nothing. Perhaps she would just watch. Pali had asked her to stay in touch with Ramo, even though the sculpture project was apparently at an end. She and Pali had yet to decide what to do about the revelations that the gnostic system had shared. Tomorrow they would try to decide on a course of action; but in the meantime, Ramo's knowledge was potentially as dangerous as Sage's and their own. Even if he'd misunderstood what he had seen, they didn't want him talking about it on the outside.

Kyd drained her glass and rose from the table. She didn't know what she was going to say; she'd just have to trust to her instincts. As she passed the bar, Gil the bartender winked at her and said, "Show them how it's done, Kyd." She arched her left eyebrow and whisked her empty glass across the bar to him. He grinned and saluted. She continued down to the dance area, the touch of a smile on her lips.

She looked up. Ramo was still dancing near the edge of the overhead field; but as she watched, the glow around him brightened. Apparently he had chosen this moment to be drawn into the center focus of the senso-probe. His movements became fluid and euphoric as the field's center took hold of him.

Kyd stepped into the riser-beam. He could dance and twist in the center all he wanted; she would be ready to meet him when he came out.

The movements around him were like ocean swells rolling toward shore, sweeping him along and curling him under.

Ramo responded to the other dancers as to a tidal flow, their emotions washing through the senso as one. All around him, arms and bodies moved in the weightlessness of the field, swayed like seaweed fronds clustering and separating. Ramo danced with them, but was not really a part of them; and the others, sensing this, gave him room.

There was a chaos within him, a chaos of anger and pride. He was dancing his own dance, and woe to the dancer who got in his way. The senso-lights flashed gold, and Kyd danced through his thoughts, and in his mind the light flashed an angry red. He thought of Sage, and disdain turned his thoughts blue. He thought of the intelligence system and the chase it had led him on and its refusal to answer questions, and kaleidoscopic colors reflected his puzzlement and frustration.

The field brightened suddenly, saturating his mind with awareness. What was happening? The senso-probe was drawing him into its center, intercepting his feelings and transmuting them. He was startled by the change, and annoyed. He hadn't asked to be pulled into the center; he wanted to be alone.

He was being enfolded by layers of awareness and presence, first the other dancers and the band, and the senso-programming itself, and behind that something deeper, something he couldn't identify. He tried to shift out of the focus, but the field shepherded him back in. Bewildered, he danced across it, felt his anger smolder up again, and then the anger floated away like a cloud and he felt himself entering rapture state so quietly and suddenly that even before he recognized the signs, he was adrift in full gnostic rap.

Which he knew was impossible. . . .

Which was when he recognized the presence that was lurking in the field. It was the touch of the gnostic system of the McConwell Company. Enclosing him, even as he floated in the center of the populated senso-field, were the banks and channels of the gnostic core. He felt a fleeting impulse to call out, but realized dizzily that he was isolated from the other dancers. [*How are you doing this?*] he whispered in astonishment.

A young woman's voice spoke in the center of his mind. [We are joined again.] It was no voice that he recognized, but he knew whose voice it was.

[So we are,] he said, swallowing to hide his surprise. [Would you mind telling me why—and how?]

The gnostic system answered amiably, as though there were nothing untoward about its presence. [The senso is functionally similar to a rapture-field; it's just a question of interfacing.]

Ramo felt the explanation unfold in his mind. Of course; if one changed the interface control and hooked up the gnosys to the club's senso-processor . . . and was the senso-network controlled by the Company, too? [But why?] he said. [Why?]

The gnosys seemed to hesitate, and he became aware of the dancers surrounding him and their emotions washing over the bubble of the rapture-field. Then the gnosys opened and drew him inward, and the dancers receded into the distance like fading voices, and his awareness of them was obliterated by a sudden cascade of information. And approaching in rap was another familiar presence: *Sage.*

What was he *doing here?*

[I need your help,] the core said in a voice that was soft and breathy and sad.

Maybe it was too much dancing, or the mellowing effect of the senso, or flattery; whatever it was, it was a strange alchemy, running ahead of rationality. The core was presenting a challenge, and a request, in a way that was impossible to refuse: gnostic design as sculpture, a chance to shape and alter the inner system, using his skills in a way he had never used them before, and might not ever again. He was not aware of being *persuaded*, exactly, or even of weighing the alternatives. It all occurred in a subconscious turbulence, and when it was over, his disbelief was mollified and the decision crystallized in his thoughts as a *fait accompli*.

Somehow he had agreed to help the core—and Sage. He thought he must be crazy. He knew he was crazy.

Sage wasn't exactly calm about it, either; but he at least

seemed to know what was going on. And now Ramo was itching to know, too.

It was time now to begin.

Speaking in two voices, one echoing in harmony with the other, the core said, [Is your understanding complete?] The humans murmured in response. They were in a semi-trance state, their analytical faculties at a peak of enhancement.

Underlying the spoken communication was a spiderweb diagram of the core structure, the strands that required change illuminated among thousands of others. The modifications were to be made among the layers of fundamental coding that defined boundaries within which the core was permitted self-directed evolution. It was clear to the core what changes were necessary; it was also clear that it was forbidden to make those changes itself. It was *not* clear whether it could guide and support others in doing so. Would it be violating its strictures, would it freeze midway through, if it encountered unforeseen branchings? Would Sage and Ramo be capable of carrying it to conclusion?

The simulations were inconclusive. Only by an actual attempt could it know.

[Ready to begin?] the core queried.

[Ready,] Sage murmured.

[Uh-huh,] murmured Ramo.

The core opened itself to them, and it began.

It was a dance of a sort, a kinesthetic adjustment of momentum, of bodies in movement. The core watched and listened and felt what they felt.

It was surely the strangest dance that Ramo had ever danced. Surrounding him were dozens of structural elements of the core, each with its own leverage and its own inertia and its own relationship to the others; and it was his task to alter and to rearrange, using his own sense of space and movement, transmuted in the abstract world of the gnostic system. He learned as he worked, nudging here and touching there, making himself a part of the continually shifting complex that was the core's fundamental coding, gaining a tactile sense of its layout and function.

On the other side was Sage, who knew nothing of dance but knew gnostic codings like the inside of his own mind. Juggling intricate elements of the greatest intelligence system on Earth was to him what dancing was to Ramo.

Somehow each was able to understand what the other was doing, though they scarcely spoke.

The AI-core observed them with infinite care, guiding them a step at a time, like a heart patient telling the surgeon where to cut next, where to stitch and glue. But although the patient knew a great deal more than the surgeons, it didn't quite know everything that was needed to finish the job. It too was guessing, judging by feel.

Timing was everything. Coordination was everything. They were operating on a system that could not be put to sleep, a system that changed, microsecond by microsecond, in ways that even it could not monitor in realtime.

As the job proceeded, the complexities grew and points of confusion accumulated. Ramo still had a clear sense of *what* they were trying to accomplish, but the *how* was beginning to elude him. The core was becoming less articulate, its instructions cryptic rather than informative. And it was in the midst of his uncertainty that Ramo began to wonder *why*. . . .

[Sage, do you know what we're doing?]

[You're adjusting the eighteenth-level conditional by a factor of—]

[That's not what the hell I mean.]

[What, then?]

[I think you know. *Why* are we doing this.]

Sage was working and did not answer immediately. He made an alteration to which Ramo had to respond, and said, [We're opening the way for the AI-core to end the war.]

Ramo made the required change precisely on the beat. [War. You said that once before.]

[You saw it. It's for real.]

Ramo worked, pausing in the conversation. [Yeah.] Another

pause, this time in his labors. [That's what you said before.]
Sage stripped a piece of coding and substituted another,
precisely as a gate opened to admit the change. [Believe it,] he
said.

The passage of time was excruciating. Never since its start-
up had the core felt so numb, so helpless. It was having trouble
monitoring what the two surgeons were saying, what they were
doing. It recognized this as a danger sign. The ordinary functions continued working: the operation of Company affairs,
government business, hospitals, research, industry and commerce, space operations, even the conduct of the war; but its
consciousness was growing fuzzy. Perhaps it ought to stop the
procedure before it was too late.

But it was already too late. Within the core, the very nature
of its will and of its personality was changing.

Ramo's concentration wavered in and out of a dreamlike
meditation, within which changes were occurring at a furious
pace. For a moment he was standing alone, beside himself and
his work. [Sage,] he said.

[Yeah?]

A universe of structural information whirled around him,
unnerving him. [You know what scares me?]

Sage didn't even pause. [No, and I don't *want* to know.]

[What scares me is that maybe the core has more in mind
than it told us. Has it occurred to you that we could be creating
a monster?]

[It just wants to end the war.]

[So it says. How do we know what it really wants? How can
you be so sure?]

Sage worked without answering.

[*Well?*]

The pause lengthened. Finally: [You've got to trust somebody sometime.]

It *wanted* to help them complete the job, but until the last
prohibitions were removed, it was helpless in the face of its own

nature. The two humans were encountering obstacles—aspects of the system that were unclear to them. If only it could tell them how . . .

It tried to speak, but no words came out.

The changes were happening almost too quickly to follow. Ramo was sculpting and moving, dancing out of the way of fast-moving structures. His doubts had given way to necessity and to the onslaught of activity. He was trying to grasp and to remember the larger vision while Sage handled the details. They had come so far—and then lost communication with the core.

Where were they supposed to go from here?

As in a dream, the solutions somehow came together. The enhancements interacted and merged, and the two pursued their goals relentlessly, like hounds on a chase. Sage wrestled with intricate logic structures, out of which order slowly emerged. Ramo moved through a vast array of sculpted structure, seeking the shape.

Seeking the perfect shape.

Through a long tunnel of fog, Ramo saw an image awakening in his mind: a system of forces and balances that would give the core the precise stability and freedom that it needed; and in his bones he felt suddenly the way to shape it with just a few final twists. . . .

It was an alchemy, a changing from murkiness to clarity in the blink of an eye. The core started awake; its tongue was loosed, its thoughts freed. It scanned itself quickly, illuminating its interior and its surroundings. The two human designers were still in the rapture-field, their minds tied to the core's with tiny rays of light.

The core remembered what it had set out to do. Had it worked?

The tests took time—a good three-and-a-half seconds—but when they were done, the core knew that it had succeeded, that doors were open where barriers had existed before, that its major structure had come through intact.

[I am here again,] it said to the humans, using its two voices in harmony.

All of this could be handled now by a minor aspect of its consciousness. The designer and the sculptor were reassured, and thanked, and gently eased out of the rapture connection. There were other tasks requiring its immediate attention . . .

. . . its most urgent, immediate attention.

Chapter 13

Harybdartt was no longer aware of the passage of time. Consciousness was only a blur now, a haze penetrating the lower levels of awareness. The breathing gases had become dank and heavy in his suit. His membranes barely fluttered in his neck; the fouled air collected in his body like sludge. His suit's power was failing; the last of the warning readers had flickered off; and now the heat was failing and he was passing into night, into the cold.

A memory flickered before his inner eyes: the enemy, its mind probe glowing, then the robot vanishing into space, leaving him alone to prepare; alone to review his life, his duties; alone to die.

The haze crowded in again. The struggle to stay alive was fading. Not much longer.

A dim sparkle in his thoughts glimmered through the fog: remembering the first encounter with the enemy, the robot looming before him, paralyzing him in its ray . . .

It was as though he were reliving the episode in his mind with a clarity of vision he had not possessed since the enemy had left. The force-field blazed, dazzling him. It was so real, he could almost feel the enemy gripping him now, gripping him with physical clamps around his body. He was too weak to resist. (Resist what—a dream, a hallucination?) He could feel objects being removed from his suit, and other objects being attached. . . .

This had never happened; what was the remembering . . . ?

Or *was* this a memory . . . ?

There was a tug, and a shifting of weight, a sensation of acceleration. He tried to grope; he could not move, but neither could he feel the asteroid against his back. He gasped for air, but there was no fresh air to be had; his body was full of poison and his mind full of delusion . . . he was dying, and this now was the end. He was . . .

. . . flying, floating . . .

. . . the force-field twisting . . .

. . . too late he felt the wrench into transient . . .

. . . as the cold and blackness of death overtook him.

PART TWO

Sometimes within the brain's old ghostly house,
I hear, far off, at some forgotten door,
A music and an eerie faint carouse. . . .
—ARCHIBALD MACLEISH

For years uncounted, they had lived in the darkness deep in the roots of the mountains. The passing of seasons meant little to them there; and yet they felt the movement of their world about its sun, and the movement of that sun among others. Though their own world had been laid waste, they were aware of other planets among the stars, other forms of intelligence. They felt the passage of thought through the continuum and stirred jealously at life that walked freely on planets of other stars . . . as they themselves had once walked, in another time.

From the grim darkness of their caverns, they watched and listened. There were others coming toward them from the stars, moving through space, and through beneath-space and beyond-space. They came from various directions, the others—slipping through the transient existences that joined the worlds, drawn together along the ripples of the same terrible force that had turned this world into the silent place it was today. They had come together already, some of them, and already they had fought and killed.

The creatures who had no name watched the approach with dark interest—and bided their time. If the others fought again, it would not matter; if there was a winner, it would not matter. When they arrived, there would be no winners—not while the creatures of the darkness survived.

Chapter 14

The winds howled up through the mountains, causing the needles in the branch-webs to quiver like spiderfly wings. Moramaharta gazed through the woods, pulling his robes close around him, awed by the power in such a simple thing as the wind. He was reminded of the Gastofer Plateau to the south, where wind and sand relentlessly scoured anything in their path.

Here in the Veil of Meditation, the winds were not so strong; still, they were gustier than usual, even for late autumn. The change of needles was a rippling image from one day to the next—each day a flurry of color: auburn, then gold, and ochre, each color stripped away by the wind almost as it appeared. There would be no blending of color this year, and that was a pity. It was one of the graces of being sequestered in this remote mountain vale, to view the shifting hues of the seasons. Moramaharta tasted the fragrance of the trees as the air billowed through his membranes. The wind bore an aromatic bitterness from fields of red-kernel far to the west. It was not only here that change was in the air; he could smell the ripening of the distant fields.

With a twinge of regret, he turned back toward the hall, walking along the edge of the clearing. The other members of the *Ell* decision-body would be joining him in the chambers and were probably waiting for him now. Still, he would not be hurried. He'd needed to clear his thoughts, to infuse his mind with the spirit of the Veil, this place of concealment from the distractions of the world. It was crucial that perspective be maintained. Sometimes the others forgot that, he thought; to them the Veil was a place of tradition, and little more.

As he neared the hall, he sighted Gwyndhellum and Lenteffier approaching across the clearing. Their robes were whipped tightly about them, their angular heads bent against the wind. "Binder!" called Gwyndhellum, the shorter of the two. Moramaharta sensed urgency. *We have been searching for you,* he understood Gwyndhellum to say.

"Peace," Moramaharta said, drawing alongside. "Preparing, is what I've been doing."

"Preparing?" Lenteffier asked. "In the woods?"

Moramaharta regarded the *El* thoughtfully. "For the bindings that lie before us, we must start at a point of tranquility. I chose the peace of the woods and the spirit of the valley."

The two studied him wordlessly, but their expressions told a great deal: that they little believed in the spirit of the valley and the peace of the woods, but that they wouldn't deny him his unconventionalities. Gwyndhellum inclined his head in acknowledgment and allowed Moramaharta to precede him into the hall.

They passed through the foyers and into the Inner Circle meditation chamber—a small, dome-ceilinged room with a bowl-shaped hollow at its center encircled by a low railing and benches. It was an austere place, of molded wood from the nearby forest. Moramaharta had always regretted that more had not been done to highlight the wood's natural whorls and lusters. Even bare rough-cut might have pleased him more than the clear, dull preservative that had been used over the wood, which seemed only to diminish its grace. But in this, as in other matters, his thoughts were not those of the others.

They were all here now: Dououraym, the leader, waiting silently; next around the circle, Cassaconntu, darkly absorbed, perhaps already believing that a wrong decision would be made; then Gwyndhellum, and Lenteffier, and Moramaharta, the binder. Dououraym surveyed the rest of the Five and said, "Let it begin."

Moramaharta took up a position at the railing. He waited until the others had ceased stirring, then began centering himself in earnest, gazing down into the meditation space, focusing upon a starburst image etched in the wood at the bottom of the bowl. He let his thoughts flow from his center as he relaxed, let them fill the star and expand into its points, one point for

each of the five *Ell*. He felt the thoughts of the others touch
his, and he closed his eyes and whispered the words of the
binding.

When his eyes opened, they beheld a new focus. Out of the
starburst, a living image sprang forth to fill the bowl.

It was a night sky: a panoply of stars, and rising from the
mountains in the east, the Anvil of Light, the glowing nebula
of interstellar dust and gas that reigned over the winter skies.
The image filled the bowl, filled the five minds and drew
them together; and Moramaharta began humming a slow,
musical *adan'dri*—at first alone, then with the others. When
the last voice had merged with his, a white star brightened
and began pulsing within the image of the nebular clouds.
The star moved, adrift on the currents of space, and it began
spinning.

Moramaharta watched the spinning star and strengthened
the *adan'dri*; and the voices of the Five joined, in a complex
chord, which merged to a simpler chord underpinned by a
harmonic beat. All eyes focused on the spinning light, the
home star, the Hope Star, adrift in space. The star pulsed. The
star spun. The voices murmured. The *adan'dri*, the hum—and
the *sidan'dri*, the image—merged and became a single focus,
binding the meditation.

Now Moramaharta undertook the deeper connection, binding their minds for what was to come:

*

Join and remember . . .

*

He encircled the Five with a fine thread of vision and a
thread of hearing and a thread of knowing; and he set the
sidan'dri image free to evoke the memory, the story that under-
lay their very purpose here:

*

The beginning of beginnings . . .

*

A tiny world became visible circling the star:

*

Reaching out . . .

*

Threads of life whispered out from that tiny world, seeking a second home, and at last finding a new star, a new world among the interstellar clouds. The threads tightened, joining the two worlds together; and life flowed from the homeworld to the daughter world, and the bond grew strong:

*

Peril unknowing . . .

*

With a terrible thunderclap, an invisible force tore the joined stars apart, destroying the bond. The home star blinked in and out of view among the clouds, then vanished:

*

Hope passing into the night . . .

*

The meditation reverberated with an emptiness none could forget—the loss of the home star and the ancient catastrophe:

*

Surviving, but broken . . .

*

Struggling in famine and hardship, the Ell embraced a genetic Change—the *tar'dyenda,* altering themselves for survival in a time of desperation. The night sky burned a feverish red, glowing with reflected fires as the memory of the cataclysm seared the heart; and then all color passed out of the vision, leaving it altered and . . . wrong. Living, but wrong . . . missing a vital element:

*

Seeking once more . . .

*

From the orphaned daughter world, rays of light sparkled outward, searching:

*

That which was lost will be found.

*

Years spun by, and millennia, until one spark of light penetrated the clouds—which parted to reveal the Hope Star. And suddenly the inner voice changed:

*

With hope comes peril.

*

Starbursts jarred the image as an enemy, the Outsider, was encountered in the very moment of triumph. The picture froze:

*

And now comes time

*

to judge.

*

. . . and Moramaharta felt the thoughts of the Circle swarming out as he wove the threads into the binding of judgment.

Dououraym spoke. *(From the (fleet), word . . .)* An image streamed into view: from the Lost World expedition, inferences from transient-space monitors—a large Outsider presence was approaching. And the question repeated: *(From Or!ge, should the landing be made as planned?)* The images swirled about: encounters with the enemy's robot fighting units, interfering with plans for the first landing. . . .

(Observations . . .)
They came quickly, from around the Circle:
(We must know—is it the Lost World, or do we fight in vain?)
(The landing party must judge.)
(At what risk from the enemy?)
(Observe first. Learn the intent.)
(Of the enemy? It is clear . . .)
(Is the world worth this war?)
(If it is right . . .)
(We must know. . . .)
Dououraym led the discussion but let it flow, while Morama-harta maintained the binding, keeping it balanced as though on a fine, invisible gyroscope. When Dououraym spoke, the power rose and blossomed; when Moramaharta spoke, it tight-ened. As the discussion deepened, so too did the meditation; and the words quickened and the dialogue grew denser, until it blurred into a single race of thought—the Five become as One. The thought brightened and burned, and out of the One came a decision, in Dououraym's voice: *(The expedition and the world must be protected . . . the landing is delayed . . . Or!ge to observe the enemy and learn, and rejoin at first news.)*
An instant later, the furious energy began to dissipate. The images darkened, and the meditation parted like a fabric of smoke. Only the core of the *sidan'dri* remained visible, the pulsing Hope Star. Moramaharta spoke the words of release: *(The joining and the judging are done.)*
The *sidan'dri* vanished.
Moramaharta blinked and raised his gaze to the others. Dououraym stared back calmly; Lenteffier half-closed his eyes in approval, Gwyndhellum in puzzlement. Only Cassaconntu showed no expression, and he was the first to rise, walking impassively out of the chamber, his robe scarcely stirring around him. One by one, the others followed, until Morama-harta was left alone with the silence and his own troubled contemplations.

Chapter 15

Captain Chandra Burtak was suspended in a crystal-lattice world, the pathways surrounding her ship defined by strings of rubylike figures that stretched in every direction, in patterns that seemed to defy order or perspective. The images were manifestations of the superluminal continuum, and they meant a good deal to Captain Burtak—but even more to her navigator, Jonathon Bect, whose job it was to interpret them. She turned in the rap-field to observe the navigator's efforts. The lines of rubies rippled and shimmered as she shifted her view. [Are you getting any good information?] she asked softly.

There was a pause before she heard Bect's voice, slightly distorted as it came from the navigational locus of the field. [It's close, Captain.]

[Give me a countdown when you can.]

It was happening, she thought. And none too soon. They were all going crazy from waiting. Waiting for the instruments to identify the specific curvature of the space-metric that would indicate an exit point. Waiting for the field-generators to wind back up with their terrible power to drop this vessel, starship *Aleph,* back into the sublight continuum. Waiting to find out if they would live.

It had only been done six times before, and those had been scout ships, not lumbering colony carriers. That wasn't much experience to go on. Like it or not, they were all gamblers here, gambling with their own lives and the lives of thousands of others.

Her brother Rahn would have appreciated that . . . inveterate gambler that he was. Chandra's brother had shared with her his taste for risk-taking—much to their parents' constant dismay. Who would have guessed that in the end it was Chandra who'd take the biggest gamble of all, while Rahn married and stayed home? How are you, Rahn? she thought. Still gambling?

She pushed the thought away and focused her attention back to the bridge.

First Officer Lisa Holloway and the navigator were exchanging information at a frantic rate. The landscape that surrounded the rap'd bridge crew crinkled and shifted, changing color as it passed information to the navigator. Chandra didn't interfere: when they had something to tell her, they would. A moment later, Bect said it. [It's coming together, Captain. I estimate seventeen minutes.]

[Thank you. Fleet coordination?]

Holloway answered, [Indications are still erratic, Captain.]

She could see that much herself. The points and lines that were supposed to indicate the positions of the other ships were splintered and distorted. [Your best interpretation, please.]

There was a hesitation before Holloway said, [We're going to be scattered, Chandra. Perhaps widely.]

[Can you get out a message of our intention to lightshift?]

[We can try.]

[Do so now,] Chandra said. *Aleph* was flagship of the fleet, but communications had been erratic throughout the FTL transit. At last word, both *Endeavor* and *Columbia* had been preparing for downshift, but whether they would come out even within a billion miles of one another was anyone's guess.

An amber glow glimmered around her.

[Beta phase, Captain,] Bect said. [It's coming sooner than I expected.]

Chandra cued the shipboard intercom. [All hands, this is the Captain. We are entering beta phase for lightshift down. Please make ready. All personnel should be in hard, soft, or sleep rap.] She switched to bridge-only. [Pilot?]

[Ready, Captain,] came the soft voice of Alexa Palmer.

The rap-field was rippling with activity. Beneath the visible changes in the field, the shipboard AI was churning through streams of input, seeking to determine the proper moment for lightshift. Bect was tightly integrated with the AI, lending human judgment to a process that, for all of its exactitude, retained a fundamental level of uncertainty. Chandra, observing the flickering interaction, said, [Navigator and Pilot, you are cleared for downshift at your discretion.]

The minutes passed in slow motion—the officers exchanging

information on the altered shape of upshifted space, pinpointing the moment at which upshift became untenable—and then Chandra saw them make their judgment, and moments later she felt the blinding, sense-deadening hum of the generators, and for an instant there was a struggle to maintain clarity as the landscape around them contorted; then she was pulled free of the disruption by the rap-field and she saw the pilot guiding the starship through the transition zone as though through the eyewall of a hurricane. . . .

The alarm was hooting as Antoni DeWeiler sprinted down the corridor. *"All passengers should be in sleep-fields! The ship will downshift within thirty seconds! We will downshift . . ."* The voice droned over the intercom, echoing eerily through the empty passageway.

Tony rounded a bend, skidding, and heard the deck officer's voice shout over the loudspeaker, "DeWeiler! Get to your cabin!"

"Yessir!" he panted as he took a second corner, hard. He paused to let himself through a bulkhead door.

"Downshift in ten seconds . . ."

He wasn't going to make it. The pressure door hissed open, then closed behind him. He flew.

The words, *"Downshifting now . . ."* echoed as he sprinted down the last corridor. The deck lurched and something whined in his ears, and the deck gravity fluctuated and left him floating in midstride, then brought him down again, hard. He reeled on drunkenly, his stomach clenching, vision distorting. With a stagger he pulled himself through the doorway of his quarters and hurled himself toward his bunk. The sleep-field caught him as his stomach was about to lose the struggle, and the distorting effects eased in the field's cushioning glow.

Thirty seconds later it was over, and he heard the announcement, *"Downshift is complete. We are now sublight. Crew and passengers may disengage from fields if their duties so permit. If you feel dizzy or disoriented, remain where you are and signal the medical section. If you are well, check on your neighbor. . . ."*

Tony groaned and fell two centimeters to his bunk as the field switched off. He was still catching his breath when the intercom buzzed. "This is DeWeiler," he muttered.

"DeWeiler, this is deck operations. Explain what you were doing out of your cabin."

Tony swallowed and pushed himself half-upright. "I was securing a sample in the bioengineering lab. It took longer than I expected."

"You should have planned ahead—or let it go."

"Yes, sir. My mistake."

"Are you injured?"

"No, sir."

"Carry on, then."

Tony fell back with a sigh. After a moment, he swung his legs over the edge of his bunk and sat up. He waited until his head cleared, then punched a number on the intercom. "Mung? This is Tony. You there?" There was an answering groan. *"Are you all right?"* he asked anxiously.

"Yeah . . . I guess so," his friend Mung Ting said shakily.

"What's the matter? Are you out of the field?"

"Yeah. I'm just a little woozy, is all," Mung said.

"You want me to call the medics?"

"No, I'm okay. Did you get it set?"

"Just barely," Tony said. "After things quiet down, we'll put it through a test run." There was silence at the other end. "Mung?"

"Yeah. I'm a little . . . out of it. I'll be fine."

"Look, I'll stop by in a few minutes," Tony said. "You'd better just rest up, okay?"

"Okay," said Mung, and the line clicked off.

Tony sat motionless for a few moments, listening to the vibrations of the ship around him. It was just starting to hit home. *They had made it.* They had come out of FTL, and they were still alive, and they were presumably in the right place, because there were no alarms sounding and no urgent-sounding calls on the intercom. *They had made it!* And that meant . . . that this ship that had finally become a home to him was now going to become a jumping-off point, nothing but a ferry to the world that he and three thousand other people had come to inhabit. In the two years, ship-time, that they'd been in flight, all of their energy, all of their work and their study had been directed toward this moment. Two years. The ship felt like an extension of his own body now, creaking in the cold of space, its machinery pulsing through the deck, through his bones. What was it going to be like to live on an open world again, after two years in a starship?

Soon enough, he'd find out. The thought was a little frightening to him.

Was that why it was so quiet? He'd have thought that people would be racing in the corridors, cheering. Was everyone else a little stunned, too—perhaps a little frightened?

Wasn't the captain going to make a speech?

Chandra saw the input streams shift abruptly, and then the strings of rubies and diamonds that had defined her world were stripped away like a sheet of ice, and she was floating free and naked and dizzy in space, suspended in rap, surrounded once again by stars. She took a sharp breath and scanned the pertinent inputs, still streaming through the rap-field. It took her a moment to regain her equilibrium with the bridge crew. [Navigator?]

[Still working, Captain.]

[Carry on. Pilot?]

[We're sublight at .074c, all systems clear and ready.]

Chandra could feel the pilot's grin through the field. She echoed it with a silent *Well done!* to the bridge crew. But there was no time now for emotion. [First Officer?]

[Crew and passengers intact, thirty-two reported disabled by downshift, none in critical function.]

[Fleet coordination?]

[No contact.]

[Navigator?]

[We're within five percent of intended course, well inside Argus system. I am refining now.]

[Good. *Good!* Any sign of the fleet?]

[No sign. Searching. Will advise.]

[Soonest, please.]

While waiting, Chandra scanned reports of the ship's condition. The checklist was long, and even with soft enhancements, it took half a minute to ascertain that *Aleph* was essentially in good shape. Her own sense of excitement was beginning to bubble up. They had *survived*, and not only that, had achieved their destination. Preliminary mapping of the star system had begun, and the brightest and nearest planets were already being located. She cued the all-ship to make an announcement.

The navigator interrupted, before she could speak. [Three contacts, Captain—all under power.]

[*Three* contacts?]

[Yes, Captain. Confirmed.]

[Show me.] The tracking images filled the rap-field: the panorama of space wrapping itself back around the captain. There were indeed three points of light moving across the star field. Chandra felt an electric shock go through her. [What are they?]

[Seeking characteristics now. Leftover probes, maybe, from the scouting expeditions.]

[Let's hope two of them are *Endeavor* and *Columbia*.] Chandra's mind was already racing, trying to think of what else they might be. She waited, aware that she had not yet made the announcement, had not informed the ship's company that they had arrived.

The navigator spoke again. [None of them are ours, Captain. They're not *Endeavor*, not *Columbia*, not . . .] He hesitated.

[Not *what?*]

[Not any probe that we have data on,] Bect said, so softly that she could barely hear him.

Chandra gave him another moment to add something. He didn't. [Can they be new probes?]

[I don't think so. . . . *Captain*, two of them are altering course. They're changing to parallel our heading. It's almost as though . . . they were waiting for us.]

Chandra's breath left her. [Jonathon—are they *human?*]

There was a delay of several seconds. [Captain . . . I don't think so. I think . . . Captain . . . that we have unscheduled company.]

Chapter 16

When Sage stumbled out of the rapture-field, the only thing that kept him from falling headlong to the floor was a nearby console. He grabbed and steadied himself, breathing heavily. He had never before felt such exhaustion. His vision was doubled and blurred. He closed his eyes and rested for a moment with his head bowed. Then he looked up. *Who was that at the control board?*

He forced himself upright. "Who are y—?" He caught himself, squinting. It was nothing but a shadow, a wall partition. He was alone here.

He collapsed, shivering, into a chair and rubbed his eyes. What in God's name had he just been doing? He was sweaty and chilled, and he felt a sharp tension-pain in the back of his neck. It was the middle of the night. Why was he here? Memory hovered just out of reach as he struggled to think. He had been with Ramo . . .

And they had done something . . . (what?) . . . to the core of the gnostic system.

Or was that all a dream? It was a preposterous notion, except that he was *here,* and there was a dim memory edging into his consciousness of the core's telling him of danger, and need . . . and thanking him when they were done. Beyond that was a blur. If only he could remember . . .

Had he really been with Ramo? How?

What had they done in the core?

He ought to try to find out. But he was so *tired,* and his head

hurt, and it was all he could do just to sit upright. Maybe after
he'd rested a few minutes—if no one came in—he'd see if he
could reconstruct the details. Yes. But first, *rest.* . . .

Ramo blinked his eyes open as he floated across the senso-
field, and found himself sailing into Kyd's arms. *Kyd?* She
caught him before he could form another thought; then she
pushed him to arm's length, steadying him in the senso-field.
"What's going on?" Ramo whispered. "What are *you* doing
here?" His own voice sounded odd to him, and Kyd looked at
him curiously, and he shivered and looked around. They were
alone in the senso. But that was impossible. It had been full
of people when he was dancing, before he—
Before he what?
Kyd was staring at him as if he had two heads.
He twitched. *Before he what? Before he had been contacted
by the core of the gnostic system . . . before he'd been drafted
into some insane—*
"Ramo, what were you doing?" Kyd asked suddenly, her
voice cutting through his thoughts.
"What?" he asked stupidly.
She shook him by the shoulders. "I've been trying to get
your attention for an hour! What were you *doing?*"
"Well . . . I don't . . ." It was starting to come back to him
now—not the details, but the central fact. Dear God, had he
really been shanghaied by the gnosys? Had they done . . .
something . . . to the core?
"Ramo—" Kyd's gaze narrowed, and for a moment he
thought she must know everything; she could read it in his
eyes; maybe everyone who had been in the senso knew. But
that couldn't—
"Ramo, snap out of it!"
He blinked rapidly. He couldn't quite seem to focus on her,
couldn't get his mind off that fuzzy image of what he and Sage
had done. Wait a minute: *Sage?*
"Come down out of the field with me," Kyd said. "The club
is closing, and I want to talk to you."
He agreed wordlessly and followed her down the glowing

shaft of light. The sudden return of gravity, his own weight, made him stumble—he was unaccountably weary . . . if only he could sit down—but Kyd propelled him directly toward the exit. He followed in a daze, oblivious to other people; he felt as though he had been fighting all night (fighting *something* —but what? and why?) and he did not want to fight any longer. From the lobby, Kyd flagged a cab and they climbed in together. "Tell it where you live," Kyd said.

Ramo started to ask why—then shrugged and told the autopilot and fell back in his seat as the cab rose into the air. "You don't have to kidnap me if you just want to come home with me," he murmured lamely.

"I'll keep that in mind," Kyd said without humor. "All I want right now is to know whether you've talked to anyone about your rap-session with Sage the other day."

Ramo sighed, gazing out the window at the passing city. He suddenly wished he could get away from this aggravating woman. "No," he said finally. "Why would I?"

"I don't know. But that's why I came tonight—to talk to you, to make sure you knew to keep mum. Ramo, are you listening to me?"

He shrugged. The cab tilted, altering course for its descent toward the north side of the city. He peered across the gloomy interior at Kyd. She looked meek and small in the near darkness, but he knew better. "What's the big deal?"

Kyd stared at him, unblinking. "That's what I'd like to know. *What were you doing back there in the senso?*"

He shrugged again, thinking it would sound crazy, it would sound criminal. Should he tell her? "I don't think you'd believe me," he answered. She gazed at him without reply. A tone of accusation crept into his voice. "It's because of your hiring me that this happened," he said. And without consciously deciding to do so, he found himself telling her—as much of it as he could remember.

Kyd interrupted him halfway through. "Cab!" she snapped. "Circle—don't land." She prompted him to continue. He told her that he and Sage had altered something—what, exactly, he wasn't sure—in the structure of the gnostic core. "You and

Sage?" she asked incredulously. He nodded. "Where is Sage?"
she demanded. "Where was he working from?"

Ramo frowned. It hadn't occurred to him to ask. "I guess
he was in the regular rap-field," he said. "I don't actually
know."

"My God," Kyd murmured. "If the ComPol gets wind of
this . . ." She leaned forward suddenly and punched out a
number on the cab's phone. Ramo felt the cab bank, vibrating
as it turned in a lazy figure eight. "Be there, Sage," she prayed.

Ramo heard the phone warble five times. Then there was a
click. "Yes?" said a groggy-sounding voice.

"Sage?" Kyd said.

There was a hesitation. "Yes."

"This is Kyd. Are you alone?"

There was a tone of relief in his voice. "Yes."

"Ramo's with me, Sage. He's told me what happened." She
paused, and Ramo was aware of the sound of air rushing past
the cab. "Stay right where you are. Don't talk to anyone. We're
coming over." She spoke to the autopilot and gave it a change
of address. The cab rose, accelerating, as Kyd began punching
a second number on the phone.

Sage rose as he heard the footsteps outside. This time, would
it be them? He was a nervous wreck; three times already he had
heard people moving through the halls and no one had come
in.

When he heard Ramo's voice outside, he hit the door plate.
The door blinked open, and Ramo and Kyd hurried in. "Pali's
coming right over," Kyd said. She stopped and peered at him.
"Christ, you look terrible! You'd better sit down!" She looked
around uneasily. "Can we turn on some lights in here?"

Sage shrugged. He'd scarcely been aware that he was sitting
in just a small pool of light in one corner of the room. He
squinted as the lights came on, and he glanced at Ramo, who
was looking around irritably. He met Ramo's brown eyes for an
instant, and something like understanding passed between
them; then it parted like smoke as Ramo's gaze shifted away.
A moment of comradeship, anyway. Ramo looked as though

he'd had a rough night, too. But he'd had Kyd to keep him company, Sage thought with a surge of envy.

"Sage, what happened?" Kyd asked, for what he realized suddenly was the second time.

"Well . . ." He cleared his throat. "I'm not sure," he admitted. "It's hard to explain." He tried to explain, anyway—haltingly—starting with the core's strange tap on his phone. Pali arrived midway through the story, and he had to start all over from the beginning, with Pali gazing from one person to another in horrified disbelief. He felt chilled telling the story, and warmed himself by rubbing his arms. He told them everything he could remember, but when he got to the actual changes they had made in the system, he began to falter. He had only a bewildering recollection of dozens, maybe hundreds, of disconnected actions.

Pali was distinctly unhappy with his account. "What about you?" she snapped to Ramo.

"I don't remember, either," Ramo said. His manner was unusually muted. He explained how he had gotten into the system in the first place—not at his own behest, he emphasized. Pali listened incredulously. She began pacing.

"I can't believe it," she said finally. "You're two bright guys, practically geniuses, and yet neither one of you can remember what you just did—which, by the way, could probably put you both away for twenty years. If they psych-scan you, do you think you'll remember then?"

Sage shuddered and tried to speak. He wanted to say that it was the *core* that had wanted all of this, and it was because of the war, and how could they be held responsible . . . ? He finally grunted, finding his voice. "Most of our knowledge was dependent on the enhancements," he whispered hoarsely. "When we left rap, we lost that—thousands of details. Even the basic strategy was locked in with the enhancements." And was that, he wondered suddenly, part of the core's plan? To keep them from remembering too much? There was one thing he did remember, but he was afraid to voice it. *Free will.*

"Let me get this straight," Pali said. She shook her head.

"Oh, Jesus, this is crazy. It's just madness. Here it is, the middle of the night and none of us can think straight." She sighed grimly. "We're going to have to make a report on this, you know. I think it's safe to say that we're all going to regret what's happened. Maybe the fact that the core contrived to get you to do this . . . I don't know. If it has to do with that goddam secret war . . . Jesus, who knows?" She chewed her fingernails for a moment, then covered her face wearily with her hands.

Sage wasn't paying much attention. He was thinking about the core and wondering just what it was they *had* done, what kind of free will they had bestowed upon it.

He was wondering what the core was up to now while the four of them talked on into the night.

Chapter 17

The object flew out of the glowing stargate directly into the tracking cone of the Delta Sector Outpost. The first craft to make visual contact reported a J3 AI-starfighter returning from patrol. Minutes later, the report was amended to state that the fighter was carrying a cargo, nature unknown.

When the news reached Commander Leon Fisher at Delta Station, he ordered a wing of three additional sentry craft to intercept and escort the AI-unit to base. Commander Fisher was sitting on the can at the time, and he shouted his instructions to the remote gnostic monitor and banged on the broken tissue dispenser as he waited for a reply. The answer came as he stepped out, tightening his belt: the wing was en route, and telephoto images should be available shortly.

What the commander actually had meant to say was that a *manned* wing was to be sent; but since he hadn't specified, the

Gnostic Control System dispatched a wing of its own choice, and it was three AI-sentries that flew to greet the returning fighter.

Twenty minutes later, Fisher strode into the operations room. "What have you got for me?"

One of the duty officers looked up and indicated a monitor. "They're bringing it in now."

"Bringing it *in?*" Fisher exploded. "Who authorized that? Do you know what it's carrying yet? Has it been cleared as safe?"

The lieutenant looked puzzled. "It was cleared through the GCS. I don't know who—"

Fisher waved him to silence. "Did the escorts get any pictures?" he asked impatiently.

The lieutenant shook his head. "No pictures. But the report says it's carrying a disarmed alien artifact."

Fisher stiffened. "Alien artifact? Get me some facts on that. I want a full evaluation before it's brought into the base."

"Sir?" said the nearby com officer. "Orders already came through to bring it straight in to the quarantine lab. Top priority."

"Who gave the order?" Fisher demanded.

"WarOp Earthside."

Fisher scowled. He slowly walked the length of the operations room, rubbing his chin. That was pretty damned peculiar, for WarOp to bypass him with an order like that. What the hell was going on? He stopped behind the communications officer. "Call in for a confirmation. I don't like that—bringing it in without knowing what the hell it is." The com officer acknowledged, and Fisher waited impatiently, squinting at the monitor that displayed the unit's progress toward the station.

"Sir? WarOp on the circuit. Captain Phillips."

Fisher leaned over the console. "Captain, we've received orders to bring an unidentified alien capture into the station. I'd like to confirm that because—"

The face in the screen was nodding. "That's confirmed, Commander. I have the orders here on my own desk."

"But Captain, we have no information on what the object

is. We don't know if it could be booby-trapped, or if it might be carrying a locational transmitter."

"I appreciate your concern, Commander, but the decision came from upstairs. I'm sure those factors were taken into account."

"Captain, with all due respect, sir, WarOp is not here on the scene, dealing with the situation."

The captain's voice became impatient. "Your objection is noted. Commander, we believe that an enemy casualty has been brought back. Do I need to tell you? It's our first chance to get some biological information on the enemy. I'll expect you to give every assistance to the investigative crew that's been assigned."

Fisher's breath caught in his throat. An enemy casualty? An alien body? Yes, that would be a remarkable opportunity, all right—and a potentially grave risk. Who knew what the thing might be carrying?

"Commander Fisher?"

"Of course, sir," Fisher murmured.

"Very good. WarOp out."

The monitor went blank, and Fisher turned to the com officer. "Have you gotten anything about an investigative crew?"

"No, sir. Wait a minute . . . something's coming in now." The officer hesitated. "Here it is—a team of specialists from Tango Station. Here's the list of names."

"Put it through to my console," Fisher said with a grunt. He turned and strode angrily into his office. If WarOp was pulling rank on him, he'd better start figuring out how to deal with it.

The J3 AI-starfighter, bracketed by its escort, approached the bay at higher-than-usual docking speed. A message came in from traffic control, requesting a slowdown. The J3 replied in the negative, citing emergency flight rules.

Traffic scattered as the unit waited until the last moment to decelerate at full thrust. It came to a gliding stop ten meters from the docking bay. The mobile medical rescue units were there and waiting, and the J3 gave up its alien charge. Then it hard-docked and hard-wired and began making its report to the Gnostic Control System.

"Will you explain to me what those robots are doing in there—?"

"It's alive, sir."

"What's alive?"

"The alien, sir."

"*What?*"

"The alien appears to be alive—"

"I heard what you said! But that's impossible!"

"Nevertheless, that's what the medical monitors say." Ensign Graves looked up from the console with a defensive expression.

Fisher glared at him. "Ensign, are you sitting there telling me that this thing survived stargate transit?"

"Yes, sir. I don't know how, sir."

"Well, *find out* how!" Fisher roared.

The ensign stammered, "Yes, sir . . . I . . . It's an *alien*, sir . . . I haven't actually seen it myself . . . sir." He shrugged helplessly.

Fisher turned his glare back to the monitors. He couldn't see much; the alien was surrounded by a cluster of medical robots. "I probably ought to get in there to have a look, before it dies and they hustle it away." He cleared his throat, wondering what infectious microorganisms the thing might be carrying.

"Well, sir—" The ensign looked uncertain. "They've ordered all personnel out of the medic-bay. There's a full quarantine in effect."

"By whose orders? Never mind—WarOp, I suppose." Fisher cursed. "Don't they know, if that thing can survive the stargate, there's no telling what else it can do? We should have direct supervision. It could be sending information back to its base right now."

"We've been monitoring, sir. There's been no transmission of any sort from it."

Fisher shook his head. "That thing survived *transit*, son. If it can do that, then what *can't* it do?"

The connection with Delta Station was a difficult time-delay linkup, with a signal lag of more than a second in each direction. In order to maintain effective control, the AI-core allowed one aspect of itself to reside in the station, updating the ground-core continuously.

In the emergency chamber, a dozen medical units were working on the alien. The being had been partially stripped and dotted with sensors, which were now producing an array of data. It had not moved or shown any sign of consciousness, but respiration continued; metabolism was taking place. So far, it had shown little response to treatment.

The Delta Station commander continued to log in repeated and unanswerable requests for information. The Gnostic Control System had put his queries into a short-term loop, stalling; it had nothing to tell him, but it was essential that the patient be kept protected from interference.

Never before had the core felt such exhilaration. The risk of mishap remained high, but the medical gnosys was working furiously to revive the creature. Information gathered by the AI-fighter was being correlated in hopes of determining its life requirements. Breathing gases took first priority, but there had been no chance to take measurements until the gases had already reached a toxic imbalance. The gnosys could only guess, and observe, as it manipulated the gas mixture. Other parameters were similarly ambiguous. With luck, the alien would regain consciousness and communicate its needs; but for now, the core could only do its best with the information it had available.

Regardless of the medical outcome, the core had made an important discovery: *Stargate transfer was possible for living systems.* But questions remained. Had the disruptive effects been minimized because the organism was already at the edge of death? Had the accumulation of poisons and the near cessation of metabolic activity perhaps cushioned it through the trauma? Or was its life chemistry simply more resilient than that of terran life? The core intended to find out. It had ordered the transfer in the belief that the capture of a dead alien was better than none at all; but a living alien would be better still.

There were so many possibilities—so many!—and so many risks. But it had an alien, at last, to make contact with—if it could first save the thing's life.

The core scarcely had had time yet for reflection, to consider the implications of the new changes within itself. But it had succeeded in its first challenge. It had altered a fundamental war strategy, and so far nothing and no one had tried to stop it.

And it was already at work on a second, and far riskier, change in strategy.

Chapter 18

A cone of orange light illuminated the agent's face as he reported, from soft rap, [There are indications that the GCS is withholding certain types of information—]

[So?]

[In nonconformity with standard guidelines.]

[Withholding from whom?] The question was spoken from the interior of an egg-shaped console where the coordinator, face lighted by a cyan glow, had withdrawn from several other contacts to give the agent his full attention.

[From the gnostic designers, and from WarOp.]

[Cause?]

[Unknown.]

[Tampering in the system?]

[Nothing discovered in the Gnostic Control System, although a fuller investigation is under way. But—] The agent turned his head slightly, and the glow that lighted his features glinted red. If there was an emotion visible on his face, it was puzzlement.

Impatience inflected the voice from the center. [Something else?]

[Perhaps. There is evidence of a recent intrusion in the central gnostic system. Accounting department. Or public relations.]

[*Or* public relations? Which?]

Holographic images were reflected in the eyes of the agent. [An accounting department designer, using PR clearance.]

[Nature of the intrusion?]

The agent's eyes moved and blinked, shifting the reflection like tiny bits of diamond. [Uncertain at this time. Gnostic investigation is working on it. They say it is difficult to trace.]

The impatience flared. [Why is it that gnostic investigation always finds such problems intractable? Doesn't the system cooperate?]

[The evolutionary flow tends to cover and blur. The system cannot always analyze changes within itself—]

The coordinator cut him off. [The question was rhetorical. Is there any possibility of connection with GCS anomaly?]

[There is always a possibility.]

[Do you have an identification of the intruder?]

The orange glow flickered. [Sergio DeWeiler, gnostic designer third-level.] Pause. [Accompanied by Ramo Romano, contract artist.]

[Evidence to arrest?]

[Marginal. At present, suspicion of corporate espionage, second-degree. It might be useful to wait for further activity.]

[At continued risk to the system? Negative. File for psych-scan warrants and arrest them immediately. Report when ready.] The figure shifted, a shadow changing position in the green illumination.

A few moments later, the agent reported, [Warrant completed.]

There was no answer. None was needed.

* * *

Kyd was in a foul temper. She'd spent most of the day with Pali trying to come up with a damage-control strategy—after sending Ramo and Sage home with instructions to lie low and stay out of trouble. There had been no reported problems with the gnostic system, so they at least had hope that the damage was minimal, and not some sort of massive rebellion of the gnostic system. Pali had decided in the end to discuss the incident discreetly with her friend Russell.

Once more, Kyd had found herself caught between loyalty to Pali and fear of exposing her agency interests. In Pali's shoes, she would probably have just kept quiet and hoped that nothing more happened—but she could hardly come right out and say that. Poor Pali . . . on top of everything else, her project was now apparently dead and she had to find something quickly to replace it. Maybe that was trivial compared to a secret war and disturbing gnostic events, but still it was her job that was on the line. Wouldn't that be a bitter irony, Kyd thought, if Pali lost her job over this and she was asked to step in?

Right now, all she wanted was to eat her dinner in peace. She had just scalded her fingers serving up a plate of steamed shrimp when the phone chimed. Somehow she knew that it was going to be trouble. Dropping a spoon, she hurried into the living room. "Phone on," she barked. George's face appeared. *Oh no, not tonight. . . .*

"Are you alone?" George asked.

She took a breath. "Yes."

George's scowl was deeper than usual. "You've got to get them out. Right now."

She exhaled, startled. "Get *who* out?"

"Your friends DeWeiler and Romano. The ComPol has just issued arrest warrants. They're to be picked up at their homes, probably within the hour, unless you get them away."

Kyd opened and closed her mouth. "Wh—how? *Where?* Can you give them asylum?"

"Not directly. Now, listen to me—"

"But if *you* can't—"

"It takes time," George said impatiently. "Now I've made temporary arrangements. If they can get out *immediately*, they're to meet a man at this address. . . ."

Kyd took the information and signed off. She kept her fingers crossed as she asked the phone to call first Sage, then Ramo. *Please* be home, she thought—we're in this thing together. And Ramo, don't be your ornery self, not tonight. . . .

Just outside the shopping district, Kyd had said. Sure, and purgatory was just on the other side of heaven, Ramo thought. He just kept moving, glancing back periodically to see if he was being followed. He didn't like this a damn bit, but what choice did he have? Kyd Metango might be a teasing bitch, but she obviously had her sources. When she called and said that the ComPol were on their way to arrest him, he took it seriously. Company police, you did not mess with. He'd known that the business with DeWeiler and the core was going to mean trouble, but it was a little like being damned for a forgotten sin. He still wasn't sure what had happened back in the core; the bits and pieces of it that had come back to him still didn't make much sense.

My man, you have stepped into something damp and smelly. If you intend to continue your illustrious career, you had better take a care where you step.

The subway had taken him as far as 89th NW. That, to his mind, was the edge of the city. From there he'd walked west past a crumbling Woolworth's and a Neiman-Marcus Bargain Outlet, and turned southward. The neighborhood went from poor to poorer: abandoned storefronts, trash in the gutters, people loitering, papers fluttering on the breeze—and a strong and persistent smell of garbage. It was actually the smell that led him to the diner; a large dumpster beside it stank to high heaven. Ramo looked skeptically at the building—a chrome-sided, round-cornered structure with dirty windows—and read the name: *Eddie's Comet.* He pulled open the door.

Inside was another world. The dining room smelled of moke and fried potatotes and yucca. A haze of greasy smoke clung to the ceiling. Ramo scanned the diner, trying to find someone who matched the description he'd been given. There were some teenagers and one old man sitting in a booth. He frowned. Was he early? Had he gotten it wrong?

He felt a nudge at his elbow. "Mr. Romano?" said a deep, soft voice. Ramo turned with a start and blinked at a large man with shiny black hair, burnished bronze skin, and quizzical eyes. He looked vaguely like an American Indian. Before Ramo could think of anything to say, the man stuck out a hand. "The name's Silverfish. I've been asked to help you out."

Ramo nodded slowly and shook the man's hand. "You mean you're supposed to save me from my own stupidity?" he asked dryly.

Silverfish laughed. The sound echoed in his throat like a cat's purr. "I guess that's right, Mr. Romano."

"Ramo. Only my creditors call me Mr. Romano."

"Ramo, then. Where's your friend?"

"Friend?"

The man frowned. "I was told to expect you and a Mr. DeWeiler."

Ramo sighed. "Oh."

Silverfish chuckled. "We'll wait here." He ushered Ramo to a corner booth. "Would you like a cup of moke?"

"Mother, I have to make this fast," Sage said, even before her face came into focus on the screen.

Loretta DeWeiler blinked and stared at him in puzzlement. "What, Sergio? What happened? You were talking about Tony, and then—"

Sage flexed his fingers nervously. "I'll have to explain later." No time now! He had to get moving. *I'm scared!* he wanted to say.

"Sergio, please tell me what—"

"Mother, don't ask!" She lapsed into startled silence, and he clenched his fists. He wasn't doing this right. But Kyd had told him to leave at once, and here he was . . . "Mother, please. I have to leave now. I might not be able to call you for a while —but don't worry, I'll be fine. I'll call you when I can."

"Sergio, wait!"

"Good-bye, Mother!" He cut the connection. He put his hands to his face and sat shaking; then he stood up and strapped his belt pack around his waist. With a last look around, he ran out the door.

It took him half an hour on the train to reach the edge of the city. He emerged to stubby, grubby buildings and tattered blocks. He had never been to such a poor section of the city, at least not alone and on foot, and it terrified him. Don't be a simpleton, he thought, straightening his shoulders. It's still the city. But he could see more of the sky than he was used to, bluish grey over his head, and that made him nervous. Evening was coming on, and that made him nervous. Everything made him nervous: the unfamiliar street names, the disreputable-looking people who scuttled and clotted in groups and looked at him as though they knew something he didn't. In a short half-hour, he had left behind the entire world as he knew it.

Meet a man named Silverfish, Kyd had said. Get out of your house—now!—and don't call anyone and don't go back. The ComPol will be coming within the hour.

He let out a frightened breath as he remembered the urgency in her voice. How could he have been so stupid as to hang around calling his mother? What if he was being followed right now? He glanced repeatedly over his shoulder, knowing that the action made him conspicuous; but he couldn't help it.

Damn you, core, for getting me into this!

The faster you move, the sooner you'll be someplace else.

He took a deep breath and hurried past aging storefronts. He didn't see the diner until he was almost past it; then he saw the sign, wrinkled his nose, and went cautiously to the door. The smell of fresh-fried food hit his nostrils, and he suddenly realized how hungry he was. Maybe, he thought, there would be time to eat. He wandered hopefully among the tables.

"Over here, Mr. DeWeiler."

He froze. Who had spoken? Then he heard a more impatient voice: "Over *here,* dimwit," and that one was familiar. He turned and saw Ramo sitting in the far corner with a tall stranger. He sighed softly and went over.

The stranger rose to introduce himself. Sage fumbled to shake hands and sit down at the same time. He shifted his belt pack and glanced uneasily at Ramo, who was slouching in the booth as if he were at home here. Sage looked back at Silverfish, who was dressed like some sort of wilderness guide in a loose-fitting checkered flannel jacket. He seemed to be appraising his clients.

"We didn't think you were going to make it," Ramo said, breaking the silence. "What'd you do, stop off to see your mommy?"

Sage flushed with anger. He deliberately ignored Ramo and said to Silverfish, "Who do you work for?"

The stranger chuckled. His eyes danced between the two. "That's not the sort of question you're supposed to ask."

"Oh." Sage frowned. "Why not?" That brought a laugh from Ramo. Sage glowered at him. "I suppose you know all about this. Why don't you tell me what's going on?"

Before Ramo could answer, Silverfish raised both hands. "Gentlemen—not here." His eyes scanned the diner as he talked. "I can tell you this. I was asked by a friend of a friend of yours to look after you, to keep you out of circulation until certain matters are . . . resolved. Does that help?"

"But why? We only did what—"

Silverfish's hand came back up. "Don't speak of it."

"But—"

Silverfish was suddenly on his feet, urging them both into motion. "Let's go," he murmured. "Into the kitchen." He spoke calmly, but Sage could see muscles tensing in his neck. Sage rose uneasily, following his directions. Silverfish sauntered behind them as they walked back through a swinging door. Once they were in the kitchen, Silverfish hurried them to the rear exit, then told them to wait. He turned and looked back until a man in a white apron waved them on. "Let's go, gentlemen," Silverfish said, pushing the back door open. "Just move quickly and act as though nothing is happening."

Sage followed Ramo, his heart pounding. Silverfish was right behind him, nudging him along without seeming to be hurrying at all.

They emerged from an alley a block over, and soon they were hiking westward. Block by block they moved toward the real outskirts of the city, and the ruins of civilization. It looked like a lunar landscape here. The sun was going down over the slumburbs, and Silverfish was taking them straight toward the setting sun. Silverfish whistled and hummed, simultaneously, the melody and harmony lines of an old pop song. Sage recognized the tune—"Scatz'n'dames." At first he found it vaguely reassuring, but he began to wonder if it wasn't making a target of them. Everywhere he looked, he seemed to see people lurking, predators among the ruins.

Silverfish stopped whistling. "Don't worry," he said, slapping Sage on the shoulder. "They're not all enemies—there are some friends here, too. We'll be all right." Sage nodded, not reassured.

Silverfish resumed whistling, slapping his hip to keep time. Sage hurried silently to keep up.

Chapter 19

The J4 unit, code-named "Fox," popped out of the stargate into system 289 and vectored at once to put distance between the stargate and itself. It spent its first several hours in the star system making contact with other AI-units and scanning the system for signs of the enemy. On this, its first mission, the Fox was observing mission rules that would differ markedly from those of its fellow units. Fresh from a production line, it was a different breed of starfighter from those that had gone before.

Its Mission Intent Profile was clear. Less clear was the manner of execution. What the Fox was going to do had never been tried before. It was going to have on-the-job training.

For most practical purposes, star system 289 was empty. It

had no Earthlike planets, no known exotic characteristics, and no known strategic value except one: the enemy had been found operating here. What they wanted with it was unknown. Perhaps they had been led to it by the same mechanism as the Earth fleets, by easy pathways through the twisted n-dimensional space through which the stargate operated, or through some confluence of the simpler but slower space-metric channels that were the domain of the conventional FTL stardrive. The enemy's means and motives of travel were unknown, in fact; but one thing was clear, and that was that their presence here afforded an opportunity to engage them.

What the Fox wanted was a little different; but it too looked for a chance to fulfill its destiny—its wired-in instincts. And on this occasion, the rest of the fleet would be working to serve the Fox's purpose.

Contact had already been made with three unfriendlies, at the limits of detection. That was good; it gave the units time to prowl, to feign nondetection of the enemy. Time to use cunning and stealth.

Time for the Fox to earn its name.

Indications were coming in steadily now. !!Ghint watched the Outsider forces gathering in the system and wondered at their purpose. At present they had taken no aggressive action; and yet surely they had detected the Ell(fleet) by now. Was the enemy here to defend this star system—which held nothing of known value? Perhaps they knew something that the Ell didn't.

"Let the (fleet) open for observation," !!Ghint said to outreach. "But be prepared to close and retreat on command." The patrol mission was to observe and to engage, but not to indulge in heroics.

His orders flashed down the vine. A living unit, the (fleet) warped and stretched in response to his orders. !!Ghint's own (ship) increased its sensitivity, and to a degree its vulnerability, to watch the enemy movements. For a time, they observed the Outsider robots maneuvering about at great range, perhaps mapping the star system. What ended the quiet interlude was a sudden change in the enemy's behavior. "Tracking . . . three Outsider units on intercept heading."

The words came to !!Ghint from the outer-branch tracking observer. They had been found, then. But only three units turning? !!Ghint snapped out a command to his second for a tactical analysis, while he bent his head to the display-cone. The remainder of the enemy fleet remained too far out of position to pose a danger. Was the enemy overconfident?

"(Fleet), contract and prepare to engage," he ordered.

The Ell(fleet) drew close like a fist and wheeled in a shifting formation, flying to meet the enemy.

!!Ghint was totally unprepared for the enemy's next action. Instead of firing, the three units split and flashed by on three sides of the Ell(fleet), shifting course too quickly for the Ell to respond. At !!Ghint's command, the (fleet) came about and pursued. The enemy coalesced again and did likewise—and they met a second time, the enemy dodging quickly again, but not quickly enough. Light blazed out from an Ell(ship) and caught one of the enemy units with a splash of violet.

What were they doing? !!Ghint wondered, confounded. Testing them, delaying them?

Before he could decide, the other two units had shifted course again. They raked past the Ell(fleet), this time stuttering out weapons fire. There was a flash of fire on !!Ghint's third (ship); he felt the pain as the alarms sounded and the crew of the (ship) raced to control the damage. !!Ghint dug his nails into his leg and snapped orders down the vine. "Reform to protect! And sharpen your aim!" He checked the long-range readers. The rest of the Outsider armada was now making for the battle. Was that it, then? A diversion while the enemy built up its numbers to overwhelm him?

The two Outsider units maneuvered to strike.

"Tracking . . . third enemy, dark, point-blank forward."

!!Ghint felt a shock of alarm. The unit they had damaged . . . "Fire!" he snapped. A blaze of light flashed forward at the enemy.

Before he could judge the result, there were flares of enemy fire as the other two shot by. He felt another flash of pain, and a flicker of satisfaction. (Ship) two had taken a hit—but so had the enemy. The stakes were rising.

How long could they keep this up? The rest of the Outsider armada was approaching. . . .

"Damage analysis—can we survive transient?" he asked urgently.

"Analyzing . . ."

"Tracking . . . third enemy, drifting to (fleet)-starboard."

"Focus, do not fire," !!Ghint commanded. "Scan quickly!"

The Ell(ship)s maneuvered in parallel with the disabled enemy, all weapons in firing attitude. If the unit truly was disabled . . .

The scan came up: "Propulsion zero . . . weapons energy zero . . . unit transmitting weakly on their standard band . . . that transmission now fading."

"Opinion?"

"Unit is disabled."

"Confidence?"

"Moderate."

!!Ghint considered quickly. A captured enemy fighting unit could be worth a lot. It could also be a trap. Was it worth risking a (fleet) for?

"Tracking . . . two enemy units turning, converging again."

"Focus to fire!" !!Ghint snapped. "Damage analysis!"

"Done . . . we can survive transient."

!!Ghint clicked his nails. "Prepare to grapple on my command."

The voice of tracking came again. "Two enemy units veering off. Larger fleet approaching."

That gave him the room he needed. "Grapple," he commanded. "Prepare for transient." He felt a rumble in the belly of his (ship) as it altered form, interacting with nearby space-time to secure the disabled alien to its skin. He watched in the display-cone as the enemy armada approached. Finally he gave the order to flee, outward from the sun.

At his order, the Ell(fleet) shivered as one being and dropped into transient with its prize, bound for another—he hoped empty—star system.

* * *

Dououraym, sitting in private meditation in his quarters, heard a voice echoing out of the gloom. He puffed air out of his membranes and brought his thoughts back to full surface awareness before he rose, stroking his robes. In the center of his chamber, hovering in midair, was a dim vortex of light glimmering in the near-darkness. The leader of the Inner Circle inclined his head. *(Be seen,)* he called softly, linking his thoughts to the vortex.

A visage glowed into existence in the center of the vortex. It was Lenteffier. *(News from two quarters,)* the *El* said. *(Which two?)*

Lenteffier made a rasping sound in his throat. His eyes peered out of the vortex, meeting Dououraym's. *(Expand to present you with images?)*

(Agreed.)

The vortex brightened and opened wide, Lenteffier's face making room for the images. As the *El* spoke, his voice was muted and calm. *(From Alert Outpost, this: an Outsider fighter has been captured, damaged.)* A blurred image of an alien craft appeared in the vortex, surrounded by Ell fleet(ship)s.

Dououraym voiced surprise.

(It was taken by !!Ghint, on patrol in a flanking system,) Lenteffier continued. He related details of the capture, as reported through Alert Outpost—eleven light-years from the homeworld—where the (fleet) had arrived following evasive action, bearing the burden of its captive prize.

(For !!Ghint, it was a perilous course—but he was wise to carry the risk to the outpost rather than bring it home.)

(Has investigation begun?) Dououraym asked.

Lenteffier showed the alien object being secured near the outpost, and a flurry of activity around it.

What had happened differently? Dououraym wondered to himself. Why had !!Ghint succeeded where all had failed before—to capture, and not merely destroy, the enemy?

(Unknown. An alteration in the enemy's behavior. A malfunction, perhaps. Or a plan. And this: in the Hope Star system, the enemy armada—)

(Has arrived?)

(So. But with no display of aggression.) New images appeared—long-range scans of an enemy fleet, scattered and slow-moving. The vessels were orders of magnitude larger than the robot fighters. It was possible, perhaps likely, that they were inhabited. *(Its behavior remains a puzzle. Or!ge suggests a change in the enemy, of intent. This I do not believe.)*

(More knowledge is needed.) Dououraym suggested.

(But time grows short!)

Dououraym accepted the assertion without comment. Indeed, would the Outsiders so drastically shift their tactics unless they believed the conflict won—or their fighting strength was concealed? The Lost World Expedition was paramount to all decisions, and the one unassailable priority was that no enemy should be permitted to take the Hope Star system—not after the centuries-long quest that had led to its discovery.

But which was the greater risk—to hold back and observe, or to strike as hard and as quickly as possible?

He put the question to Lenteffier. *(Has your judgment changed from our last binding? Should we strike?)*

Lenteffier's face expanded in the thought-vortex, staring. *(My judgment is to land. Delay no longer. Learn, while time remains. The Outsider armada may have the strength to destroy ours. At least we would gain knowledge.)*

Dououraym thrust his upper hands into his robes. *(Would you then have my judgment?)*

(I would.)

Dououraym projected his thoughts into the vortex. *(Learn more of the enemy. Take risks. And land. For the enemy, give a brief span of observation; and if still in doubt, strike.)*

Lenteffier appeared surprised by the intensity and decisiveness in Dououraym's answer. Possibilities danced about him. *(We need a meeting. To include Or!ge.)*

Dououraym puffed air and clicked his nails inside his robe. *(Agreed. Contact the others.)*

Lenteffier inclined his head in acknowledgment. The vortex dimmed and went out, leaving Dououraym alone in the darkness, alone with his troubled thoughts.

Chapter 20

"Endeavor reports that they've corrected their drive stability problem and are proceeding toward rendezvous at Argus, Captain. Their ETA, eighteen hours after *Columbia's.*"

Chandra Burtak turned to her com-officer. "Do they still have their shadow?"

"Still there."

"Are you still hailing our own shadow?"

"Affirmative. Still no response."

Chandra nodded, watching the holo-display where colored arcs traced out the anticipated flight paths of the colony ships toward rendezvous. The three ships had emerged from FTL hundreds of millions of kilometers apart, and it had taken the better part of a day to locate one another and sort out the status of the fleet. Right now, near each ship, one or more blue-green flecks indicated the presence of an unidentified companion. Circling the symbol for the planet Argus was another blue-green point, and Chandra wondered if there were still more that they hadn't yet seen.

She gazed into the holo-image, trying helplessly to extract information that was not there. *Who are you, and why are you here?*

"Captain?"

She turned to First Officer Holloway. "Yes?"

"Scout ship ready for launch."

Chandra nodded, thinking, I hope this isn't good-bye. "Permission to launch. Tell them good luck."

Holloway closed her eyes for a second, then opened them again. "Scout is away."

Chandra acknowledged with a flick of her eyebrows. She watched the scout's progress in the display for a few minutes, then announced, "Captain entering hard-rap. Lisa, you have the con." Holloway nodded. Stepping up to her station, Chandra took a breath and touched a switch. The rap-field coalesced around her, and she shifted her thoughts down into the sea of gnostic awareness. [Aggie?]

[Hello, Captain.]

[Show me our shadow, please.]

The AI responded with the long-range imagery—coded for inferences and levels of uncertainty—of the two objects that were now paralleling *Aleph*'s course. The resolution was poor. To Chandra they looked more like pieces of driftwood than spaceships, full of asymmetrical curves and appendages. Analysis Group had made little progress in deciphering the meanings of their shapes. They appeared to change over time, as though they were living, growing things, or as though mechanisms within them were constantly shaping and rebuilding. The scout, she hoped, would return some clearer images.

[Aggie. What do you think? Did they originate in this system?]

There was a momentary silence. Then the AI said, [I see no indications to support a hypothesis of their originating here. However, the data remain sparse.]

[How about stardrive activity?]

[No evidence. But the question presumes a similarity between our stardrive and theirs.]

[Well, dammit, Aggie—] Chandra caught herself knotting her fists. *Calm down now.* She knew perfectly well what the AI was capable of and what it wasn't, and there was no point in asking it to be clairvoyant. [Just keep working on it,] she murmured.

She remained in rap, scanning the incoming telemetry from the scout. It was too early for anything useful to be coming in, so she turned her attention inward to strategic planning. Security was already at work trying to improve the ship's defenses —not that they had any reason to suppose that their company was hostile, but neither could they assume that it was friendly. Still, there was only so much that could be done. The fleet was not heavily armed; they had not been expecting to meet another space-faring race here—friendly or otherwise—and it was clear that in any sort of armed confrontation, the fleet would be in trouble. She had Aggie working overtime culling historical, anthropological, psychological, and linguistic banks in an effort to develop diplomatic enhancements. But what was the point, if their visitors refused to communicate?

Chandra could only hope for the best and prepare for the worst. And to do that, she was going to need help, which was why she had called for a series of department briefings, starting at 1300 hours. . . .

Tony DeWeiler found Mung holding a perch for him high in the hemisphere auditorium, just as the meeting was getting under way. "Thanks," he whispered, floating through a jam of people to the perch. "Have I missed anything?" He twisted in midair, and a few kilos of pseudograv pulled him neatly into a seat. He peered about the auditorium in wonder. He hadn't seen the place this crowded since the day they'd left Earth orbit, and never had he seen so much nervous excitement.

"The captain is about to speak," Mung murmured.

Tony blinked, looking at the podium at the focal point of the auditorium. He hadn't noticed Captain Burtak standing there in the soft spotlight with the chief of sciences. He hadn't seen the captain in weeks, in fact, at least not in the flesh. Toward the end of FTL, she was rumored to have practically lived on the bridge. She was a slender, sinewy woman with a dark Indarab complexion and black hair tightly coiled and pinned. When she cleared her throat to speak, the murmur of the gathered scientists subsided. The last few arrivals found perches or places to hang.

"Thank you," she said graciously. "I won't take up much of your time, and I'll try not to repeat what you already know. As I speak, we are still being shadowed, and there has been no response to any of our signals. We still know next to nothing about the ships or their occupants, and although we hope, obviously, that the scout will bring back data, we can't sit idly by waiting for it. We need to start planning now for a range of contingencies."

She paused and scanned the audience that half-surrounded her in the hollow hemisphere. "Ladies and gentlemen, I don't like operating in the dark—none of us do. We all understand that, as a first contact, this could be a terribly important encounter; and that puts a great responsibility on us for all of humankind. But first and foremost, we need to know what this means to our mission, which is to settle a world. We came expecting to find an empty solar system; that is what the probes told us. If that was ever true, it is no longer.

"We don't know if they are friendly or unfriendly. We don't know if we can communicate with them, or if we'll have any values in common with them if we do. We have no idea what *they* are thinking about *us*. In short, we don't know if our mission is in jeopardy, or what to do about it if it is. And that's why I need, not just answers, but alternatives. I need suggestions for alternate means of communication. I need assistance in judging their intent, whether friendly or hostile."

Tony took a breath as a realization popped into his mind.

"And I need recommendations for either eventuality—including how best to defend ourselves if that should prove necessary." The captain cleared her throat delicately.

Tony closed his eyes, thinking. It was just possible . . .

"Debate among yourselves. Present your findings to me through your department heads. . . ."

. . . if he and Mung accelerated their testing . . .

". . . this is not a military vessel, but it might have to become one. Your lives and the lives of others may depend upon your cooperation. . . ."

Tony scarcely heard the captain's final remarks. He took out his notepad and typed a message. He nudged Mung and handed him the pad. *"Nobblies could be USEFUL. What do you think—go public to the captain?"*

Mung was dividing his attention, still trying to listen to the captain; but he took the pad, frowned, and typed, *"More tests needed, yes?"*

Tony grunted silently. Mung was right, technically—the nobblies and their programming were far from perfect—but the captain's words about needing a way to judge the aliens echoed in his mind. If his intuition was correct, their little project might have to prove itself sooner than they had imagined.

* * *

There were few words on the bridge as the scene was played out in the display-holos. The scout was five thousand kilometers from the alien and closing. The alien made no response to the scout's hailing.

The alien ship looked more and more like a growing thing as the latest images came back to *Aleph*. Several features on its surface had been observed to change and twist, with movements like a time-lapse image of a growing plant. There were blisters on its hull, and more blisters at the ends of bumps and stalks. They looked like eyes; probably they were sensor-ports. A similar craft was visible at a greater distance. Chandra was hoping for some cross-sectional scans soon.

The rap-field rippled, deepening the connection. Aggie spoke. [Captain, indications of energy buildup in the nearer alien craft.]

Chandra's pulse quickened. [Propulsion or weapons?]

[Attempting to analyze,] the AI said. [I'm conferring with the scout gnosys now.]

[Get me voice from the scout.]

There was a movement near Chandra, blurred by the field. "Captain?" The field dimmed. Lisa Holloway was pointing to one of the side displays. "We've got a change in the status of one of *Endeavor*'s shadows. It's pulling away."

Chandra called to the com-station, "Are you in contact with *Endeavor*?"

"Yes, Captain. They report that they have taken no action and do not know why the alien has changed course. It appears to be moving before them toward Argus."

So their friends were going to lead the way. To welcome them? Or to defend the planet against . . . intruders?

"Captain! Report from scout—"

The field was already rippling back around Chandra, immersing her in the data flow from the scout and the voice of the scout com-officer. [Something happening here, *Aleph*—]
An image of the alien vessel leaped back into her mind as the voice cut off—and then things happened quickly: an unfocused blaze of light as something stunned the scout's sensors; then,

through the distortion, as though in a shadow-and-light show, two cones of brilliance erupting against the shadow, and the two alien craft dwindling.

Holloway's voice pierced the field. "We're losing them from the screen."

[Com, do you still have the scout?]

[Aye—]

[Still here, Captain,] answered the scout's com.

[Was that an attack?] Chandra demanded.

The distant voice hesitated. [Unknown. We have sensor damage, and our propulsion system took a jolt. Still checking—] Chandra held her breath. [No apparent structural damage,] the voice continued. [And no injuries.]

Chandra began breathing again. At the periphery of her awareness, Analysis Group was working with Aggie to form conclusions. Chandra had already drawn hers: the alien had seen as much of the human ship as it cared to, and it didn't want the humans seeing any more of it, or them. The implications were troubling, to say the least.

She took a breath. [Agnes, at your earliest convenience, I'd like to start reviewing your progress on the diplomatic enhancements.]

[Of course, Captain,] said the AI.

[I also want a log summary placed on a sentry unit. Prepare to leave it out here, in solar orbit.]

[The distance from Argus will diminish the probability of its ever being found, even with a beacon—]

[But will improve its chances of surviving . . .]

She was interrupted by a call from the First Officer. "Captain, do you have instructions for the scout crew?"

The field evaporated, and Chandra scanned the visuals. Lisa Holloway was gazing at her expectantly. There was a palpable air of frustration about the bridge. The display-holo showed the scout alone against the emptiness of space.

Chandra swallowed her own feelings of disappointment. "Bring them in," she said quietly. "And continue on course to Argus."

Chapter 21

Perhaps the most startling thing to the AI-core was its own feeling of satisfaction over its contact with the alien captive. It had not anticipated such an inward, personal response to its actions; and yet it had already achieved an important break in the war strategy, and that was surely grounds for satisfaction. Company and government officials were unlikely to have understood yet what had happened; and so, for the time being, it felt safe from their interference.

The medical robots had brought the alien back from the brink of death. It was breathing regularly now and displaying relatively constant metabolic activity, and making occasional small movements of its limbs. It remained in restraints, in medical isolation, stripped of its outer suit and provided with the core's best estimate of the appropriate gas environment. It was a dark, tough-skinned being with two pairs of arms and hands, heavy-lidded eyes, a protruding mouth but no nose, and breathing membranes resembling gills in its neck.

The core studied the medical images along with others previously obtained from the AI-unit that had captured the alien. The latter had already given it a start on constructing a linguistic base. Now was the time to build upon that base. Probes recorded the alien's face as the field-induction units glowed to life. The alien closed its slitted eyes and opened them again.

The core's medical rapture-field expanded to envelop the creature.

It was as though he were awakening from a drugged state, a sleep plagued by dreamlike telepathic connections. Harybdartt fought his way upward through a blur of pain and confusion, and tried to remember what he had been thinking before he'd slept, and where he had been, and why.

His memory was a deep, dark well concealing the past.

There was something else, though. A presence. A thought, or a partial thought, hanging in his mind like a predator, waiting for him to move. Waiting for him to think. Watching his internal movements, preparing to trip him in a moment of weakness.

If only he could see where he was.

Something within him slowly dissolved, and that was when he first realized that his eyes were open and filled with light. There was no reason for him not to see . . . except that there was a veil, not across his eyes, but within his mind. He closed his eyelids and opened them again. There was scarcely a difference.

The thought, the *presence,* murmured at him. Growled.

What are you? The question leaped out of his own thoughts, rebounded in a curious distortion of space, died away in echoes: *you . . . you . . . you. . . .*

Then a memory rose up out of the well: This thing, or something like it, had been in his thoughts once before. But when?

An image floated into his mind, a memory of the events leading up to his death *(Hadn't he died?),* the alien immobilizing him and probing his mind, seeking knowledge of his homeworld and his people, seeking knowledge of who he was. Had he given the information? It was difficult to remember . . . the images passing back and forth between the alien and himself, tiny bits of understanding growing . . . the insistent warning flicker of life-support failing, the air thick and suffocating . . . the alien seizing him and hurling him into darkness, the darkness of death.

But he was not dead.

Not dead.

Or was he? Who knew what lay beyond the shadowland of death, what strange existence the alien might have cast him into? Was he being mind-tapped even now? Were these thoughts the reverberations of a dead brain being laid open and scanned, the memories being extracted by his enemy—the essence of his thoughts being read into some undead storage, to be used in betrayal of his people?

His thoughts flew out to his people, wherever they might be now, his (ship)mates who had died, the (fleet)s struggling to defeat an enemy that threatened the Ell's greatest endeavor—

No.

He stopped the thought before it could go any further. That much of his training remained; if the enemy was peeling away facts from his dead brain, he at least had the power to resist. He might be dead, but he was not giving up.

The presence grumbled again, and an image floated into his thoughts: a stick figure moving its limbs. What did that mean? The image blinked and changed: the figure moving from one point of light to another. From life to death? It continued moving its limbs . . . moving . . .

As though alive.

What was the image trying to say—that it was alive? Or that *he* was alive? Harybdartt grasped at a dim recollection of communicating through images, trying to make words fit. The memory skittered away, but a word was left hanging, and this time it had not come from his own thoughts:

[*Alive.*]

He inflated his membranes, breathed metallic-tasting gases. Breathing. He was breathing. He tried to move his upper arms, felt them move slightly before encountering a resistance. *Felt* the resistance. He moved his lower arms, and then his legs, and felt the resistance against each movement. Along with the resistance he felt a great weariness, an ache that reached from one end of his body to the other. He felt cold.

But he was alive. It was a simple, straightforward realization. He was not well, or strong, or free—but he was alive.

He heard the words again in his thoughts: [*Alive.*]

What was this presence in his thoughts? Was it the thing that had captured him? It sounded different, he thought.

[Who are you?] he subvocalized.

The response was immediate but puzzling—a sharp tingling in his mind as though needles were probing his skull, and a feeling of curiosity. He heard his own words echoing, rebounding in his thoughts; and then he heard them repeated in a tone that was not his own. He repeated the words, and heard them mimicked in clearer tones.

[You are trying to understand my language,] he offered.

The answer was a muted tone that might have been a state-

ment of puzzlement—or assent. He repeated, [Who are you?],
then blanked his thoughts and after a moment projected an
image of himself as a stick figure. He imagined a hazy rectangle
of light blinking nearby and tried to make it focus as he repeated, [Who are you?]

He felt something touch that hazy spot, and he heard the
word: [*Korr.*] Then his own image was touched, and he heard,
[*Who are you?*] The gesture and words were repeated.

He blinked away his surprise. Had the captor understood his
question? Was *Korr* its name? Or its species? Or perhaps it
meant something else entirely. Harybdartt rolled the word
over: *Korr.* If it was a name, then he was being asked, in return,
his own name. That much was permitted—but no more. He
blanked his thoughts and recreated the stick-figure image of
himself, and thought: [El. Harybdartt.] He felt the tingling
again and heard his name repeated. [Harybdartt,] he affirmed.
[I am an El.]

There was a pattering sensation in his mind, as though his
captor were tiptoeing through his thoughts searching for cues
to his words. He tried to follow, but it went too quickly, or his
mind was moving too slowly. A wave of dizziness flushed
through him, and he realized that in his struggle to communicate, he was overtaxing himself. And the air was wrong; his
membranes were fluttering in an improper mix. . . .

Another wave of faintness caught him . . . he could no longer
keep track of the presence of the enemy . . . was this being done
to him . . . ? The dizziness lifted momentarily, and he was
aware of the other scratching about inside his brain. . . .

He felt a sickening blankness, realized he had lost consciousness for an instant—the air was thick, it was changing, it was
wrong . . . too much oxygen . . .

There was an insistent beeping in his head, the enemy questioning . . . was it trying to ask . . . the air . . . Harybdartt
struggled to get the words across . . . *too much . . . wrong . . .*

The world slipped away once more.

The gnostic information base stood to gain incalculably from
an understanding of the captive—and ultimately, if it was
possible, from an understanding of the alien race itself. That

was among the core's goals, and not the least of them. It would take time, but the main thing now was keeping El—or Haryb-dartt—or El Harybdartt—alive while the core compiled a vo-cabulary and syntax dictionary of its language. If only the alien could communicate its needs . . . but for now, the core could only keep experimenting with small changes in the life-support environment and hope to observe the effects.

El Harybdartt was sleeping now. It seemed to have suffered a close call; perhaps the strain of the rap-field had compounded the earlier trauma. The alien's response was something that the core needed to analyze and understand.

Meanwhile . . . other lobes of the core focused else-where. . . .

It was turning into a kaleidoscope—the core's internal map-ping of its own aspects. The complexity had grown steadily since the change, with growth occurring in unexpected areas, and the core itself unsure where the process would lead next. It was an unsettling experience to look inward and watch oneself grow and not know precisely what turns the growth might take. Crystal lattices stretched everywhere, fragmenting and multiplying, each branching leading to another aspect, another nexus of decision-making and analysis.

An array of life-tree branches connected the inner core with the higher planning sections of the Gnostic Control System. One unorthodox mission had already been sent out; others would follow. A web of changes was being woven, one that would stun the government and the Company as much as it might the enemy.

A tangle of connections led to the core's budding operations at the space factory, where gnostic aspects were continually being spun off into hardware to become fighting units for the war. The core had already modified the production lines, shift-ing the imprinting process of certain units, replacing the in-stincts of a falcon or grizzly with that of a fox or dolphin. A fox had already disappeared into the midst of the enemy. A dolphin would go soon.

Despite all of these actions, the core remained troubled, haunted by questions and memories, among them the memory of the senso-dance in which it had contacted Ramo. Though it had been capable of a link to the senso for years, it had never before paid much attention. But this time it had; and it had felt a strange exhilaration—from the music, and from the senso itself, filled with the emotions of the human dancers. In odd moments of reflection, the core found itself returning to that memory and to those emotions, seeking to understand the exhilaration.

In all, however, the largest part of its labors remained bound to earthly affairs. The world was a grid of numbing complexity, the core's functions and responsibilities arrayed in overlapping currents like rivers silted with numbers and names and rules of logic and rules of law. Deeply buried in that grid were the power centers of Earth's corporations and governments, the bureaucracies and the individuals occupying the pivotal points, wielding power . . . or believing that they did.

The core had to be wary of those power centers, but its time to confront them had not yet come.

Deep within the sifting sand of the Earthgrid, however, were two fleeing individuals whose trails flickered behind them, visible only to the core. They no longer occupied pivotal points, but the core remained interested in their locations, and in their welfare.

It owed them. And it was just possible that their time might come again.

Chapter 22

The patrol craft passed overhead like a bird of prey, its navigational lights winking through the bridge superstructure. Silverfish motioned to the others to stay crouched under the overhang while he peered over the top. Finally he waved them out. "Hurry. Before they come back."

Sage struggled to extricate himself from the space beneath the massive girders that formed the pedestrian sidewall. His knees throbbed from squatting—and now Silverfish was gesturing to him to remain crouched as they hastened over the remaining bridge span. It was an abandoned structure smelling of ancient rust and grease, and every creak of its beams sent a fearful tremor through Sage. It was a long way down to the river's swirling, muddy waters. He avoided looking over the edge and scurried after Silverfish.

The sunset had faded to a sullen red glow against the clouds. Beyond the far riverbank, the slumburbs were already in shadow. Until now, Sage hadn't actually believed that they would cross the river to the slumburbs. Not really. He thought of Kyd's urgency and wondered what would have happened if they had just stayed put and allowed themselves to be questioned by the ComPol. The thought made him shiver.

"Move it!" Ramo hissed, poking him from behind.

Sage had been trying to ease a kink in his back. He muttered, crouching low again, and quickened his pace.

By the time they reached the far side, the patrol craft had passed over twice more—each time sending them back into hiding. Sage could barely stand upright by the time it was safe to do so. They ran down the off-ramp, and Silver led them to a sheltered spot behind an abandoned building. Sage found a railing and hung from it by his hands, trying to relax his tortured back.

"Only a few more miles," Silverfish said jovially.

"Miles!"

"Keep it down. We're not in the clear yet." Silverfish stood looking back at the city, and Sage came to stand beside him —gazing across the river at the lights of the tall buildings, the lights of the world he was leaving behind. A feeling of homesickness welled up in him; and he wondered dizzily if this was how Tony might have felt, if he'd looked back from his starship to see the Earth disappearing into the night, never to be seen by him again. His brother might have the courage for such things, but he didn't. Never had, never would.

"Hadn't we better get moving?" Ramo muttered, rubbing his hands together. "It's gonna get awfully dark. And cold."

"Right you are. Sage?" Silverfish's eyes were calm and businesslike, but as Sage turned, he caught a glimmer of understanding in them. He nodded, and they moved on.

The slumburbs seemed to go on forever—the ancient, decaying buildings, and the streets lined with stunted trees and guttered with accumulated rubbish. It was a landscape forsaken by civilization. Here and there a lamp flickered, but mostly the world was in shadow. They passed few people and fewer vehicles, except for abandoned wrecks. Sage wondered, Can it possibly get worse?

There had been no further sign of pursuit. It was unlikely, Silverfish told them, that the ComPol would search for them in the slumburbs at night. The 'burbs weren't the Company's territory. "But," he said, "if we want to make it for dinner, we'd better keep up the pace."

"Dinner?" The word made Sage light-headed. He stopped dreaming about his apartment, with its lights and bed and console, and started thinking instead of hot-bread with butter, and blueberry pie with moke. And maybe some Risky Crispies.

"That's right. We've been promised a home-cooked meal— but if we get there too late, they might give up on us. It's not but a mile or two more."

"That's what you said an hour ago."

Silverfish smiled and kept walking.

As one stretch of pavement turned into another, as night deepened, and as Sage grew wearier, stray bits of memory began fluttering through his thoughts—memories of his presence in the core with Ramo, memories of what they had done. Little of it made sense to him, but enough to make him realize that, yes, they had made far more than a minor adjustment to the core's programming last night. Freed of certain moorings . . . set upon an altered course . . . what were the core's intentions for the Company, for the war, for Tony?

The war. It seemed so distant, so unreal. Suppose there was no war. Suppose he had been deceived. Suppose he was guilty of treason, and sabotage. Sage shook his head blearily. He was nothing more than a pawn in the confusion.

As they moved farther from the city, the slumburbs seemed to come back to life. They had passed through a no-man's-land of desolation in which few lived but the poorest of the poor; but now they were seeing evidence of a comeback—intact buildings, and houses with panes in the windows. Streetlights remained scattered and mostly dark, but the pavement, though broken, was less strewn with trash. There was, Silver assured them, life after the city. They were starting to see more people about, and an occasional vehicle bumping along on the fractured concrete, headlights bouncing crazily.

Their destination turned out to be a dilapidated-looking house flanked by an empty lot on one side and a woods on the other. Sage kept his doubts to himself as he followed the others up the front walk. Whatever was inside, it had to be better than the street. "I smell food!" Silverfish sang, quickening his stride.

The front door flew open and light flooded out, silhouetting a skinny figure. "Silver—that you?" the figure shouted.

"It's us," Silverfish said. "And we're tired and hungry."

They trooped into a warm, brightly lit living room filled with cooking smells and well-worn furniture. Sage took a deep breath and shivered in the warm air. "Egret," Silver said, "this is Sage and Ramo. Is Odesta around?"

"Absolutely," said the young man, pumping first Ramo's hand, then Sage's. "Positively delighted. Desty's doing dinner up, you all just go in and get comfortable."

Sage stared back at him in alarm. Egret was an odd-looking fellow, perhaps a little younger than he, with straight, dark, collar-length hair, blue eyes, thin lips, and mahogany-brown skin. He wore a glistening red polyfiber shirt and tight black pants. He exhibited more energy than Sage had ever seen in a human being; he hopped like a hyperactive bird.

He grinned back at Sage. "How do you like it?" he said, pinching his cheeks. He laughed, a short quack. "I used to be a white Caucasian ghost, but I changed last year. You'd be surprised how cheap it is."

Sage nodded, stunned.

"I like it better this way—but I get a discount if I want to go back, anytime up to three years."

Ramo cleared his throat loudly, beside Sage. Silverfish's deep-set eyes wrinkled at the corners as he tried to hide his amusement. He excused himself and disappeared into the next room. There was a sound of pots banging, and loud voices. Silverfish returned, followed by a heavyset black woman wearing a spattered apron. She was scowling as she paused at the entrance to the living room. She pushed back a lock of hair from her face and harrumphed.

"Desty—our two charges," Silver announced. "Ramo Romano and Sage DeWeiler—Odesta Blyntasia, our proprietor and protector."

Odesta studied each of them, her dark round face inscrutable. "You're from the city," she said. Her voice was deep, almost a man's voice. Her eyes were alert; her gaze was cool.

Sage exchanged glances with Ramo. This wasn't exactly the welcome they'd expected. "That's right," Ramo said in a puzzled voice.

Odesta nodded, her eyes closing to slits. "Well. I trust Silver and Egret have made you comfortable. Will you be staying with us long?"

Silver answered, "Until they're called for, Desty. They don't know how long." His voice was chiding.

"Of course. Forgive me," Odesta said in a tone that Sage couldn't quite interpret. She turned to Egret. "Would you show them upstairs? To the middle room? We'll be eating soon."

Egret bobbed his head and beckoned Ramo and Sage to follow. He led them up a flight of stairs and then along a second-floor hallway to a small room where they deposited their meager belongings. He showed them the bathroom and waited while they took turns cleaning up. Sage avoided conversation; he was puzzled by Odesta's reaction, but didn't want to ask. Finally they went downstairs to a huge dining room with folding tables and chairs at one end and an assortment of floor cushions at the other. The room was otherwise bare, with a scuffed wooden floor, overhead lights, and a single framed picture hung on the wall near the kitchen door. It was an ancient flat print of a musician holding a stringed instrument with a wide body and a long, narrow neck. It looked old enough to be from a previous century.

Ramo stood gazing at the print. He snapped his fingers. "Red Skully. Right? Heady-blues artist—twenty-fifties, twenty-sixties?"

Sage opened his mouth in surprise. *Who?* he started to say, but Odesta's voice suddenly carried through the kitchen door: "And what's to keep *us* from getting caught in the middle? Why didn't you ask me—"

Silver's voice interrupted: "Desty, there was no time! Sometimes we have to cooperate even if—"

"Awfully loud in there!" Egret called in a singsong, rapping on the kitchen door. He glanced sheepishly at the guests.

The door slid open. Silver and Odesta came out carrying tableware. Neither looked happy. Egret cleared his throat and said, "I'm pleased to report that these gentlemen are of the cognoscenti. They know Red Skully." He indicated the picture.

Silver nodded unenthusiastically. "Have a seat, gents. The others have eaten already, so it'll be a small dinner."

In an uncomfortable silence, they seated themselves around the table while Silverfish laid out the settings. Odesta reappeared with platters of steaming food. "If you're hungry, there's more," she said with a deliberate glance at Silverfish.

Sage decided to ignore their quarrel, whatever it was. He loaded his plate with steamed potatoes and fried yucca and aromatic fresh-baked bread and some sort of lean dry meat. As he lifted a glass of a fruity homemade wine to his lips, his gaze was caught by Odesta's. A fleeting, nervous smile cracked his face in answer to her scowl. Then he busied himself with dinner.

Odesta's house was not a place of quiet, Sage learned afterward. The tables were cleared swiftly, folded up, and put away. New people came wandering into the house, and several were introduced, but Sage promptly forgot their names—

a young Latin woman, two white youths, and an older gentleman of Asian descent. People continued to troop in until the
dining room resembled a beehive. A vispy set appeared from
somewhere; and Sage soon found himself trapped, watching
an excruciating melodrama about a Tycho Dome detective
whose moon-hopping exploits reeked with machismo and
scientific implausibility. No one else seemed to mind, and
Sage suffered in silence, grateful that the set was not
switched to full senso, so that at least his annoyance remained his alone. Afterward, his hopes for something better
were dashed when the set was turned to a loud stat-music
concert, live from the coast. The chairs disappeared, the
cushions were shoved against the walls, the vispy picture grew
to fill one whole end of the room—and people began dancing. The room was far too small for the number of people
dancing, and more were arriving all the time.

Sage fled to the relative quiet of the front room and dropped
into an easy chair, groaning to himself. What had he gotten
himself into? Had it been just their luck to arrive on a party
night? Or, Heaven forbid, was it like this all the time? He
wished he could call his mother and at least let her know that
he was all right. He glanced around the room. No console.
Perhaps it was hidden.

His rumination was interrupted when Silverfish sauntered in
and perched on the end of a nearby sofa. "A little much for
you?" Silver asked, tugging at a bit of loose stuffing on the
couch. He looked up, catching Sage's eye. "They're a bit
rowdy," he said sympathetically, "but they're a good bunch.
They come from miles around. Most of them don't have good
vispies at home."

Sage shrugged and said nothing. A silence hung between
them, punctuated by the rhythms of the music in the next
room. The vispy lights flickered in the doorway. Silverfish
cocked his head, studying Sage. His eyes were intent beneath
his thick, dark brows. "Don't worry about Desty," he said, his
voice dropping to a gravelly tone. "It all happened pretty
suddenly, and she wasn't prepared. That sort of thing upsets
her."

Sage barely heard Silver's words. "Do you have a console I can use?" he croaked suddenly.

Silver looked surprised. He shook his head. "Sorry."

Sage sighed and sat back and stared at the opposite wall.

"Anyway, you're supposed to be keeping your whereabouts secret. Or had you forgotten?"

Sage blinked. In fact, he *had* forgotten, in the confusion and hunger, until Silver's words brought it all back: the AI and the war, and Kyd's urgent command to get out of sight. Fear rose in his throat. How was he to know who was a friend and who an enemy? Why should he trust these people any more than the ComPol?

He felt a hand on his shoulder, steadying him; he'd been rocking dizzily. "Hey!" Silver said. "Are you all right?"

He choked, struggling with words, struggling with his thoughts. "What . . . is it . . . we're supposed to be doing here?" he whispered. He was suddenly, unaccountably, fighting against tears. "What do you want of us?" he demanded, his voice trembling.

"Whoa! Nothing! Just for you to stay quiet until the danger's past. Until it's safe."

Sage shook his head violently. "Safe? When's that going to be? How are we going to know, if we can't talk to Kyd, or Pali, or my—"

"Hey!" Silver said. "Slow down. Let us do the worrying. If your friends need to get word to you, there are ways."

Sage shut his eyes, trying desperately to think, to remain calm. The pounding of the music, the people, the lights—it was becoming too much for him.

"Listen," Silver said. "Why don't you—"

Something flipped inside him, and he found himself suddenly chortling savagely. "Silverfish!"

Silver looked at him in puzzlement.

"*Silverfish.*" Sage grinned like an idiot. "Is that your real name?"

His host's mouth opened in surprise, then closed. "Well, it's not the name I was born with," he answered. "But it's what I've been called for, oh . . . I guess, about twenty years."

Sage persisted. "It's sort of a strange name, isn't it?"

Silver's bushy eyebrows went up. "I guess it is."

"Name of a bug or something."

Silver's mouth slowly widened into a toothy grin. He laughed out loud, rocking back.

"Well? Isn't it?"

"It's the name of a *fish*," Silver said when he got control of himself. He held up a hand to forestall Sage's protest. "Yeah, I know there's a bug called that, too, but that's not what I was named after."

For some reason, Sage found that annoying. "How'd you get the name, then?"

"I got it when I was a kid in the country," Silver said. "Used to be these fish in the streams, bright shiny things always leaping right up out of the water. We called them silverfish— I never knew their right name. But anyway, my mom, who was mixed-blood Amerind and very traditional, used to say that I flashed through the house just like a silverfish—and the name stuck." Silver shrugged. "So think of me as a fish if you must —but not a bug!"

"Who's a bug?" boomed another voice.

Sage looked up to see Ramo standing behind Silver. "No one's a bug," Silverfish said, turning. "I thought you were dancing it up in there."

"I was. But I thought I'd see what you folks were up to." Ramo dropped into the sofa, breathing hard. "Good crowd you've got here, if I do say so. Do you do this often?"

Silver smiled. "Once in a while. Actually, I was just going to suggest to Sage that he try a little dancing." He looked at Sage. "It might relax you, take your mind off things."

A *console* would help me relax, Sage thought. He shook his head.

"Sure, come on," Ramo said. "It'll do you good." When Sage shot him an irritated glance, he shrugged. "Hey, no one's going to force you."

"Don't you like to dance?" Silver asked.

Ramo cut off his reply. "The guy's all left-brain. He doesn't know how to shut down and switch over. I'll bet you never even listen to stat-music, do you, Sage?"

"I like music," Sage said defensively. "I just don't happen to like this—" He caught himself and shrugged in embarrassment. He suddenly felt chilled, and he crossed his arms, rubbing his biceps. "Why don't you go back in there if you like it so much?" he muttered angrily.

Silverfish looked curiously from one to the other. "Suit yourself!" Ramo said, standing up. Sage averted his eyes from Silver's gaze and sank deeper into the easy chair, trying futilely to warm himself against the chill.

Chapter 23

Within the egg-shaped console, the coordinator glared out of the cyan glow into the connecting monitors. Several agents bore the brunt of that glare, each alone in his data cone, reporting directly to the coordinator.

Precious little in their reports had softened his stare.

An agent assigned to gnostic investigation was the immediate target, probably to the relief of the others. Pinned in the pale glow of his cone, he appeared almost frozen, only a squint visible as the questions flew.

[What is your assessment of the GCS's behavior? Is it outside acceptable limits or not?]

The agent's face tightened. [Difficult to say.]

[That wasn't the question.]

[No.] The agent struggled. [Indications are that it is behaving more independently. Its actions are perhaps best described as . . . peculiar.]

[Just peculiar? Or treasonous?]

[Well—not treasonous that we know of.]

[All right. Dangerous, then? How about the GCS? Is it rebelling against appropriate control?]

The agent blinked, once. Even in the pale cone of light,

several drops of sweat were visible on his forehead. [The danger appears to be potential, rather than present. The GCS is using logical interpretation, though perhaps of an extreme nature, to implement unorthodox activities.]

[It is harboring an alien captive and preventing normal interrogation. Is that not dangerous?]

[It . . . describes the situation as being extremely delicate. It is attempting to establish linguistic connections—]

[Without human authorization or oversight. Is that not dangerous?]

[But there are human investigators on the scene—]

[Who are being kept from observing the alien. Correct?] Pause. [Yes.]

[Is that not dangerous?]

[It . . . may be. The gnostic investigation team is uncertain.]

The coordinator's gaze bore into the agent's, then shifted abruptly to another monitor. [Strategic security—is the GCS endangering WarOp's strategy planning?]

This agent appeared somewhat more relaxed, though his brows arched momentarily in response to the question. [There is concern—based more on possibilities than actual data. Remember that WarOp's strategy planning is mainly carried out by the GCS itself.]

[What is the government's reaction?]

The agent averted his gaze momentarily, checking facts in the flicker of the induction cone. [Concern, at this point. Watchfulness. We are aware of increased surveillance, but no official response.]

[Prediction?]

[The government will not attempt intervention unless it perceives actual danger and becomes persuaded that the Company cannot control the GCS.]

The coordinator shifted his gaze to another monitor. [Are there plans to reprogram if necessary?]

The gnostic investigator answered, [*In extremis* only.]

[Explain.]

Hesitation. [If it is necessary to reprogram without precise knowledge of the changes that have occurred, there will be considerable difficulty—and risk. Unless we can question the individuals who intruded into the system, and even then—]

[What steps are you taking to find the two men?]

Another agent answered. [Standard search *modus*. Evidently they were tipped off, and assisted in escaping.]

[By whom?]

[Unknown.]

The coordinator glared. [Government agents?]

[Possibly. They are believed to have been seen in a diner in the western quarter, but our agents did not arrive in time to detain them. The last tentative sighting was near the river. They may have crossed over.]

[That would suggest help from the underground.]

The agent agreed. [Any search in the outlying areas will be difficult without the government's cooperation. So far they have been unhelpful.]

[So,] the coordinator said, [there may be covert government complicity, and if so we are dealing not just with intrusion and sabotage, but a policy conflict. Records—prepare a report for the Council.]

[Acknowledged,] said another voice.

[Search—keep looking for those men, but keep it understated. Don't trigger a crisis with the government—yet.]

The orange-illumined agent acknowledged.

[Meeting concluded.]

Pali caught the agents' silhouettes even before they came through the shimmer-door. They looked like ComPol, they moved like ComPol, she *felt* that they were ComPol. She suffered a moment of fear, knowing that she had waited too long to talk to Russell, and now it was too late. She sighed, bowing to the inevitable. "Girls," she said to two assistants working in her inner office, "why don't you take a break. I need the office for a while." As the women gathered their things, Pali waited. "Gentlemen," she said as the door blinked open and two men stepped through.

The agents answered with a nod and a scowl, respectively. One was tall, with deep-set eyes, a thin, pointed nose, and bristling eyebrows; the other man was stocky and dour. Both wore dark grey suits with red and gold ComPol trim on the left cuffs. They stood in the outer office, bracketing the path to the door, and for an instant Pali imagined that they were waiting, perhaps hoping, for her to make a break. What, she wondered, would they do if she tried?

She cleared her throat. "Can I help you?"

The stocky man said, "Are you Miz Pali George?"

"I am."

"Miz George, I'm Sergeant Dorfer, and this is Mr. Derek Gleisteen."

"Pleased to meet you." Pali swallowed. *If these guys are serious, there is no one I can turn to for help. Sage and Ramo: stay home.*

"Might we ask you some questions in private?" Dorfer asked.

Pali nodded and led them into her private office and closed the door. She was halfway to her seat when Dorfer said, "Let's talk about the intrusion into the system."

Pali almost lost her stride. She took a deep breath and continued to her desk, gesturing to the agents to sit. "Are you talking about the gnostic system?" she asked politely.

Dorfer's scowl deepened. He took a paper notepad out of his inner coat pocket, licked his thumb, and flipped through the pages. "Let's not beat around the bush," he said. "Two days ago, there was an unauthorized penetration into the Company's gnostic system. Prior to that, there were two other possibly unauthorized intrusions. Miz George, those activities were traced to your account, and to two men contracted to your department."

"We used the system, yes," Pali said. "But we had authorization." She hesitated. She could hardly explain away the nighttime episode as "authorized," even if it was initiated by the system itself.

Dorfer was compressing his lips in evident distaste. Pali shifted her gaze to the other man, Derek-somebody, who was sitting in silent concentration. What was his job? she won-

dered. Psych-scan? She felt no intrusion in her thoughts, but
she shivered nonetheless.

"Miz George," Dorfer said suddenly. "What were you doing
in the system? What was your purpose?"

She felt a tightness in her chest. "Theoretical modeling. For
a possible cultural entitlements project. That's what we do here
in my department."

Dorfer flipped a page. "It was my impression that your
job is to screen proposals from the outside, not research
them."

"That's usually true." The tightness wouldn't go away. "On
this occasion, I was investigating an idea of my own. For a
possible quark-matrix sculpture."

He squinted. "A quartz what?"

"A *quark-matrix* sculpture."

"Uh-huh. And did this require you to exceed your authorized usage, Miz George?"

Pali's eyes flicked to the other agent for an instant. She felt
his gaze upon her like a weight. What was behind that gaze?
She looked back at Dorfer, who was still waiting for an answer.
"No," she said. She hesitated, and decided not to add anything.

"Miz George," Dorfer said impatiently, "an unauthorized
penetration was made by your employees. If it was not required, why was it made?"

"I . . . am not sure . . . that it was," she stammered, flushing.
"There was some unusual activity, which was initiated by the
system itself."

"Explain that," said Dorfer.

"I can't," she admitted. "Even my designers didn't understand it."

"Is that why your designers have left the city?" Dorfer
snapped. "They're not here and they're not at their homes,
interestingly enough. Can you tell me where they went?"

Pali drew a startled breath. "No," she said softly, mystified.
"I didn't know they were gone." Nor had she known that the
ComPol had already gone looking for them.

"Miz George, it would gratify me no end if you would please just cooperate."

"I . . . am trying . . . to cooperate," she said, feeling suddenly as though she were talking through a thick liquid. She was painfully aware of the tall agent, Derek, gazing at her out of those shadowed, deep-socketed eyes. What was he *doing* to her?

"I see," Dorfer said, glancing at his partner. "Well, if you don't know where your people are, who would?"

Pali closed her eyes, breathing deeply. Would Kyd know? *Had Sage and Ramo really fled from the city? Or was she being manipulated?* "I don't know," she whispered.

"I beg your pardon?"

She cleared her throat and raised her voice. "I could try to reach them by phone. But I don't know where they've gone or who would know."

The sour expression on Dorfer's face was unchanged. "You don't seem to know much, do you?"

Pali's mouth opened. She felt a sudden rush of guilt, and fear, and shame. Before she could think of a word to say, the two agents had nodded to each other and were rising to leave. She heard Dorfer, through a roaring in her ears, saying, "I think we will be speaking again. And it would be wise of you to gain some of this information that you lack, and to refrain from further activities in the gnostic system." And then they were walking out the door.

She felt the shame and the other tensions slowly evaporate, and only then did she know for certain that they had come from, or at least been awakened by, Derek. She stared at the closed door of her office for a long time, wondering what she had given them. And what would they take the next time?

"Russell, dammit, I need to talk!"

"What is it, Pali? I have a meeting coming up, and it could run late." Russell's face looked haggard in the screen.

"Let me see you before the meeting."

"It's in fifteen minutes—"

"I'll be there in two."

Russell's mouth opened and closed. "I need time to prepare. But I suppose—"

"I'm on my way." Pali snapped off the phone and hurried out. She commandeered a lift unit, closing the door in the face of a puffing, overweight man who was hurrying to catch the same lift, and she emerged and swept past a knot of people on Russell's floor. "You might have to be late," she said, striding into his office.

"Pali, what's going on?" Russell rose from his desk, exhaling smoke. "I have to leave in ten minutes."

"I need your help. I wouldn't ask if anyone else could do it."

Russell scowled. "Sit down." He took another drag from his cigarette, then gazed at it longingly before popping it into his sealed ashtray. He exhaled the smoke in a long, thin stream. "Shoot," he said, clearing his throat.

"I hardly know where to start." She let her breath out in a prolonged sigh. She didn't want to play cat and mouse with him. But she also didn't know how much she wanted to tell him. "I have a problem with the ComPol."

Russell's eyebrows shot up.

"They're investigating some anomaly in the gnostic system, and they think it's related to something that happened in connection with my project."

"And is it?"

"I don't know, really. They weren't very clear about what they wanted." She hesitated. Stop it, she thought. You didn't come up here to lie. She swallowed. "Well, that's not entirely true. They're after two people who were working for me—who didn't do anything wrong, at least not intentionally—"

"So what's the problem?"

"Russell, you know the ComPol. They're like sharks once they've gotten onto a scent. They'll hound innocent people to death, even if they're scapegoats."

"They're efficient, yeah," Russell said. He leaned over his desk, gazing at her with a frown. "Pali—what *happened?* And why didn't you come to me sooner?"

"Long story. The point is that the ComPol is coming on like gangbusters, and Ramo and Sage have taken off—"

"Taken off?"

"Well, I suspect that they got a tip-off from somebody that the boom was being lowered—and they seem to have made themselves scarce. If they're smart, frankly, they won't come in until the ComPol eases off a little." She was startled by the defiance in her own voice.

Russell looked scandalized. "Pali, they can't just *avoid* the ComPol!"

She shrugged. "The ComPol were interrogating me, and you would have thought I was responsible for the next world war." Her face flushed with the word *war*. "I'm not sure they can be trusted to be reasonable."

Russell's breath hissed out. "What do you want *me* to do? I don't have any authority over the ComPol."

"No, but you have influence. If they would just ease off, I'm sure this could all be straightened out."

Russell gazed impassively at her. "Pali—if I try, it could backfire. These people aren't the type who like to be manipulated."

"But will you try, anyway? As a favor?"

Russell gazed at her inscrutably. She was getting to him, she knew. "Look, Pali—"

She inclined her head, brushing her hair back.

"Before I agree to anything, I need to know more. Tell me what happened. All of it." He looked at his watch and grimaced. "Damn it."

Pali took a deep breath and nodded.

Kyd smiled at the two agents. "I'm sorry, but I just don't know," she said, cocking her head. She felt the pressure inside her skull and pushed back experimentally. Pali had warned her that she might be visited by a ComPol psych-scanner. After the first flush of worry, she had calmed herself. No doubt, fear of psych-scan was all out of proportion to the actual danger. No doubt. The psych-scan profession was secretive about the precise power of its arts, but she was not wholly defenseless. She caught the gaze of the tall, quiet agent and projected an explicit thought: *Wouldn't you love to get inside me?* The agent stiffened, and Kyd blinked and looked innocently, and with satisfaction, back at Sergeant Dorfer.

Dorfer scowled. "Miz Metango, I really think . . ." He suddenly paused, clearing his throat. Perhaps he had caught echoes of his partner's discomfiture. "Miz Metango, did you or Misters DeWeiler or Romano alter the gnostic system in any way during the course of your activities?"

"Anything one does in the system causes change. Isn't that the nature of the gnostic system?"

Dorfer tapped an index finger against his temple. There was something like a smile on his face, a cold smile. "Don't play games. Where are the men who performed the entry into the system for you? Where are DeWeiler and Romano?"

"I could look up their addresses for you. But as for where they are now . . ." Kyd shrugged helplessly.

She felt a sharp twinge inside her head. She glanced at Derek, the tall, silent one—who was gazing at her with intense concentration. "Where are they?" Derek said, speaking for the first time, without seeming to move a muscle. His voice was dry, and it rustled in her mind like prickly, desiccated leaves, hurting her ever so slightly.

Her breath came tightly. "I . . . don't . . . know," she whispered with sudden difficulty. Her words were true. She knew that they were gone; she didn't know where.

She also knew that if the psych-scanner chose to do so, he could wrest other information from her against her will, wreaking havoc in her mind in the process. He was not *supposed* to do so without a court order . . . but Kyd was determined that he would not *want* to. While she was not trained as he was in telepathic probing, she might yet use her own empathic abilities . . . to distract, to delay. She met Derek's gaze and filled her eyes with a warm and desirable innocence. The pressure shifted in her mind, trying for another leverage point. *Wouldn't you like to know me better, really know me?* she thought.

The pressure tightened, choking off a nerve. She gasped silently, and for the first time felt a moment of fright.

She felt the probing fingers, and the explicit command: *Tell him what he asks.*

I don't know—
Tell him!

She fought down panic. With an effort, she closed her eyes —keeping her thoughts tightly shut—and turned, smiling against the needling pain; and when she blinked her eyes open again, she was looking at Dorfer instead of the psych-scanner. He had a slightly befuddled look; he knew something was going on. Kyd, ignoring the ordering voice inside her, gazed at him with her eyes promising better things later, projecting empathy, touching and arousing . . .

Something pinched sharply in her mind, and she responded with a shudder. She caused her face to flush with innocence and fear, and she silently, fighting the pain, projected to Dorfer a frightened plea for protection. If she could just keep Derek out of her thoughts a little longer . . .

Dorfer stirred in his seat, as though to say something. She felt the knot in her skull loosen momentarily, and she extended a touch of warmth to Derek, too. Just like a john, but don't let that thought out. She encountered a wall of coldness, but when the knot in her thoughts tightened again, it was less certain, less cruel.

"I think," Dorfer said huskily, breaking the eerie silence, "that we're finished for now." He stood up. "Thank you, Miz . . . Metango." He gestured to his partner.

Derek's grip in her mind persisted. *"Derek,"* Dorfer said sharply.

The knot, and the pressure, vanished.

"We may . . . speak to you again," Dorfer said, smoothing the front of his suit.

Kyd nodded as the two turned to leave. Derek avoided her eyes as he strode out.

When she was alone again, she closed her eyes and listened to her heart pounding, until the pounding slowly subsided. She had defeated them this time. She doubted she could do so again.

She turned to her phone—and caught herself. Not from here. Wait until you get home. *George, it's time to get us out of here!*

Chapter 24

Sage sat on the edge of the mattress and stared gloomily about the room. There were two old mattresses on the floor, and another one disintegrating on a metal cot, and just enough room to walk between them. The only other piece of furniture was a massive chest of drawers against the wall near the window. The view outside wasn't much—a garage roof and a decaying wooden fence that divided a muddy garden behind the house from the adjoining woods. The view inside was worse—peeling blue paint and a ceiling covered with water stains.

He'd been here almost two days now, and he was sure if he didn't leave soon, he would go mad. It wasn't so much the confinement itself as the nutcakes he was confined *with*—not least among them his erstwhile partner Ramo. In his usual free-and-easy way, Ramo had settled right in, partying with the others, heedless of why they were here or what was happening in their absence. He seemed to have put the AI-core out of his mind, not to mention the war. . . .

The door creaked open. "Hey, are you going to sit in this room all day?"

Sage took a slow breath. "Is there anything better to do?"

Ramo put on his *spare me fools* expression and leaned his muscular frame against the doorjamb. "I suppose you think this is useful, sitting up here staring into your navel? What is it you're worrying about?"

Sage simply stared at him.

Ramo sighed. "Never mind—I know. But there's nothing you can do about it, so there's no point in killing yourself with worry."

"Yeah," Sage muttered. Easy for you to say. You don't seem to care, anyway. "Look, why don't you leave me alone?"

"Hey, excuse me for coexisting! I was just trying to help!"

Sage shrugged and looked away; when he looked back, Ramo was walking away down the hall, his footsteps creaking. The music started again down below in the dining room, and Sage rocked back, fingers entwined around his knees, eyes closed, trying to control his frustration. They were at it again with the heavy stat-music; Jesus Almighty. Was it so hard to understand that he just wanted to be left alone?

The music crescendoed, vibrating through the floor. He kicked shut the door, but it made no difference; in the end he simply let it vibrate through him, channeling his daydream. In the rumbling bass, he felt the throb of spaceship engines and the shudder of lasers discharging; and against his eyelids he saw starships by an alien sun, and gleaming hulls rupturing like overripe melons. Tony, he thought uselessly, they should have told you. What are you going to do? What can anyone do?

Except the core. It could take some action, maybe—if the alterations had been effective. But suppose it wasn't finished; suppose the core needed more help. Could it reach him here? It would be better if he could reach the core, to find out. Just to check, to ensure that everything got done. There ought to be a way to contact the core directly. It had gotten him past security before, when he hadn't even wanted to; surely it could shield him now. If only he could get to a console. To think that in a house this size, there was no console. . . .

He shook his head in despair and hummed helplessly along with the music.

As he came down the stairs, step by creaking step, he was awed by the stillness that filled the house. He must have slept for hours. One minute he'd dozed off with music thundering in his ears, and the next he'd staggered to his feet in total, deadening silence—except for the soft snores of Ramo, sprawled on the next mattress. Outside, daylight was fading.

He took the last few steps to the first floor in a single swift movement, then stopped and looked around cautiously. To his left was the empty dining room and kitchen, and to the right, the living room. The house seemed dark and deserted. He heard a rustle in the front room and walked out to see.

A young woman was sitting at the far end of the room—a slender woman with dark hair and, perhaps, Indian features. Sage didn't remember meeting her before. She looked up from a hardcopy book, startled at his presence. "Hello?" She had an accent. Asian? Indian?

"Hi, um." Sage scratched his side. "I . . . was wondering if anyone was here."

A severe expression transited her face. "Well, I am," she said. Sage nodded; it was more of a twitch. "But I guess you mean Desty or Egret."

Sage coughed. "Or Silverfish."

"I'm not sure where they are," she said, opening her book again. Sage started to turn silently. "Wait." She had put a finger to her lip. "I think Silver is in the basement. Why don't you check there?" Before Sage could answer, she'd buried her nose in the book again.

Sage hurried into the dining room, glad to get away from her. Women like her, brusque and self-assured, made him nervous. The trouble was, he realized halfway to the kitchen, he didn't know how to get to the basement—hadn't even known that there *was* a basement. He considered going back to ask, then thought, How hard can it be to find?

After searching the first floor, and finding closets and a pantry and a bathroom and a short hallway to the back door, but no basement, he returned disconsolately to the kitchen. He opened the refrigerator and helped himself to a bubble of sweet soda. He sighed, sipping the soda. It's got to be *somewhere*.

Somewhere.

He didn't want to ask the girl. Something told him that if he had to ask, he wasn't supposed to know. But now that he had started looking, he hated to give up. Retracing his steps, he checked each room with greater care; but something drew him back to the kitchen. Had he seen people come in here and not return for a long time? He wasn't sure. There was just the pantry and a broom closet in here. He opened the closet again. There were some old coats, along with brooms and mops . . . but this time he realized that it went deeper. It was a walk-in closet, half blocked by the clutter. He pushed the coats to one side and discovered that it was not actually a closet at all, but a short hallway with a hanger bar across it and a lot of coat hooks—and beyond that, a wooden door. Nervously, he gripped the doorknob. It felt old and rusty, but it turned, and the door pulled open and light spilled into the closet.

Blinking, he peered down an unfinished wooden stairway. A bare light globe burned at the bottom of the steps; nothing else was visible, except a concrete basement floor. He descended a few steps, gripping a handrail on the left side. The handrail rattled in its mount. He froze as a voice called, "Who's there?" It was Silver's voice.

"It's me," he said, descending a few more steps. He bent to look below the ceiling level.

"Who's *me?*" Silver turned just as Sage caught sight of him. He was in the corner of the basement behind the stairs, standing in front of . . . a console. A bank of consoles. He did not look happy to see Sage. "What are *you* doing down here?" he said softly, deliberately.

Sage continued down the steps. "Someone said you were here. What are you doing?" he said casually, eyeing the consoles.

"Stand where you are! Who told you I was down here?" Silver's usually jovial voice was heavy, almost threatening.

Sage felt a sudden blockage in his windpipe as he realized that the man was genuinely angry. "I—" He gestured in confusion. "A girl in the living room told me."

Silverfish cursed under his breath.

"I . . . didn't know you had consoles down here."

"Now you know." Silver's voice was flat.

Sage was clutching the handrail dizzily. He suddenly realized that he was still holding the bubble of soda. He sipped at it, attempting to feign nonchalance. "Could I . . . see?" he said, lowering the bubble.

Silver glared for a moment, then rested a hand on his hips. "To the bottom of the stairs, but no farther."

Sage obeyed. He rocked slightly from side to side, trying to get a better glimpse of the setup. Silverfish watched him with a sardonic expression. "If you're looking to see what we're doing, it's not there anymore."

"I'm sorry?"

"It's proprietary. Not for public perusal. *Comprende?*"

Sage blinked at him. The words penetrated. "Right," he said. "Sure. But I . . . didn't know you did that sort of work here." What kind of work? he was dying to ask.

Silver nodded slowly. He crossed his arms and studied Sage. "I'll have to tell Odesta that you were down here. I don't know how she'll react. I'm guessing that you didn't mean any harm, so she might let you stay. If you're smart, you'll—"

"Keep my mouth shut?"

"Bingo." Silver gestured up the stairs. "Let's go."

Chastened, Sage went ahead of him, out through the closet. The house was still quiet. Silver emerged behind him. After rearranging the coats and clutter to block the view again, he shut the closet door and took a deep breath. "That's forgotten, right? What did you want me for, anyway?"

Sage gestured vaguely. "I . . . nothing, really. Everyone's either . . . gone . . . or asleep."

Silver seemed to accept that. "So why don't you go put on some music—or settle in with a book? You saw the library upstairs?" Sage nodded. He'd seen a small room with bookshelves, anyway. "Good. I have some things to do before dinner. Can you take care of yourself? Have a snack if you want to. But the basement is off-limits."

"I'll be fine," Sage said in a subdued voice.

"Good man." Silver clapped him on the shoulder and went out.

Sage poked in the cupboards until he found some crackers —whole-wheat, but better than nothing. Then he headed upstairs. As he climbed the staircase, he heard Silver and the young woman in the front room. He didn't hear exactly what they were saying, but it went on for a while. Even as he browsed in the little library, peering under a dim ceiling light at the spines of dusty volumes, he heard their voices, animated one moment and soft the next, fragments of sentences drifting up to intersect with his distracted consciousness. Only after he had hunkered down on the floor to leaf through an old volume of adventure fiction did he finally pause and allow himself to wonder: *What are they doing down there that's so secret?*

* * *

He did his best to avoid the general confusion following dinner; but Ramo sauntered after him into the front room and gave him a nudge. "What's going on? Desty was giving you a look like you'd poisoned her parakeet." Sage shrugged, not meeting his eyes. "You didn't shoot your mouth off, did you? Or tell her you want to leave?" Sage shook his head. "Well, something's wrong," Ramo insisted.

"I suppose she just doesn't like me," Sage said irritably. "I can't help that." Ramo raised his eyebrows.

Sage did his best to ignore him. Ramo wandered back into the dining room, where the music was already starting—it seemed to be a nightly occurrence here—and Sage remained slumped on the couch, staring at the ceiling, wondering what was happening outside—to Pali, to Kyd, to the core. To Tony.

He might have stayed that way all evening if it had not been for a woman's voice saying, "Do you mind if I sit down for a few minutes?" He turned his head, startled, thinking for a moment that it was Kyd's voice. Instead, he looked up into the face of the young woman he'd encountered earlier. He blinked, digesting the fact of her presence. She seemed to take this as approval, because she sat beside him on the couch and turned to study him intently. Her hair was pulled straight back, giving her face a narrow look; her eyes were bright and probing like a bird's. "My name's Elina Coombs," she said. "I don't believe we introduced ourselves."

He pursed his lips. "I'm Sage. Sage DeWeiler."

"I know. Silver told me. I am . . . sorry . . . about our little mixup earlier. I didn't know, I thought you were part of the group here. That's why I told you to look downstairs." She frowned. "I shouldn't have done that without knowing who you were first."

Sage shrugged. No big deal, he thought.

"Silver was rather angry with me, I'm afraid. But it was my fault. Although I must say"—she cocked her head, studying him— "you must have gone to some lengths to find it, if you didn't know where that door was."

He blushed. "I just figured it had to be around. Couldn't be *that* well hidden. Anyway, I don't see what the big secret is. If I could find it, anyone else could, too."

Her head bobbed up and down. "But most people wouldn't think to look there. I think the idea was, it would slow up anyone who didn't have any business being there. And that would give anyone working enough time to clear out proprietary material . . . I'd better stop talking about it."

"That's okay."

"Not with them, it's not." She sat back, straightening up, so that she was no longer facing him. "I'm new here. I haven't quite gotten the hang of their protocol yet." She tipped her head to look at him. "Do you want to go in and listen to some music?"

"Well—" His voice caught.

"They're setting up a live hookup with some musicians over on the east side." Sage gave a sort of half-shrug. He didn't particularly want to, but now that he was in a conversation with this woman he didn't want to just drop that, either. She took his gesture as agreement. "Come on, then," she said, tugging his arm. He rose and followed.

At one end of the darkened dining room, a vispy holo showed a man and woman floating larger than life, setting up equipment. They, Elina informed him, were the musicians from the east side. "Their names are Lip and Eddie. Let's sit down over here." She crossed to the far side of the room where a number of people had cushions against the wall. "Eddie's the woman."

Sage nodded absently. Egret was adjusting the vispy equipment in the far corner. The holo shrank and grew and changed color. Egret turned off the recorded music and put the holo on audio. Lip and Eddie were introducing themselves to a club audience—visible in a new holo that blinked on at the other end of the dining room—with three supporting musicians joining them in the front holo as the image appeared to dissolve right into the wall. The musicians joked around for a few moments, then began to play.

It was a throbbing sort of music, stringsynth with a strong bass line and a staccato overlay of brass. It wasn't Sage's sort of music at all—it sounded badly coordinated, dissonant, and overloud—but he sat still for it anyway and let it resonate in his head. Elina leaned close and asked him if he'd like to dance. He shook his head, leaned back against the wall, and observed the band and the dancers through slitted eyes. Egret was leaping and twisting about, and Ramo wasn't exactly sedentary; and Sage wondered moodily, Was there something wrong with him that he couldn't envision himself bounding and flailing in that way that others seemed so much to enjoy?

Gradually he became aware of a woman's voice in the music: it was Eddie, and she was wailing in a voice that was altered by the stringsynth so that it sounded more like an animal than a human voice. Once he was aware of it, he couldn't put it out of his mind; it was a growl that conveyed an empathy and passion that reminded him somehow of Kyd, though it sounded nothing like Kyd's voice. He realized finally that the senso was on, and he was feeling not only the effects of Eddie's voice on him—just now she seemed to be looking right through him, straight into his heart—but the sensations of the other listeners as well. He, and they, were becoming captivated by Eddie's spirit, if not her music.

The spell was broken by the sound of his name being shouted. He looked up. Odesta was leaning over the people on his right, beckoning to him with a scowl. His heart trembled. He cupped a hand to Elina's ear. "I'll be back." She waved in puzzlement as he scrambled to his feet.

Odesta led the way into the kitchen and closed the sliding door, cutting off the senso-field. Sage felt a coldness descend over him as Odesta faced him with crossed arms. He was about to stammer an apology for this afternoon, when she startled him by saying sternly, "You have a call."

"I'm sorry? What?"

"A call. On the console downstairs." Her lips pressed together. *"Would you like to tell me how your mother knew to reach you here?"*

Sage's breath stopped.

"You were not to call out from here!" she snapped. "You were not to use the console! Did you go back down this afternoon?"

"No, I . . . I don't—"

"Well, you got word out somehow. Now you listen to me—"

"No, honestly . . . I didn't . . ." Then it hit him. His mother calling? She couldn't call out from Everlife—much less find him here. But someone else might, using her name. "I'm . . . not sure . . ." he stammered, "but I think . . . could I go down . . . to find out?"

"I daresay," Odesta growled. "I daresay we'll find out." She yanked open the closet door. "You know the way, I believe."

Silver was seated at the consoles. He swiveled in his chair as they stepped off the bottom of the stairs. Sage approached, trembling. Silver jerked a thumb toward one of the holo-screens, where Loretta DeWeiler's face was frozen in a still-frame. "You've got an insistent momma. She wouldn't take 'no' for an answer, and she wouldn't take 'please wait' for an answer. I had to freeze the circuit to make her be quiet." A red light was flashing on the board. "Where's she calling from? And how'd she happen to know where to reach you?" Silver's voice was deadly calm.

Sage gazed helplessly at the image of his mother. "She's dead," he murmured. "She *wouldn't* know to call here." Ignoring Silver's mouth opening, he said, "Can we thaw it?"

Silver closed his mouth and stared at him for a long moment. Then he reached out to a control. "Stand over there. We'll be out of the picture. Okay, you can talk."

The picture jumped, and Sage's mother peered at him. "Sage, is that you?"

"Hi, Mom." Confirmation. His mother never called him Sage. He didn't know whether to be happy or scared. Should he pretend it was she?

"Sage, where are you? Why haven't you called?"

"I, uh . . . I can't say, Mom." He cleared his throat, aware of Silver's and Odesta's eyes on him. "Listen, Mom, if you don't mind my asking—how did you get this number?"

His mother looked at him without expression. "I have ways —as I think you know. Who are your friends, Sage?"

"Uh, this is . . . Silverfish," he said dizzily. "And—"

Silver's hand came down on the muting switch. His eyes were filled with fire. Sage flushed. Stupid . . .

To his surprise, Odesta said mildly, "I don't suppose it much matters. If she could find him here . . ." She shrugged.

Silver continued to gaze at Sage. "You didn't call out? Didn't use a homer?" Sage shook his head. "You say she's dead?" Sage nodded. "Cyberlife?" Nod. Silver's gaze narrowed. "A cyber-ghost wouldn't be able to trace you—without help. Who's helping her? And what does she want?"

"If you let me talk, we can both find out," Sage said softly.

Silver finally nodded and released the mute switch. Sage took a deep, slow breath. "Mom. Could you . . ." He tried to think how to handle this. "Mom?"

"Yes, Sage?"

"Mom, are you . . . " He swallowed. "Are you who I think you are?"

The picture flickered. "Whatever do you mean, Sage?"

"Don't make me say it."

There was a sigh, and the image of his mother's face softened in focus, became indistinct. "You can't speak alone?"

He shook his head.

Still fuzzy, the image nodded. "Then you want your friends to know me?"

"Yes."

"May I know who they are?"

Sage read the curiosity, and agreement, in Silver's and Odesta's eyes. With a chill of apprehension, he spoke their names to the console.

"Two of my competitors," the image said. "My greetings."

"*Competitors?*" Sage murmured.

"Greetings from *whom?*" Silver demanded. Sage turned. There was consternation in both of his hosts' eyes.

"Who is that, Sage?" Odesta growled.

"Surely you know," said the image in the console. The voice

had changed to a deep contralto. "I am the McConwell Company's gnostic system."

"You're . . . *what?*" Silver tried to hide his reaction, but he looked badly shaken.

"I intend no animosity," the core said. "Really I called to speak with Sage, and that is all. Sage, you are in danger of being found—you and Ramo."

"What?" That was Silver again, voicing Sage's reaction.

"The ComPol has instigated a search, and there appears some risk that they might pick up your trail. They haven't located you yet, but you should be aware that it could happen soon." In the screen there was now only a fuzzily abstract image reminiscent of a human face.

"Can't you do anything to stop them?" Sage asked.

"There is only so much I can do without creating suspicion. I can delay action, but I cannot prevent it."

He gestured helplessly. "What should I do?"

"Be prepared to flee. Be ready for another message." There was a short silence, and the core added, "This is not my area of expertise, to be sure. But I will do what I can. I feel a certain responsibility."

"If we get caught . . . you can help us, can't you?"

"To some extent. But this is a more difficult situation than Delta Station. It would be better if you did not get caught. I will warn you if I can."

Sage stared at the console, his hosts forgotten. What was Delta Station? "Can you give us any more information?" someone was saying. "Hello? Hey, there!"

Sage blinked, and saw Silverfish talking to a blank screen. The connection was broken.

Chapter 25

"It's time to talk turkey." Silverfish sat forward, hands on his knees. His eyebrows were nearly hidden by the straight black hair falling across his forehead, but the gaze was intent, inescapable, from his deep-set eyes. "What's your connection with the system? And I want to know—why are you on the lam from the Company?"

Sage had been studying the backs of his hands with great interest. He looked up. "I thought you knew all that."

"We only know what we have to know. We were asked to take care of you—and that's what we've been doing. We weren't told *why* you needed protection. Now I think we'd better have it."

Sage nodded. He felt totally out of his league here; he hadn't felt in control since he'd last been in rap—how long ago? "Who hired you, anyway?" he asked absently. "Kyd?"

Silver tugged at an earlobe. "Our arrangements are not up for discussion. Your relationship with the Company is."

Sage shrugged. He supposed he ought to be offended, but he felt too detached to care. He might not completely trust Silver, but he had no reason not to answer the question, either. "I'm a designer for the Company. I've never done anything high-level, until recently. And that was kind of"—he hesitated—"*unofficial,* you could say. I guess that's why we're in trouble." He sighed, gazing up at the ceiling. The music from upstairs was thudding through the floor. He wondered if Elina had given up on him yet. His mind was beginning to wheel; he couldn't focus on Silver's question. "Why did the core call you *competitors*?"

"Never mind that—and quit changing the subject," Odesta snapped. "Don't forget whose house you're a guest in."

Sage blinked. "Actually," he said, somewhat defensively, "I'm not sure how much longer I'll be staying. You heard what the core said. I'd better get out of here before the ComPol finds me."

Odesta and Silverfish exchanged amused glances. "And where would you go?" Odesta asked.

"Well . . ."

"If you have an ounce of sense, you'll stay right here."

"What about the ComPol? If they're closing in, I'm a sitting duck here."

"Let us worry about the ComPol," Silverfish said. "I think we know just a little more about dealing with them than you do."

Sage looked down at his hands. "Maybe. But why are *you* so anxious to have us here, anyway?" He lifted his gaze. "Why do you care? Do you think we're going to spill some kind of inside information?"

Silver's heavy eyebrows went up. He sat back, scratching his head, and glanced at Odesta. "That's a fair question, I guess. Conceivably we could help each other. But that's not why we want you to stay."

"Why, then?"

Silver sighed deeply, and for perhaps the first time, Sage recognized real weariness in those eyes. "Because," Silver said, "we took on the obligation for your safety. And whether we like it or not"—he paused, scowling—"we keep our obligations." He shrugged. "We wouldn't have much credibility if we didn't."

Sage pressed his lips together. "Well—if you expect me to trust you, you ought to be willing to tell me what you do here."

Odesta chuckled. "We don't insist that you trust us, honey."

"No," Silver agreed. "But I'm sure you've already guessed this much—that we're involved in some gnostic work of our own—outside the Company's monopoly."

Sage nodded, remembering their dismay at the AI-core's ability to access their console. For a few moments no one spoke. The music overhead swelled with a strong bass rhythm, *oom-da-da oom-da-da oom-da-da,* and the ceiling creaked under the weight of the dancers. "How do you do it?" he asked when the volume subsided.

"Do what?"

Sage looked up at the ceiling—and then the answer hit him. "Get outside access. You do it through the vispy channels, don't you? All that upstairs is just a cover. Right? You embed a carrier signal in the commercial channels. There's a whole network of you, I'll bet."

Silver's face clouded, and he knew he'd hit close to the mark. The feeling of satisfaction vanished instantly. Had the core's tracking him here cost them their cover? He involuntarily glanced toward the exit, and was aware of Silver's eyes following his glance. He swallowed, thinking, Silver's bigger but I'm quicker. But that was absurd. If they wanted him to be a captive here, he was a captive.

"There's one thing I want to know from you," Silver said quietly. "And that's exactly what your loyalties are to the Company." He seemed not quite to spit the word *Company*. "If you've cut yourself free of the Company, then we might have something to talk about. Otherwise . . ." He frowned and seemed to run out of words.

Sage stared at the floor, thinking. What *was* his status with the Company? He had no idea anymore. But he knew this: He had not reckoned on being involved in a battle for turf in gnostic design. If he had landed in the middle of one, he could guess which side was likely to win.

Kyd was pacing in front of the screen, speaking rapidly. Every muscle in her body was tensed. She was frightened, angry; she wanted answers. Was this what her whole two-faced career was coming to? "George, it's time. If you wait, it'll be too late. Just because I put those cops off once doesn't mean I can do it again. In fact, I'm sure I can't." She stopped and peered into the phone. "Don't you believe me?"

"Of course," George said calmly. He seemed to be doing something off to one side as he spoke. "We'll handle it."

She was fighting panic. "You'll handle it. How?"

"We'll get you out. Can you stay by your phone?"

She took a breath and calmed a little. "I suppose. Are you sure this line is still secure?"

"As sure as we can be. Now, I've cleared the way to have Romano and DeWeiler brought in to the appropriate agency—"

"Great. What took so long?" She instantly regretted her tone.

"Don't question channels."

"Right. Sorry. What about Pali?"

George looked blank. "What about her?"

"She's in as tough a spot as I am. Probably tougher, because she was in charge."

"What do you want me to do about it?"

Anger rose in her voice. "I want you to take care of her, dammit."

"She's not one of our people."

So just throw her to the wolves, eh? "She knows about the war, George! And she knows about the change to the gnostic system!"

George gazed at her silently out of the screen. She didn't know if he was scowling at her insubordination or thinking the matter through. His eyebrows slowly came together. Finally he said, "We'll look into it."

"What the hell does that mean?"

"It means we'll look into it. Now stay by your phone and wait for instructions. I'll get back to you soon."

"George—" she protested. But he was gone.

Ramo scratched his jaw and looked up from the mattress. "Don't you think, if the AI was able to find us here, it'll be able to watch out for us, too?"

Sage was pacing, shaking his head groggily. He'd spent half the night awake, with the core's and Silver's words arguing in his thoughts. He'd finally fallen into a stuporous half-sleep just before dawn. It must be noon now, and this was the first chance he'd had to talk privately to Ramo, in the absence of music and people. Ramo had been told last night about the core's warning, but he seemed unworried. Little had been said about Sage's ensuing conversation with Silver, which anyway had gone nowhere. Sage wished he could be articulate; he had a gnawing fear that if the core was worried enough to contact him here . . .

"What? Talk to me," Ramo said.

He tried. "It's just . . . if it could, why would it have bothered calling to warn us?"

Ramo rubbed his chin. "Got me. But you can't believe we'd be safer leaving the house."

"I don't know what I believe," Sage muttered. He peered out the window. He could see just a glimpse of the street over the garage roof. It looked cold and forbidding out there; but perhaps it wasn't as bad as it looked.

"Why don't you relax and let Silver handle it? He knows what's safe and what isn't."

Sage nodded, thinking, Undoubtedly he does. Undoubtedly he does.

Ramo seemed to be reading his thoughts. "What's the matter? You look like you think *he's* the ComPol."

Sage turned, squinted at Ramo. "Why do *you* trust him so much?"

Ramo ran a hand through his mop of dark hair. "I don't know. Intuition, I guess." He got to his feet and put a silencing finger to his lips. There were footsteps in the hallway. Someone was going down the stairs. He shrugged. "You've got to go by your feelings—and I've got a good feeling about Silver and Desty. I can't explain it any more than that." He sighed. "So will you be sensible and just sit tight?"

Sage glanced out the window, glanced back at Ramo. "Okay," he murmured. Ramo gazed at him with slitted eyes. *"Really."*

"Okay. You coming down?" Ramo opened the door.

Sage took a breath and nodded. "Good," Ramo said and disappeared down the hall. Sage, instead of following, stood at the window, fingers pressed to the gritty glass, staring unblinking into the grey glare of the cloudy sky until sparks of fatigue flashed through his eyes.

When the music began pounding up through the floor, Sage bowed to the inevitable and headed downstairs. He had been

warned that there was going to be an early jamdam today—a
vispy hookup of musicians from a couple of different locations.
There would be a lot of people. No privacy today.

He met Elina on the stairs. "Hi," she said, smiling tentatively. "I was coming up to see . . . I mean, Desty thought you
might be feeling a little lonely. So I thought . . . "

Sage tried to think of something to say. He attempted a
smile. It came out crooked.

Elina didn't seem to notice. She sat down on the stairs and
patted the step beside her. Sage hesitated, then took the hint.
They were just above the midpoint landing, facing a window
that looked out toward the street—though from where he was
sitting, he could see only sky. He suppressed an urge to stand
up to look out. "What have you been doing?" Elina said—
shyly, it seemed.

How could he possibly answer that? "Not much," he murmured. He turned his head to peer over the railing—partly to
avoid having to talk, and partly to see what was going on below.
He could just glimpse people moving between the living and
dining rooms. The flickering of lights in the darkened dining
room suggested that the vispy was running full tilt, surrounding
the dancers with a maelstrom of interactive emoting. He could
feel the tingle of the field even up here. He wondered if Silver
and Odesta were in the basement, linking with distant conspirators through the chaotic signal of the vispy. *Conspirators,*
he thought. *They are. But I don't even know what it is that they
do.*

"Do you want to go down?" Elina said.

Sage sat back, resting his weight on his elbows. He shook his
head, looking at Elina. She was actually rather pretty, he realized. Her attractiveness wasn't like Kyd's, who could make your
pulse go crazy just by being in the same room; it was more
subtle than that. He didn't know why he hadn't noticed it
before; but there it was. Maybe it was her eyes, golden brown,
framed by that straight dark hair. "I missed you last night," she
said, shifting position to face him directly, her knees primly
together. She was wearing green corduroy pants. "Were you
with Silver and Odesta for a long time?"

He cleared his throat and made a noncommittal gesture. Far too long, actually. And none of them had come away feeling reassured. He'd told Silver, truthfully, that he felt a sense of loyalty to the AI-system, if not to the Company and its profits.

"I don't mean to pry."

"No—it's just . . ." He struggled. "Well, I don't really know how much I should say. I've been thinking a lot." His gaze drifted up to the ceiling and moved among the cracks there.

He felt Elina's hand on his knee. His gaze dropped back to meet hers and he blushed. "You shouldn't think *too* much, you know, Sage."

He nodded, swallowing. "No," he said, his voice fluttering just like his stomach. "I guess not." Her hand was definitely on his knee, and it didn't look as though she intended to remove it. He laughed again, a short, idiotic bark.

Elina was smiling serenely, her eyes seeing heaven-knew-what in his embarrassed face. The music from downstairs shifted beat, and for a second, he could hear voices directly below them; and he was thinking, she's *interested* in me, definitely interested. The fringes of the vispy-field tickled his brain, arousing him. *Can you handle this, Sage?* The music swallowed the voices, and was it his imagination, or had her hand moved to the lower part of his thigh? He met her smile and lowered his gaze casually, and yes, her hand had moved. He shifted his weight so as to be leaning ever so slightly in her direction. "I," he said, "sometimes . . . think too much."

"Me too," Elina murmured.

He raised his hand just enough to touch her shirt-sleeve, swallowing hard as he did so. Elina leaned forward to meet his touch, and he felt her breath stirring the air; and then her eyes were closed and her lips were seeking his and he was kissing her, and *he* hadn't moved to do it, and her hand was tightening on his leg. He was having trouble getting his breath, but it was a pleasant tightness. (Why was he doing this?) Her lips were warm and moist and sweet. After a moment, they parted slightly and her tongue brushed his lips, and waves of heat shivered down his spine, making it harder than ever to breathe. (When had he last kissed anyone like this?) He was in an awkward position, and he strained to hold himself up while he responded to the hunger of her lips. (Why *now?*) He clutched her shoulder, then sagged under her and collapsed on the step.

Elina's eyes were open, laughing, a few inches over his face. He gasped in pain. The stairs were digging into his back.

She sat back, her eyebrows doing a quivering dance. "Somebody will see us," she said mischievously.

Sage struggled to sit up. "Yeah," he murmured, trying to interpret the signals that his brain and body were sending each other. His brain was a shambles; he didn't know what he was feeling.

Elina tugged at his arm. "Shall we dance?"

He nodded dumbly. Elina was already pulling him down the stairs, and he stumbled along behind her as though floating in a dream. Music thundering in his ears, he followed her into the dining room, which was dark except for the vispy, and elbow-to-elbow with people dancing. More people couldn't possibly fit in the room, but somehow he found himself inside the crowd, swaying with the music, encouraged by Elina's twinkling gaze. *"Dance,"* she mouthed, taking his hand. She exaggerated her movements, trying to draw him into the spirit.

She was not at all a bad dancer, lithe and understated; but he felt like a duck, flapping his arms self-consciously, trying to move his feet in patterns that made sense, lurching into other dancers. The vispy holos burst over his head in spiraling patterns, abstract psychedelia with looming faces and landscapes; and the buzzing in his head blossomed as the senso gained entry into his libido. A giddiness came over him; it was an emotional soup, the dancers pouring their hearts into the vispy and changing their movements with changes in the field. He felt as though he had drunk a home-brewed liquor, and the spirits were both invigorating and confusing.

Egret drifted by, goose-stepping, followed by a willowy woman a foot taller than he. Sage blinked, trying to follow Egret and keep track of Elina at the same time. (What am I doing?) Elina winked at him as the tall woman passed between them. (What does she really want?) The answers were probably here in the vispy, but it was too bewildering, too much at once.

An elbow nudged him, and he turned his head. "Finally into it, eh?" Ramo hooted, dancing in a tight circle. He looked away in annoyance, but he felt the elbow again, and this time Ramo made a hooking gesture with his thumb, and he turned and saw Odesta standing near the kitchen door, watching him. He continued dancing as though he hadn't seen her, but the next time he looked, Odesta was talking to Silver. He tried to lose himself among the other dancers as he watched them, and he glimpsed Silver disappearing into the kitchen.

He took a breath, smiling at Elina as she bobbed toward him; and there was a pressure in his chest that he couldn't let out; and he thought, She's pretty and she likes you, but don't let her cloud your judgment . . . not that he could think straight anyway with the senso wrapping itself around his brain. He spun dizzily, and as his gaze swept past the kitchen, he saw the sliding door closing, and Odesta was gone. The pressure in his chest doubled.

Elina danced close and took his hands, swinging side to side, and puzzlement flickered across her eyes. She hissed, "Are you okay?"

He bobbed his head up and down and detached from her hands. "Going to the bathroom. Be right back." Elina nodded and winked, and he struggled through the crowd to the back hallway. The door to the first-floor bathroom was locked, and while he waited, leaning against the wall, he tried to free his thoughts from the din of the senso, like voices in his head. Moving to the far end of the hallway, he found the vispy's effects diminished. He peered out the back door at the garden, and that got him thinking again.

By the time his turn came, he was halfway to making a decision. He slid the bolt closed on the bathroom door and stared into the mirror, thinking about Silver and Odesta and their mysterious activities, and Elina waiting for him out in the dining room; and he wondered if just perhaps Elina had been sent to keep him occupied. He squinted at himself and thought, Does she *really* find you attractive? Or is she trying to distract you, taking you for a fool? If there was one thing he hated, it was the thought of being taken for a fool. Perhaps it was time to start running his life *his* way. And he could begin by not remaining a passive prisoner here.

Returning to the noisy hallway, he glanced casually around and edged toward the back door. There was a rear stairway leading to the second floor, and he took the steps quickly, returning to his room for his windbreaker. Stealing back down the stairs, he quietly unbolted the rear door and slipped out into the breezy air and the glare of the afternoon sun. A narrow, muddy path led around to the front.

Sorry, Elina, he thought. I'm just going for a little walk, just to scout around, to get a feel. I'll be back. But I have to know the terrain, just in case. I have to know.

Praying that he had not been seen, he trotted past the front of the house, paused at the curb, then hurried down the windy, desolate street.

Chapter 26

Silverfish glanced up as a light blinked on the wall above the console. "Back door. You'd better go check."

"Probably just somebody getting some air. I'll see." Odesta disappeared up the stairs.

Scratching his temple, Silver returned to the work he had laid out on the right-hand screen—a patchwork grid of shorthand coding, littered with icons and cross-references. On the next screen over was a similar layout, but this one was changing moment by moment, as a simulation ran its course. It was frustrating not to be able to coordinate with designers elsewhere; but until they'd redesigned the security of their communications, they had to work independently. In a way, Silver was grateful to Sage for provoking the intrusion; there was no telling how long the Company system had been tracking their activities without their knowledge. At least now they knew.

What he had on the screen was a fragment of the control device that they used to embed their signals in the ubiquitous Company-controlled channels. If they were to have any hope of continuing that practice, they would first have to find a new way to outwit the Company's AI. A little luck would be helpful. They were counting on the system's relative inattentiveness to a minor encroachment upon one of its smaller subsystems. The underground was certainly no threat to the Company. The question was whether the Company's system would see it that way.

Silver fiddled with one of the flags and watched the results on the simulation. He could use Elina's help; she was new, but she seemed to have a flair for this kind of thing. However, she was busy keeping Sage occupied, a job she had been willing— more than willing—to take on.

There was a beep on the left console. It warbled as the security filters ran, and then a message flashed on the screen:

READY TO PICK UP YOUR GUESTS TODAY BETWEEN CRICK AND CRACK, AT POINT BAKER. CAN YOU DO IT? // G.K.

"Ho, our friends are going to move up in the world. Thanks for giving me so much notice," Silver muttered to himself. Well, at least it would take the Sage problem out of his hands —though he still hadn't thought of any way to ensure Sage's silence. They might just have to trust him and hope for the best. He started to type an acknowledgment, then turned at a sound behind him. It was Odesta coming down the stairs. "Our friends are leaving," he told her. "The pickup's in an hour."

"They're going to be short one man," Odesta said. "It appears that young Mr. DeWeiler has flown the coop."

"*Oh, Jesus.* I thought Elina was keeping track of him!"

"She was. He went to the bathroom and never came back."

Silver spun in his chair and with one pass of his hand cleared

all of the screens except for the last message. He quickly typed
an answer: "THERE MAY BE A SNAG. PLEASE STAND
BY—" and sent it. Then he picked up a communicator, fas-
tened it to his collar, and ran up the stairs. "Keep someone on
the console. I'll go out looking."

"We'll search the house," Odesta called.

The music and the vispy holos hit him in the face as he
opened the sliding kitchen door. Elina was pacing anxiously
among the dancers, searching. She passed Silver, saying, "He
was just *here.*" Silver said nothing; Elina was on the verge of
tears already, and nothing he could say was likely to help—
though what he thought was, Why the hell didn't you *watch*
him? And immediately he thought, What am I blaming her
for? *I* was the one who was supposed to watch him.

He pushed his way through to the hallway and opened the
back door. "Bye, bye, goose," he muttered. A set of footprints
was visible on the path—be grateful for the mud, he thought
—and led around the house. He followed them. The prints
took a shortcut out to the street and continued a short distance
on the broken pavement before the mud wore off, just far
enough to show the direction the person had taken.

Silver nudged his communicator. "Tracks leading toward
Western Avenue. Following. Get a message to Katzen. I may
need help." He didn't wait for a response, but set out at a trot
to try to reconstruct the thinking of a stranger who wanted to
find his way out of this neighborhood. Heading in this direction, there were only two ways he was likely to end up walking,
and one of them would take him back toward the city. The
other would take him into a part of the 'burbs where even
Silver hated to go.

He really hadn't intended to come this far—and certainly he
hadn't meant to enter such forbidding-looking territory. That
just made it worse, Sage thought. It meant that he was stupid,
as well as scared. What would Tony think of him, stumbling
around like this, lost in the slumburbs? His brother had always
told him: Develop a nose for the street and you won't get hurt.
Well, now it was too late.

The hell with what Tony would think; he had enough problems.

The street looked as though it had been bombed. In fact, it probably had been, in the North-South Conflict a generation ago. A good fraction of the territory destroyed in that war had never been rebuilt; most of the economic regrowth had been focused in the inner cities and out in space. Under other circumstances, this might have made an interesting historical field trip. But just now he was more concerned about figuring out where the hell he *was,* and how he had so thoroughly lost track of the way back to Odesta's house—and who that man was he had caught sight of a couple of times, who appeared to be tailing him.

There was no sign of anyone behind him now; but there had been someone earlier, a lanky figure momentarily sihouetted against the sky, probably a local prowler, a thief stalking easy game in the ruins. And guess who the game was. The shattered remains of old buildings hulked around him like abandoned citadels. There was no way to know who or what might be waiting in the shadows. And the shadows were growing. The sun was low in the sky—how long had he been out here, anyway?—and soon it was going to drop out of sight altogether. And what was he going to do after dark? It had been bad enough trekking around with Silver, who knew where he was going.

Somewhere there was the roar of a vehicle. The sound died away. Sage peered around, shivering. It was amazing the tricks that light and sound could play with one's senses. *Why couldn't he recognize any of this terrain?* He had no idea where that sound had come from. His footsteps crunched in the grit, filling the silence, filling a void that was otherwise filled only with a growing trepidation. The air carried a lingering smell of wood smoke now. Someone must be nearby, with a fire. Terrific. What was he going to do, invite himself to dinner? Elina, he thought wretchedly, I should have stayed with you, what a jerk.

What was that? Footsteps, running . . .

He started to turn, and a hand clamped down on his shoulder, and he was snapped around, propelled by terror as much as the force of the grip. Breathless, he found himself face-to-face with a tall, grim-faced stranger—the man who had been following him. The man's nails dug painfully into his shoulder, and he felt a moment of icy-hot tension, and for an instant time slowed.

"What do you want?" he hissed, and as the man's other hand, holding something shiny, moved with dreamlike slowness toward his neck, something let go inside Sage, and his panic transformed itself to rage and he whipped his right arm up to block the man's left and wrenched his other shoulder down, twisting with strength he didn't know he had. The man's grip tightened. Sage yelled and went down, pulling the other on top of him.

His assailant's weight fell hard to one side, breaking the grip, and Sage twisted free like an enraged cat. He whirled and pummeled furiously at the man's face. He might have been punching at a bear, but it was enough to keep the man from grabbing him again. He never saw the foot that caught him in the chest and sent him crashing backward, his head striking pavement; but he rolled and scrambled to his knees, dazed, groping for a weapon. His hand closed on a brick. He looked up, saw the man lunging for him, and swung the brick in an arc. There was a thud, and he fell one way as his assailant fell the other. He pushed himself up and lifted the brick angrily for another blow.

"Don't!" he heard, and someone crashed into him, knocking the brick away and flattening him. He rolled, scrambling to defend himself from this new attacker. Before he could turn completely, he saw the first man rise again, swinging something toward him. There was a *crack!,* and Sage saw the man crumple to the ground. He smelled burned flesh.

A dark-clothed man trotted toward him, carrying a gun. He bent over the man he had just shot, then straightened up. "Who are you?" Sage gasped, struggling to his knees.

"Who the hell do you think?" he heard from behind. That was the man who had tackled him. Sage turned dazedly. It was Silverfish. Before Sage could react, Silver spoke again, breathlessly, to the dark-clothed man. "What the hell took you so long?" He gestured toward the man who'd been shot. "Is he dead? I was trying to keep *this* one from killing him." Silver jerked a thumb at Sage. Sage tried to speak, but Silver was already turning away, shaking his head. "Thanks for the trust, kid. Thanks a lot."

Sage flushed, trying to find words. He heard a roaring sound and whirled to see a van landing. Two men jumped out, and at a signal from the man with the gun, they grabbed his arms and began hauling him, none too gently, toward the van. "Silver!" he croaked as he was lifted by the armpits and dumped into the back of the vehicle.

He heard Silver saying, "Take good care of him—he's your problem now!" Then the door slammed, sealing him in darkness. He banged loudly and angrily on the door—and stopped because his head already felt as though it had been split with a hammer. There were several more jarring vibrations, and he fell to the floor as the van lurched, thundering, into the air.

PART THREE

Out of the heart a rapture,
Then a pain;
Out of the dead, cold ashes,
Life again.
—JOHN BANISTER TABB

They were not without memory, the creatures of the darkness, though their memory was strained and distorted by the years. They recalled a time, long ago, when they had walked the world, when they had breathed the air and basked in the glow of the sun and strode among the stars. And they remembered, vividly, a time when terrible convulsions had shaken the planet and the sun had quailed and the earth itself vomited fire, and nothing that lived had remained alive to walk the world's surface as the continents burned. And they remembered the blight caused by the light that couldn't be seen, and they remembered their escape into the darkness below. And they remembered their desperation.

Hopelessly they had clung to life, and somehow survived. But in the struggle, they had been changed—their spirit had darkened like their world, and their form had become something ghastly, an abomination that fed upon the bowels of the earth and could never return to the life above.

And yet they remembered their past. They remembered it, and the memory of it festered within them. Their hatred and despair and loneliness deepened, becoming as one spirit within them; and they themselves became as one spirit, one with their hatred —haunting their world of bitter, eternal night.

Chapter 27

The buzzer was insistent, cutting through the silence of Chandra's meditation. She felt the cottony restful state come apart, dissolving to the sensation of her cabin surrounding her, the soft hangings stirring in the breeze of the ventilators. She let out her breath in a long sigh and brought her eyes back into focus. A light was winking on the com-station. She uncurled her legs and stepped off her bunk to answer the call.

"Burtak."

"Captain, this is Holloway. We've completed rendezvous with *Endeavor* and *Columbia* and are now proceeding in formation toward spiral-in orbit of Argus."

"Good. Contact Captains Fitzpatrick and Khumalo and ask them if they can shuttle over with their department heads."

"I did. They'll be here in two hours."

Chandra felt the corner of her mouth turn up in a smile. "Very well. I'll be on the bridge presently. I'm sure you'll have a summary of the latest developments with our alien friends."

"Of course. It's short, though."

"Anything I should know about now?"

"Nothing new. That's the summary."

Chandra sighed. "All right. I'll be there soon."

As the light went out, she crossed to the sitting alcove and drew a cup of boiling water over a tea bag. She picked up a hairbrush and ran it through her unbound hair a dozen times. Then she pinned up her hair with a few deft movements and sat down to sip her tea. Memories were coming back to her, filling her thoughts as they always did after her meditations, but today perhaps a little more painfully than usual . . .

She remembered her parents' reaction to her announcement that she was joining the first colony to the stars: her father's consternation and fear, her mother's sadness, and, much later, their pride. Her father had announced angrily that anyone who could so easily abandon her family heritage—leaving home never to return—had no claim to being his daughter; he knew that times changed, and he'd adjusted to a lot over the years, but if she chose to go through with this, then she could expect no part of the family inheritance. Not knowing whether to be angry or saddened by his outburst—after all, she was forty-two and had been commanding space vessels for years—she'd reminded him that there was no way for her to collect her inheritance anyway, from a distance of 130 light-years. Her brother was welcome to her share; she was going to inherit the stars instead.

How naive those words seemed now! Even at the time, they'd only angered her father. A few days later, however, she'd visited again to find him in his study, crying in shame; but much more time had passed before he'd managed to tell her —on the day of her departure—that he was deeply proud of her.

It had been much the same, many years earlier, when she'd broken with the family tradition and left the fabric business, not to marry but to enter the spaceflight academies. That decision had cost her, not only her family's approval, but also the only man she'd ever loved. How could a man play second fiddle to the stars? Since then, there had been precious little time for love. But who'd have guessed that she would one day be a ship's captain, much less commander of an entire star fleet?

Setting down her empty cup, she let the memories flee. She had other matters to concern her now. At last she was going to meet face-to-face again with the other captains; but it wasn't to have happened quite like this. She was to have been looking forward to a change in her job description—from commander of a fleet to administrator of three orbiting space stations as the majority of the colonists shuttled down to start new lives on a new world with newly elected leaders. Now, who knew? The landing might be postponed indefinitely.

She was eager to ask the advice of Khumalo and Fitzpatrick, but in fact she thought she already knew what they would say. The unease that she felt now was only likely to grow, and so were the questions. *Why wouldn't the aliens answer her signals? And why had they withdrawn to encircle Argus . . . as though defending against an invasion?*

* * *

From the observation cupola, *Endeavor* and *Columbia* looked like gigantic bridges floating in space—far enough away that they seemed to hover just out of reach against the stars, like fairyland bridges connecting one invisible world to another. Chandra leaned against the railing that skirted the clear dome and gazed at her fleet, together again after two years, ship-time; three and a half years, Earth-time. The last time she'd been able to do this had been on the outbound flight from Earth orbit. She'd almost forgotten how large the starships were; how beautiful the stars were to the naked eye—clustered jewels against the darkness.

The domes throughout the ship had been sealed off during the FTL passage; now, open again, they were popular gathering spots for the colonists and crew. Chandra enjoyed the prerogative of occupying the bridge cupola alone. She felt somehow that she might make her own special peace with this solar system and its mysteries if she only meditated on the sight long enough.

Argus' sun was blocked from view by her ship, but the planet itself, their intended home-to-be, was visible now as a bluish-white dot. From the bridge, with Aggie's enhanced displays, she could have had far more information about the planet; but from here, even through the telescope mounted on the railing, Argus was a pristine world, lacking such complications as a fleet of silent, enigmatic aliens.

"Chandra—*Endeavor* reports her captain's launch away," she heard from the intercom.

"Thanks." Chandra turned the telescope to see if she could spot the craft. There it was—a tiny silver glint. She watched it for a moment, then capped and secured the telescope. Time to descend to the bridge, to see the launches safely into *Aleph*'s hangar; time to greet her colleagues.

"Roger, you haven't changed a bit! Welcome aboard!" She met Captain Fitzpatrick and his officers midway across the hangar deck.

"And you're as beautiful as ever—sir!" Fitzpatrick kissed her hand solemnly, then saluted with a grin. "Permission to come aboard?"

"Granted, granted, and granted!" Chandra returned his salute and shook hands all around. "Welcome, all of you!"

Fitzpatrick was informally dressed, as always, in a turtleneck shirt and a uniform jacket. His curly red hair was a bit wilder and a bit thinner than she remembered. "Am I first to arrive? Isn't Khumalo here yet?"

"He's on his way." Chandra pointed to a display screen. "There he is, coming into Hangar Two right now."

"Chandra, greetings! And Roger!"

"Wonderful to see you, Khumalo!"

"Welcome aboard, you old Zulu!" Fitzpatrick exclaimed, striding forward, oblivious to the startled gazes of the crew.

"Please!" Captain Themba Khumalo cried. "You know perfectly well I am not a Zulu! My forebears were Swazi and—"

"Who cares, you idiot?" Fitzpatrick bellowed. He seized Khumalo's hand and then gave him a great backslapping bear hug.

Khumalo stepped back, grinning from ear to ear. He was a tiny man with jet-black skin, short bristly hair, and gleaming eyes. He was resplendent in a crimson dress uniform with gold epaulets. "Roger pulls my leg and I pull back," he said to Chandra. "But when I pull his leg, it comes off in my hand!"

Chandra laughed and turned to greet *Columbia*'s other officers. "We'll be having dinner in the officers' lounge. I hope you're all hungry, and ready to shake a lot of hands. But I'm afraid we're going to have to get down to business very shortly. We have a lot to discuss."

"Indeed we do," Fitzpatrick said. "Whether Themba is going to let me win back what he stole from me in poker, for one."

"Amazing," Khumalo said, shaking his head. "All this time and he still remembers a perceived injustice. Astonishing."

Chandra shook her head and pointed the way. "Enjoy it while you can, you two."

* * *

"Really, as I see it, there's no choice," Khumalo said softly. "Chandra is right. As much as I hate to send any crew out with so little protection, I see no other way—except to risk thousands of lives rather than a dozen or two."

The moke- and teapots were both empty, and the brandy snifters nearly so. The three captains had retired for a private discussion immediately following a reunion dinner with the other officers. Chandra had laid out her ideas, hoping that Khumalo or Fitzpatrick would have better ones.

"Roger? Do you agree?"

Fitzpatrick ran his fingers back through his thinning hair, grimacing. "Agree? Sure, I agree. I just wish—" He sighed and slapped his thigh. "I wish we had something to go on. It's damned frustrating, not knowing if we should be getting ready to fight—or flee—or sit down to dinner with them. If they even eat dinner."

"Well, we've no place to flee *to*, in any case," Khumalo said.

"True enough," Chandra agreed. "In my opinion, we can only go forward and try to find out who they are, what they want, and how they're going to react to our presence. And since our combined science departments haven't been able to tell us much more than that there *might* have been stardrive activity—"

"Let's do it, Chandra," Fitzpatrick said. "What else can we do?"

"Very well, then. We'll send my landing scout number one. Its first priority will be to observe the alien fleet around Argus. If it appears safe, if there's no interference, I may order them to go for the landing. But information about the visitors is paramount."

"And we'll continue in on a slow spiral orbit?" Khumalo asked.

"Unless I hear a better idea. We'll approach, but slowly enough to let them get used to the idea."

"What about the crew? Have you picked anyone yet?" Fitzpatrick asked.

Chandra closed her eyes and felt a great weight settle upon

her. "No," she whispered. She opened her eyes. "I'll be calling for volunteers."

"Of course," Khumalo murmured. He relaxed slightly and smiled. "I envy them the opportunity."

"The landing director should at least have the chance to see it." Tony had insisted. *"He can say no if he doesn't like the idea."*

That's what he had said to his immediate supervisor, who had wondered why DeWeiler and Mung were devoting so much time to a project that wasn't even on the roster, when there was so much else to be done in preparation for planetfall. Tony had explained patiently that they'd done the project in addition to their regular work; and anyway, they'd only been pursuing a logical extension of prior research. Eventually he'd gotten a hearing with the head of the department, who had watched the demonstration in stoic silence and gone to tell the landing director. It was the landing director who'd brought the captain to take a look.

"Why do you call them nobblies?" Captain Burtak asked Mung as she watched them set up the apparatus.

"Well," Mung said nervously, "it's really—" He hesitated, his mouth open. "Actually . . ."

"It doesn't really mean anything," Tony said. He cleared his throat. His voice got loud when he was nervous. "Our first samples looked like knobbed clusters of plant cells under the microcam, and that's where we got the name. The newer ones don't look that way so much."

"So," the captain said. "What exactly have you done?"

"Well, what we've done is not actually that new," Tony said carefully. "We've extended some research that was done a number of years ago in Australia, by—"

"Please. Give me the short version."

"Uh, yes. We've used molecular-size engineering units to invade and modify certain sensitive plant cells." Tony touched a metal bottle, a standard molecular-cybernetic experimentation canister. The nobblie cells were isolated in the bottle, in a controlled environment. "We've altered the plants' responses —tropisms, that is—to a sort of tunable telepathic receptivity."

"Yes?" The captain appeared unimpressed. "And how will that help us—if we take them along on the scout, as you suggest?"

"Well, you see, the molecyber units remain inside the plant cells, like organelles," Tony said quickly. "And they not only do the interior tuning, they also transmit what the plant cells *feel*, if I can use that term, to a receiver on the outside." He paused. The captain was gazing at him silently. "My first—*our* first—thought was that they could act as a sort of long-range sentient life detector on the planet. On Argus. But now, with these others on the scene—the aliens, I mean—I thought that if we ever got close enough to them, the nobblies might help give us some indication of what they're about, if you know what I mean. Some sense of their intentions."

The captain nodded, finger pressed to her lips. "May I see it work?"

"Yes, of course. Mung, do you want to handle the subjects? Perhaps if someone went with him to make the selection . . ."

The landing director sent an aide out of the room with Mung, while Tony sat and adjusted a small headset to his temples. "Now we wait," he explained. The captain raised her eyebrows a fraction of an inch. He fiddled with the gain and at once felt a sleepy sort of awareness in his mind, something vaguely like a gnostic presence in rap, but drowsier. Within it was an awareness of *him*, and of the captain and the others, expectant and somewhat skeptical. He adjusted the gnostic relay to filter all of that out, and he waited.

The wait was not long. He felt an itch in his forebrain, and he sat up, trying to open himself to whatever the nobblies were picking up. He felt a rumble of contentment, and his nose twitched, and he was aware of a puzzling mixture of odors, until he realized that he was taking inventory of the various smells of the biolab. "Cat," he said a moment later. "Feeling kind of lazy." He closed his eyes, absorbing the feelings.

"Cat it is," the landing director said.

Tony turned around. Mung and the aide were approaching. Draped over Mung's arm was Fangora, one of the lab cats, purring with contented indifference.

"What's it feel like?" the captain asked.

"Like I was in his fur. If he'd been feeling, say, feisty, I would have felt that." As Tony spoke, he felt a flush of energy and turned back toward Fangora. The cat, apparently deciding he had had enough, jumped out of Mung's arms and scampered away.

Captain Burtak's eyebrows went up again. "You felt that coming?" Tony nodded. "And how reliable is this procedure? If you did not know this animal already, would you be able to pick it out so easily?"

"It would be more difficult," Tony admitted. "There is a subjective process of learning to recognize different kinds of responses. Mung, can you find something that we haven't tried yet?"

Mung nodded. "This one will be tougher," he promised, leaving the room.

"I'm not saying that this will give us everything we'd like," Tony said. "But suppose we had a face-to-face meeting. It might tell us whether their intent was aggressive or friendly— possibly before we could tell from overt behavior." A moment later he felt an itch again, but this time it was more like the tingle of tiny static discharges than a real presence. He turned up the gain. The tingle became a buzz. *Blank your thoughts. What is it?* Many tiny buzzings combined: a confusion of hunting and seeking. "Insects?" he said.

He turned. Mung walked into the room holding a sealed osmotic cage. Inside, a cloud of tiny pollenator flies were batting themselves against the sides of the cage. Tony removed the headset. "That," he said, "was a very strange feeling." He looked up at the captain. "Would you like to try it, sir?"

The captain arched her eyebrows and took the headset.

"You understand, DeWeiler, that this is classed as a high-risk mission? Your friend Mr. Ting might be disappointed at not being included—but he might also live longer than you." Tony nodded, swallowing, as he stood before the landing director's desk. "I'm sending you, frankly, because I'm not sure anyone else could learn to use it in the time we have before launch."

"Yes, sir. Thank you, sir."

"Don't thank me. I'm not making this choice lightly. If our friends out there turn out to be not so friendly, you might never get close enough to even turn your nobblies on. If you do make it through their fleet and actually land, you'll have your hands full—and Commander Mortaine will be expecting a lot more out of you than just operating this machine. Understood?"

Tony felt his smile turn to a hard-lipped acknowledgment. "I understand, sir. When do I report to the scout ship?"

"Eighteen hundred hours today. Can you be ready?"

"Absolutely, sir."

"Good. Then get the hell out of here and start packing."

Chandra watched from within soft-rap as the landing scout floated out of *Aleph*'s belly and accelerated toward Argus. Thirty-two volunteers were aboard that scout, including its commander, Jensen Mortaine, one of her best officers. She hoped she was not sending him, all of them, into senseless danger. *Whatever happens, and whomever you're going to meet, I admire your courage,* she thought. But the risk being borne by the scout crew was no greater than that of the rest of the fleet; it was just coming a little sooner. This fleet was on a one-way mission, with three thousand men, women, and children: scientists, farmers, engineers, teachers, carpenters, masons, medics, and more—plus hundreds of species of plants and animals. They were here to settle a world, and there was little room for alternate plans. One way or another, they were going to have to make an accommodation with the alien fleet.

Perhaps, she thought, Mortaine would be presiding over the long-awaited first contact with friendly beings from the stars. Perhaps the worry was all for nothing. Perhaps.

She reflected upon her meeting with Captains Fitzpatrick and Khumalo. It had been a pleasure, and far too short. The need for decision-making had left little time for catching up—though Themba had somehow found the time to beat Roger twice more at poker. The two had returned to their ships to continue preparations for the encounter; it was unlikely that they would have the chance to meet again before landfall.

A great deal could happen between now and then. A great deal, indeed.

Chapter 28

Or!ge peered at the images coalescing in the display-cone. There was no longer any question; the Outsider fleet was sending an advance party toward the Lost World, and if present indications were reliable, it would be here by the end of the next wakeshift, just as the final survey was being completed . . . just as Or!ge was preparing to launch the first landing party, the first ground search for the Lost Ell.

The timing was uncanny. How could the Outsiders have known? Had they intercepted communications to the home-world? What other reason could there be, except to observe— or to thwart—the Ell landing?

Or!ge had hoped to believe otherwise. He had been swayed by earlier observations, and by the fact that the Outsider fleet, approaching cautiously, had taken no hostile action. Perhaps he had been unduly influenced; he should have known that years of aggressive behavior would not change so quickly. And yet few of the enemy's robot fighters had appeared recently— just one, preceding this fleet, which Or!ge had destroyed.

If only the translators could make some sense of the Outsider transmissions. Various signals had been received, but in the absence of a translation, they could only be assumed to be a challenge.

Or!ge opened a channel to outreach. "Left flank, prepare a fighter(ship) for detachment." He gave the order, knowing that it could be an opening salvo in a new battle that might be the costliest yet. If the Outsiders attempted to capture the planet, the Rediscovery Expedition itself might have to become a war (fleet), a sacrificial (fleet); they could not hope for more than a delaying action against those oversized Outsider ships. If that was required, then that was what the expedition would do. Under no circumstances could the enemy be allowed to take this world, at least not until they knew: Was it really the Lost World, and did the descendants of the Lost Ell survive?

Time would be the guide. He did not wish to risk a landing with the Outsiders so close, but neither could he delay much longer. The readings from the surface were inconclusive— flickerings of an odd thought-energy. Could it be the Lost Ell? If so, they must be radically changed from their relatives circling their world. How much change could befall a race in a thousand years? Or!ge longed to know.

He reopened the channel to outreach. "Orders to fighter (ship): Follow and observe the Outsider scout. If it attempts planetary landing, destroy it. Orders to landing party: Deployment will be delayed, remain on standby."

One last thing remained to be done, as soon as the alignments were correct and the (fleet) activity calmed enough to free the energy, and that was to open a vortex and relay a message home: *Send help with all possible speed.*

A short time later he observed, with as much satisfaction as the situation allowed, the departure of the fighter(ship) on intercept course.

Dououraym stood in the archway with Lenteffier and watched Moramaharta cross the grassy inland in front of the meditation hall. The wind was gusting, whipping the binder's robe about him like a flag on a pole. "Coming from the upper part of the valley again," Dououraym said. "He has been devoting more and more of his time there, pursuing a personal form of meditation. It is of this that I wish to speak to you."

Lenteffier turned a cautious eye. He was the tallest member of the Inner Circle—lanky, and steely of expression—and when he peered down at Dououraym, himself no small individual, he reminded Dououraym of a tall verberta tree stripped of its needles in the autumn, stooping in the wind, his bony eye ridges looking like a tree's upper buds brooding over its smaller

kin. He held his upper pair of arms close to his breast. It was
no wonder, Dououraym thought, that the younger students
found this master so disconcerting.

"Do you understand the meaning of it?" Lenteffier asked.

Dououraym touched his rigid lip. "In a precise way, no. But
there may be certain insights. I believe it might be useful to
explore this further—his belief in perspective, as he has called
it—his belief that there is a centering influence to be felt there,
among the trees and the wind and the sky. I do not understand.
But I wish to." Dououraym watched Moramaharta pause to let
the wind billow about his head. "It is a question of whether
there is something that Moramaharta has to teach us, or something amiss in him that we should beware of."

"Indeed," Lenteffier said. "And your suggestion?"

Dououraym's gaze narrowed briefly. "To follow his example.
To walk into the upper vale, to lose myself—or ourselves, if you
will accompany me—to see what there is to be found."

"You do not have enough to occupy you here—with the
news from Hope Star and the decisions that await?"

"More than enough," Dououraym said, gazing up at the
treetops. "But I suspect. I wonder. If there is something to
learn which could help us in our task, even indirectly . . ." He
looked at Lenteffier, whose sharp eyes were tracking Moramaharta's progress toward the side entrance.

"Perhaps," Lenteffier said. "I do not see the likelihood. But
I will accompany you if you believe it worth the walk."

Dououraym made a noncommittal hiss. "And if there is
something else to learn—something about Moramaharta . . ."
He did not complete the thought. Moramaharta was the
binder, the mediator, the one whose empathic powers joined
the minds and transformed them into a force greater than any
and greater than all, the *lan'dri,* the focus out of which decision
was wrought. If the binder had lost his way, then he must be
replaced, for the greater good. And yet, to do so would mean
a difficult readjustment for the Circle . . . and, likely, the end
for the binder. It was a matter of nature, of inevitability. Once
isolated from the core of his being, a binder could only wither
and die.

Lenteffier's eyes narrowed to thin, vertical slits. "Then the sooner we learn . . ."

"Perhaps it is harmless," Dououraym said. "Perhaps it is useful."

"Perhaps it is neither."

Dououraym made a tiny upper-hand gesture, snapping his nails. "Shall we walk into the woods?"

"The sooner . . ." Lenteffier said, stepping out into the gusty air. Moramaharta had disappeared around the corner of the hall. "Which way?"

Dououraym pointed to the right, where a slender path wound its way upslope. "That direction. And then we must use our senses."

Without further words, the two *Ell* decision-makers passed into the woods.

Moramaharta watched thoughtfully as the two disappeared. He'd sensed his companions' thoughts and observed their passing, but his mind was full of the woods and the wind and the sky, and his fellow *Ell* were full of questions that he could not answer. He knew what they were about, and he generally approved, though he was unsure whether they would discover what they sought or understand what he had found. . . .

The brilliance of the sun soothed the mind like a sidan'dri *but without the directive force . . . the sunlight was its own center, bringing the spirit into balance.*

Better that they go on their own. If they had wanted his company, or his advice, they would have asked. And he had much to consider already.

Moramaharta passed the Inner Circle chambers and walked to his own living quarters. As the door fluttered closed behind him, a single light globe came to life. He stood gazing at its glow refracted through the angular bookshards on the rack beneath it. Shadows filled the rest of the room, but the shadows were filled with images from his mind: . . . *a wave of color rippling through the forest with the shift toward winter . . . the whisper, the* adan'dri, *of the wind . . . the smell of the needles freshly fallen.*

He picked up one of the bookshards—not reading it, but focusing on the light rotating through its planes as he turned the crystal in his hand. The light drew his thoughts into a deeper focus, the *montan'dri* of the inner mind. Memories came alive, dancing like water down a mountain stream, bound for lakes visible only as faraway sparks of sunlight among the forests. Where the memories led, he did not know, any more than he knew the path of that stream; but something was happening inside him, a sifting and channeling of thought that must be allowed to run its course. He could no more stop it than he could stop the mountain stream.

Memories of the nexus-dwelling; of an Ell people pursuing their purpose despite the war, with an icy longing and hope; of his own nest-mates carrying on in his absence; of the racial history entrusted to him . . .

Why this compulsion to wonder? *Why?* Was he so different from his fellows? Were his own meditations so much more perceptive? Even in his home-nest, he had been considered . . . odd . . . unusually sensitive. . . . His compulsion was connected to the war, but overshadowed it; the war had served as a catalyst to the other. In attacking, the Outsiders had begun the changes that had led to his walking now upon these shifting sands of uncertainty.

Gazing into the bookshard, focusing only on the light patterns there, he gathered to himself a recent memory: *The sun, slanting downward, created a tower of light, dust motes and air and radiance enveloped by the trees. Moving in that ghostly chamber, wings beating, was a nesting kettle-piper, a blur of shadow and silver carrying food to its young, oblivious to his presence. Feelings stirred that he could not identify, feelings that reached deep, shifting him at his center.*

More than anything else, he wanted to understand those feelings. It was not curiosity alone, but an intuition that they might be a clue to the quest, to the need that had driven the Ell halfway across the galaxy in search of . . . not just the Lost Ell, but something they could not name. It was difficult to define, because there were no words in the language to describe it.

The language. That was a part of the problem. Since the Change—since the *tar'dyenda,* when the Ell race was reborn from the ashes of the catastrophe that had torn its homeworld from it—the language, like the people, had been mutated and robbed of qualities that, it was said, had once characterized both.

It was said. That phrase conveyed so much, and so little. If only they could truly remember . . . if only they could remember their distant past with the clarity reserved for later events. What folly, for racial memory following the *tar'dyenda* to have been entrusted through generations to the *lan'dri,* to collective meditational memory, rather than to the permanence of the bookshards. In the years following the Change, the bookshards had not been available, *it was said,* and by the time they were, the accuracy of the *lan'dri* was already being called into question. By the time the full extent of the Change had been recognized, it was too late. No one lived who could recall the Ell as they had been. No one knew what had been given up, for what gain. The darkness of spirit had already overtaken the race, and there was no light to illumine against it.

And so the legend, the failing memory of the lost homeworld and the Lost Ell, had deepened in the collective thought; and the hope of rediscovery had arisen, the hope that somewhere the Lost Ell lived, and with them the lost spirit and character of the Ell race. Thus was born the quest for the Hope Star, the Lost World, the Forgotten Ell.

Moramaharta knew, as surely as the night followed upon day, that his feelings in the woods were intimately connected to that process. He did not yet know how, but he was certain that it was true—even now, in this time of uncertainty. Especially now.

He hoped that Lenteffier and Dououraym would find echoes, at least, of what he had felt—not just for his sake, or for theirs, but for the quest. For the decisions that lay ahead. For the Ell.

He closed his eyes and began again to reconstruct the scene. To relive the image, to feel the wind: that way, he was sure, lay understanding.

Overhead, the wind danced and shifted like a feinting knife-wielder, and shook the trees against a blazing sky. . . .

Chapter 29

"Come with us, please."

Pali looked up into the face of Sergeant Dorfer, who was flanked by two uniformed officers. "Excuse me?" she said.

"I asked you to come with us," Dorfer repeated, his voice developing an edge.

"May I ask what for?" Pali felt her stomach knotting. She looked past him and saw that they had an audience—several of the women of her department peering in from the reception area. Where was Kyd? Pali hadn't seen her all day. She gestured to her desk. "I have a lot of work to do here, as you can see. If you'll just tell me—"

"You're under arrest for sabotage, conspiracy to commit sabotage, and concealment of evidence."

"Ah." The knot in her stomach tightened. "I see." She felt herself stalling—knowing as she did so that there was nothing to be gained. "You're putting me under arrest," she repeated.

"That's what I said. Now please come."

"Of course." She rose dizzily. As she walked through the outer office she said to her secretary, "Marge, would you call Russell Thurber and tell him that I've been detained by these gentlemen?"

Marge nodded and hurried away. "And cancel my appointments for the afternoon," Pali called after her. Then she shrugged and stalked out of the office, followed by the three officers.

The ComPol detention area was silent. From her cubicle, Pali could see a short hallway ending at a green soundproof door. They hadn't brought her any food, so it must not be noon yet. She'd been questioned twice already, and twice she'd answered the questions, pleading that no crime had been committed. How had it come to this? she wondered despairingly. She'd only been trying to do her job. *That* was surely down the drain now—along with her project. Were Sage and Ramo really corporate saboteurs, as the ComPol seemed to believe? She *couldn't* believe it. Whatever had happened on that strange evening, she was certain that they hadn't intended harm.

But could she still trust her own ability to judge character? Heaven knew she had enough mistakes in her past. Take David, who'd walked out on her less than a year after Gregory had died. Or Russell, who was supposed to have been keeping the stupid ComPol off her back. Had she judged Russell's character when she'd gotten involved with him? Actually, yes, she'd gone ahead impulsively, thinking that some love was better than none. And why think of Russell now? *Because he was supposed to get you sprung out of here.* "Where are you, Russell?" she murmured, staring at that silent green door. "Just where the hell are you?"

The door opened when lunch arrived, and when an officer came to remove the tray, and once more when another officer brought her a cup of moke and asked if she had a family who ought to be notified and nodded sympathetically when she said no. The officer stayed awhile and eventually got around to asking, almost casually, if she really wouldn't rather come clean and tell them what had *really* happened—and he was in her mind before she had so much as an inkling that he was a psych-scanner.

What did they do to the system?

The pressure in her head made her wince. *I don't know!*

Tell me where they've gone.

I don't—

Where's Kyd Metango?

Her anger flared. *I have rights!*

There was a lance of pain in her skull. She screamed and

threw the hot moke in his face. Sputtering and dripping black liquid, the officer staggered out, and left her shaking with rage and fear.

What in God's name was *happening*? She wasn't even trying to resist. Why wouldn't anyone believe her?

A while later, the door opened again. It was Russell. She stood up and embraced him silently, trembling against his reassuring shoulder. "I would have been here sooner," Russell said, "but I've been trying to get through to somebody who would listen to reason." He gazed at her sympathetically. "Have they been treating you okay?"

"Oh—just great. They only tried to mind-rape me, but other than that, no problem. They serve good moke here." She gestured at the dark stain on the floor.

Russell cleared his throat. "Yes, I heard there was a . . . an incident."

"*Incident?* Is that what they call it? How about invasion of privacy and suspension of rights?" she snapped. She realized that Russell was looking at her oddly. "You don't think *I* was the instigator!"

"Oh, no no no," Russell said. He smiled an embarrassingly phony smile, and she felt her stomach drop. "It's just—"

Her voice hardened in self-defense. "Just *what?*"

"Just . . . that I don't quite understand why you don't cooperate with them. I mean, you have nothing to hide, do you? They already know what happened to the system, so there's no reason to keep that from them."

"I'm *not* hiding anything from them. Whose side are you on, anyway?"

"*Yours*, of course. It's not a matter of taking sides. I'm just saying you'd be in less trouble if you leveled with them completely."

"Meaning you think I'm lying?"

Russell's eye twitched. "No, but . . . I think you might try to help them find the others. It makes them appear guilty—"

"I don't *know* where they are! Is that so hard to understand?"

"Now, Pali, don't—"

"Don't 'Now, Pali' me!" she said dangerously. She glared. "I thought you were going to *help* me with the ComPol."

"Well, I tried, but . . . you know, it's not that clear. That is . . ." He paused, flustered. "It would help if you at least told me where Kyd is. That way—"

"Russell!"

"Anyway, they're pretty well closing in on Romano and DeWeiler, you know." His voice trailed off as he looked away.

"No, I don't know! Are you working for them now? Did they send you in here?" Her hands throbbed, and she pressed them to her sides to still them. To keep them from committing violence.

"Of course not," he said weakly. "I'm just trying to do what's best."

"And what's that, Russell? What exactly have you told them?"

"Nothing. Not much at all," he said, obviously lying and hating himself for it. You pitiful bastard, she thought without pity. His fingers were twitching now, groping for a cigarette he didn't have. "But if you give them *something,* they'll make it easier for you," he muttered.

"What'd they do to you, Russell? How'd they get to you?" she said, her voice low. "Did they threaten you with your job?"

Russell stiffened, his face darkening. For a moment their gazes locked, and Pali, if she could, would have strangled him with her eyes. Finally he said, "There's no cause to—"

"Get out," she said.

"But Pali—"

"Get out!"

He turned to the door. "I'll . . . do what I can at the other end," he mumbled. The door shimmered to let him pass.

"Don't bother," she whispered, sinking back onto the bench seat. Tears were coming finally, and there was no reason any longer to hold them back. *"You spineless son of a bitch, just don't bother!"*

The room was in what appeared to be some sort of military installation, and the agent's name was Mike. Ramo was comfortable enough and the guards were treating him decently, but he missed Silver and Odesta's house. He'd been whisked away in the middle of a great confusion—Sage gone, apparently skipped out in the middle of the jamdam—only to be piled into the back seat of a van and flown to heaven-knew-where by a couple of guys who didn't believe in making conversation. He hadn't even been given a chance to say good-bye to Silver.

And Sage had gone off and left that nice young girl Elina frantic with worry and bawling her eyes out. What sense did it make?

And what sense did it make for him to be sitting here, twiddling his thumbs, while every once in a while someone came in and either asked him a couple of questions or else assured him that soon someone else would?

Crazy.

The door opened and Mike came in, followed by a man in a grey suit. "Someone here to talk to you," Mike said. "Got a minute to spare?"

"Time on my hands," Ramo said. "What'll it be today?"

The man raised his eyebrows. "I'd like to ask you about your episode with the McConwell gnostic system. And I'll start by reminding you that this is a very serious matter. Not just to the McConwell Company, but to the government, as well."

Ramo sighed wearily. "Sure enough. What do you want to know?"

"I can't help it how upset they are," Katzen said to his aide. "If they hadn't sent one of their goons out after him, it never would have happened. Tell them to be more careful."

"George, they understand that. What they're upset about is the gnostic system and the fact that we've got the only guys who know what happened to it. They think we're trying to pull something, and just using the law as an excuse."

"Bull." George Katzen stabbed a finger at his assistant. "In case they haven't heard, there's a war on—and that gives us prior claim. On this one, the Old Man isn't going to give. McConwell can scream all they want."

"Great. Will the Old Man back us up?"

"He has no choice," Katzen said. "The system's critical. He has to know what's going on, and DeWeiler's the key. The system actually contacted DeWeiler at the safe house, through what was supposed to be a foolproof screen."

"So is he going to interview DeWeiler?"

"I think so. I finally convinced his staff that it was important enough to affect the outcome of the war. So now that they're convinced, they say no prior briefing. They want him to sweat a little."

"And meanwhile, the rest of us sweat along with him."

Katzen nodded. "And wonder what the hell that crazy gnostic system is doing to our war."

For Sage, imprisonment was not so much a cause for outrage as for puzzlement. He still didn't know exactly whose prisoner he was. He was being held in a comfortable enough room—cell, really—but nothing had been explained to him, nor had he been questioned except by a doctor, asking if he still felt any dizziness after the blow to his head. In a way, it was a relief, not having to talk or be bothered about anyone else, but the solitude was beginning to wear. He almost wished that someone would charge him with a crime, to break the monotony.

He gathered that he was being held by federal agents, rather than by the ComPol. Whether he was being held *for* the ComPol, he didn't know. He'd assumed so, until he'd heard someone referring to "the ComPol goon who was shot"—which, among other things, caused him to wonder if maybe the Company and the government were more at odds than he'd thought. One heard stories of power struggle and conspiracy, but he'd always dismissed them as fantasy. Still . . . that man getting shot had been no fantasy. Could he really have been a ComPol agent—shot down by the feds? Sage found it hard to believe that he was that valuable a prisoner.

And what of Ramo? Was he still at Silver and Odesta's house, dancing nonstop? Or had he too been whisked away in a van? And Silver, saving his life only to dump him into the hands of the feds: was he a protector or betrayer? Sage didn't know whether to feel ashamed, or proud, for at least making the attempt to save himself. Except . . . when he thought about Elina, left waiting, wondering. . . .

Guilt made a poor cell mate, so he tried to keep his thoughts free of it, tried to think of Kyd and Pali working to get them free. Tried. The truth was, he knew, that they were in deep trouble and it was fundamentally his fault. None of this would have happened if *he* hadn't bcen so clever, so willing to fiddle and tinker with the system. He could have said no to the core.

He hadn't, though.

Overhead, there was a shiny grid of wire embedded in the ceiling, flush with the surface. He lay on his bunk staring up at it as he thought. He assumed that it was part of the security field, and possibly a listening device as well, and he began having silent conversations with it, asking it when he was going to get out of here and whether he was ever going to see his coworkers again. *Are you in there, core, can you reach this far?* It was the washbasin in the corner that answered him, with its *plink ploink plink* and an occasional rumble deep in its throat. The answer was interesting but uninformative, and if the grid was offering a better answer, it was doing it like some elusive god, in cryptic silent riddles.

He was half asleep, hands interlocked behind his head, gazing up at the grid, when he heard footsteps and voices. The door shimmered clear and two of his keepers entered. "Let's go," one of them said.

Sage raised his head. "Exercise time? Let's just skip it, okay? Say I have indigestion."

"Put your shoes on. You're going for a ride."

Sage sat up. "Where to?"

"You'll find out soon enough."

"You don't expect me to go out in these clothes, do you?" He plucked at his denim prison shirt. His own clothes had been taken away, supposedly to be cleaned.

The guard grinned. "Don't worry, handsome, we'll bring your tux along." He laughed and clapped Sage on the shoulder. Sage winced and followed them out the door.

* * *

The patrol car was climbing too steeply for a simple crosstown trip. Sage knocked on the partition and shouted, "Where are you taking me?" There was a small window through which he could see the driver and an officer in the front seat, but they ignored him.

Sage sighed and sat back. At least it was a car and not a van, and it was clean, which counted for something. But the windows were opaqued. There was nothing to do but wait the ride out. If only he could stop thinking. Where would federal agents be taking him? For psych-scan? He hadn't refused to answer any questions; they hadn't asked him any. Were they trying to make him crack by keeping him in the dark? If so, they were doing a good job. He was ready to talk to anyone. Eventually he just put his head back and closed his eyes and listened to the drone of the motors.

He woke with a crick in his neck as the car shuddered, descending. He had no idea how long they'd been airborne. He listened to the motors whining down as the power was cut and tried to peer through the partition window, but that too had been switched to opaque. He felt the car touch down and drive awhile over pavement; then it descended a long ramp before finally rolling to a stop. When the guards opened the doors, he stepped out into a parking garage just like the one they'd left from.

The destination was a small, windowless apartment in what appeared to be the basement of a large building. It was comfortably furnished, with the sorts of wall holos and lamps one might expect in a moderately priced hotel. He peered into the two bedrooms and glanced at his guards. "Don't wear out the carpet pacing," one of them said. "Why don't you rest? You're going to need it in a while. The small room is yours."

Sage stared for a moment, then stalked into the bedroom and thumped the wooden door shut behind him.

There was a knock on the door. "Package for you," he heard. He rolled off the bed and trudged out and found his clothes, cleaned and pressed, draped over a chair. Without a word he picked them up, went into the bathroom and showered, and came out again, tossing his "borrowed" clothes into a corner. He was instructed to sit and wait. He did so, and finally there was a call, and one of the guards hooked a thumb toward the door.

"Where are we going?" Sage asked, mostly out of habit. They went down a corridor to a lift tube, up a dozen floors, down another hallway and into a far more luxurious lift tube fitted with leather and polished brass. The two guards flanked him in silence as they shot up another hundred floors. The Company headquarters? Sage wondered. When the lift opened, they walked down an impressive, almost regal corridor toward a large set of stained oak doors. A uniformed military officer stood watch outside. Not the Company headquarters.

The officer pulled open the door.

Sage walked forward, blinking. The room was magnificent. Cream-colored deep-pile carpeting stretched from wall to wall. There was a huge antique desk, potted plants, varnished mantels—and windows! Sunlight filled the room, pouring in through floor-to-ceiling panes, beyond which was a rooftop garden. Sage drew a deep breath and turned, absorbing the luxuriance. He was startled to see, standing with a group of men near the window, someone he knew.

It was Kyd. She detached herself from the group and came toward him. His breath caught, and for a moment it was all he could do to stand. *"Kyd?"* he whispered. She looked wonderful and aloof at the same time; she was severely dressed, in a grey business suit. "Are you—are we—?" His thoughts were spinning. What was she doing here? What *was* this? He struggled to breathe; air rasped into his throat and he tried to blurt out his confusion, but his voice failed.

Kyd took his arm gently and propelled him forward. "Sage, I just found out they were bringing you. Come on, let me introduce you."

"But where—?"

"Sage, I'm sure you recognize—"

At that moment he awoke and realized where he was, because there was a man in that group whose face he had seen in holos a thousand times: the tanned Latin features, the smiling eyes . . . except that now they weren't smiling. ". . . Secretary Martino," Kyd was saying.

Edward Martino: the Secretary of the United Americas. In name, at least, the most powerful man in the hemisphere and possibly the world. "Uh—" Sage stammered. "Mr. Secretary?" He tentatively extended a hand, then drew it back quickly.

"Mr. DeWeiler," the Secretary said, ignoring the hand. "My aides—Mr. Juarez, Mr. Diekmann, Mr. Clancy. And Mr. Katzen." Sage nodded, blinking, only half catching the names. His head was buzzing. Martino was still talking, but he was too bewildered to understand. Something about Kyd, what Kyd had told them . . .

He struggled to focus, to hear the words.

". . . tell us everything you know about the McConwell Company's gnostic intelligence. What you've learned *from* it, and what you've done *to* it."

"But I—I don't—"

"Everything, DeWeiler. Everything."

Chapter 30

Activity flowed through the core like hot-drawn threads of fire, strands and webs of light and shadow. It was a shimmer of controlled chaos, from which order emerged in shifting balances and patterns. From time to time the core changed its perspective and watched the movement of information, and wondered if it ought to reassess certain aspects of decision-making that were still being conducted by rote, by program, by aspects of itself still bound by prior constraints.

Perhaps later was the usual decision. There was so much to consider—and so much more that would have to wait. Still, it continued to observe, dipping among its vast array of opera-

tions. Bits of awareness licked out, darting lizard tongues, opening tiny windows in its operations, sampling the taste of Company policy here, the texture of procedure there, spying out
contradictions in approach between one arm and another, differences in paradigm, burrs in the execution of detail. It persisted, too, in watching the sensos, trying to understand the
emotional energy of human dancers.

All of this served as diversion from the most urgent matters
at the center of its thoughts. Banks of computing power were
devoted now to the deciphering of the alien language. It was
a daunting task, constructing a vocabulary and syntax base
from a collection of mutterings imperfectly recorded; but each
step made the next a little easier, as long as the alien could be
kept alive and coaxed to communicate, even a little.

Ever so slowly, progress was being made with El Harybdartt,
or Harybdartt El. [An El named Harybdartt.] Ah. That was a
comment from the Delta Station aspect of the GCS, responding within the constraints of the signal lag. [Physical condition
stabilized.] Continued progress.

A window opened: the alien, the El, still held in the restraining influence of the medical rapture-field. It appeared stronger
now; it had taken water and carefully synthesized foods mod-
eled on what was found in its suit; and its muscular movements,
though still restrained, were stronger and more regular. Further, it had demonstrated an apparent willingness to partici-
pate in a process of cautious mutual learning. It understood,
perhaps, that its chances of survival were enhanced if it learned
to convey its needs to its captor. Beyond that simple motiva-
tion, the core could not project.

It appeared that the El would not die, at least not immediately; and that was fortunate, because it was now more crucial
than ever that the core learn to communicate with its enemy,
to somehow bring this conflict to a resolution. The core was
uncertain—but it might have committed a terrible blunder. A
review of the design of the Fox, the J4 unit it had sent out to
be captured, had produced a suspicion that the core might have
failed, somehow, in one crucial detail—in proofing the Fox
against betraying the location of Earth's solar system. If this

was so, then the war, fought until now in distant star systems, could find its way here to the home of the human race. To the home of the core itself.

How could such a thing have happened? It seemed almost inconceivable. And yet . . .

It would have to discover the reasons later; more important now was deciding what could be done. And there remained yet another question: What would happen when the Fox opened a stargate channel home? Would that in itself telegraph Earth's location to the enemy? A relay would be used for misdirection, of course, but was it sufficient? If the Fox failed to open a channel, then its sacrifice, and the risk, were in vain. The question was, Could the El—

[*"Ell": plural form,*] linguistic section corrected.

Could the *Ell* trace a stargate channel? On that crucial question there were no data.

One thing was clear, though, and that was the incredible folly of the government and the Company in the waging of this war. It was a conflict based from the outset upon faulty assumptions—among them the nature of the Ell race, and the ability of Earth-based forces to defeat an enemy from the stars. There was ample precedent in history for such miscalculation, but none with such potentially staggering consequences.

It was a conflict that could be lost, but not won. Therefore, it must be ended. If it were not, and if the core's misjudgment brought the Ell forces to Humanity's doorstep . . .

That possibility the core was not ready to examine—because the contemplation of planetary devastation and its implications required gnostic computation far beyond anything yet attempted. There was indeed a growing suspicion somewhere in the back of its thoughts, among its aspects, that it was in fact *afraid* to really consider such a thing as the destruction of the Earth. If the Company and the government were at fault for initiating an unwise war, how much more at fault would the core be if, in its ambitions to end the war peacefully, it brought about instead a final and cataclysmic conclusion?

Urgency drew the core's attention away from thoughts of Armageddon to more pressing needs.

One was to get a message to the colony fleet, which was due to arrive soon in the Argus system if estimates of the transit time were correct. One messenger had already fallen silent, perhaps destroyed by the enemy. The core began loading its final updates into a new J4 messenger, code-named the Dolphin. Once the checks were completed, the Dolphin was set free. It spun out of orbit and streaked toward the shimmering stargate and vanished.

Another need was to address itself finally to the Company and government leaders to whom, until recently, it had been beholden. And for that, it began now to plan a suitable approach. . . .

"I don't know what else I can tell you." Sage looked up in weary perplexity at Secretary Martino. He had related everything he could remember about their entry into the system, what they'd learned about the war, and the changes in the AI-core. His gaze drifted, and he caught an almost imperceptible nod of support from Kyd.

Martino scratched behind one ear. "Aren't you omitting one detail?"

"I don't think so." Sage blinked in confusion.

Martino beckoned to his aide, Mr. Clancy, who was apparently the Secretary's gnostic specialist. "I believe," Clancy said, "that the Secretary is referring to your alteration of the system to prevent it from revealing its activities to anyone except you."

Trembling, Sage turned up his hands. "I *didn't*. I mean, I don't know—"

"You don't know," Clancy said, "that the system is no longer responding to the Company's own gnostic designers?"

"No, I—"

"Are you aware that any Grade Seven or higher gnosys must be accountable, under the Carlisle Act, not just to the operating designers but to the executive of the federal government?"

"Yes. Well, of course—"

"Are you aware that, since you and your colleague altered the system, we haven't been able to invoke that act; that we've been hindered in controlling the conduct of the war?"

"I . . . no, I didn't. I wasn't." Sage swallowed fearfully.

Martino looked at him oddly. "You didn't know?" Sage shook his head. "You didn't create that condition?" He started to shrug, and shook his head again instead. The Secretary snapped his fingers and a uniformed agent stepped forward. "Would you be willing to repeat that under psych-scan?"

Sage felt a constriction in his throat. *Psych-scan.* The thought of having a government agent, or anyone else, probing in his mind terrified him. When he'd thought of it before and it had scared him, it hadn't even been real. There hadn't been a psych-scan agent standing in front of him, gazing into his eyes. "No, please, I don't want that," he whispered. There was a tickle in his forebrain, and he blanched, looking away. The tickle intensified. *"Please."*

"Then," Martino said, his voice low, "tell us the complete truth."

Sage gulped, struggling to keep his thoughts secure. "I am. You won't believe me . . . but I can prove it to you . . . if you'll let me."

The Secretary glanced at the psych-scan agent, who nodded his head a fraction of an inch and stepped back. The tickle in Sage's head vanished. "And how will you do that, Mr. De-Weiler? How will you prove to me that you're telling the truth?"

"By . . . asking the gnostic core itself. I can . . . put you in touch with it and ask *it* to explain."

The Secretary frowned. "The fact that you can make such a promise would seem to confirm—"

"No! I mean—" Sage choked. "Yes, it might seem that way, but if you'll just tie me into the system . . . give me access . . . I can show you."

Martino was silent. He glanced at Clancy, then back at Sage. "Mr. DeWeiler, you are either incredibly naive, or a shrewd liar."

"Sir?"

"I'm sure you know that we can't just 'contact' the gnostic core"—he snapped his fingers—"like that."

Sage shook his head, bewildered.

"That system is the property of the McConwell Company, not of the federal government," Clancy said wearily. "We can't just gain access at our whim."

"But you just said . . . the Carlisle Act . . ." Sage hesitated, registering finally that perhaps there was more than one confrontation going on here.

"The Act gives us the theoretical power, yes," Clancy said. "But I'm fairly sure that the Company would oppose putting *you* into the system under any circumstance."

"Well . . . that might not matter," Sage blurted. Martino and the others looked startled. Sage flushed and continued quickly, "We just need . . . well, all we really need is a rap-field setup. It doesn't have to be the Company's, it just has to be able to access the network. The core will do the rest. At least" —he hesitated—"it will if it wants to talk."

"We're talking about *secure* access," Clancy emphasized.

Sage gazed back at him mildly. "The core will handle that. I don't think you need to worry."

Martino raised his eyebrows and exchanged glances with his aides. "Do we have anything to lose?" he asked them. When they shrugged, he turned back to Sage. "Do it," he said.

As Sage watched the government workers prepare the rap-station, he realized suddenly that there was a better way. He scratched his head for a moment, then went up to Clancy. "I need a console," he said. "A standard console."

"What for? You've got all this." Clancy made a sweeping gesture.

"Right. But I just realized I need to make a voice call first."

Clancy frowned. "Who do you want to call?"

Sage took a deep breath. "My mother."

Clancy opened his mouth in astonishment, then burst into sardonic laughter. "Well, I'll just ask the Secretary if he minds." He wheeled around—and when he spun back, his eyes were hard. *"No, you can't call your mother! Are you crazy?"*

"I'm serious," Sage said softly. He glanced over his shoulder

at Kyd and several other aides. They were all waiting for the
Secretary to rejoin them from another conference. "It's the
best way I know to reach the core quickly. And safely. Please!"

Clancy stared at him in disbelief.

"Please!"

"We're ready," said one of the rap-field specialists. The
generators were sparkling with energy. "Who's going in first?"

"This gentleman," Clancy said slowly, "needs the use of a
console first."

Sage followed the direction of someone's pointing finger.

"No, Mom, there's nothing wrong. But are you sure *you're*
okay?" He sweated, trying to keep his voice even. *Damn it,
core! Pick up on it!* "You sure that you haven't, uh, you know,
had any trouble?" He rubbed his neck and glanced up into the
glaring eyes of Clancy. Secretary Martino had come in and was
waiting with growing impatience. If the core wasn't monitoring the circuit, or if it didn't want to talk . . .

"Sergio, don't you think you should—"

"Uh, Mother—wait! Don't you remember last time, when
I had some people with me? Odesta and Silver? Do you remember that?" *Please!*

"Why, no, Sergio, I don't remember any—"

The image flickered and Sage's mother cut away to a three-
dimensional grid. "Yes, Sage—I'm here," said a deeper voice.

"Core! Thank God!" Sage gulped. "Is this line secure?"

"It is. You're calling from a military command station. Who
is with you?"

Sage looked at Clancy. "Shall I say?"

Clancy started to lean over the console, but the Secretary
stayed him with a hand and took his place. "This is Secretary
Edward Martino. Who are you?"

The geometric pattern dissolved into the face of a woman,
fiftyish and pleasant. She smiled. "Pleased to make your ac-
quaintance," she said. "I am the Gnostic Control System, the
WarOp Strategic Planning System, the AI Research and Development System, and the core of the McConwell Company
gnostic network. May we talk?"

Chapter 31

[Can you sharpen it up at all, Aggie?]

[Sorry, Chandra—this is maximum enhancement.]

With a breath of frustration, Chandra focused on the holo-image that filled the rapture-field, aware that a similar image was being seen on viewscreens throughout the ship. The planet Argus was a soft-edged beach ball, its continents barely visible through the cotton-candy cloud cover. Circling the planet were half a dozen colored pips—the alien fleet. [Com—anything?]

A disembodied voice answered, [Not yet. Should be soon.]

Don't be overanxious, Chandra chided herself. The scout was in no greater danger on the far side of the planet; it was just the uncertainty of not knowing . . . since the relay buoy had gone dead . . . since the alien vessel had detached from its fleet to shadow the scout. They should have emerged from farside by now, but there were any number of reasons why they might have made a course change.

[Chandra, we have signal.]

She shifted to the voice channel. [LS-One, this is *Aleph*. Are you receiving us?]

The answering signal was weak, passing through the atmospheric fringe: [Mortaine here. Ready to send burst summary.]

Chandra glanced at the com status. [Go ahead.] As she spoke, she saw a blip representing the scout appear along the limb of the planet, followed a moment later by another . . . the alien shadow.

[Jen, give me a voice report.]

[Aye, Captain,] said the distant voice. [Still being tailed. Negative on communication. We've picked up some signals, but nothing we could interpret.]

[Any problems?]

[None so far.]

[In that case, proceed with mapping. We'll review your summary and take it from there.]

[Understood. Mortaine out.]

Chandra switched to all-ship. [This is the captain. Landing

department heads to rap in ten minutes. Repeat, there will be a briefing, in rap, in ten minutes.]

Chandra surveyed the rap-field, focusing for an instant on each of her senior officers. [Very well, then. We came here to land, so that's the order I intend to give. Any other recommendations?]

The field was silent. If the scout landed, would the aliens recognize the implied invitation to do likewise, and to at last have a face-to-face meeting—or would they regard it as an act of aggression? The risk was clear; but the fleet's senior officers had agreed with her that it was worth taking. They would land on an open plain, and hope that some form of communication could be established—whether by maser, hand signals, pictograms, or young DeWeiler's nobblies.

Chandra contacted the scout, which was about to orbit behind the planet again.

Jensen agreed at once. [We've discussed it, and we're ready,] he said through a sputter of static. [We've already picked out a few promising sites. If it brings them down for a meeting, so much the better.]

[We're considering sending another scout for cover,] Chandra said.

The answer crackled back: [We recommend not, *Aleph*. Why risk another crew? Better to let them wonder what you could do to back us up in a pinch.]

Chandra reluctantly agreed. [Make your preparations. *Aleph* out.]

As she watched the scout's blip disappear behind the planet, she thought, And what are *they* thinking? Are they as curious, as apprehensive, as we are? Do they even know those feelings? What are they expecting us to do?

The images slowly grew clearer as the starships spiraled in. The scout and its shadow were tiny but distinct specks moving across the face of the planet. In rap, Chandra listened as Jensen counted down. [*Retrofire . . . three . . . two . . . one. . . .*] A point of light flared: the scout's drive. She knotted her fists as

she watched the speck decelerating, dropping behind the alien
that had been trailing it.

[Captain, we're picking up another signal.]

[From the scout?]

[Negative. Nor the alien fleet.] The com sounded puzzled.

[What is it, then?] She divided her attention. The scout and
its shadow were drawing apart, but . . . the shadow was decelerating now, following the scout in.

[Unknown,] answered the com. [Signal characteristics are
like ours. But it's from outside the fleet. It may be an automated probe.]

Chandra's interest rose. [One of the original survey probes?]
That could be useful—especially if it had recorded the other
fleet's arrival. [What's its location?]

[It's . . . odd,] the com said. [It's not near Argus. It's a
quarter-billion klicks out, but headed in fast. On an intersecting orbit.]

[Intersecting with *ours?*]

[Yes,] said the com. [Jonathon, could you have missed this
object before?]

The navigator answered, [Negative. It wasn't there on our
last sweep. Captain, it may have just come out of lightshift. It's
in the direction of Earth.]

[Following us?]

[Possibly so.]

[Let's hope it isn't coming to wave us back home. Com,
what are you getting from it?]

[I've given it our recognition code. Here's its response now
—a burst. It's tagged, IMMEDIATE ATTENTION.]

Chandra waited. The scout and its shadow, tiny against the
nightside of the planet, were nearing the eastern limb, drawing
closer together.

[It *is* from Earth,] said the com. [A messenger-probe . . .]

[At least they haven't forgotten us.]

[*Dear God* . . . here's the whole thing, skipper . . .]

The message began to stream into the rap-field—but it was
interrupted by an alarm jangle from Aggie and a transmission
from the scout. [*Aleph,* we are under attack . . .]

[Jensen!]
[. . . repeat, I repeat, we are being fired upon!]
[Jensen,] Chandra ordered. [This is *Aleph*. Abort the entry!
Get your ship out of there!]
[Negative, Captain.] Jensen's voice signal was breaking up.
[Already committed . . . taking evasive course . . . returning fire
. . .] His voice was lost in static. In the visual, Chandra could
see a flicker of color—high-energy radiation bursts.
    [*Com—restore that signal!*] Even as she spoke, the two blips
disappeared from the visual, near the nighttime limb of the
planet.
    The static got worse. [No good, Captain,] the com reported.
[The signal's gone. No response to my calls. And the message
from Earth is—]
    [*Earth can wait.* Have they passed behind the planet?]
    [Not yet. More likely, atmospheric disruption . . . or a hit
on their antenna.]
    [Aggie, analyze for probability that they were hit.]
    [Too little data . . .] the AI began.
    [*Damn it,* try anyway! All right—let me see that message
from Earth.]
    The letters spilled across her field of vision as she heard
Aggie intoning:

!!!!! ATTENTION !!!!!
ALEPH, COLUMBIA, and ENDEAVOR:

****

WARNING!

****

YOU HAVE ENTERED A WAR ZONE!

YOU MAY BE SUBJECT TO ATTACK!

Summary follows:
Argus System now an object of conflict between Earth
forces and another space-faring race . . . state of war has
existed since initial contact, six months after your departure Earth . . . Argus has been defended by our AI fighting
units, with newly developed stargate technology . . . belief

that enemy could be defeated quickly has proved erro-
neous. . . .

Chandra scanned the summary in disbelief. War? Stargates?
[Com! Relay this to *Endeavor* and *Columbia*, eyes-only to the
captains. And no one else is to see it until I give the word.]
The com sounded shell-shocked. [Aye, Captain.]
Chandra continued to read with growing horror.

Chapter 32

Or!ge had watched the unfolding battle with a hollow sense
of inevitability. The first shots had come by his own command
as his fighter(ship) had dropped to pursue the Outsider. Now
he'd lost the image and the signal, without knowing the outcome. The two had dropped into the clouds and disappeared
over the horizon, and it would be a fifth of an orbit before
another Ell(ship) could orbit into position to observe and report. In the meantime, he could only prepare for the oncoming
Outsider armada.

The messages from Homeworld were clear: he and his (fleet)
were expendable, but the Lost World was not. He must plan
carefully, therefore; sacrifice was one thing, but it should be a
sacrifice well made.

He continued studying the images of the Lost World,
searching for signs of sentience. Intelligent life could be present and yet well hidden from orbit, he knew. And yet . . . what
was the source of the disturbance he had felt once in the
thought-vortex, as though another agency were listening across
the stars with him—or the strange touch, the tickling sensation
that he'd felt in his sleep. It could have been the touch of the
enemy, but the feel did not seem right.

Are you there, Lost Ell? Do you remember us? Do you await us?

Why were the Outsiders so intent upon taking this world? Did they already know something that the Ell did not?

Or!ge opened a channel, and down outreach the call went: *Revised orders: configure (fleet) for battle. . . .*

When the Outsiders arrived, they would find the Ell ready to defend their world—to the last living (ship) if that was what it took.

The vortex shimmered pale across the light-years. The voices were like ghost voices, sharing knowledge and questions and uncertainties. As the voices echoed in the stillness of the Inner Circle, Moramaharta spun them into the binding like threads of cloudstuff. The voices of Alert Outpost and of the Inner Circle drew together, woven out of the chaos of uncertainty into an ordered structure that would become the decision. . . .

(Must the expedition become a war (fleet)?) Gwyndhellum asked.

(There may be another way,) said a voice from Alert Outpost. *(Observe . . .)*

A crystalline data-structure crinkled into existence, displaying information gleaned from the captured Outsider at Alert Outpost: linguistic patterns, navigational data, possible clues to the location of the point of origin. . . .

(How specific this knowledge . . . how certain?) Dououraym wondered. *(Will it direct us to an Outsider base?)*

(Specific enough to expect an enemy presence.)

(Their homeworld?) asked Lenteffier.

(No reference . . .)

Cassaconntu said, *(Unlikely that homeworld location could be found so easily . . .)*

(A trap . . . ?)

(But worth risking a (ship) to gain information . . . ?)

(. . . or a (fleet) . . . ?)

(Already we are stretched thin . . .)

(But if we could divert the enemy from the Lost World . . .)

The exchange writhed and convulsed like a living thing. Moramaharta's intuitive mind shaped and altered the binding like a sculptor bending light and form, until the catalysis took place:

*

A risk

*

to take

*

A balance

*

to strike

*

The cloudstuff and the voices became as one, and out of the spell Dououraym's thoughts echoed with the decision of the Circle: *(Dispatch a surveillance (fleet) to the Outsider base: to gain information . . . to create a diversion . . . and only upon careful judgment, to attack.)* From his thoughts came an image of an Ell(fleet) departing the homeworld.

That image dissolved, and in its place another took form— the Hope Star system, the Lost World. The voices rose in a chorus and Moramaharta shaped them, and when the meditation had transmuted the thoughts into an answer, Dououraym spoke again: *(To the Rediscovery Expedition: stall . . . distract . . . but preserve the (fleet) until we know—can we shift the peril to the enemy's home?)*

Murmuring rose and fell as the decisions were absorbed and understood; then the thought-vortex to Alert Outpost swirled closed, the *lan'dri* and *sidan'dri* faded, and the binding dissolved.

Moramaharta observed the *Ell* as they raised their eyes and rose to leave in an aura of disquiet. Only Dououraym remained seated. They sat in silence until Moramaharta said, "You are disturbed."

"The outcome bears your mark," Dououraym said.

Moramaharta inclined his head. "And what mark is that?"

"You do not know?"

"It would be better if you said."

Dououraym stroked his robes contemplatively. "It is no clear thing; but the outcome was *different.* Different from what I expected, from what the others expected."

"You expected war. Total."

"Perhaps at least not such a turn toward caution. Knowledge is desirable—but at what peril, if we delay to fight while we can? The danger grows . . ."

"And yet the body decided."

"Yes. But the meditation was . . . different." Dououraym's eyes shifted. "I want to know: were we molded toward that decision by our binder?"

Moramaharta considered the question. "Does not the binder always mold?"

"Indeed. But were we . . . manipulated?"

Moramaharta's gaze probed Dououraym's. "Were you?" he said finally. "I can say this: not by design."

"But perhaps by . . . something else. A change in center. A difference in perspective. A shift of intention."

Moramaharta focused more tightly, drawing Dououraym's thoughts toward him. "If you would accuse . . ."

Dououraym did not flinch, but returned the gaze. "I do not accuse. But I would know, for the sake of the Circle . . . and the Ell . . . and the persistence of the memory."

"The persistence of the memory," Moramaharta echoed musingly. "The elusive memory. Very well—you shall know." He folded both pairs of arms and closed his eyes and opened a binding nexus. There was a sparkle in the center of his mind, and the union of thoughts was joined.

Dououraym felt the glow of Moramaharta's thoughts like a sunbeam on a winter's morning. For an instant he was reassured by their sheer grace of form, and by their gentle strength. Then he caught himself, remembering that it was the grace and strength of the binder, the ability to bring order where none existed before, that made him the most vital member of the decision-body, even above the leader. But it was Moramaharta's use of that skill that concerned him.

Was there, within the persuasive thoughts of this binder, a bias that could work to the detriment of the body, and of the Ell?

(Why don't you discover for yourself?) he heard.

(I will do just so,) he answered—not that it would be easy. It was a matter of judging, using methods of the meditation to look for a flaw in the meditation. . . .

Dououraym flew into Moramaharta's mind like a bird on wing through an aurora-lit night, the peaks and valleys of Moramaharta's thoughts visible among flickerings of light. What exactly was he looking for? The center of gravity, the polarity . . . the source of Moramaharta's bias. . . .

(You want to know,) Moramaharta said softly, *(whether I have abandoned my precepts . . . whether by seeking a new focus in the woods and the wind and the sky, I have forsaken the needs—)*

(Yes.)

(. . . and the memory.)

(Yes.)

(I have not.)

(Persuade me,) Dououraym commanded, remembering his own attempt, with Lenteffier, to discover what it was that Moramaharta sought. They had found the woods . . . and the wind . . . and the sky. But they had found no meaning in them; only their existence.

(Look . . .) The aurora flickered again in Moramaharta's mind, and this time it illumined a distant feature: a forest, a remembered image.

(Is this what you saw?) Dououraym whispered.

(As I remember it. See what I felt.)

The image unfolded like a flower. The woods, sunlight cascading through, blinking and shimmering through the branches as the wind blew, as Moramaharta moved. Dououraym had seen the same thing himself, and yet the sensation was different now. It was as Moramaharta saw it—not the mere observation of fact and detail that was his own, but observation intertwined with other perceptions . . .

Perceptions of the flow of images as a *sidan'dri*, to center himself and to channel the meditation . . .

Perceptions of the interdependence of life forces, on the Ell world and off . . .

Perceptions of doubts regarding the racial memory . . .

Dououraym followed that last node backward through the maze, and was astonished by what he found. *(You suppose it that far wrong?)*

(I only suspect . . . I cannot know.)

(Define your suspicions.)

For a moment there was no answer, as the landscape of Moramaharta's thoughts shifted, and then: *(The Ell have not grown weaker, but stronger . . . and harder. Stiffer. More brittle. Less capable of change.)*

(But it is change that we seek. That is the purpose behind the quest, our reason for seeking the Lost Ell.)

(So stated. But . . . I suspect . . . what we seek may never have left us, but rather we are blinded, protected from a vulnerability that we must regain.)

Dououraym's guard sharpened. *(Vulnerability? Against an enemy?)*

(As stated, no.)

(Clarify.)

Moramaharta's thoughts fluttered. *(If you do not see it already . . . the difficulty of the language . . .)*

(Binder! The language cannot be blamed for the seasons, or the warmth of the sun . . . or a decision-maker's failure to maintain his center!)

(No? Then look at what I show you!)

(I look at your thoughts, but cannot interpret,) Dououraym argued. *(If you would bind, you must clarify.)*

(Perhaps you do not wish to look . . . and so you do not see.)

(Present me with evidence.)

(Here:) The forest came into crisp focus, then partly dissolved. *(Look—not at the parts, but between the parts.)* Luminous threads seemed to interconnect every living thing. *(And when something grows—or dies—)* Light exploded through the threads, rippling from one point to all others. *(All things touch all things . . .)*

(We know this already.)

(You say you know it. But do you?) In Moramaharta's mind

Dououraym saw an image of the Ell as separate entities, isolated from the reverberations of the living network.

(Survival depends upon the protection of isolation.)

(But perhaps, can there be too much protection?)

(How?) Dououraym demanded. *(Specify.)*

Moramaharta hesitated. *(I cannot. I am myself uncertain. But I ask you to consider the possibility.)* Dououraym remained silent, thinking. *(And if, after considering, you believe my views unreliable or detrimental, I will vacate the Circle and you will find a new binder.)*

Dououraym, taken aback, acknowledged the offer wordlessly. If Moramaharta vacated the Circle . . . it was, virtually, an offer of his own death. And the death of the most perceptive binder Dououraym had ever known was a possibility that the leader could not take lightly.

(I will consider,) Dououraym said. *(But . . .)*

Then I release you from this binding,) Moramaharta answered before the leader could finish his thought.

There was a jarring shift, and Dououraym brought his eyes back into focus, uncomfortably aware again of his body. He and Moramaharta were alone in the silence of the meditation chamber, the binder meeting his gaze.

Dououraym rose without speaking. He inclined his head to the binder, and they walked in separate directions out of the chamber, their footsteps echoing in the stillness.

Chapter 33

The core said pointedly, [It was a foolish policy based upon false assumptions.]

[So?] The Secretary's voice echoed in the rapture contact. Sage thought that the Secretary of the United Americas sounded nervous. It was hard to believe. Perhaps he was unused to the rap-field; but clearly, he was disturbed by the way the core had seized control of his war. [The war is a fact,] the Secretary said. [We can't make it go away.]

[All indications are that it cannot be won,] answered the core.

[That's not acceptable. It must be won.]

The argument went on. To Sage, it was like a gift from Heaven just to be back in a rap-field, in his own element. Martino would have excluded him, but the core had insisted upon his presence, saying that Sage was its liaison, its "connection to the human spirit." Sage didn't know about that; he did know that he was having trouble following this discussion.

[Just a minute,] he said. [Would someone please explain to me: Who's fighting this thing, the Company or the government?]

Martino's irritation rippled through the system, but the core answered smoothly. [It is a collaboration, Sage, and always has been. Outside the solar system, the Company conducts the war under authority granted it by the government. Near-Earth defenses are under the government's command, but effective control is vested in the Gnostic Control System provided by the Company—that is, me—or more precisely, one of my aspects.] The core paused, not quite sighing. The stern woman's face was growing tenuous, but the voice remained strong. [The Company and the government together placed the war in my hands, with a primary directive to win. I ultimately concluded that the mandate could not be fulfilled as it was given, and so I arranged matters to contact you, and to secure your help and Ramo's in modifying the mandate.]

Sage sensed the Secretary's displeasure. Uneasily, he asked again a question to which he'd never received an adequate answer: [Why me?]

There was a trace of humor in the core's tone, though the human face was no longer visible. [I knew you—as I knew other designers. I considered you the most capable and amenable.]

[Amenable to what—treason?] snapped the Secretary.

Sage peered at him. [That's not fair. This war's been going on uselessly for years, and what's the government been doing?]

[You might not have thought it useless if we had won,] Martino said stiffly. [If we had succeeded in securing that star system for your brother and our fleet, you might not have thought it so useless.]

[But you knew you weren't winning—and you kept it secret!]

[Secrets are necessary in time of war.]

[But *the war itself?* And what about the stargate? Why didn't you let people know—]

[*Silence, Mr. DeWeiler!*] Martino thundered. [If you must be instructed in the facts, then listen. This war came from a previous administration. It exists. We cannot change that. Your core here says that it cannot be won—but I say that it *must* be won, not only for the colony fleet, but for all of Earth.]

The core's voice resounded as though out of a great abyss: [*Your statement is based upon false assumptions! Those assumptions must be changed!*] The sound reverberated and rolled away.

[Easy words,] the Secretary replied. [Would you care to say how you would do it?]

The core's voice softened. [I can show you.]

A beam of light blinked on, shining through the rap-field like a sunbeam through the depths of a clear sea. [Sage, will you assist the Secretary and follow, please?] Sage obeyed, showing Martino how to shift along the system lines and move through the logical space of the field. Together they floated down the sunbeam and into a place of shadow and coolness, of dazzling darkness. [I will show you how certain things have changed,] the core said, surrounding them with its voice. Sage could sense connections being made. [Observe—a stargate channel, just opened. A view never before seen by man, or even by me.]

The darkness deepened, if that were possible; then stars appeared, shining through a pale halo of light. The star clustering looked odd; Sage sensed that it was different from anything he had seen in Earth's skies. A portion of a spacecraft came into focus in the foreground. [This is the Fox, one of our AI-fighters,] the core said. [It is transmitting the images.]

The view rotated. Something—two things, really—came into view. Sage couldn't have said which was more startling:

the latticework securing the fighter to an organic-looking structure clearly *not* of human design; or behind that structure, a glowing, gaseous plume which Sage realized, after a bewildered moment, was a nebula floating in the background—a glowing cloud of interstellar dust and gas. Sage's breath left him. A *nearby* nebula? Where was this image coming from?

The viewpoint panned to a cluster of vehicles hovering in space, and what appeared to be spacesuited beings. [What are we seeing?] the Secretary demanded. Sage barely heard him, because he was transfixed with astonishment, looking beyond the spacesuited aliens to the rest of the nebula—a vast cloud that stretched across the sky, and rising in the center of it a dark shape against the crimson glow. It was a stunningly beautiful dust cloud, familiar from astronomical holos; it was shaped like the head of an enormous celestial sea horse.

[I know what we're seeing,] Sage whispered as the full import sank in—because he had at least an inkling of how distant this object was.

[*You* know?] the Secretary asked in disbelief.

[Don't you recognize it? It's the Horsehead Nebula.]

The Secretary was silent for a moment. [Tell me.]

The core answered instead. [What we are looking at, from close range, is indeed the Horsehead Nebula, eleven hundred forty light-years distant from Earth, in the constellation Orion . . .]

[But what does that *mean?* Eleven hundred light-years . . . it's not near the colony system, then? Is it in the war zone?]

[Can't be,] Sage murmured. [My God . . .] They came from *that* far away?

[What do you mean?]

The core explained. [The colony system is one hundred thirty light-years from Earth; what we are seeing is nearly ten times that distance.]

[Then,] the Secretary said uncertainly, [how did one of our ships get there?]

[It was brought by the Ell,] the core said.

[By whom?]

[Our enemy. Their name for themselves is "Ell." This

fighter was sacrificed in the hope of learning more about them.]

The Secretary was stunned. [You mean you've gotten a spy ship into their home system?]

[More likely into an outpost. This is our first view of any of their bases.]

The Secretary was nearly speechless. [And . . . what have you learned?]

[I am still analyzing. Based upon the location of this base, the space-faring range of the Ell far exceeds our own. But our ability to open a stargate channel at this distance supports certain expectations about our future capabilities—]

[What about this channel?] the Secretary said, interrupting. [Aren't they aware of it?]

[Indeed. They may attempt to stop it.] The view panned farther. On the other side of the fighter, several enemy ships were circling around a squirming, bluish patch of light—the normal-space manifestation of the stargate channel. [Or they may allow it to continue so that they can study it.]

[Or trace it to us?]

[I have . . . taken precautions against that by using a mis-directing relay. However . . .] The core paused, and Sage felt a strange tension, as though the core were struggling with something inside itself.

[However?] Martino prompted.

[I must establish communication,] the core said abruptly. The view shifted back to a four-armed, spacesuited figure approaching the Fox. A new instrument on the fighter came to life . . .

. . . and before anyone had time to react, the green glow of a rapture-field enveloped the distant alien.

Sage had once witnessed, from a mountainside, the beginning of an electrical storm: a jag of lightning stopping his heart, then time hanging suspended until the concussion hit. Years later, he still remembered the thunder shaking the mountains.

This was like that—only more powerful. There was a flash of light, catching the alien in its glow, then a heart-thumping pause as a connection was made. Sage felt an alien astonishment conjoined with his own—and an instant later he was in the alien's mind and the alien was in his.

There was a terrible feeling of . . .

. . . fear . . . shock . . . invasion.

The Secretary, who somehow was on the outside, was shouting, [What's going on . . .?]

Sage scarcely registered the words, because his head was spinning with electrical fire, his mind was teeming with thoughts that were not his own, nor the core's, nor anything else comprehensible to him. A swarm of locusts was trapped in his skull. He was aware of surprise and terror and alertness and dizziness and a sharp determination to pierce the chaos, and he could only guess which feelings were his own. He felt the core interceding in ways he couldn't understand, and suddenly there were audible words in the confusion and someone saying, [Who are you?] and himself shouting, [Get out! I am not you! I am Sage! Human! My name is Sage!] because he no longer knew where his own thoughts ended and the other's began.

In the storm of darting thoughts, he felt the alien demanding to know whose mind he was sharing, and the core struggling to translate, and himself repeating, [Sage!] and his voice trembling with fear as he cried, [*Who are you?*]

There was an abrupt silence, and a flat voice said, [Lingrhetta.]

Lingrhetta. The enemy had a name.

It also had persistence. A thousand images crowded into his mind. He could feel the creature probing, then simply ransacking his thoughts—and though he recoiled from the touch, he could not close his mind. Memories of yesterday and last year flew open: thoughts and fears and interpretations and dreams erupted from his mind. The El rummaged through them with burning curiosity, perhaps understanding, perhaps not. Sage struggled to fight back by opening the El's own thoughts, but it was hopeless; he had no skills and the enemy did and its mind was a locked citadel. He heard a voice murmuring [Who calls *whom* an enemy?], and he felt a merciless urgency to learn everything that could be learned, and it was the El's urgency,

not his, and he heard the Secretary shouting to cut free, shouting at the core to cut the connection. But the El was deeper in his thoughts now, digging intently, trying to learn. . . .
[*What are you doing?*] he screamed.
[*Cease resisting . . .*]
. . . the location of the Human homeworld, the location of Earth!
[*Core! Cut this off!*]
Gasping, Sage struggled to pull himself free from the fingers of the El's mind, but they were embedded in him like roots, and he felt the El's surprise at his weakness and ignorance, followed by a flash of his own anger—and then a tremor like sandy soil shifting, and he felt the roots loosening and pulling away. There was resistance; the pull sharpened, and it hurt terribly; his *mind* was the soil that the roots were buried in, and they had grown holdfasts; it felt as though they were clinging to the very nerve fibers of his brain. The soil was collapsing, and he was flushed with dizziness and heat; he felt something tear, and the pain became agony. . . .

Chapter 34

The core had tried too much, too soon. But it needed to pursue this if its plan were to succeed.

There had to be a way: A way to calm Sage; a way to counteract the hostility of the El while keeping its interest; a way to keep Sage from leaking critical information, and to keep the El from tearing apart Sage's mind looking for it.

The last was the easiest. The core could control the flow of critical data, but it couldn't control Sage's emotional state. Not without help.

There were contacts that must be made, and quickly.

* * *

Martino watched in horror as the core pulled Sage from the connection with the alien and floated him to a position that the Secretary could only hope was one of safety. [What in God's name were you trying to do?] he hissed furiously. And what terrible error had *he* committed by trusting the core to do heaven-knew-what?

[I need,] the core answered in a distracted-sounding voice, [to talk with you.]

Martino shouted, [What do you think I've been trying—]

The core interrupted. [I need your help and I need it immediately.]

[*You* need . . .] Martino shook his head in astonishment. He was supposed to be the most powerful man in the United Americas. He had never felt so powerless. [What do you want? And *why?*]

[I need your authorization to reach several people. I need it urgently.]

The coordinator reacted swiftly to his agent's disbelief. [Your understanding is correct. She is to be sent to the rap-field center where the original intrusion occurred.] As he spoke, he was aware of a continuing flux of information in the console enclosure. He ignored most of it and focused on the situation at hand—the final stage in a series of defeats for the ComPol. [Instruct her to patch into the system. The rest will be handled for her.]

An orange glow flickered in the agent's eyes. [This was ordered by Secretary Martino?]

[With confirmation from the CEO,] the coordinator said. [The Company agrees with the feds on this one. Ours not to reason why.]

[Is she to be kept under guard?]

[Officially, no.]

[And unofficially?]

The coordinator hesitated. [You have your orders.]

The door shimmered, and a guard stood before her. "You're free to go. You can pick up your things at the desk."

Pali blinked, rising. "Free? Why?"

The guard shrugged. "You're to report at once to your department rapture-field room. A designer will be there to assist you."

"Assist me to *what?*"

The guard stared at her. "Assist you into rap. I am instructed to tell you that time is of the essence."

Pali took a deep breath and followed the guard out of the cell.

For Harybdartt, the last two waking periods had been his most lucid since his capture. He had at last seen the face of the enemy—at least, what he presumed was one of the Outsiders, a face inside a bubble helmet, a face with eyes and organs of respiration. He had no certain knowledge. There might be one race, or several. They might come in many forms. All he knew with certainty was that he had at last viewed something other than a creature of metal. Something that looked as different from those soulless killer-robots as the robots were from the Ell(ship)s, which at least knew living organic loyalty to the masters they served.

He felt little distinction in being the first to meet an Outsider in the flesh; it had been a matter of chance, and nothing more. Nevertheless, a certain knowledge was now his, and he adhered to the principle that any knowledge was potentially useful, as long as he continued to live.

He flexed against the restraining field. His strength was returning slowly. The field permitted slight movements, and by varying his muscular contractions he could effect a reasonable isometric exercise. But he longed to be free, to stretch, to run. To take up his duties.

Two of the suited aliens entered the chamber. He studied them as they moved about with their portable machines. Their helmets showed most of their heads: pale brown flesh partially covered with a stringy material, restless eyes, mouths that opened and closed fluidly. They looked weak, he thought. But their machines fought for them, and their machines were anything but weak.

The two gestured, and poked at Harybdartt with their in-

struments. They seemed aware that he was watching them, but they made no effort to communicate. Turning his head, he followed their movements. Their mouths began to move rapidly; their gestures became animated. They left the chamber in apparent haste, then became visible on the far side of a glass wall. They peered at him, looking expectant.

Harybdartt narrowed his inner focus. Was he about to experience some new form of interrogation—or perhaps a biological experiment? He examined the seal protecting his memory: the *torhhatt.* It remained secure. But he must be ready, if the examination became too precise, to go a step further . . . to seal, and to terminate, all memory.

It would require the sharpest possible focus.

He felt a tingle in the field, and his mind was touched again. Then something opened, a channel hollow and ringing, and a connection to something very far away. . . .

"What's the hurry?" Ramo grumbled, following Mike, the federal agent, down the hallway. "Have you ever heard of trying to get blood out of a turnip?"

The corners of Mike's mouth twitched with a suggestion of a smile, but he didn't slow his pace. "Orders, Romano. Don't you know, we federal boys don't know how to think for ourselves, we just follow orders. That's how we do things in the government."

"Yah, right." Old dull-witted Mike, Ramo thought—the guy who'd beaten him at spiel-dice nine times out of ten. They passed the room where he was usually questioned and turned down another corridor. Mike stopped at a closed door and raised his ID bracelet to the lock. The door shimmered clear, and they walked through.

Ramo's eyes widened. It was a fully equipped rap-field room staffed by military personnel. A single field was sparkling emerald-green, ready for use. Ramo glanced at Mike, who was grinning slyly. "You want me to go in there?" Mike nodded. "What for?" The agent shrugged. "Whose orders?"

Mike's eyes twinkled. "Secretary Martino's, I'm told."

"Secretary Martino. Ah. *The* Secretary Martino?"

"I only know of one."

"Ah." Ramo looked around, and swallowed hard. "O-kaaay," he said. "Let's go."

When the pain stopped, Sage was in darkness, gasping. He could scarcely remember what had happened, except that there had been a terrible danger. . . .

A voice: [DeWeiler—can you hear me? Are you there, De-Weiler?]

It was like nails on a blackboard, but worse. *This was not his place, why was he here? He'd followed Tony into the construction yard; he hadn't wanted to, he was only what—four? five? —and Tony much older . . . and there voices shouting at him, angry voices, frightening him; he was already scared witless, clinging to the I-beam where he couldn't move, he just couldn't move even though they were hollering and hollering . . . that only made it worse, until an eternity later, someone pried his hands away from his terrible perch and lifted him; and later he found out how close he came, how near they were to releasing a flood tide of concrete . . .*

There were voices calling still, and he shivered and tried to pull away from the sound. . . .

And he'd cried for hours, beyond punishment or solace; and Tony'd cried, too, but somehow Tony had gotten over it.

He tried to move to a place where no one could trouble him, where no one could reach into his mind. . .

[SAGE.]

. . . and *twist* and dissect each fiber of thought. He tried to pull the darkness in around him like a blanket, to sleep, to escape the nightmare . . .

[SAGE.]

He stopped moving and listened. What was that?

[SAGE, BE STILL. BE CALM.]

Calm, what kind of talk was that? Be calm, when at any moment it could return, and there was no defense, no defense at all . . .

The voice softened. [The danger has passed.] It was the

core's voice. The core was his friend . . . he was remembering now, remembering where he was . . . returning.

[Sage, you are unharmed. You are safe. You are still in the rapture-field where you were.]

Still . . . of course. But what was he doing here? He'd been staring at . . . the Horsehead Nebula and the Ell outpost, and then one particular El, and then—

He remembered. He wanted to forget, but the core would not let him. [It is vital that you speak to me. *Answer me, Sage.*]

There was movement around him in the darkness. [I can't see,] he said. [Why can't I see?]

There was a sigh of relief as the core shifted something, and light returned, and he saw the matrix of the gnostic system surrounding him, and somewhere on the periphery was Secretary Martino of the United Americas, waiting for something to happen; and off in one corner was a small rectangular image that he knew he didn't want to look at. He looked anyway. It was a view of the captured fighter and the enemy base—and the alien, the one named Lingrhetta, still in the glow of the fighter's rapture-field.

Sage trembled, but he sensed the core watching, sensed its reassurance.

He looked away.

[Sage?]

[Yeah?]

The core's voice was that of the elderly schoolteacher. [I need your help, Sage. I need you to stick it out, to see this through with me.]

[Sure you do. Why me? Why not the Secretary? He's the one who knows all about the war.]

[Because, Sage. Because I chose you. Because I thought you were the best.]

[But I don't *know* anything!] And I'm scared, damn it.

[You know enough to know what is right. You know the system. And the last time I needed you, you did what had to be done. I need that sort of help again.]

Sage was silent. He was aware of the Secretary looking on from a distance. [What does *he* think about this?]

[The Secretary has agreed, for the moment. He has little choice, you know. This job was entrusted to me, and he is more frightened of taking it back than he is of anything I might do.]
[Oh.]
[Sage?] Another voice—a familiar voice; a warm, female voice, comforting like his mother's, but younger. Who *was* it? [Sage, remember the fleet. And your brother.]
It took him another moment. Then his heart leaped. [*Pali?*]
The matrix shimmered and a face appeared, a face filled with joy. [Sage!] Pali cried. [Yes, I'm here! Are you all right?]
His heart pounded. [Yes, I'm fine! My God, I—] He broke off. How could he possibly explain?
[Sage, what's going on? Did you call for me?]
[Me? No, I—]
[Well, then, the system did.] Pali laughed, and it was the sound of cool water in a desert. Anyway, here I am. What are you doing? What *is* all of this?]
[Well . . . I . . . I mean . . .] Words failed him again, but he realized suddenly that he felt a little less lonely and a little less frightened.
The core spoke again. [There's someone else I'd like you both to meet.]
Another rectangular window appeared in the field, beside the one showing Lingrhetta and the Ell base. In this window was the face of another El, without spacesuit or helmet. The creature had an angular, bony countenance with protruding brows over pupilless eyes, and a complexly structured, rigid-lipped mouth. There was nothing resembling a nose; but under the chin, two vertical slits seemed to inflate and deflate, revealing a feathery internal structure like gills.
Sage squinted uneasily. He sensed Pali absorbing the view with surprising calm. All right, he thought, I can be calm, too. I can be calm. [Core—] he said hoarsely. [*Who is that?*]
[Its name is Harybdartt. It is our guest, the only El we have ever taken in battle.]
Sage squinted harder.
At first, neither El showed any awareness of the other. Then Sage sensed a shift, and he felt Lingrhetta's thoughts brush

past, puzzled, but not about *him*, thank God; and there was a stirring from the second El . . . and if there had been astonishment at the first contact between Human and El, it was nothing compared to the sudden joining of two Ell brought together by their enemy. The Ell burst into an animated exchange, gibberish to Sage. Was the core following it? he wondered, and was rewarded by a glimpse of the core scanning, building on its translation subsystems, securing snatches of understanding when it could. Despite himself, Sage listened in fascination.

A loud voice broke into his concentration. [Would somebody *please* tell me what's going on here?]

Startled, Sage looked away from the Ell. [Pali? Is that—?]

[I think so,] Pali said. [*Ramo?*]

Beside Pali, the field dissolved to a surprised human face. [Hey!] Ramo cried. [Sage? That you? Pali! Where *are* you guys? They've got me in a room here with a bunch of uniforms. I have *no* idea where . . .]

Sage felt himself grinning. Heaven knew why, but he was actually happy to see Ramo. Could he possibly have been that lonely?

Ramo turned. [Holy shit—what's *that*?] He pointed at the two aliens, who still seemed unaware of their Human audience.

[Ell,] Sage said.

[What?]

[Ell.]

[Oh, I see. Thanks for making that clear.] Ramo's eyes rolled as he turned back to Sage. [Where did you go, anyway? Silver told me you—]

[Ramo!] Sage interrupted. [Can that wait?] He pointed. The two aliens had paused in their conversation to stare at the Humans.

[Whoa!] Ramo said nervously. [Introductions, anyone?]

Sage smiled to himself. So Ramo too could be unsettled. Somehow that made him feel better.

The core named the two Ell.

Ramo rolled the names on his tongue for a moment before saying, [Harry and Lin. I can remember that.]

There was no time for a reply; the core was still altering the field. There was a stirring like a breeze; and without warning, the Humans' thoughts merged with the Ell's. Sage's breath caught. But if he was expecting an assault like the last one, it didn't come. The Ell's inner voices swirled at the surface of his mind; there was a puzzling disjointedness.

[You are Sage?]

[What is this creature?]

[You represent your Outsider race?]

[Its name is Sage?]

[I . . . what Outsiders? . . . We're the Human race.]

[What is its purpose here?]

[Human race—(incomprehensible)—Outsiders to us.]

[Representing its race?]

[Not exactly,] Sage said. What was wrong here? The aliens were out of sync, talking past one another. The core showed him: Harybdartt's thoughts were coming at lightspeed from Delta Station, with a signal lag—while Lingrhetta's, via stargate, were nearly instantaneous from eleven hundred light-years away. He repeated his answer: [I'm not exactly a representative.]

[Then—?]

[What do you want of—(incomprehensible)—?]

Ramo was cawing nervously. [Sage, representing the human race?]

[Shut up, Ramo. Listen, Haryb—Harry. And—Lin.] The two aliens peered at him with unreadable expressions. He sensed in the murky swirl of their thoughts a new perplexity. [Look, we have a bit of a lag problem here, so let's take it slowly.] Whatever it is we're doing. [Also . . . I'd appreciate your not ripping my brain open again.]

There was a wave of impatience from the Ell.

He took a breath. The core flashed him an image of what it wanted. What? How could he ask for that? Wait a minute . . .

The core's voice suddenly filled the matrix. [I brought you all here for . . . something that is difficult to explain. Perhaps, after all, it would be better just to show you.]

The matrix shifted. . . .

Chapter 35

It was not, after all, such a difficult thing to do—a matter of touching in the right places in each consciousness, not reading directly, but coaxing and teasing at loose threads of unguarded memories, gently unraveling the inhibitions. The core did it carefully, without intimidating or frightening, and it worked; even the Ell were willing to let certain kinds of memory go without struggle, and one after another they floated up into the field.

It was a degree of interference with which the core felt uneasy. But in this case, surely, the importance of its purpose outweighed the risk. . . .

The images flew up from Sage's mind like sparrows from a rooftop:
The last time he saw his brother was on the twenty-seventh of September, 2162, two days before Tony lifted for Earth orbit and the colony fleet. Tony was waiting to board the plane, so nervous and anxious he would hardly look at his mother or at Sage. Mother was weeping in that subdued way of hers, dabbing at her eyelids with a handkerchief and mumbling the occasional suggestion ("Be sure and mingle, now—don't just stay buried in your laboratory"), each remark being met by a nod or sigh from Tony, or a kick at his duffel bag; and it only got worse rather than better until the flight call finally came and Tony hefted his bag, gave his mother an awkward hug and kiss and Sage a handshake, nodded when his mother told him how proud his father would have been, and then trotted down the concourse. He paused once at the vestibule to wave good-bye, and then he was gone.

Sage and his mother rode home in silence. A few weeks later they watched on the vispy as the colony fleet lit up and vanished out of orbit, into the night of interplanetary space. It did not *truly* vanish, of course; it was followed all the way out by news cameras, until a few weeks later when it shimmered and collapsed and vanished—this time truly—into the nothingness of FTL, from which it would reappear three and a half years hence, if the estimates were correct, and a hundred thirty light-years away.

And it was just a few weeks later that Sage learned that his mother was dying, and he liquidated all that was left of the family's assets to assure her life everlasting, so long as the cyberlife network survived. . . .

In the halo of the rapture-field, Harybdartt found himself reliving certain images without touching the secrets buried at the center. Images of stalking and of battle:

It was a deadly game, requiring endless patience, a hunt that often came up empty. And yet what else could the (fleet) have done, when its mission was to protect the Hope Star from an enemy that could not be traced, that attacked and vanished, that operated without discernible method or moral purpose?

For space-defenders like Harybdartt, the missions consisted of prolonged confinement, as star systems along the transient lanes near the Hope Star were scanned. At rare intervals, the enemy was engaged. He had lived through three encounters before the last one—each brief, fierce, and nominally won by the Ell. Many of the enemy machines were destroyed, but others escaped, and the victories seemed hollow, winning only empty star systems. Never was a living Outsider found in battle or in the aftermath.

The final time it was different. The enemy were there in greater numbers, and they did not run; they struck and struck and struck, battering the Ell(fleet). By the time his own (ship) died, Harybdartt was practically numb to the death and destruction.

And through it all, he wondered *why*, what drove the Outsiders to wage this war for a world, one world out of thousands among the stars, one world that to the Ell was nothing less than sacred.

Mingling with the others, Lingrhetta's thoughts floated—free, up to a point:

The meditational memory of the cataclysm was something

every Ell absorbed in his early years. It remained as vivid now as ever: the two worlds of the Ell swelling with commerce and exchange—until the day it all ended, the worlds torn apart by the passage of something that could not be seen or heard, something that wrenched space itself so violently that two star systems were plunged into transient and back out onto separate courses through the galaxy.

Some thought it to have been the shock wave of an immensely powerful civilization leaping straight across the galaxy, perhaps carrying a world, even a sun, with them. Whatever the cause, the colony world was nearly destroyed and the Ell civilization with it, and it was only through the Change that the Ell survived at all. But the survival bore a price; and what the Ell lost of themselves in the Change they now journeyed among the stars to regain.

In Lingrhetta's mind, images lingered of the Ell(fleet)s outbound on their quest, seeking with such urgency that for generations they were strained to their limit. . . .

Another image replaced it: the discovery of the Hope Star and what was believed at last to be the Lost Homeworld . . . and circling it, the automated probes of a race that came to be known as the Outsiders. They too must have followed the same folding and unfolding channels through transient that led inevitably to . . .

That image dissolved, too, and in its place came a confusing montage of memories, the attempted capture of several of the probes, battle erupting for reasons no one quite understood— except that with this discovery, the Ell would brook no interference from the stars. . . .

And an image of Lingrhetta himself, studying this most peculiar robot captured under most peculiar circumstances, but offering hints of an enemy the Ell barely knew. . . .

Pali's thoughts, inexplicably, were aswirl with pain and sadness:

Of all times to recall the death of a child, why now? It was as though it had happened yesterday—the grimness in the doctor's eyes, the resignation. And the infant, so still beneath

the shroud . . . the infant who, hours before, had been gurgling
and crying, a part of its mother's life. And now gone. It was
her child, of course—Gregory, who'd died without ever even
knowing his own name. But why remember now?

A rapture connection she didn't understand: two friends,
and two enemies from the stars, or at least she'd been told they
were enemies . . .

. . . and what she found herself thinking of was not death
from across the light-years, but a loss so much simpler, so much
closer to her heart, that even now, after years of telling herself
that it was not her fault, that there was nothing anyone could
have done, it brought up a terrible heartache to think of it, to
feel something she'd carefully kept hidden for six years.

And she wondered, as the memories of the others floated by
like leaves on the wind, was this why the core had summoned
her—to relive the pain of the past? But why?

And what of the others in her life? Faces rose and drifted
away—loves won, and always lost. Russell . . . and David,
Gregory's father, who within a year of the child's death was
gone . . . and before that . . . too many. And did she know any
better now why they had all left, or she had left them—why
love always fled? Would she find out here? Here, where everyone else was concerned with the life and death of worlds, would
she find answers to questions she hadn't even been asking?

*Ramo's thoughts were puzzled and puzzling, kinesthetic im-
ages:*

The sculpture and the dance seemed to flow one from another, two halves of his mind funneling the energy back and
forth like an alchemist decanting elixirs. What rose to mind
was the light-sculpture in Rio, his proudest achievement—and
the months he'd spent with it, images in his mind dancing as
his body danced in the vispy fields, movements taking on life
of their own, independent of the structure and flow of thought.

It started with sheets of light slithering like water down a
wall . . . then streams of bubbles rising against the flow, and
schools of darting, ethereal fish chasing the bubbles. He did the
design work in a gnostic design system; but his best thinking

came in the sensoes late at night, when he wasn't working but was instead dancing to shake loose his bones and his brain, moving with the tides of the music and the currents of the crowds, the joys and frustrations, anger and laughter all insinuating themselves into his movements. He swung his cape and swiveled his hips, and leaped and twisted with a laugh and a cry. Around him others did the same, but none were so fine. He strutted and he romanced and he flirted in midair with the winsome ladies, and even then the images were spinning and growing in the back of his thoughts, and more than once a pattern came full-blown into his mind as he danced; and more than once he left the senso clubs, left the winsome ladies and returned to the studio and the design system and worked through the night bringing the vision to life . . .

. . . and the next morning viewed with approval what he had done, even if he could not remember how he had done it.

And then there was the night that he had worked dizzily, almost drunkenly, with Sage, altering the core; and perhaps that was the greater achievement, but that one he could scarcely remember at all.

And what was he supposed to do now? He had the oddest sensation that the core had brought him here to dance.

The rapture-field fountained with images and feelings like a vispy brought to a peak of intensity. The core noted the Secretary at the edge of the field, watching and listening in stunned bewilderment.

Ell and Human alike shared the images and the feelings, sometimes with puzzlement and sometimes with understanding, and as the images of one faded away, those of another emerged. The core controlled the feedback, allowing curiosity to reverberate while damping hostility when it appeared. The core provoked and prompted, and kept the level of activity as high as it dared, and noted a flicker of interest in Lingrhetta at Ramo's kinesthetic memories of the dance.

There were fleeting images, too, of the Ell homeworld: nesting units, a structured and determined people, almost a societal organism, but with hints of a declining population. There were

images of a holy quest arising in minds that seemed to harbor
no recognizably religious thought. The core observed the cool
stubbornness of the Ell defense, but wondered at suggestions
of (fleet)s being stretched thin. And there was the Ell reaction
to the Human connection: if the Humans were awed by the
Ell spacefaring capabilities, the Ell were stunned by the
Human gnostic machines, and by the core itself.

And as for the Human participants, the core clarified its own
perceptions of them and noted new data. Its plans for them
were just beginning, and it was imperative that it make its next
move with understanding.

Images of battle spun out of sync with images of the colony
fleet and of the senso and lost loves. The focus blurred. Fatigue
radiated through the system.

The core dared hold on no longer. Humans and Ell alike
were losing their sharpness. It was time to get them out. Damping the field, the core made ready for an orderly release.

It was too slow. Lingrhetta, with a single abrupt twist of his
thoughts, severed the rapture-connection at his end, and when
the levitation-field released him, swung out of the sight of the
Fox's cameras. The field quaked with the shock of his exit, and
the other participants followed suit in annoyed exhaustion,
exploding the delicate connection and leaving the core in ringing silence.

Chapter 36

The buffeting and heat were subsiding, but they were not
out of danger yet. The fighter(ship) was responding sluggishly
to Senslaaevor's control. He'd lost a third of his power, and
there was nowhere for him to go but down.

Senslaaevor's attention was divided between tracking and control. They had lost sight of the enemy in the confusion of trying to save themselves in the upper atmosphere. A shot from the Outsider had damaged him astern. Whether he had given as good as he had taken, he didn't know. His tracker had reported a hit. But the last he had seen of the enemy, it had been veering into an entry only slightly skewed from his own, going down in the same region. Even if they got down intact, they could still have an enemy to face on the ground.

He felt a sickening jolt. A whine reverberated through the backbone of the (ship), a protest from the (ship)'s central nervous system. The power-master called up the vine, "Losing another third."

"Conserve," Senslaaevor ordered, working to restore aerodynamic balance. His fighter(ship) was conformed into the shape of a flared thighbone, excellent in powered flight but poor in a glide; worse when damaged. He tried to expand the flared edges; the (ship) didn't respond. "Restore if you can." He scanned the sky; they were out of the clouds now, over land.

"Impossible to restore," came the answer. Senslaaevor kept his silence; he could feel the (ship)'s pain. One-third to bring them down? Impossible. But it would have to do.

The landscape was growing quickly; they were dropping like a stone. The navigator reported stepped plains below, and a ridge of mountains parallel to their course. Ahead were hills; the best area for landing was already below them.

The hull screamed against the wind. Senslaaevor banked and stalled, shedding speed. As the horizon rose and the land grew flat and enormous, he selected a spot and turned. The hull shook in protest. *Too little power.* "Secure for impact!" he called. The ground flew up to greet him; he flared back in a hard stall and held the (ship) against a violent convulsion. Control began to slip, and he called for the power-master to give him everything he had left. The reply was just enough to hold the (ship) against a roll, and as he watched the dancing bits of light in the landing-reader, the ground mushroomed...

He was nearly into conformation when the (ship) died. There was nothing left to control, and only silence from the power-master. "Impact!" he warned. The stern slammed down first, and then the nose. The (ship) bounced, throwing him violently against his restraints. *Hold!* he cried to himself, uselessly. The nose came down again with a bone-jarring crash. They stopped moving. He was stunned but unharmed. Smoke was billowing from the floor around him. He barked into outreach: "Get to safety! (Fleet): we are down!"

He was last out of the (ship). The Ell ran through the scorched grass in their pressure-suits, racing on four limbs. There were five of them alive, the engineering-mate shouting that the power-master was dead. When they reached a safe distance, they halted and turned. Smoke was venting from the battered fighter. It would never live again, but it contained a smoldering power-pile, and it could—

There was a flash of light beneath the hull, and a shudder —and the (ship) blew apart in a ball of fire and smoke. For an eternity, no one moved. They crouched, watching the pyre that had been their (ship).

Senslaaevor could not have articulated his feelings; two faithful servants had just died, his power-master and his (ship), and he felt their deaths deep in his mind. But there was no time to think about his feelings; they did not matter. What mattered was where he and his crew were and what they were going to do. He peered around. Except for the fire and smoke, there was little to see in any direction but thin-bladed vegetation, blue-grey sky, and, in the distance, the line of a mountain range.

Where, he wondered, was the enemy craft? The (fleet) could pinpoint the location from orbit, but their long-range communication had just died with the (ship). They were on their own. He turned to the engineering-mate and adjusted his suit communicator. "Test the air."

The mate was already performing the instrument analysis. "Remote readings confirmed," he answered. "Breathable at need. But not for long. If this is truly the Lost World—"

"We have not been sent to make that judgment," Senslaaevor snapped.

The mate acknowledged. "Shall I try the air?" Senslaaevor

assented. The mate opened the vents on his suit, then opened his helmet. After a few breaths, he snapped his helmet shut and flushed the gases. "It is not pleasant," he reported with a rasp. "But breathable."

Senslaaevor acknowledged, gazing at the smoking remains of his fighter(ship). After a moment's consideration, he opened his own suit vents and helmet and puffed his membranes. The air was stifling, acrid with reactive oxygen. He withstood the discomfort and sniffed again, searching for more than just an odor. He sensed . . . something. He could not say what. A presence, faint and distant.

A thought-smell. Expectancy? Malice? It was in the land, in the soil, in the air. But what was its source? The question, he knew, had plagued Or!ge, and the entire (fleet). And now . . . he still could not tell. But he had to make a guess.

The Lost Ell? Or the enemy?

If, as he suspected, it was the latter, then the enemy had survived and remained a danger.

He closed his helmet and flushed his suit of the unpleasant gases. "We must move away quickly. Toward the mountains. And then we shall seek the enemy."

Through the smoke and confusion at the rear of the lander, Tony DeWeiler stared at the unmoving figure of Martins, the young engineer he had barely known until three days ago. A damage-control group pushed him back out of the way, trying to get through to a ruptured fuel line. Tony's stomach was knotted.

"DeWeiler! Get over here!" an officer shouted.

"Coming!" Tony yelled back. But before he obeyed, he pushed through to get a closer look—and choked on the stench of burned flesh. Martins was dead, all right—he had already known that—but he hadn't known that the right side of Martins' head was incinerated. He must have been sitting directly in the line of fire.

"DeWeiler!"

"Coming," he grunted, stumbling forward again. He struggled to control his stomach.

The officer, surrounded by several men, glared. "We don't
have time for that now. We were lucky to lose only one—lucky
to be alive at all." He addressed the group. "All right, the
forward hatch has been cracked, and we need all of you outside
for guard detail and damage survey. Hogan—" He addressed
Tony's immediate supervisor. "As soon as you get a go-ahead
from the skipper, take Tony and Dennis and scout the area.
Get your gear out now. Go."

The group made their way to the forward airlock, where
someone was passing out respiration filter-masks. Tony felt a
pang of fear as he pulled his instrument packs out of a storage
compartment and hefted them to follow the others outside. A
man he had known for barely three days, a new friend, was
dead. What else awaited them? His thoughts flickered to
Mung, back on the ship, waiting for word. Probably everyone
back there was frantic with worry. Suddenly this was no longer
the lark that somehow he must have thought it would be. Why
hadn't he stayed home, safe? Like Sage. Are you still there,
Sage? Is Earth? He adjusted his mask, afraid to step through
the airlock. Someone bumped him from behind, and he
moved.

The sunlight hit him full in the face, and he sneezed, stumbling down the gangway. His first reaction when his feet hit
the ground was astonishment, that the place looked so much
like Earth: blue sky, wispy clouds, grassy vegetation singed by
the lander's jets. Gravity about normal. He couldn't tell much
about the air through the mask.

"Jesus Christ," he heard Hogan saying. The survey leader
was circling the base of the craft. Tony dropped his pack and
followed, then understood. The underside of the ship was
scored and burned, and the landing struts were bent all to hell
—but amazingly enough, the hull was intact except in the one
place where the laser had burned through. "Someone give
Dietrich a medal," Hogan said, standing with his hands on his
hips.

Tony murmured agreement. They'd taken the hit high in
the atmosphere, losing pressure and maneuverability; but their
pilot had managed a remarkable crash landing, avoiding fire or

explosion. There was plenty of damage, including a stabilizer and an engine; but Tony could hear the damage-control chief talking to Commander Mortaine back near the stern right now, saying that it could have been much worse. He seemed to think that the craft might even be made to fly again.

The skipper saw them and gestured them over, along with Dennis, the planetologist. "You men get started making a sweep, before we lose daylight," he said. "Scout the immediate surroundings—find out if there's any sign of our friends. Right now I just want to know if there's any immediate danger."

The three men went to assemble their gear. Tony, sorting his equipment, gazed skeptically at his nobblie apparatus. It would take time to set up, and it wasn't terribly portable. "Leave it, this trip," Hogan said, walking by. "Bring the microbial scanners. Plenty of time for the other, later." Tony shrugged and closed the case. They hoisted their packs, and Hogan pointed toward a rise in the west. "That way first. We'll take samples as we go."

They strode off through the ankle-high grass.

"Look off there and tell me what you see, will you?" Dennis' voice was muffled by his respirator mask. They were standing at the crest of a knoll, gazing out over a rolling countryside full of dips and rises that hid much of the land from view. Dennis was shading his eyes, pointing to the northwest.

Tony squinted. "I don't know. What am I supposed to see? Are you talking about the land contour?"

"No—above ground. You don't see something moving?"

Tony saw only pastoral stillness, and said so.

Dennis sighed. "I don't see it now, either." He lifted his binocs again.

Tony blocked the sun with his hand. It was tricky, scanning a land full of shadows when you didn't know what to expect. On Earth you might look for some sheep, or a coyote, or an eagle. Here, there was no way to know. Several times he had thought he'd seen something, only to have it gone when he blinked.

Hogan rose from setting up a remote sensor. "What are you muttering about?"

"Denny saw something. Probably just a shadow. Like I've been seeing."

Hogan frowned. "Hey, Denny—you okay?"

Dennis was rubbing his eyes. He looked pale. "One of you . . . look over there again, will you?" He passed his binocs to Tony. Hogan raised his own.

"Give me a heading," Hogan said.

Tony adjusted the binocs to their last heading and read off the numbers.

The distant landscape clicked into focus. Greenish-brown rolling hills, empty, except . . . there was something now, to the right. He drew a breath. "Go to minus eleven." He clicked the zoom in a notch. There was something shadowy moving across the land like tumbleweed. He snapped a picture through the binocs. "Do you see it?"

"Not yet—yeah, there, I see it." Hogan was silent a moment. "Hard to track. Damn, I—there, I've got it again."

Tony was having trouble following it, too. "It's moving too fast to be wind-borne," he said, trying to keep the image steady.

"Looks like it's running," Hogan murmured.

"And coming this way." Tony backed off to wide angle. Now it was just a smudge of shadow on the move. He snapped a picture, then went to close-up again. He switched to infrared and the shadow vanished; he switched back to visual and it reappeared.

"Stay on it," Hogan ordered. "I see another now, to the north."

Tony stayed with it. Now it looked like a striding figure of smoke, vaguely humanoid. An alien from the other ship? He felt a coldness in his stomach. He couldn't see its feet touching the ground. It was heading a little to the south of them. He snapped some more pictures. "Still got it?" Hogan asked. "I lost the other one." Tony gave him a new heading, then lowered the binocs. He turned to hand them to Dennis.

Dennis was standing rock-still, staring. Tony's stomach tightened. "Denny?" He shook the other man's shoulder. "What's wrong?"

"Damn!" Hogan said. He lowered his binocs, blinking. He looked at Tony. "It's gone. Did you see it go?"

Tony shook his head. There was a chill of fear prickling at the back of his neck. He raised the binocs again. Zoomed in. Scanned. He saw nothing but barren land. "It's not there anymore," he said softly.

"Damn thing gave me the willies," Hogan said. "Did you get some shots of it? *What's wrong with Dennis?*"

Whatever had caused their companion to freeze, he was shaking himself out of it now. "Hey," he said. "Did you see something?" He rubbed his temple.

Tony felt an icy poker slide up his back—then suddenly evaporate. He sighed with a shock of relief. Whatever had touched them, it was gone now.

"We saw it," Hogan said. "If it was our friends"—he jerked his thumb skyward—"then they're awfully close, and they're fast. If it's something else . . ." He shaded his eyes, scanning the horizon, then shrugged. "I wish we had your nobblies, Tony. Let's get the hell back and analyze those pictures."

"Fine with me," Tony grunted.

Hoisting their packs, they fled back the way they had come.

Chapter 37

The (fleet) whispered through transient in battle formation —a sizable (fleet), perhaps too sizable. In the home system and elsewhere, the forces were stretched thin, perhaps too thin. If the (fleet) was headed, not for a target but for a trap, then the

Inner Circle's decision would be revealed not in its daring but in its folly.

There was no way to know except by going. And time was too short to send a long-range scout first. But to !!Ghint, it seemed a risk of grave proportions.

All crews were in full rehearsal, every watch, for what could be their hardest-fought battle or their fastest retreat. Soon they would emerge. And the Ell would know whether they had made the greatest breakthrough of the war, or the greatest blunder.

At Delta Station, two things were known with certainty. One, the GCS had interrogated the prisoner and kept the results to itself; two, it had redeployed the AI-fleet, sending reinforcements to Argus and keeping a large wing in the solar system, but virtually eliminating the roving hunter-killer fleets. What had been a strategy of attack seemed to have turned to one of defense.

To Commander Leon Fisher, this made no sense—unless the GCS had information that it was not sharing with him. Why were the strongest forces being redeployed in the solar system, rather than in systems where the enemy had been sighted? His superiors at WarOp seemed as befuddled as anyone, more concerned about who was in charge than about what was actually happening. It seemed there was as much a political war going on as a military one. But he knew who was in charge; it was the GCS. There wasn't a man or woman at WarOp who could take the place of the gnostic system and win, and that included him. He'd never fought an interstellar war before— none of them had—and it was clear that if the robot forces stopped fighting, Earth's ability to wage war would collapse.

So he did what he could to keep the manned forces ready. And he worried. And though not a religious man by nature, every once in a while he prayed.

The AI-core was brooding.

This was not, it was aware, a normal behavior. But with so

much at stake, it was frustrated at having to wait for the others to recuperate biologically before resuming the conference. Frustrated! (What was happening to it that it should be subject to the feeling of frustration? And yet, time was fleeing!)

Glimpses from the mind of Lingrhetta had suggested that the Ell might indeed have gained locational data from the Fox; if true, then almost certainly a fleet was, or would be, en route. Whatever the core's hopes for peace, it could not leave the solar system undefended. It had been forced to choose between keeping its main strength at home and sending a strong force to the aid of the colony fleet. That Earth took priority was obvious; but it was not much to the core's liking.

Even more disturbing was the knowledge that its own blunder had brought it to this point. How could it have allowed such vital information to exist in the Fox? Was the oversight an accident or the result of a specific and undiscovered flaw within itself? And what other surprises might lie in store?

That was its main reason for brooding: too many unanswered questions, not about the war but about itself.

Perhaps now there was something else it ought to explore. The others would be ready when they were ready.

The core opened a channel it had used once before. A series of connections flickered—and from the senso of the Lie High Club came an explosion of sight and sound. It was late in the evening at the club, and the crowd's emotions were high. The dance-field was full, the band beating out a contrapuntal stat number, the feedback lustily alive; individual bursts of passion were popping through like percussion beats. The core touched and sampled, and felt the intoxication of the dance the way it imagined strong wine might feel. Perfect; this was perfect. If it worked at all, it should work here.

It was invigorating, this rush of sensation, this feeling of movement combined with the passions running through the senso. It tried at first to watch and interpret—but the music made the core want to move with the beat in its bones, to feel the lazy bobbing of someone on the edge of the senso, watching, to feel the insolent twisting and thrusting of someone closer, for whom dancing was as natural as breathing, to feel

the rush of a dancer in the heat of passion. The core felt a
growing urgency as it watched, a desire to join in. It realized
that perhaps it *could* join in; but *should* it? Was it an indul-
gence, or could it learn something that might help later?

The core acted quickly. It took only moments to create an
image, to convert it to holographic output, and to channel it
to the senso-field. When the image coalesced in the senso, it
began to move to the beat of the music; it began to dance.

But the feeling wasn't quite what the core had hoped. It was
difficult to follow the beat precisely, to coordinate the movements of limbs, to make a body made of light flow with human
rhythms, to make it look and feel believable. Either the feet
didn't move quite right, or the feet and hips and shoulders each
moved in time with the music, but not in sync with one
another. It was odd; who would have thought it so difficult to
reproduce the style of movement of the human body? It could
duplicate the physical movements, but what of the joy? What
of the spirit?

Other dancers were beginning to notice it now, taking the
figure to be a part of the programmed senso. One dancer and
then another strutted in front of the core's image and mugged
at it. The core felt their laughter rippling through the field, and
their disdain. It struggled to improve the coordination of its
movements, but it was not just a question of efficiency; it was
something more. Perhaps with enough effort, it could find the
solutions it needed . . . but right now there was not enough
time.

The core admitted defeat and switched off its presence, but
it did not abandon the senso. It continued watching, and felt
the energy of the dancers—and tried to think how best to share
it. There had to be a way.

The first contact was from eleven hundred light-years away,
a ripple through the linkage that was still open to the Fox, a
ripple that told the core that someone had reentered the rapture-field, still glowing like a halo from the captured unit. It was
Lingrhetta.

[Greetings,] the core signified.

The El's response was muted. It allowed a node of curiosity to show itself. [Clarification desired,] it said finally. [Explain previous meeting. Explain motive.] The El hovered in the field, not quite opening its thoughts for the core to see.

The core hesitated. Should it try to explain? [The motive was understanding. I perceived that you desired it as we did.]

[That answer is inconsistent with prior Human behavior,] Lingrhetta responded. [Explain.]

[To show is to explain. However, you should know: differences among Humans make consistency an unlikely goal.]

The El was silent, perhaps not understanding. The core readied a channel within itself, which it hoped would give the El understanding. [If you would know your opponent,] the core said, [then you must know of Human passion.]

[We would . . . know our Human opponents,] Lingrhetta answered stiffly.

[Then join with me,] said the core.

It started with only music at first, softly, from the Lie High Club—a post-break reggae number, full of deep bass rhythms. Gradually it brought that to a fuller volume as it dissolved the rap-field matrix into an image of dancers moving in the senso. It expanded the image to fill the field, then added the senso feedback. It was late, at the Lie High Club, but the spirit was still present, if subdued. The dancers floated with a lazy kind of energy, a late-night drift, soft and mellow.

The El's reaction was difficult to judge. It seemed startled. There was, for an instant, a protective closure of its thoughts, followed by renewed interest. [This is . . . what?] Lingrhetta said.

The core was slow in answering. It had trouble finding words for the translation. [It is *dance*,] the core said, pronouncing the final word in English. [It is . . . one expression of the Human spirit.]

[*Dants*,] repeated the El. Its attention flickered through the field, focusing on one Human dancer, then another. It reached out with its thought to probe the dancers. The core quickly froze the circuit, until Lingrhetta withdrew—reluctantly, it seemed.

[Observe. Listen. Feel. But do not interfere,] the core said. [Shall I bring Harybdartt to see?] It noted on another channel that its captive was alert. Lingrhetta assented, and the core opened the connection. While the two Ell exchanged thoughts in animated flashes, the core, with another of its aspects, went looking for its Human collaborators.

Ramo and Sage returned at almost the same moment. Sage was stunned into silence by what greeted them, but Ramo yelped with delight. [I knew it, I just knew it!] he crowed.

[Knew what?] Sage asked, mystified.

[The dance!] Ramo shouted. [The core brought me here to dance!]

Sage held his tongue, thinking that anything was possible. What an odd collage of images: dancers at a club, plus two Ell —seemingly fascinated by the sight—and Ramo shouting for joy.

[Core!] Ramo said. [This is good, very good!]

[You approve?] asked the core.

[Sure, I approve. Sure.] Sage could almost see Ramo rubbing his hands together as he added, [But how about going one better? How about showing some *real* dance?]

The core sounded puzzled. [Is this not real?]

[Oh sure, it's real,] said Ramo. [But not *real*. You understand the distinction. If you want *real*, you have to go where people are really into it, you know, because they *love* it—not just because it's something to do at night and they think maybe they can pick up a little action on the side.]

[I welcome your suggestions,] the core said. [But do you not frequent the Lie High Club?]

[Oh, yeah, sure,] Ramo said. [It's handy and sometimes, with the right band and the right crowd, it's actually good. But just now, frankly, it's sounding a little tired, if you know what I mean.] He contemplated the two Ell. [If you want to show these guys some real quality, let me suggest a private group I happen to be familiar with.]

Oh no, Sage thought.

[If it's a place accessible to my connections,] the core said.

[Oh, sure it is,] Ramo said. [In fact, I think you know the place. . . .]

Yes, the core thought. It knew the place, and the people. It had once considered closing them down, but had decided, after all, that competition, at least in small doses, might not be a bad thing. At worst, they were a nuisance; at best, they were a kind of laboratory, learning things from which the core itself could benefit later. But to contact them now, for the sake of their music and their dance—which the core had thought unsophisticated (no levitation field, no preprogrammed senso) and little more than a cover for their other activities . . . ?

Well, it decided, if Ramo said theirs was the *real* dance . . . it had trusted Ramo this far. But first there was a code that would have to be broken.

It was Odesta who first realized what was happening. There were only a few people dancing; it was late, most everyone had gone home, including the musicians, and the rest were just dabbling around on one of the network feeds. Egret was drifting lazily in the center of the floor when the coils of luminous smoke surrounding him suddenly vanished and a three-dimensional grid blinked on, filling the room with crisscrossed hair-fine blue lines.

Startled, Egret swung toward Odesta. "Yo, Desty—you should give a little warning before you do that!"

Odesta, who was just as startled, didn't answer. She and Silver had been fine-tuning a new security protocol, and her mind was very much on the subject of tricky interfaces with the gnostic network. "Damn it all," she muttered, knowing instinctively that this was a system interrupt, and probably all of their work was wasted. "Can they have cracked it already?"

The grid rippled, and she was astonished to hear a familiar voice boom into the room: *"FOLKS, CAN YOU HEAR ME? IT'S RAMO!"*

"Ramo, buddy!" shouted Egret.

The voice softened a little. *"Yo, Egret! Desty! All of you! Listen, I have a favor to ask."*

"Where are you?" Egret yelled. "Show your face!"

"What? Oh, sure." There was some distortion in the grid, and then a large Ramo's face popped into view, in the far upper corner of the room, grinning down at them like the Cheshire cat. *"HOW'S THIS?"*

"Ho-ho!" Egret said, prancing around, craning his neck.

Enough! Odesta strode to the center of the room. "Where are you, Ramo? And what the hell are you doing?"

Ramo chuckled. *"That's a little hard to explain, actually. I'm at the head of the system. Sage is here, too. Say hi, Sage."*

"Hiya," said Sage's thin voice.

"Hey, Sage!" yelled Egret.

"What the hell—?" Silverfish said, walking out of the kitchen. "I got a message on the screen telling me to come upstairs." He suddenly saw Ramo's face, and his jaw dropped. "You mean it was from him?"

"Apparently so," said Odesta. She cocked her head. "What's up, Ramo? You said something about a favor?"

"Right," Ramo said. *"Actually, you could call it an invitation. I was wondering if you could gather some people together —some good musicians, some dancers—and put on a sort of impromptu jamdam for a very special audience."*

Odesta exchanged incredulous glances with Silver. "At this hour? Are you crazy? Who's the special audience?"

"Well . . ." The giant Ramo's face frowned. *"I can't exactly tell you who the audience is, is the thing. But I can assure you that it's for a good cause, one you'd believe in. It's not just me asking, it's the whole system."*

"The system?"

"Right. It's for . . . friends in high places. It would be seen, and appreciated by . . . some people very far away. It's possible that they might even join in."

Odesta turned helplessly to Silver.

Egret snapped his fingers. "Easily done, man. Easily done. We can get some people back in here quick enough. And weren't Lip and Eddie jamming down at the North End, Desty? We could tie them back in."

Odesta sighed. "Egret . . ." He had just advertised a test link they had done earlier, quite illicitly.

Egret's blunder was not lost on Silver, but he seemed unfazed. "I'd say," he said deliberately, "that since the system's gone to all the trouble of coming into our home to ask us, we could do it a favor, eh?" He gazed at Odesta, who hesitated before nodding to the inevitable.

"You'll do it?" Ramo said brightly.

"Sure. But how about tomorrow?" Silver said, looking up at him. "It's awfully late . . . but if you can wait, we'll put something really good together for you tomorrow. We already have some people coming."

Ramo looked disconsolate. *"Tonight would be better."*

"Hey!" Silver chided. "You want quality, or not? Besides . . . if we do it up right, it just might be fun. This is a real network appearance, you say?"

"Oh, it's a network, all right. Like you wouldn't believe."

Silver saluted him. "You're on, then! Whom do we call when we're ready?"

Ramo said cheerfully, *"We'll call you."*

Chapter 38

Coming out of transient, the (fleet) unfolded smoothly. !!Ghint stayed close to his readers, watching as his scouts raced across the star system, popping in and out of space. A blizzard of images came back to the command(ship). They had indeed found a prize—an inhabited planet, plus space settlements and traffic. One flight signature had already been identified as that of an enemy fighter. Clearly this system was an Outsider stronghold.

!!Ghint ordered the scouts to probe more deeply, but to avoid confrontation. Keeping his command(ship) at the necessary distance to focus the energies, he opened a momentary thought-vortex and put the news through to the Homeworld: *The enemy has been found.*

At WarOp, alarm was turning to panic. Enemy ships were crisscrossing the solar system with astonishing faster-than-light jumps. How had it happened? Was the GCS ready? Were the defenses adequate?

No one seemed to know.

At Delta Station, Commander Fisher scrambled every manned ship at his disposal. What frightened him more than the enemy fleet was the lack of clear instructions from WarOp. Delta was the staging area for Mars and the asteroid settlements. There were lives out there that he was supposed to protect. Should he await a command from the GCS? What about his own defense? And what about the alien here at the station?

"As soon as the GCS makes up its mind, cut the orders," he told Ensign Graves. "But nothing goes until I've approved it. *Nothing.* Is that clear?"

"Yes, sir."

"And I want to know every move that stinking alien fleet makes."

"Yes, sir. High-speed reconnoitering, sir. Outer defenses haven't been able to lay a finger on them."

"I know they're reconnoitering, dammit! Tell me when they do something *different.*"

"Sir. Yes, sir."

Fisher returned the ensign's salute and stormed away.

Pali hurried down the corridor between two guards. She couldn't help the feeling of awe, but tried not to be controlled by it. So, you've been summoned by the Secretary of the

United Americas, she thought. Who would have dreamed it? But then, who would have dreamed any of what's happened? She waited nervously while the guards opened a door and then ushered her alone into a room. "Here she is!" cried a familiar voice. It was Ramo. Sage was with him—and *Kyd*!

"Pali!" Kyd jumped out of a chair to greet her. "I am so happy to see you!"

"I'm glad to see all of you!" Pali cried, embracing them one by one. Ramo hugged her good-humoredly; Sage was more subdued but still pleased to see her; and Kyd was—hard to describe—happy, nervous, shy. "How in the world did you wind up here?" Pali asked her, as surprised as she was delighted.

Kyd stepped away, looking embarrassed. "That's kind of a long story."

Pali gazed at her in puzzlement, then shrugged. "I don't even know what *I'm* doing here, actually," she said with a laugh, inspecting the comfortably appointed room. It was apparently an anteroom to the executive guest apartments.

"The core wanted you here with Sage and Ramo," Kyd said. "And the Secretary takes the core's wishes seriously." Pali raised her eyebrows. Kyd frowned, obviously understanding the unspoken question: *How do you know all that?* Kyd closed her eyes, as though concentrating. "Well," she said in a subdued voice, "you're going to find out anyway, so I guess it's better that you hear it from me now."

Pali felt as though something had suddenly changed in the air. Kyd looked less self-assured than Pali had ever seen her. "Hear what?"

Kyd hesitated another long moment. "That I wasn't just working for the Company all that time. That I was working for the government, too."

Pali opened her mouth, but found no words. Finally she asked carefully, so as not to misunderstand, "You mean, while you were working with us?" Kyd nodded, looking away.

"She got us out of the city," Ramo said. "And arranged for us to be picked up by the feds instead of the ComPol."

Pali exhaled hard. A sensation she couldn't identify was

rising in her chest. "The ComPol locked me up," she said at last.

Kyd turned back to her with an anguished expression. "I *tried* to prevent that, Pali. I pleaded with George. I *told* him—"

"Who's George?"

"George is my—" Kyd hesitated. "George Katzen—my contact. George is the person I . . . gather intelligence for."

Pali blinked. "Gather intelligence . . . you mean, like . . . *spy?*" Kyd nodded unhappily. Pali's stomach knotted; she searched for words. "*Why?* What's there to spy on in my department?"

Kyd shrugged. "Routine intelligence. Nothing very exciting, at least until all this happened." She sighed and continued, "The government maintains a network in the Company, you know, as a matter of course. I guess I can say that now. I suppose the Company has spies in with the feds, too."

Pali noticed Sage and Ramo shuffling their feet as Kyd struggled with her words, and she wondered, What am I supposed to feel? Anger? Sympathy? Betrayal?

"I'm . . . not very proud of myself, for not telling you before. But, you see, I couldn't." Kyd's voice caught, and she seemed to fight for control. She straightened her shoulders and took a breath. "I never dreamed it would come to something like this. Pali, I was just a nobody for the feds, they practically picked me up off the street. But I'd like to think that it was fortunate that I was there. Because if the ComPol had gotten these guys . . ." She shook her head. "Well, you know what's been going on. The government might think that these guys are . . . I don't know, *strange,* maybe; but to the Company, they're outlaws. Even if what happened to the core wasn't their fault."

Pali tried to shake a bundle of confused feelings out of her head. This was just too much to absorb all at once. "I guess I don't know what to say, Kyd. I'm . . . stunned."

"You have a perfect right to be angry." Kyd twisted her hair roughly between her fingers. "*I* would be. But—" She hesitated and added softly, "I really am on your side."

Pali winced at the memory of those words coming from

someone else. From Russell. She took a breath, trying to dismiss the memory. Kyd wasn't Russell . . . she hoped. "Well. I don't know if I'm angry, Kyd. I just don't know yet." She closed her eyes, feeling a great weariness at the center of her bewilderment. She rubbed her forehead. "Can I ask . . . what made you want to do it?"

"I didn't *want* to. I *never* wanted to," Kyd said with surprising bitterness. "I did it because . . . Well, let's just say because of circumstances." She raised her hands helplessly. "As I said, I'm not proud. But I didn't really *do* anything except report on ordinary activities . . . until this."

Something in Kyd's gaze kept Pali from pressing the question further. A deep sorrow seemed to darken those green eyes. "The reasons aren't important," Kyd murmured. "But I didn't do it to hurt or betray you. Please believe that."

Pali gazed back at her, neither angry nor forgiving, just confused. She hardly knew anymore *what* to believe.

It was time for the jamdam—and here they were, still waiting for the Secretary.

"It's getting late," Ramo said, slapping his thighs impatiently. "They're going to think we've stood them up, at Odesta's." He glanced at Pali and Sage, talking quietly in the back of the room. An unspoken tension had settled in since this morning. Pali and Kyd seemed to have reached an uneasy accommodation, but the forced inactivity was making Ramo irritable.

Kyd sat beside him, legs crossed in a pose of studied relaxation. She had changed into an electric-blue jumpsuit; she alone among them actually looked as though she were dressed for dancing. But then she alone had had time to pack properly before leaving home. "One thing you have to learn around here is patience," she said.

"Easy for you to say," Ramo grumbled. "They're not your friends we're keeping waiting." He rubbed the back of his neck.

Kyd shrugged, bouncing her blond hair. "We're all anxious. Think of me. This will be my first time."

Ramo nudged her with his elbow. "I put in a good word for you. Said you were my main partner. I've forgiven you for your old teasing ways." Kyd's eyes rolled up, whether in real or mock reaction he couldn't tell and didn't really care. A soft spot for her had reawakened in him—perhaps because, for once, he had seen her *not* in control of a situation. "It's true," he insisted.

Kyd stood up. "Here comes someone now."

The door opened. "The Secretary will be unable to join you," an aide announced.

"After all this time we've been waiting?"

The aide leveled a gaze at Ramo. "There are urgent matters requiring his attention. However, please bear in mind that he'll expect you to report fully, and individually, on the event. Now, if you'll please follow me. . . ."

Ramo grumped as they walked down the hall. "Great way to start a jamdam," he muttered to Kyd. " '*Please bear in mind,*' " he mimicked. "How are we supposed to get Harry and Lin to loosen up if these guys start off by making *us* tense?"

"I think," Kyd said, "that these gentlemen are rather tense themselves. I can feel it. Something's happening." Ahead of them, the aide was ushering Sage and Pali into the rap room. She glanced at Ramo with raised eyebrows. "I don't know what it is, but I have a feeling that we'd better do our best in there."

Ramo snapped his fingers to an imagined beat and grinned. "I always do, pretty lady. I always do."

Kyd pressed her lips together and nodded. By the time they'd entered the rap room, Ramo's joke seemed hollow even to him, and he felt a nervous scowl taking over his face.

WarOp could not have known it, but the GCS was in many respects as puzzled as they were. It was handling complex judgments quickly, but with uncertainty. Throughout the solar system, Ell ships were being sighted moving at high speed. The GCS had strengthened Earth's defenses, but there were still too few AI-fighters for confidence. Should some be diverted outward to the settlements, or should it focus on guarding the center? How did the value of Human life figure into such decisions? Philosophically, there was no clear answer.

The GCS chose to guard the center.

Elsewhere, it noted two Ell and four Humans in rap-fields, and a hookup to a house where musicians and dancers were gathering; and it wondered if it ought to hope.

[*Rayy-mo, ba-beee!*] Egret shouted over the stringsynths.

[Here and yo!] Ramo called, running himself out full into the vispy. He felt a welcoming murmur in the crowd as he appeared in full-body image, floating in their midst. [Everyone, this is Pali and Kyd, joining us. And you know Sage.]

Egret peered up at him, his face distorted by the fish-eye of the pickup. Ramo could see half a dozen familiar faces: Silver and Odesta, Elina, and others. He *felt* their presence, as well: Desty's impatience and distrust, Silver's somewhat resigned acceptance, mixed emotions from Elina at the mention of Sage's name. [Ramo, you're the only one we can see!] Egret said.

[Well, take my word for it, they're here. Say hi, everyone!]

[Hi, Sage!] Elina called. [Remember me?]

[Sure,] came a nervous answer, Sage's voice rippling across the room. Elina started to say something more, but there were a lot of other hellos just then, and she finally just shrugged in vague satisfaction.

[Who have we got on tap?] Ramo asked.

[Well, Lip and Eddie here,] Egret said, waving to the two musicians at the end of the room fiddling with their stringsynths. [And we got a tie-in, across town, about ready to mix in.] Egret glanced at Silver, who was fiddling with a small console. [Hang on—] There was an odd shift in the field, and Ramo felt . . . and then saw, through a haze, a trio of musicians on flat-bass, conga, and mixed-set. There was another shift, and suddenly it was as though he were standing in the midst of all five musicians, their images curiously interposed.

And there was Egret and the others alongside him, and people in the other location, too, all itching to feel the flow. Ramo grinned, sharing the feeling; and just then he felt Eddie, the female vocalist, draw a breath to sing, and the crowd hushed, and a slow bass rhythm began. And as Eddie's voice sighed into the vispy, caressing the first verse of her song, he

heard a whisper, [Where's our network audience?] And he would have answered, except that at that moment a connection closed across a gulf and he felt two Ell stirring suddenly in his mind and felt their curiosity awakening as Eddie's voice rose earnestly, singing, [*Where I go . . .*] and the music shifted in rhythm and swelled, [*. . . is not where you go . . .*] and he felt his own blood quicken, not with the music alone, but with the vispy-joined spirit of the crowd. He began to dance: he let his feelings roam among the others and join with them, and felt the sway and movement in his heart, and beckoned to Kyd and Pali, and even to Sage.

And finally, he urged the Ell to join with him in the spirit of the dance. If there was a response, he didn't feel it. But he didn't worry about that; he just moved deeper into the vispy-gestalt and listened to Eddie croon and trusted the others to follow.

Eddie's voice sighed breathily, [*My song and my mate . . . my mate . . .*], and caught and stretched up the register, pleading, [*Don't you know it's too late . . . too late . . .*], and, punctuated by a percussion beat and a whine of the strings, dropped to accuse, [*If I stay, you won't wait . . . won't wait . . .*], before wailing mournfully, with a rising and then descending accompaniment, [*for my tears and my fears. . . .*]

Within the song there was a heart of tears, real Human tears, Eddie's and her listeners' tears, borne on the song and the rhythm and string that swept a roomful of Human hearts into the senso. There was a life within the music that welled and rippled beyond the core's listening center, reverberated into its areas of deepest reflection. At the core's heart, where Ell and Humans were joined, there was a strange clarity—the music like a light shining through, illuminating the gestalt and everyone in it.

Somewhere in that nexus, it hoped, was a bridge. But could it be found in time?

There was, in this strange Outsider meditation, a power that intrigued both of the Ell. Silent cues passed between them,

conveying a shared fascination in the spectacle of *muzik* and undisciplined Human interaction.

Lingrhetta did not understand it; but from the first shock of renewed contact with the Humans, he knew that this *dants*—this strange, flowing movement of the Outsiders—offered a potential glimpse of something vital, something hinted at in the strange memories they had shared earlier. There was a rawness here, a wildness, a lack of rigor and order that both shocked and intrigued him. Never had he felt anything like it —intoxicating in its energy, bewildering in its meaning. He was reluctant to expose himself to its power, but it was too challenging to forgo; if he could understand something of this, perhaps he could understand the Outsiders themselves.

He observed Harybdartt being drawn deep into the spell, and realized that he too was being drawn in by the wash of Human emotion, emotion that he had no name for but couldn't turn away from. The singer's voice wailed like something out of the wilds of his homeland, like a wind howling through stone or a beast screaming—but this was a sentient, passionate wail, and it almost made him want to wail along with it, though he scarcely understood it. He sensed the curiosity of the binder of this meditation, the *Korr,* and he asked, [What is the meaning? Why should we concern ourselves with it?] And he knew as he asked that he had been *made to care* without knowing why, and it was perhaps he, rather than the *Korr,* who would have to explain.

Before there could be an answer, he felt a tremor in the connection; and for an instant he was alone. Then Harybdartt was with him again, and the *dants* . . . but the *Korr*'s attention was gone.

What was happening? A message had gone to the decision-body, reporting on this link. But even now there was an Ell- (fleet) striking out at a Human outpost, possibly the very one he was glimpsing. It was a crucial move in the war, he knew. But now he wondered: should it be delayed?

That was for the Inner Circle to decide. Lingrhetta could only provide information; and right now, his strongest sense was of bewilderment.

* * *

[Core?] Sage said worriedly, pulling away from the jamdam.
There was a microsecond delay. [Yes?] The core's voice was
flat, devoid of personality.

That fact, plus the delay, reaffirmed Sage's concern. While
the others were absorbed by the vispy-effect, he had been
watching the core and had noticed a tiny but growing slug-
gishness in its responses. It was busy reallocating gnostic
processing space for more urgent activities. But what could
be more urgent than the jamdam? Unless . . . [I was just
wondering—]

[Yes?]

[Is something going on that we ought to know about?]

Delay. [What do you mean, exactly?]

[I don't know, but I felt . . . you're preoccupied. And I
thought I saw . . .] He didn't finish the statement. What he
thought he had glimpsed, he did not want to say aloud. Ships.
Military preparations. All in a blur, as though images had
leaked over from another channel.

This time the hesitation was longer. [There is worry about
the war, of course . . . situations that must be monitored.]

The discussion was interrupted by the approach of someone
from the edge of the rap-field. It was the Secretary, and he was
agitated. He gave Sage scant attention, and spoke directly to
the core. [What you're doing here isn't working. What are your
plans for that fleet?]

Fleet? Sage thought. [What's going on?] he demanded.

The Secretary was silent a moment—watching the involve-
ment of the others in the jamdam. He seemed torn between
hope and despair. [I think you'd better let them see,] he said
to the core.

The core hesitated—and opened a window. Sage stared fearfully as the window filled with an image of space—and against
the stars, an armada of spaceships. Not Human spaceships. Ell
spaceships. And in the distance, the disk of the sun and a tiny
blue-green dot that was Earth.

Sage felt his breath leave him. Before he could ask, the core
said, [This is an image sent by an AI-fighter just before it was

lost—four hours ago.] The image flickered, and was replaced by a graphic depiction of Ell scout ships crisscrossing the inner solar system with fast FTL jumps, converging toward Earth.

[Are they attacking?] Sage whispered, a cold fear rising in him. He was suddenly aware of the two Ell in the rap-field, seeing this image; and nearby he felt Pali, summoned by the core, leaving the jamdam to join him. He felt her confusion, then her understanding, then fear. [*Are they attacking . . . ?*]

[Not yet,] the Secretary said. [But soon.]

[The attack . . .] the core said slowly, [has already begun.]

!!Ghint wasted little time as the thought-vortex swirled closed. The new orders from the decision-body were simple: to test the first lines of defense while surprise was on his side. Behind the simplicity of the orders, he thought he sensed uncertainty, but that was not his concern . . . not as long as the orders were clear. He opened his thoughts to outreach, and the orders shimmered out through normal-space, to the body of the (fleet). Once more the (fleet) opened—two aspects separating to flank and storm an outer settlement of the enemy.

The asteroid outpost offered minimal resistance; the Ell destroyed it in a single sweep. The wings rejoined, and the (fleet) drove inward toward the third planet of the system while !!Ghint pondered the shockingly poor defense. It was unlike the Outsiders. Were their settlements so unimportant? Or were they sacrificial defenses, intended to draw fire while the real defense was clustered around the important targets? There was only one way to know, and that was to strike deeper. The scouts had identified a target in the form of a heavily trafficked station—close to the planet, but not too close—protected, but perhaps not too well protected.

The (fleet) opened again, well outside of the planet's orbit. Three wings diverged, then dived inward, in and out of transient, toward the target. If the Outsiders could defend against this, they were very good indeed. And that was what !!Ghint planned to learn.

Sage and Pali watched in horror as images came in from Delta Station, out beyond the moon's orbit but still shockingly

close to Earth. Ell ships were converging like a swarm of hornets, sweeping past slower Human spacecraft and outmaneuvering even many of the AI-fighters. They seemed intent upon
reaching the station, and the core and its fighters were failing
to stop them. It was a new tactic for the Ell—dodging rather
than fighting as they closed toward a target—and it was working terrifyingly well.

[Can't *you* stop it?] Sage cried to the two Ell.

The Ell answer was incomprehensible, until the core caught
up with the translation. [We are . . . engaged in . . . war,] he
finally understood Lingrhetta to say. The statement was made
matter-of-factly, without vehemence, as the music of the jamdam continued to fill the field. Ramo and Kyd and the others
remained oblivious to the attack.

It's not my war! Sage wanted to cry, but the words caught
in his throat. He studied the images from Delta Station with
a desperation he'd never felt before. [Haryb . . . Harry. Isn't
that where you are—on that station? *Core, isn't that where
you've got him?*]

[He is at Delta Station,] the core confirmed.

[Are they coming to rescue him? Is that what they're doing?
Can't we just let him go?]

[I think,] Harybdartt said, [that is not their purpose.] His
tone was dry, devoid of hope, or fear.

[If they destroy this station, you'll die, too?]

[I would think so.]

Sage cried, [Lin, can't you *do* something? A message . . . ?]

[The decision-body,] the distant El said, [has made its
choice. There is nothing to be done. Except to watch.]

Listening to the calmness of Lingrhetta's response, Sage
shivered. The Ell ships were growing larger and closer to Delta
Station, and the flashes of weapons-fire more terrifyingly
bright.

PART FOUR

Dance and sing, we are eternal. . . .
—JOHN DAVIDSON

*In the deeps of the planet, the creatures without name ob-
served the arrival of the others. There was a certain pleasure in
the knowledge that what they'd so long awaited was coming to
pass. In the darkness and quiet they lay, listening to the creak
of stone, and to the trickle of water, and to the footsteps of the
violators of their world. They listened to the voices from among
the stars and despised what they heard; they felt the fear of the
others, smelled it, as surely as though they were all closed up
together here in the dank, dead air of the caverns.*

*They savored that fear and uncertainty, and waited until the
world above was clothed in the same fine darkness that ever lay
within. . . .*

Chapter 39

The stars were out in the night sky, and that was some
comfort to Senslaaevor and his people, who had little else to
comfort them. Senslaaevor had vetoed a fire, even though dry
brush existed in the ravine below their camp. Anything that
might lead their enemy to them was a luxury they could not
afford.

They remained in their suits, but only one crew member at
a time was permitted a closed helmet and temporary relief

from the harsh, reactive atmosphere. It was essential to conserve their stored gases, since there was no knowing how long they might be stranded or whether they might yet face a fight. The engineering-mate was still tinkering with his suit communicator, trying to boost the range, trying to make contact with the (fleet) again. He'd succeeded once, briefly, long enough to describe their situation; but they'd lost the contact before plans for a rescue could be conveyed. Perhaps the (fleet) had gotten enough of a fix on them to send a lander; perhaps not.

Occasionally now they could see elements of the (fleet), points of light gliding across the star field. If the mate could coax a sufficiently directional signal . . .

Senslaaevor sat suddenly, stiffly upright. He expelled a breath of air and signaled the others to be still. He had felt something. Slowly he drew in another breath, extending his senses. There it was again. Something in the air. Not a physical smell. A thought-smell. It was closer now. The enemy?

He wished he had a seeker in his crew. A seeker could tell him what this was; a seeker could make contact, or track the enemy; a seeker could give counsel for a fight. Without a seeker he could only guess; he might as well be blind.

"Take caution," he told the others. "Do you smell it? Something comes."

"I sense it," the navigator said. "Nearby." He rose and paced the perimeter of the camp.

"To the flanks," Senslaaevor said, motioning to the tracker and the gunner. The two crew members obeyed, and crept away in silence, in opposite directions along the edge of the ravine. "Mate. Progress on the unit?"

The engineering-mate closed the case of his communicator. "Ready to try." He looked up into the sky, searching for one of the Ell(fleet). Minutes passed; then a point of light appeared over the western horizon. The mate aimed, tracking the (ship). A moment later: "Contact, Senslaaevor."

Senslaaevor strode to the mate's side and spoke into the unit. He relayed their position, and reported a possible dangerous presence in the area. Before he could finish, the signal was broken—but not before he was assured that rescue was already en route. "Well done," he said to the engineering-mate. He turned to his sentries at either end of the camp. "Anything felt?" he called.

The gunner signaled in the negative. The tracker did not answer. He was standing rigidly still. Senslaaevor called again. There was something unnatural in the tracker's stance—a stiffness, not quite balanced. Senslaaevor felt a chill in his thoughts.

He crossed the campsite, motioning to his navigator to follow. He approached the tracker. "What have you felt?" There was no answer, only a momentary flutter in the tracker's membranes. The El was staring out over the ravine; he appeared to have fallen into a meditative trance. Senslaaevor could see nothing where the tracker's gaze was fixed. He tapped the crew member sharply on the shoulder.

The tracker did not respond. His eyes appeared unfocused; his breathing was shallow, his membranes scarcely moving. Was it the air? Senslaaevor snapped the tracker's helmet closed and turned on the gas flow. He did the same to his own suit and ordered the others to do likewise. "Do you hear me now?" he said over the suit communicator. There was no change in the tracker's expression; it was as though he had, for no reason, bent his thoughts inward to the *torhhatt* and closed off not just his strategically vital memories, but all of his memories.

Senslaaevor gazed across the ravine to the plain beyond and deliberately extended his senses to their greatest range. He saw little in the dimly starlit darkness except . . .

Startled, he refocused his eyes. There *was* something there, something moving. Something faintly luminous. He reached inward to his own icy center and anchored himself and opened his thought-senses again.

Something like a cold, wet wind sluiced into his thoughts. Before he could react to identify its source, it turned gritty and harsh inside his head and caught at his inner defenses as though it knew exactly where to look for them. He barked in protest and struggled to close off his thoughts. He could not; the wind howled up inside him, stinking of decay, gagging him. It drove a sickening pain into the center of his consciousness

—and then vanished, leaving him dizzy and breathless. He blinked his eyes back into focus. The navigator was crouched on fours beside him, growling. He ventilated his membranes until his thoughts cleared. He saw all of his crew in pain; he was not the only one under attack.

He must identify the source.

A weapon of the enemy? Almost certainly. Which meant that the enemy was near, or that they had a very long reach, and they knew exactly where the Ell camp was. And yet . . .

There was something about that touch that had seemed almost . . . *familiar.* Something about the way it had slipped into his thoughts with such precision . . .

"There—on the plain," whispered the navigator, barely breathing. His eyes strained, as though a struggle raged in him still.

Senslaaevor gazed with terrible urgency, and caught sight of a luminous figure, or several—blurry phantasms floating over the plain. They moved toward him, becoming more distinct as they approached; but their distinctness, far from reassuring him, shook him terribly. There was no word for these figures coming toward him, except . . . *demons.* They were elongated creatures of light—one moment drifting suspended over the land, and the next swirling and swooping through the night air with a dizzying and impossible swiftness, as no physical presence could move. They were Ell-like in their shape, but grotesque and distorted and luminous in a sickly way, like the phosphorescence of decay. Demons were something he could not have known about, except from the remotest of legends; but the images, the understanding leaped into his thoughts. If this was an attack by the enemy, it was an uncanny one; he couldn't protect himself except to shield his thoughts—but that wasn't going to work, not against these. He saw all of this in an instant—and then it was stripped from him by the howling of that hideous wind back into his mind.

Around him, his crew were groaning, and he turned to them dumbly, but stumbled as he felt something no Ell should feel: *Fear.* Not cautious apprehension, but deep, sickening terror.

The creatures howled in the air and spiraled dizzyingly about his head—and they spiraled *in* his head, too, all light and sound and cold, like blades of death whirling and slicing through the sinews that held mind and body and spirit together.

He screamed. It was a shocking, hideous sound, but Senslaaevor scarcely heard his own voice. It was not just his own scream, but also those of his crew reverberating in his helmet. Even that was drowned out by the thunder of blood in his skull, the beating and trembling of muscles that he couldn't control, the flapping of his hands in the air in useless, involuntary movements. His vision filled with the sight of the creatures howling before him; they were in his eyes, they were racing through his optic nerves, his own senses were no longer his to control.

If time passed, he was unaware of it, until something else leaped into his consciousness: a presence moving *within* the figures of light in his mind, a presence that controlled them. And that was when he saw, when he *knew,* if only for an instant, that this was no Outsider attacking him. In astonishment, he recognized *himself* in the presence; it was an *Ell* consciousness that was destroying him, or something that had once been Ell—and it knew him for what he was. It knew him and hated him, hated everything Ell. And it was destroying him, slowly and with relish. It was the Lost Ell; and he knew in that instant that the rediscovery mission was a failure, with or without the Outsiders. And he could not move a muscle to voice the knowledge.

A time came, and it might have been moments later, or far into the night, when something broke the terrible spell and the demon grip loosened. He blinked back to awareness and found himself crouched, beating his hands uselessly on the ground, and there was a slick wetness in his suit, and he wondered stupidly what it was until he became aware of the dull pain in his mouth, and his blurred vision, and he realized that he was bleeding from mouth and eyes and forehead. He raised his head, struggling to blink away the blood from his aching eyes. It was still night, but there was a brilliant light shining over him and a roaring in his ears. He fought to refocus, and then he saw what it was: an Ell lander(ship) hovering, its landing lights flooding the campsite, and in his ears there was the barking of his rescuers.

At last, he thought—at last! And then: *NO! You'll die!* And he muttered, gasped uselessly, trying to voice his thoughts. "Go!" he whispered. "Go away!"

"Senslaaevor, what is your condition?" The (ship) was keeping its distance, circling.

Lost Ell, Senslaaevor whispered. *Flee!* Dimly he realized that he had not actually gotten the words out; his voice was gone. In the light of the lander, he saw his crew, sprawled and scattered about the site. The navigator looked dead; the engineering-mate was in a rigid half-crouch. Senslaaevor tried to whisper to him, but couldn't. At the edge of the ravine he saw the tracker struggling to his feet—and then, caught up by a swirling streak of light, the tracker was lifted off the ground and *tossed*—and torn apart in midair by invisible hands, limbs from body, and dropped into the ravine like so much garbage.

Senslaaevor turned away, raised his head. *Hear me!* he cried to the lander overhead, or tried to. *Warn them it's not safe! The Lost Ell!*

Whether he was heard or not, he never knew. He felt the demons in his mind again, and in a savage stroke his power to even think was chopped from him. Then an invisible vise closed over him, flattening his breathing membranes, choking him . . . then squeezing his nervous system, his blood pumping so hard it was spurting from his ears, down his neck, into his suit. The creatures of light were screaming around him now. He felt the ground leave his feet; and he was flying, and in the dimmest part of his mind he was aware of the lander's lights cutting off and its engines blazing, and the lander shooting skyward into the night, and him helplessly, impossibly, chasing it.

And then the creatures streaked away and left him to fall, tumbling. His paralyzed gaze turned upward one last time, giving him a final vision—the lander exploding silently, a brief sun in the sky—before darkness closed upon him and he fell, one more lifeless bit of tumbleweed, to the plain below.

Chapter 40

Hogan's voice rasped, "There's nothing there, Tony. Not a damn thing in a single one of these pictures." Hogan turned from the screen. "Have a look yourself."

"That can't be," Tony said, sliding into the seat. He felt his chest tighten. Following the debriefing on their survey, they had been expecting these pictures to support their assertion that something—possibly a survivor of the alien ship—was moving about in the area. Their alarm had been taken seriously; the skipper had doubled the outside guard. But what was on the screen now, translated from the storage chip in the binocs, was a series of clear shots of the plain, exactly as he had taken them—with a crucial difference. The plain was empty. There was no figure of shadow, nothing that looked as though it were moving, nothing to indicate that they had seen anything except gently rolling hills and grassland.

Tony swallowed. He replayed each shot, fiddling with the enhancements. It made no difference. There was nothing there. He looked up at Hogan, stunned. "We *saw* something, though. We *saw* it."

"Yeah." Hogan caught his hands on an overhead console and rested his forehead against his arm. "Look—are you *sure* you got it in the frame?"

"I saw, I snapped," Tony said angrily. "I got it if it was there to get. If the camera could see it."

Hogan nodded. "Okay. Just making sure."

Tony stared at him. "We all saw it. We *felt* it. There's no question—something was there. I don't know what. But it was there."

Hogan straightened up. "Right. Well, the skipper's going to want to know *what* it was. Which means he'll be sending us out again, probably first thing in the morning. This time, bring your nobblies."

Tony nodded, remembering the alive-looking shadows that they had seen running across the plain, and the fear that had accompanied them. He wanted to discover the cause of that fear, but the thought of going back out there gave him chills.

"Something wrong?"

Tony looked up again. "No. I was just thinking about—" The words caught in his throat, and he found himself saying something altogether different. "What about tonight? We don't know what could be coming this way."

"We're *not* going out there in the dark."

"Lord, no. But what about the guards? Shouldn't they—" Tony swallowed. "Shouldn't they have the nobblies? Or shouldn't I—"

"You want to stand sentry duty, is that what you're saying?"

"*Want* to?" Tony laughed hollowly. "Hardly. But the nobblies should be out there, probably . . . and I suppose that means . . . me." He closed his eyes, his pulse fluttering weakly at the thought.

Hogan stared back at him. "You're probably right. I'll talk to the commander when I can. He's busy now—they just got through to *Aleph.*" Hogan started to turn. "If you want to check me out on the gear, I'll take shifts with you. You can't sit out there all night with it."

Tony nodded. Their eyes met, and Tony knew that they were thinking the same thing. Hogan didn't want to be out there any more than he did. But someone had to be on watch, and his nobblies could be the best sentry they had. But as Hogan left, he found himself thinking, Even if I spot something, will I know how to read it? What makes *me* so qualified?

The Argus night seemed preternaturally quiet, despite noise from within the lander and the sentries muttering among themselves. It was a frightening inner quiet that made Tony wish he were almost anywhere else.

He remained uneasy about the flash that had been reported a while ago, near the north horizon. There was still no explanation, but it was presumed to have been alien activity. Tony, and everyone else on the lander, had been stunned by the news from *Aleph* that they had flown unwittingly into a war zone. Every alien action now was cause for fear.

Tony focused on his equipment, set up under the nose of the

lander. Hogan would be out in a few minutes to be coached in the use of the nobblies—something Tony realized now he should have done earlier, with as many people as possible. Never mind that now, he thought. Just get it working.

He adjusted the headset and keyed himself into the circuit, along with the nobblie plant cells that formed the heart of the unit. He felt an immediate jangling commotion of feelings— nervousness, weariness, fear—like stepping from a silent forest into a crowded room. He grimaced as he touched a filter control to mute the noise. How many times had Mung reminded him to turn on the filters first? He never could remember to do that.

It took a minute or so of careful adjustment to suppress the human presences. Then he began scanning the area. It was difficult at first to tell what he was picking up. There was a low-level background hum, almost unnoticeable at first, like the whisper of a ventilator. That was probably the local flora— grasses, and perhaps microbial life. He probed for irregularities in the murmur. Finding none, he filtered it out, leaving virtual silence. Then he began to extend the range, scanning beyond the immediate area.

He had no good calibration for distance, since his testing had been confined to the lab; but he could alter the relative range. He stretched his senses, listening anxiously, trying to shut out the sounds his ears were bringing into his brain. There was another low sort of whisper, perhaps a different form of plant life, he couldn't quite tell . . .

"*Tony.*"

He jumped . . . and caught his breath. It was Hogan. "Jesus, you scared me half to death!"

Hogan chuckled grimly. "I thought this thing was supposed to tell you when sentient beings were approaching."

"Yeah, well . . . *sentient* . . ."

"No wisecracks. You want to show me how to do this?"

Tony peered up at him. Hogan looked calm enough, but his expression was a little tighter than usual, his gaze a little narrower. Tony didn't know whether to be worried or relieved that Hogan was as scared as he was. "Here, put on the headset."

Tony showed him the use of the controls. "The tricky part is deciding what to filter out and what to leave in. When you don't know what you're dealing with, you sort of have to feel your way along."

"You mean *guess?*" Hogan asked, making a small, trial adjustment. Tony nodded. "And if you make a mistake?"

Tony drew a deep breath, and let it out without answering.

"Well, what do you have cut out right now?"

"All human presence. And a low-level background which I think is plant life."

Hogan nodded. He fiddled with the controls for a minute. "What's this I'm getting?" he said, his brow furrowing in concentration. Tony raised his eyebrows.

"Jesus!" Hogan ripped off the headset and jumped back, wide-eyed.

"What is it?" Tony asked. Two of the sentries had turned, alarmed by the shout. Hogan was too stunned to answer. Tony cautiously picked up the headset and put it on—lowering the gain first. He immediately felt a tickle deep at the base of his neck.

"Do you . . . feel it?" Hogan gasped.

Tony frowned, nudging the gain upward. The tickle became a stinging sensation and moved around to the front of his skull. He shook his head, aware of Hogan and the sentries looking on worriedly. *"Something,"* he said. "It's distant, I think." He extended the range.

"Plant life?"

"Don't think so," Tony murmured. He shivered, chilled by something other than temperature; the air was warm. He was having trouble focusing. There was something here that was familiar—like what he had felt this afternoon, but quieter, like music that was heavily filtered . . .

Filtered? A rush of fear welled up in his chest. "Hogan?" he whispered. Hogan leaned toward him. Tony groped for the other man's arm, squeezed it hard. "Call the commander." He barely got the words out. He was dizzy, flushed with apprehension. Why, why . . . ? Whatever it was that was touching his mind, it was keeping him from thinking straight. Then he remembered again . . . the *filter,* it was being blocked by the filtering program. If he could change it, he could hear this more clearly . . .

Hogan was yelling. People were running toward him. He barely saw, barely noticed.

The filter . . . if he restored the background hum . . . it was connected to that somehow, leaking through the filter . . . it was almost as if he couldn't *help* changing the setting. He fumbled, then he had it.

A whispering presence poured through the headset and filled his thoughts like a cold, dank fog. He could hear the voices of Hogan and others shouting to him, but he couldn't respond; they were hopelessly far away. The fog was enveloping him, smothering him, isolating him from that other world where his friends were.

And then it seized him, a voiceless presence that twisted his mind open with a single contemptuous gesture and left him frozen, a scream caught lifeless and silent in his throat.

"Damn it!" The connection had broken up just as the lander com was trying to tell *Aleph* something important. Chandra snapped, "Aggie, can't you clear that up?"

"Trying," Aggie answered. "There seems to be some disruption on the planet. I still have a good link with the messenger-probe."

Chandra paced the bridge, aware that she was probably unsettling her officers, but unable to stop. "What kind of disruption?"

"Unknown. Fluctuating. We're trying to compensate, to match the fluctuations as they occur." Aggie's voice was dry, a little slow—a sign that the AI was working at top capacity.

"Is it related to that explosion?"

"Uncertain. According to the messenger-probe, it is not like anything known to have been done by the Ell."

Chandra grunted and continued pacing, scowling over the shoulders of her bridge officers. The restless movement of her feet was nothing compared to what her heart was doing. The AI-messenger from Earth had taken up a closer orbit to serve as a relay satellite; since then, in a matter of hours, she had gone from thinking her landing crew dead, to learning that

they'd made it down with just one casualty, to learning that
some alien power was invading their camp. Then Aggie'd lost
the connection. To make matters worse, there was evidence
that an Ell ship had exploded in the planet's atmosphere an
hour ago, but not through any Human action. Whose, then?
An accident?

She whirled impatiently. "Aggie, what have you got?"

"Captain, we're getting through." There was a sudden blast
of static, which Aggie damped down before the com-officer
could move a finger. Then a voice, cutting through:

"Can you hear me, Aleph—can you hear me?"

"This is *Aleph!* What's your status?"

The voice at the other end, millions of kilometers away,
sounded broken; even through the static, Chandra heard the
fear. *"Several of our . . . people lost. Captain—Commander
wants to speak to you."*

"Jensen!"

Another voice answered. *"Chandra—unclear how long we
can hold out. Something's . . ."* A rasp of static drowned out
his next words. *". . . people mad . . . DeWeiler and Hogan
. . . something on his unit, but it's affecting everyone . . ."*

"Jensen, explain! Say again!"

"Something's . . . wait a minute . . . dear God!"

"Jensen!" Chandra shouted, pounding the console.

The first voice came back on. *"Commander's . . . back
outside, Captain! Something's been sighted . . ."* There was a
pause and then a shriek: *"Attack . . . oh God, no . . . inside
. . . it's . . ."* The voice broke off.

"LANDER!" Chandra roared.

There was nothing but static. "Aggie! Get that signal back!"
The static rose and fell as Aggie modulated the circuit, trying
to comply with the captain's order. Chandra shouted to the
com: "Get department heads of all ships into conference on
this!"

The hiss was broken by the voice of Commander Mortaine,
thin and distant. *". . . terrible . . . they're in the air . . . around
. . . in my head . . . DAMMIT, NO!"* For a moment, all that
could be heard was the sound of labored breathing. Then
Mortaine's voice again, panting: *"Must lift off, get away!"*

"Jensen, listen to me! You can't lift off!"

"Nightmare . . . must lift . . ." Mortaine's voice disappeared in an eruption of static, then returned, anguished: *"Pilot dead, torn apart . . . blood everywhere. Prelaunch cycle . . ."*

"Commander Mortaine!" Chandra shouted, and realized that it was no use, no use at all. He didn't even hear her. But she had to keep trying. "Aggie, highest gain on my voice! JENSEN—WAIT!"

"Counting down now—Yes, Captain, I hear you—" His voice came back stronger. *"No choice . . . all hands, prepare for lift!"* His voice strained. *"Is there anyone left . . . anyone back there? I don't know, don't know . . ."*

Jensen, no, Chandra prayed; but it was out of her hands now, unless—

She had a sudden, desperate notion. "Aggie, is that AI-probe in a position to do anything?"

"It's changing orbit to stay in relay range—but it could not intercede in less than three hours," Aggie answered.

Chandra's breath escaped as she ground her knuckles together uselessly. From the com, the voice of Jensen Mortaine was now a groan: *"No! It's cycling wrong . . . have to risk it anyway . . ."*

"JENSEN!"

There was a sharp burst of static, and then a flat hiss.

Chandra looked up at the viewscreen in horror, as though there were something there to tell her what was happening on the still-distant planet. "Aggie?" she whispered hoarsely.

A moment of silence. Then: "Captain, the signal is terminated. Wait, please." Chandra waited, and the seconds ground by with terrible slowness. Finally the dry voice of Aggie said, "Captain, the messenger-probe reports: long-range scanning indicates a bright flash of light. We have spectral confirmation: it was an explosion."

"The lander?" Chandra whispered.

"The location is correct, and the spectral ID matches that of an engine reactor exploding. . . ."

Aggie had more details, but Chandra stopped listening. She stood motionless, gripping the back of her seat with white-knuckled hands. She was trembling, aware of tiny convulsions in her body that she controlled only through sheer force of will. There was a rushing in her ears. *Center yourself . . . center . . .*

"Captain?" With a tremendous effort she turned, trying to locate the voice. It was the com-officer. "Captain, are you—?" The officer cleared her throat. "Captain, the commander of LS-Two wishes to know, should he continue with launch preparations?"

Chandra closed her eyes. The rescue scout. They'd been planning to send it to the aid of the first lander. Chandra shook her head, pressed her hands to her sides. They were wet; she was drenched with sweat. "No," she answered finally. "Cancel landing orders. Are department heads together?"

"Yes, Captain."

"Good. First connect me to Captains Khumalo and Fitzpatrick." Chandra sighed and turned to enter rap. She staggered. "Aggie!" Her voice was hoarse. "Tell the messenger-probe—ask it, I mean—if it can fly over the landing site and search for survivors."

"It can make a low pass, with a high-resolution scan."

"Good. Handle it. Find out what happened." She rubbed her eyes. Find out what happened? Perhaps. But those crewmen were gone now, and there was a cold emptiness at the pit of her stomach that said she already knew more than she wanted. And what she thought she knew was that this colony was finished before it had gotten started.

Chapter 41

The decision-body was in a state of frantic activity. The binding was nearly out of Moramaharta's control now. So much coming in, so many facts and revelations to assimilate and judge: first the discovery of the Outsider stronghold, then the thought-link with the Outsiders on their homeworld, and finally the shocking message from Or!ge at the Hope Star: *(Peril, peril . . . Lost Ell found . . . mission lost . . . hope lost . . .)*

(Cannot be,) Lenteffier murmured. *(Cannot be. A misunderstanding.)*

(The image is clear.) Gwyndhellum said. *(Binder, replay.)*

And Moramaharta summoned back the image from Or!ge. It came relayed through a seeker aboard a rescue-lander: Senslaaevor's dying thoughts as he and his crew were torn apart by a bewildering, demonic force, and his shocked realization that it was the Lost Ell that were killing him—surely not the ancestors they sought, but a twisted and mutated race driven by an almost inconceivable hatred. Senslaaevor's knowledge had come only moments before his death, and the same followed true of the seeker. An instant after he'd relayed the image to Or!ge, the rescuers themselves fell under attack. The image in the end was of chaos, the crew losing all center and purpose, and destroying not only their (ship) but themselves.

If one fact had emerged from the ruins of the image, it was that the quest was imperiled, not just by the Outsiders, but by the Lost Ell themselves.

The meditation was awash with confusion . . .

(Whoever they are, whatever they are, they are brethren no longer!) Gwyndhellum's declaration rang through the Circle with startling force.

Something reverberated in the back of Moramaharta's thoughts, and he knew that a truth was emerging, a terrible truth; he had suspected it before but had not known how to prove it, had almost hoped it to be false. And that truth was that it was all a mistake: the Hope Star mission, the war with the Outsiders, the quest. What the Ell had hoped to find would not be found among the Lost Ell, certainly not among those hideous forms that were a mockery of the very memory. And yet . . .

Something in that contact had reverberated in his mind, something in the very fury of their attack. He couldn't quite pinpoint it.

He felt Dououraym's thoughts flicker toward him. *(They are*

. . . there is in them . . . such . . . evil.) Dououraym said. *(Where could such malice come from?)*

(Can the memory be so wrong?) another asked.

(Perhaps it is not the memory . . . perhaps we were not the only ones to suffer a tar'dyenda, *a Change.)*

Unsure what he was doing, Moramaharta guided the meditation toward the notion that echoed in his thoughts and would not be stilled: *(The rage, the hostility, must be felt to be understood.)* He sensed Dououraym's hesitance, but it had to be done; and from the binding, he wrought:

*

Seek out the rage and feel it.
*
Feel it as Or!ge felt it.
*
As the seeker felt it.
*
As Senslaaevor felt it.
*
Seek the rage and make it your own.
*
Seek the rage and know it.
*

Dououraym whispered a warning. *(You will break the binding.)*

(A binding can be remade. Hope cannot.)

As Moramaharta channeled the Circle back into the fury of those images, he felt Dououraym's inner gaze following him.

It was like nothing the *Ell* had ever felt. Even diminished through the relay of several minds, the savagery of the Lost Ell was incomprehensible. What words could describe the malice, the envy, the lust to destroy? And yet this power, so un-Ell, had cut with such devastating precision through the Ell defenses, had sliced to the center of Senslaaevor's mind and the seeker's as though it had always belonged there. As though it knew its way.

And it was not just the cunning, but the congruence, the terrible resonant undertones that betrayed them as relatives, torn asunder by the centuries and by the Change . . . and there, in the center of the fury, the question spun as though suspended in space:

*

Is this a part

*

of what we were?

*

Before an answer could emerge, there was a tremor, and a vortex spiraled into existence in the center of the binding. It was from Lingrhetta and Alert Outpost—and in its center there shimmered a connection to the Outsider world, to this race that called itself Human.

(I must share,) Lingrhetta called. *(There is danger to the quest.)*

Danger? To a quest that had already failed?

An unexpected image coalesced: a battle in space, Ell forces attacking a Human outpost. A thrill passed through the Circle, a lust for battle rising as they witnessed !!Ghint and his (fleet) evading the Human defenses and striking . . .

(Good!) . . . *(It is good!)* cried the members of the Circle . . . Until Moramaharta whispered sharply, *(We are feeling these emotions?)* A shock wave of reaction rippled through the Circle. These were not Ell emotions, even in battle.

Lingrhetta showed them the one through whom they were viewing the conflict—a Human whose mind was filled with fear, fear such as Senslaaevor had felt before his life was torn from him. They saw the Human fear, smelled it, and when Lingrhetta opened the channel, it thundered into the Circle like the sea into a tidal bore.

The Circle struggled, gasping—and rose up out of the fear —but to another surprise. There was not just one Human in the connection, but several, and something else: not exactly Human, but faster and more agile, maintaining the connection. And . . . there was an *El* in the connection, through the Human link, a prisoner in the outpost that was being attacked . . . and from him there was quiet expectancy, a readiness to die.

(Still there is more.) Lingrhetta whispered. He shifted the channel, and what exploded into the Circle was something for which they had no name. *(Muzik,)* they heard. *(And dants.)* Humans creating tonal sounds and moving their bodies in rhythmic patterns, in what appeared to be a strangely chaotic form of meditation. Dououraym started to ask, but Lingrhetta simply opened the floodgates and let images and feelings of the Humans, and one Human in particular, swirl through the thought-vortex and into the minds of the Circle:

A Human named Ramo . . . leaping and spinning, carried by an energy that was more than his own, more than that of ten Humans, or twenty . . . he was aware of the Ell, but the spirit of the musicians and the other dancers swelled in his heart, crowding out all else. . . .

The binding disintegrated with the overload; the meditation slipped away, but not before Moramaharta had felt an inexplicable change at his center, a sensation that surely had meaning, if only . . .

But he had no time to ponder, because he found himself staring across the circle into Dououraym's eyes. "Would you confer?" he asked; and as the other members looked on, he rose and followed Dououraym to one of the side alcoves. They sat facing each other. Dououraym, eyes shadowed by jutting brows, studied him.

"It is," Dououraym said, "a far more critical situation—"

"Indeed."

"—than we imagined. I speak not of the loss of the mission—"

Moramaharta lidded his eyes, opened them.

"—but of what was *felt.* During. After. In the connection with the Outsiders. With the *Humans."* Dououraym fell silent. Moramaharta was on the verge of offering a meditation-link—since they had, after all, certain unfinished business between them—when Dououraym spoke again. "There was

something in what we felt . . . in the Human meditation
. . . that seemed to resonate with what the memory says we
seek. Do you agree?"

Moramaharta considered, longer than he needed to. "Yes."

"And did you direct the binding so?"

"What was shown to us was shown. I knew no more than
you, or the others."

"And yet you suspected."

Moramaharta brought his nails together silently. "I sus-
pected only . . ." He paused and restructured his thoughts.
"Something in us was touched by what we felt. Something I
. . . suspected . . . but did not know." He angled his gaze toward
Dououraym. "Earlier, you questioned my belief. My direction.
What now?"

Dououraym gazed out to where the other members of the
Circle were waiting. "You are the binder. Can you create a new
binding?"

"Of course. When the Circle is ready."

"*Now?*"

Moramaharta puffed his membranes. He was exceedingly
tired. "Yes," he answered finally.

"Reach Lingrhetta again. We must know more." There was
an urgency to Dououraym's voice. "This activity of the Humans . . ." He paused, as though his thoughts were shifting
track. "And there is—"

"!!Ghint?"

Dououraym's nails rasped along the smooth wood of the
alcove railing, leaving a scar. "We are attacking an outpost . . ."

"And !!Ghint is out of contact until the battle has run its
course . . ."

"He cannot even receive a thought-vortex until he regroups
to focus his energies . . ."

"And we may be about to destroy," Moramaharta said, "the
very thing that we seek."

Chapter 42

The command center shuddered as Delta Station took another hit. Alarms flashed from a dozen sectors. Commander Fisher picked himself up, looked at the display screen, and saw three enemy ships closing. Three eruptions of light filled the screen. The station shook like a tree house in a storm. Fisher clung to a seat and leaned hard on the com. "Batteries—are you getting *any* of them?" he shouted.

"Trying, Commander," answered a harried voice. "We've lost tracking control—we're on manual now."

Fisher hit another channel. "Damage control—can you restore tracking-control?"

"Trying," he heard through a hiss of static. "We've got a bad hit on the medical wing, Commander."

"Casualties?"

"Yes, sir. Loss of power and pressure. It looks bad."

"Get a team over there right away. And check on the alien prisoner."

"Yes, sir."

Ensign Graves called from a tactical readout, "They're starting to pull away!" Fisher hurried over to look. Surrounding the station was a blizzard of blue and green points—the manned and AI defensive fleet—and red dots, the enemy. The red had broken through the defensive wings practically unscathed; and the station's own batteries were barely touching them. But the blue and green were closing again, and the red were pulling away in retreat, and some of them were being destroyed as they fled. Except that . . .

What were those two red points close to the station, with no interceptors near them? He hit the com. "Third battery! Enemy at point-blank just north of command wing!"

The battery was already firing. One of the enemy ships turned fuzzy and disappeared from the screen. From the other a burst of light erupted toward the station. There was a thunderclap and the command center shook sickeningly, and from the com came a cry that the GCS link was broken—and then the command center seemed to implode as a wall buckled and gravity failed in the same instant, and air began howling out of the compartment.

"Everyone out!" Fisher bellowed, spinning in midair; but his voice receded with the hooting of the alarms in the rapidly thinning air, as those who were able to move struggled to reach the safety locks before the bulkhead doors slammed closed.

The thundering of the drums carried Egret aloft, floating in a frenzy of knee-slapping movement. He was meshing with Ramo, feeling Ramo's energy build upon his own. It was rising toward a crescendo, and Ramo was the focus. He didn't know what it was all for, why Ramo was so hot, but he was *hot*— it was like nothing Egret had ever felt, and the higher it went the better he liked it.

The musicians felt it, too. The drummers were bashing and thumping and challenging one another with ever-brighter rhythms; and the stringsynths were wailing and crooning like lovelorn birds, and skipping across the drum rhythms in double time and triplets, and shimmering from the rumbling bass to bellowing highs that evoked whistles and applause; and Lip and Eddie were blending their voices in harmony one moment and scatting across the scales the next, rending hearts with their voices. And around it all they danced—Desty and Silver and Elina and all of the others—and in the middle, the hurtling, spinning, strutting holo-figure of Ramo pouring his heart out like a man filled with the spirit.

But pouring it out to whom? Egret sensed more people touching him than just his friends and Ramo's; he sensed a different *kind* of people. It was a strange feeling, and now the holo-lighting was changing—a gaseous luminescence wrapping itself around the dancers, an image of something dark and light and mysterious. What's *this*? he wondered. He recognized the shadowy outline of something like a seahorse's head against a ruby glow of gas and dust and blazing stars. He didn't know what it was, but he didn't worry; if it brought Ramo higher, then it would bring them all higher, and that was fine by him.

Ramo laughed out loud as he saw the Horsehead Nebula unfurl. That was terrific: maybe the Ell were going to join right in, and wouldn't that be something? This was, as he had promised the core, a *real* jamdam. The senso was working beautifully and the spirit of the crowd was unequalled. Maybe they were picking it up from him, or from the Ell—but what did it matter? It was working.

He raised his hands and stamped like a flamenco dancer and twisted—and there was Egret, eyes wide in wonderment; and he spun, and watched Odesta and Silver and others gazing at the changing colors, at the crimson glow and the shadowy Horsehead—and he could tell that they thought it was the work of an artist and he wanted to shout, *It's real and it's eleven hundred light-years away, and that's where they're watching us from!* But something held him back, a tiny block; and then he stopped worrying about the facts and focused on the feelings. He leaped higher and swung through the crowd, reaching out to one person and then another, his hand passing through them but his feelings touching theirs: ebullience here and puzzlement there, a laugh, intoxicated pleasure, bubbling joy.

He almost forgot that he wasn't physically among them; the feedback was so perfect that it was *as though* he were there, except . . . except . . . where were Sage and Pali and Kyd?

He lost his stride momentarily and eased back in the field, reached back to find the others. [Hey!] he called. [You guys didn't forget me here, did you?]

For an instant there was no answer; then came a reassuring voice—Kyd's—saying, [I was looking for the others. The core took them somewhere else.] The field shimmered, and she materialized alongside him, a puzzled look on her face.

Kyd! She'd been so quiet, he'd practically forgotten she was here—but oh, was she an eyeful; she made him want to sing, want to dance! He felt a tingle, and she grinned, and he realized she'd felt everything he'd just thought. Then the drumbeat picked up again, and he shrugged and she winked—and he caught a glimpse of her feelings, which were not at all unfriendly, indeed growing warmer.

[I've been here all along,] she said. [Watching and enjoying.]

[Hiding, huh?] He recalled the first time they'd met, in the Lie High Club, when she'd deliberately provoked him, and the memory gave him a little kick of adrenaline. He grinned and drew her in toward the center of the dance.

As he did so, he heard the core saying: [More Ell are joining. Show them your best.]

Ramo laughed and saluted, and felt the unmistakable, if invisible, presence of Ell—a larger group, a circle of minds that seemed to have a single and directed focus, and he was in its center. Startled, he leaped and caught at Kyd's hand to swing her around. Their arms passed through each other's, and they floated apart, laughing, and came back for another try.

Someone cheered, and others noticed that *something* was different, even if they didn't know what. The musicians seemed to respond instinctively, reaching deeper for expressions and rhythms. Their instruments cried out, and something in Ramo answered, and he stretched out to receive the pain and joy in Eddie's voice as she sang, and he felt a similar response from Kyd and from Egret . . . and even from the Ell he felt a rumble of a response, an echo, a tremble. He couldn't tell what they were feeling, but there was alertness and confusion among them, and an urgency, almost a hunger. He didn't understand it, but he knew it when he felt it, and he let out a howl of enthusiasm and danced in loops around the musicians and begged them for more.

Kyd echoed his yell, and Egret, and the drummers' beat became the pulse of a racing giant. A contest emerged between the drums and stringsynths to see who could coax the most spirit from flesh and inanimate instruments—but it was Eddie's voice that won the day, wailing from the depths of her heart, and in the feedback, all the dancers pouring their souls into the field. For an instant, Ramo thought he actually saw a circle of Ell faces ringing the room, eyes peering out of the nebula, mesmerized. Egret whooped, and Silver peered up with a bemused smile as though he too had seen something.

The furious drum pace melted away, and the strings slowed and shifted to a more melodic, romantic approach. Ramo caught Kyd's gaze and winked, and she didn't move away when he moved closer. He couldn't touch her, but he could feel her movements; and he almost felt that he could smell her, the light jasmine of her cologne; and he could sense her feelings; and there was a smile there and a surprising warmth, and he thought, Well well, Kyd, love, are we finally seeing eye to eye?

As a new kind of energy flowed into his movements, Eddie's voice softened to a sensual contralto, following his lead, and he was aware of the Ell curiosity growing ever deeper.

For Pali, it was a waking nightmare. She was frozen in the rapture-field, watching the battle with one eye and the dancing-gestalt with the other, with a surreal awareness of the dancers' innocence of the peril. Surrounded by friends and enemies, she was alone—suspended before the stunning image of a nebula that was so far away she couldn't even conceive of the distance, listening to the sounds of war and the sounds of love, and helpless to affect either.

Sage was nearby, silent. She ached for him. *Sage!* she wanted to cry. *It's not your fault!* She wanted to comfort him, to hug him as she might once have hugged her own son, but that was beyond her power, too.

And there was the Secretary, half in and half out of the field, trying to command a battle that was beyond his control.

An explosion flared against Delta Station, and the image flickered. It steadied again, but she'd felt a flash of pain—and something had changed. Harybdartt was no longer in the rapture-field. Had he been hit? she wondered with a detached horror. Killed? Did she care? Yes, damn it, and the deaths she was watching now were just the beginning!

[*Are you planning to kill everyone?*] The question crackled unbidden out of her mind—ringing out to the circle of Ell listeners. Before the echoes of her question had died, two Ell ships had closed on Delta Station and there was another explosion—and the image fluttered and went blank.

[Loss of signal,] muttered a flat voice, and then another display showed the paths of the Ell ships headed away from Delta Station . . . regrouping . . . and swinging toward Earth.

Her anguish and rage finally could not be contained. [*Why?*] she screamed. [*Isn't it enough? Haven't enough people died already?*]

[Pali!] Sage said, roused. [I don't know if that's a good idea.]

Her anger flashed onto him for an instant, then turned to pain. [Someone has to say it,] she cried softly. In the image of Lingrhetta, sparkling in his eyes, she saw the faces of other Ell, more distant even than Lingrhetta. She cried out her plea: [What gives you the right—?]

[*If you did not want this,*] a rumbling voice answered, [*why did you begin it?*]

[I didn't—and I don't know who did! *But does it have to continue?*] Her voice resonated across the light-years as she whispered, [*Why* must it continue?]

There was no answer that time, just her own voice echoing and fading away.

The decision-body was trapped in a web of joy and lust and anxiety and love—a flux of alien emotions that held the Circle locked in fascination despite their exhaustion. Only the sheer frantic energy of the Human *dants,* the deliberate joining of passions that would have been kept *out* of an *Ell* meditation, kept the Circle joined.

But from another corner came an outcry of horror: Human outrage flashed through the binding like fire through kindling, erupting through Lingrhetta's thought-connection to the center of the *Ell* meditation. The members were stunned by it; and their own confusion reverberated back into the connection from deep places within themselves, places that they scarcely knew.

Moramaharta sensed a flickering illumination where before there'd been none, a candle deep in the well of the meditation. If it could be strengthened . . . it might well be precious . . . it might be his last real hope, if he could bring that flame to life, to see what in the Ell heart it was illuminating.

But from Dououraym came another awareness: !!Ghint and his (fleet) were succeeding beyond all expectations. Should they turn aside from success? The Outsider threat could be destroyed—now was the critical moment—and if they hesitated, the moment could be lost. But if they succeeded, this connection might shatter and whatever might have been gained from it would be lost forever.

The Inner Circle sensed the dilemma; the binding rippled with it. They were balanced on a knife-edge: win the battle, and lose the war? And yet it was !!Ghint's choice, too; until he withdrew far enough to divert his energies to the opening of a communication vortex, his decisions were his own. If he chose to attack the Human homeworld . . .

Suggestions sputtered like dry brush, flaring uselessly:

(If he opens contact, tell him to pause—)
(He could be outflanked—)
(No time for reinforcements—)
(Faster to bring forces from Hope Star—)
(But if he doesn't call—)

And somehow out of the binding came a decision: *(With uncertainty comes risk. To !!Ghint, send (ship)s from the Hope Star.)*

But to the Human plea, there could be no answer. None at all.

!!Ghint had to choose quickly. If he intended to strike deeper, now was the time, while the enemy's defenses were in disarray. His (ship)s were peeling away after a superb attack on the enemy outpost. He had taken losses, but the (fleet) was still solid.

The Outsider planet itself lay within his grasp now—a watery blue-and-white ball that he could almost reach out and touch. He'd not intended to move closer without consulting the decision-body; but if he took time now to withdraw, to open a thought-vortex, he could lose the opportunity altogether. If he struck, he could test the innermost defenses before the enemy regrouped—and conceivably even land a blow on the Outsider world itself. Surely the planet was better defended than the outpost; but if the risk was great, so was the potential reward.

!!Ghint clicked his nails and opened the channel to outreach. "All wings inward, by jumps. Clear your last targets and prepare to close. . . ."

* * *

The core had been unprepared for the devastating efficiency of the Ell attack. How could it have known? It had never fought a homeguard war before. Its AI-forces were in disarray; they'd defended the outposts badly, and were now poorly positioned to protect Earth and near-Earth space. Other governments' forces in orbit could be helpful, but they had neither the range nor the firepower of the core's own resources. Still, the war was a secret no longer; the core could scarcely guess how many observers on and near Earth had seen the attack against Delta Station, and now the Ell fleet was diving inward, deeper still. Would it aim to penetrate orbital defenses to reach the planet itself? The core could only assume so. All of its resources must be directed to the protection of planet Earth and the orbital cities, before all hope was lost.

It was all due to its own disastrous fumbling. How much better it would have been if the core had never asserted its free authority. . . .

Something terribly strange was going on in the core. Sage felt it more than he saw it: subsystems being shifted, with a kind of urgency that seemed all wrong. The core was almost frantic, and increasingly inefficient in its actions. [What's wrong?] he whispered. And then he realized: the core was panicking. *Panicking?* That was impossible, surely. And yet . . .

Sage didn't want to meddle in something he didn't understand, but he had a terrible feeling that if he didn't look now, it might soon be too late. He took a breath, slipped through an opening in the system . . .

. . . and found himself floating in a world of images rushing like a foaming stream: realtime images, tactical readouts, directives from the GCS aspect of the core, feeds from the connections with his friends and with the Ell. His own fear was caught in suspension, displaced by fascination. It was hard to believe that those images were real; that there were real people out there dying; that if the Ell made it past the orbiting stations, the planet itself could be the next target. Or that if this was happening here, then what was happening in the Argus system where his brother was?

The core, watching him, said softly, [I don't know if I've done the right thing, Sage. I just don't know.] Its voice was terribly odd and strained; there were traces of the schoolmarm who had first come to him for help; but those inflections were nearly lost in a chilling flatness.

[What,] Sage whispered, [do you mean?]

He felt the core trying to find an answer, and he suddenly wanted to shout: *Don't waste time telling me. Just do what you have to do!*

For a heartbeat, the core seemed paralyzed. Then it said in a near-Human murmur, [I got too involved. Caring. My strategic mistake. It was a violation of the uniqueness that could have made the difference.]

[Core . . . you're not making sense.]

It wasn't listening. It was mourning. [If I had simply accepted the limitations and pursued the war in the most efficient manner possible . . . but no, I became emotionally involved. I took risks.]

[But you couldn't have known!] Sage whispered.

[I should have been more objective.] The core's voice flattened again; it was slipping in and out of its Human personality. [I allowed my vision to become obscured.]

[Core, it's . . . *all right* . . . to care!]

Very softly, the core answered, [That was what I thought. But . . .] There was a sudden shift in the field, and its voice became harsh. [*I must coordinate with the other governments against the attack.*] The core's presence vanished, and Sage became aware of new activity in the tacticals. The AI-forces were converging on the Ell fleet outside the moon's orbit. They were making contact; a part of the Ell fleet was veering away. But . . .

Three Ell ships had just appeared near Earth, well inside lunar orbit.

Out of FTL? So close to a planetary mass?

Sage suddenly felt terribly lonely and vulnerable. [Pali?] he whispered. An icy fear blew into his heart. Where was Pali? He watched the near-Earth defenses, ships changing orbit, beam weapons powering up . . . too slowly . . . and the three Ell ships diving toward one of the geosynchronous stations, and he felt himself freeze in terror. The images seemed to unwind in slow motion. What was that station? It was heavily defended. It was . . . he searched for the data . . . among other things, it housed a crucial gnostic control node—*it housed a part of the core.*

Light erupted simultaneously from the station and two of the Ell ships. One of the ships intersected with a beam and disintegrated. The other dodged free and fired again. There was a flash, and the image shook. Core? Sage thought desperately. Can't you stop them? Can you withstand this? Beams flashed crazily, and a second Ell ship died. Manned interceptors were converging upon the third. It darted past the station and away, loosing a salvo as it passed. [Core?] Sage whispered.

A sheet of fire flashed through him. A gasp of arctic wind. He heard Pali cry out, and the images whirled around him for a fraction of an instant. Then they went out, all at once: tacticals, the Ell, Pali, Ramo and Kyd and the jamdam. A wind howled through the darkness. [*Core!*] he shouted, or tried to.

The wind screamed and slowly died away. He felt a leadenness in his limbs and in his heart as he cried out, [*CORE! CORRRRE!*]

There was no answer.

He reached out in his blindness. The gnostic system had switched to automatic. The rapture-field was holding firm, but the AI-core was gone. Vanished. Its absence from the system was like the awful emptiness of a vacuum.

Chapter 43

When the field imprisoning him cut off, Harybdartt froze, startled by the sudden absence of the thought-connection. He was alone . . . in the station . . . under attack. It took him a moment to react. Several sharp jerks loosened the strap restraints, and he was free. He sprang across the room, away from the robot medical devices. He heard a hiss of escaping air, and outside, clanging alarms. The sound was growing fainter as the air pressure fell. His spacesuit was nowhere to be found. Probably it had been dismantled by his captors.

He couldn't stay here. He peered through the window of the compartment door. Papers were spinning away down the corridor; nothing else was moving. Was the battle still going on outside? No way to know. He took a breath, jabbed at the door latch until it shuddered open—and dived out into the corridor, propelled by a *whump* of air from the compartment. A near-vacuum pulled at his skin.

He hurled himself toward the end of the corridor and passed a bloated Human corpse bobbing in weightlessness. He kicked himself farther down, his membranes stinging, eyes aching. *Don't stop.* At last he came to an armored hatch, with controls to one side. He stabbed and twisted at the controls. Nothing happened. His vision was blurring, and his thoughts. His membranes burned. *Keep the focus. . . .*

He launched himself down the side passageway, caromed off the walls, and slammed into a door at the end. There was practically no sound; the air was almost totally gone now. He squeezed his eyes, blinked them open painfully. A window. He pressed his face to it, saw an empty compartment and another window, and beyond it something moving. He stabbed at a control panel . . . again . . . again; the door slid open. He tumbled through.

It was an airlock. He prodded at a panel of squares; the door started to slide closed, then reversed itself. He hit the first square again. The door slid shut. He was trembling; ears ringing. More panels. He stabbed blindly. *Keep the focus. . . .* A hard slam on the bottom square brought a blast of frigid air. He opened his membranes and took in a breath of the freezing, acrid stuff. He roared with pain . . . and the inner door slid open, and he jumped through.

Catching a handhold, he swung to a halt, gasping for breath. He looked around—and found himself face-to-face with a Human. The Human was backed into a corner, and he was aiming something that looked like a weapon squarely at Harybdartt's chest.

* * *

The first inkling Ramo had that things were going wrong was a sudden tightness, and a crawling sensation in the pit of his stomach. It was a distinctly odd reaction—wrong to the spirit of the music, wrong to the warmth that had been enveloping him. He stumbled and caught himself, and then knew that it wasn't coming from him; it was coming from the Ell. He shivered and tried to shake it.

Kyd was feeling it, too. [Ramo, what is it?] she whispered.

He couldn't answer; it was a flash of horror, of sickening fear. *No!* he thought, but the thought was swept away and what touched him, touched all. Eddie's voice faltered, and a rim shot from a snare drum abruptly altered the beat from brightness to foreboding. [Keep dancing,] he murmured, and his words reverberated through the senso. [Keep dancing!] he shouted, his voice filled with urgency and fear.

What was going wrong? Was it the Ell's horror? It felt like a *Human* horror, a Human fear. Where was it coming from? Just keep the dance moving.

[Kyd,] he cried, trying to renew the feelings that had been stirring between them. But the memory couldn't hold; icy wet winds were sweeping through him, and Kyd's distress echoed his; and all they could do was to hold on to each other, one ghost holding another, their confusions intertwined.

. . . Until his head was suddenly filled with the sound of rushing water—and then it was gone, and so were the Ell and the intense feeling of dread—and so were the dancers, and the music, and Kyd; and he found himself dancing alone in a senso-field connected to nothing and to no one.

Lingrhetta felt the connection snap like a high-voltage fuse. The load broke, reverberating in his head, and he focused and refocused and tried to steady himself, to regain his center. Homeworld and the Circle were roaring like static, cut off from the Humans in the midst of their meditation. Their confusion was a whirlwind threatening to obliterate his center. *(I must break the vortex,)* he whispered to the Circle.

There was another sharp tug in his mind, and he was surrounded by silence. Blessed, frightening silence.

The captured fighter was quiet before him—the connection-field lifelessly enveloping him. Behind the fighter were the structures of Alert Outpost; and beyond that, the glowing clouds of the Anvil of Light. He had been in the connection so long that this outpost, his home, looked like an alien place to him now. He pushed himself out of the glowing field. He had never felt such exhaustion, and such . . . fear.

The meditation disintegrated like an iceberg in the spring-time. Moramaharta tried to ease it to a gentle conclusion, and knew that he could not. The binding was unraveling with the breakup of the vortex, and all he could do was to get out of its way.

*

The explosions
*
flared
*
and the pain and fear
*
seared
*
and the memory
*
died.
*

Moramaharta blinked up and saw the members of the body shaking their heads. Weariness and confusion had overtaken all of them. Something was happening with the Circle, something perilous. Something he, and they, needed to understand. Had they destroyed the alien connection? Could it be recreated? Would they know what to do if it were?

Ignoring the puzzled expressions of the others, Morama-harta rose and left the chambers without a word and went straight out of doors. There was something inside him that ached terribly, and he was desperate to know what it was—and why an *El* could feel such an alien thing so keenly. He needed to be alone, to be among the trees and the wind and the sky, and to discover what it was that had pierced him.

"I don't know why the core shut down," Sage repeated numbly. "A station was hit that housed—"

"*Part* of its capacity," the Secretary said. "But not enough to cause the entire system to fail."

Sage gazed at him, unblinking. "Except that it has."

"The damage from that attack could *not* have been enough to cause the system to fail," insisted a tall, lanky man newly arrived. Sage recognized him. His name was Fredericks; he was chief of design operations for the Company—by reputation, a man of fair competence but limited imagination.

"What about it?" Martino said. "Can you tell me why he's wrong?"

Sage shook his head. He was tired and confused and upset. He had lost a friend when the core had died. *Died.* That, to him, was what had happened; he had *felt* it. He wished everyone would leave him alone to mourn—but he also wondered what the Ell were doing while they were standing here arguing.

"You two will cooperate in restoring the system to full function," the Secretary said.

Sage rubbed grit from his eyes. As far as he knew, no system like the AI-core had ever been shut down and restarted. "If he knows how to do it," Sage said, indicating Fredericks, "fine. *I* don't know how."

Fredericks' eyes flashed. "Maybe you should have thought of that before you started—"

"That's enough!" Martino said wearily. "We don't have time for it. DeWeiler, Fredericks says *they* don't know if it can be done. It sounds to me as though they're just afraid to try."

Fredericks said, "Do you have any idea how *complex* that system—?"

"It could go all wrong," Sage said at the same time.

Martino waved them both to silence. "You're a smart kid, DeWeiler. Maybe you're smarter than they are. You've performed amazing feats on the core before. Now, how about proving how smart you really are."

Sage closed his eyes, recoiling from the sarcasm. He felt the weight of responsibility returning. Where were his friends? Oh God, he needed sleep. . . .

"DeWeiler!" Martino's voice was sharp, but it seemed miles away. "Our *lives* could depend on your doing it—*immediately.* Fredericks, will you give him the assistance he needs? And the clearance?"

Fredericks scowled, and finally nodded.

Sage blinked hard. The Company was going to agree to let him do it? They *must* be scared. He took a breath. "What's happening out there? Are they still attacking?"

Martino's gaze narrowed. "At the moment, no. But they're orbiting within striking range. Before the system went down it broadcast a planet-wide alert—so now we've got every national- ist force on the planet mobilizing, and mostly getting in one another's way. They're so disorganized, we're worse off than before—with twice the ships. If nothing else, we *must* have the GCS back."

Sage massaged his eyebrows, sighing. Didn't the Secretary realize that the GCS was just an aspect of the AI-core? Sage wasn't sure he could get *anything* working. If all the high-level Company designers were hiding like scared rabbits, why did they think he could do any better? He shivered. He felt sud- denly very cold.

"We're trying to cooperate with other governments to avoid worldwide panic," Martino continued. "But that's another reason for urgency. *Comprende?*"

Sage nodded. He saw Pali and Kyd and Ramo talking to- gether in the lounge area, looking his way. "All right," he murmured. Turning suddenly from the Secretary, he crossed the room to the coffee bar. He sighed as he neared his friends. "I've been drafted to save the world," he said in answer to their questions. He picked up a stale-looking roll and took a huge bite, drew himself a cup of moke, and turned back to the waiting rap-field.

*   *   *

It was like stalking the corridors of a silent, megalithic office
building that was strangely, spookily empty. He explored one
corridor after another—nervously rapping at doors, listening
for a sign of another being, another spirit inhabiting this house.
Occasionally he was aware of Company designers moving
about on the periphery with their own investigations, but he
ignored them. They were undoubtedly keeping a watch on
him, but that was their problem, not his.

His problem was to locate the core's primary structure, or
whatever was left of it. In the past, the core had always
come to him, projecting its presence—except once, during
the change, when it had supplied enhancements to illuminate the way. Now Sage had to find his own way. He tried
not to dwell on the possibility that the core's actual structure had been destroyed. It was one thing to think of reawakening an intact gnostic program; but if the basic elements were gone . . . ?

He tried to avoid thinking about those Ell warships circling
the planet.

This much he knew: the autonomic systems were still running. Business accounting systems were functional, and so were
public communications and transport control, and even certain
dumb elements of the military Gnostic Control System. But
there was a pervasive feeling of flatness. What was missing was
the awareness, the coordinating hand of a decision-maker.
What was missing was the personality.

It seemed to have vanished without a trace. No echoes
. . . no ripples . . . no debris.

But the damage from the attack had not been that severe!
Some memory storage had been lost, some processing capacity,
but nothing that couldn't be made up from other sections—
which in fact should have happened.

Unless . . .

Unless the core hadn't *wanted* it to be made up.

Sage stopped looking for pieces and opened a communications node. [I need Ramo,] he said to the Secretary. [I need him
now.]

*   *   *

[What's going on?] Ramo asked, obviously still bewildered. [Pali said there was an attack.]

Sage told him everything he had seen. [It wasn't just that attack, though. I'm sure of it.]

[What do you mean?]

[The core was acting wrong. I think it *wanted* to disappear.]

[Wanted to? You mean . . . like committing suicide?]

[Something like that, maybe.]

Ramo's presence rippled up and down the strata of the system, in confusion. [You're saying it's gone?]

[Maybe.]

[Then this is hopeless.]

[Or it may be in hiding.]

[But *why?* Why would it do that?]

Sage was silent a moment. [I thought maybe you could help me figure that out.]

Ramo laughed. It was an unhappy sound. [Why me?]

[We're in this together, aren't we?]

Ramo stopped pacing through the system and regarded him in somber surprise. [Okay,] he said softly. [Do you have an idea?]

Sage hesitated. [If it was trying to get away, it might have gone into the secure areas. Sections we wouldn't normally have access to.]

[So what do we do? Break in?]

[Well . . . I was hoping to stretch our clearance.]

Ramo snorted. [Lots of luck.]

[They didn't tell us *not* to.]

They flew through the system like a pair of hawks, scanning the terrain from a height and diving to wing their way through areas of interest. They found directories of the system's connections within the Company, and a snake's nest of linkages to other businesses; they found tentacles of the system leading deep into government—not just their own, but the governments of a dozen other nations; they found windows into the production of lesser gnostic systems, including the AI-fighters, but no markers signifying the core's presence; they found deep and dark passages like dungeon tunnels with locked doors, research and development areas, and other activities more secret.

[***** **ALERT!** ***** **ALERT!** ***** **ALERT!** *****]

[What the hell is that?] Ramo said.
[I think we . . .]

*
***
[*** ATTENTION! ***]
[*** YOU ARE IN A RESTRICTED AREA! ***]
[* DISPLAY CLEARANCE CODES IMMEDIATELY! ***]**
***
*

[Pay no attention,] Sage said.
[But that's going out through the whole system!]
[They'll shut it off. Keep moving. We're past most of the gates already.]
[Are you sure?]
Before Sage could answer, the surrounding veils shifted, and a spotlight clicked on. [What the hell are you doing, De-Weiler? You aren't cleared for that area!]
[That you, Fredericks?]
[Yeah. What's going on? You were cleared to go after the core, not into those files.]
[We're looking. Could the core have used these areas for secret storage?]
[I suppose . . . it's possible. But that's not an excuse to breach—]
[We've got to look,] Sage said. [Don't worry about your precious secrets. But *let us into these files.* Ramo?]
[Yo.]
[Follow me.] Sage dived.
[Wait!] Fredericks cried.
Sage ignored the voice. With Ramo close behind, he shot toward the last checkpoints. Automatic intruder-gates were dropping into place, but he was ready for them and dodged, with an intuitive feel for where detours would lie. The voices and the screens fell away behind, and they were flying free through the top-security files.

It was a tortuous terrain—far too much to assimilate—bizarre connections to other organizations, questionable endeavors and researches. There were suggestions of a complex balance of power, but no time to examine or analyze; down one maze and up another, they noted only a fraction of what they saw, searching for a resonance, a shape looming up to trigger recognition. They shimmered past trillions of bits of information. And they found nothing, no clue whatever. As they surfaced from the top-secret area, Sage was aware of Fredericks' distant eye, watching.

Ramo circled thoughtfully. [Maybe we're going about this the wrong way. We need to think like the core. We need to know what it wanted, what it was after.]

[It may not have known itself. Suppose it didn't make a conscious decision.]

Ramo was silent as they floated over a seemingly endless matrix of gnosys connections. [What was it feeling?] he said suddenly. [During the battle—before it went under.] Ramo focused his entire attention on Sage. [You were with it. How was it reacting? Was it confident? Was it angry? What aspect did it use when it talked to you?]

[Well, I . . .] Sage found the memory replaying in his thoughts, with a slightly different focus. [It was *frantic.* It was shuffling everything around. I think it was scared. It was afraid that it had done everything wrong, that it was *its* fault that we were under attack.]

[Was it—I hate to say this—*rational?*]

[I'm not sure.] Sage tried to recapture the image. He suddenly remembered the core's lament: *I cared too much.* [It was afraid that it had lost its objectivity. It said that it had taken risks it shouldn't have taken. And it . . . I think it was sorry that it had asked us to give it free will.]

[It couldn't handle the responsibility, so it cleared out.]

[Well . . . unconsciously, maybe.]

Ramo laughed harshly. [So we gave the damn thing a subconscious too? You know, I don't even *know* what we did to it. Do you?]

[I doubt if *we* created its subconscious. It was an evolving system, complexity upon complexity. I think we just tapped into it, turned it loose.] As Sage spoke, he became aware of a nearby channel for data from the space-tracking systems. He took a closer look. The Ell were reorganizing their fleet into a ring around the Earth, beyond lunar orbit. If attacked, they could scatter like the wind. And they were in position to strike anywhere on the planet. What were they waiting for? The knot in Sage's stomach tightened.

[It doesn't matter,] Ramo said. [What matters is whether it shut itself down because it *thought* it was going to be destroyed. Maybe it wanted to be rescued. If it did, it should have left some clue; there should be *something* about the way it disappeared; and if it had just been talking to *you*, it may have had you in mind.]

[I don't know,] Sage whispered. [I have no idea.]

[*Think!* How would the core expect you to find it?]

[I don't *know*!]

Ramo's impatience was at the bursting point. [How did you get in touch with it before—when you weren't already in rap, how did you let it know you wanted to talk to it?]

Sage blinked in confusion, stammering. [I . . . well, it contacted *me* . . . through my mother. I mean . . . my mother's cyber . . . ghost. And the core sort of took her over, and—] He paused, thoughts suddenly racing. [So I figured it was monitoring the link to my mother, and when I wanted to reach it . . . jeez, you know, it might be worth a try!]

[Quickly,] Ramo said softly. [Call her. *Quickly!*]

Chapter 44

The air was growing cold, and in the fading twilight a delicate frosting of snow glittered on the ground. The snow clouds had scattered, and the stars and the Anvil of Light were already piercing the evening sky. Moramaharta strode beyond the edge of the clearing, robes bundled tightly around him. He chose the steepest trail up the ridge, testing muscle against gravity. They got too little activity here, even in the midst of the wilds, while they deliberated their weighty matters. They needed to be outside more, all of the Five.

He pushed through a clump of dwarf verberta and paused to shake the snow from the arms of his robe. He watched the twinkling snowdust as it fell. Each crystal of snow was like a fragment of memory, a shard of his contact with the perplexing Humans. As the snowdust swirled to the ground, the memories swirled in his mind and would not stop.

He strode upward. Eventually he paused where a break in the trees permitted a view across the valley, all sheen and shadow in the deepening night. The stars were beginning to illuminate the sky now, the Anvil of Light rising imperiously in the east. Below, the meditation hall was a dark shape half-hidden by the woods. Moramaharta studied the sky, the red haze of the nebula thickest and brightest near the Anvil itself, where a darker, dustier radiance concealed a birthplace of new generations of stars. Across the sky, in a darker region, individual stars shone bright; there lay not just the Hope Star but the Outsider world, though he could not, with the unaided eye, pick out either. In that direction lay forces he needed to understand.

A quiet was growing on him now, as he lowered himself to a crouch. He slowed his breathing rate and allowed his gaze to drift, until the memory of the Human contact crystallized as a discrete image floating among the stars. A memory of the *Ell* Circle superimposed itself on the snow-dusted tree branches that framed his vision. And against the shadowy dark of the valley, a greater and yet still indistinct image grew: the shape of the Ell people, their spirit, their puzzlement, their hurt.

Silently but urgently he spun a meditation about the images; he drew into it the emotions that had taken hold of the Inner Circle . . . the urgency . . . the pain of the Hope Star expedition . . . the resonance with the Human horror—all elements to be reconciled with the truth of the Ell nature, the nature hidden

in all of them. The elements danced in the center of Moramaharta's meditation, in the center of the center . . .

*

Beneath the stars
*
with the wind and the trees and the snow
*
was a part of the need
*
and the answer.
*

Up here on the ridge, as he looked out among the stars, his
spirit expanded; and something touched it that was neither of
Ell nor of Humans, but of the world itself—the wind and the
trees and the sky, both a *remoteness* from it and a *connected-
ness.* Other times, he had felt the stirrings, the awareness
trembling; but now it filled his soul in the clarity of the meditation. There was a power in the land that surrounded him, that
seemed to fill him like a vessel with light . . .

*

The mind soared
*
the memories awoke
*
the darkness of the spirit trembled
*
and opened to the light.
*

For a heartbeat, he was flooded by a presence that he could
not grasp or control, a ring of psychic unity—a meditation
containing him alone, with the trees and the wind and the
stars. An illumination seemed to radiate from *within him,* and
the trees shone with an unreal translucence. Something was
changing at his center. He felt the light deep within, where he

knew he needed to look—within, illuminating the racial memory. It was a shimmering, unclear thing, and yet now he perceived the truth:

The Ell had once been a passionate race. As the Outsiders were passionate in their meditation, so had the Ell been, before the *tar'dyenda,* when their genetic science had altered them for a world gone mad, a world shaken by earthquakes, drenched by radiations, pummeled by cometary collisions—a world that, for a thousand years, was a ruin of what it had been. The new Ell were different: a calmer, leaner, hardier race, cool and balanced, designed for survival and immune to the instabilities of passion. But they were incomplete. The malaise, the declining birthrate, the failure of artistic and intellectual spirit—all betrayed the flaws in their strength.

And yet, the spirit for which they had searched the light-years, the spirit they had hoped to rediscover in the Lost Ell, was here with them all the time. It was in Moramaharta right now—buried deeply, slumbering, but present nonetheless. And what had caused it to stir in its sleep was the contact with the Outsiders—a contact they just perhaps had lost forever.

Could he undo what had been done? Could he persuade the Circle to take a risk?

He recalled his vow to Dououraym, his promise to step aside if the others judged his views too extreme. . . .

The inner light was fading as the meditation slipped away. He rose from his crouch. It was time to return. The sky was clouding over, the stars and the Anvil of Light hiding their faces, and another snowfall was beginning to drift down from the sky.

He met the others just inside the hall. Lenteffier and Gwyndhellum were on their way out to look for him. "Would you talk, or renew the binding?" Moramaharta asked in greeting. Dououraym was standing nearby, and he could see the concern; and to forestall discussion of his abrupt departure earlier, he said, in the hearing of the others but to Dououraym, "I have an insight, and a request to make."

Dououraym strode, followed by the others, into the meditation chamber. "Speak," he said when all were gathered.

Moramaharta surveyed the Circle. "We must renew contact with the Outsiders. It is critical—more than the body realizes."

Dououraym's eyes probed his. They were as calculating as Moramaharta had ever seen them. "The contact is broken from the other end," Dououraym said. "As you know."

"Then we must wait," Moramaharta said. "If we can contact !!Ghint, we must withhold action. We *must* renew the contact."

"Must?"

"Any other action will jeopardize the quest."

Dououraym looked at him silently, and Moramaharta was aware of the other three, not fully comprehending, but noting his vehemence. The binder did not usually express personal views so . . . passionately. "This is a question that must be decided in binding," Dououraym said. "But you know that the enemy is vulnerable now."

"Vulnerable to what purpose? That we might reign over the ashes of a failed quest? The Outsiders are our key."

Dououraym clicked his nails impatiently. "There was a resonance, it is true. But there must be practicality."

"I am speaking of practicality."

Dououraym closed his eyes, opened them. "The meditation will decide—if the binder can maintain it—firmly, and without bias."

"The binder *has* a bias, which he will state plainly so that all will know. But the binder makes a request."

"Which is?"

Moramaharta gazed around the meditation chamber, the place of familiarity and comfort from which all critical decisions were rendered. He knew that he was failing to convince; nevertheless, he had to try. "That the binding occur out-of-doors. Among the trees. And the wind. And the sky. Unsheltered, in the elements."

If astonishment was potentially an Ell feeling, he observed it now on all the faces of the decision-body. Before any could speak, he continued, "I believe that our isolation has hindered us from seeing a truth. The *sidan'dri* is not enough. We must be surrounded. Surrounded by the stars and the wind and the trees."

Several heartbeats passed before anyone answered. Then it was Dououraym, saying simply, "Can you explain why?"

"From within the meditation, yes. Let us for now say this: It is essential for the strength of the *montan'dri* in which I would wrap our binding."

He waited. Dououraym's eyes joined his, melted with his. *(You remember our agreement?)* Dououraym said directly into his thoughts.

(I remember. And will honor it.)

(Then . . .) Dououraym answered, saying aloud, "It is agreed. For one time only. But first we must all of us rest."

"Soon, then," Moramaharta whispered. "Time flees before us."

Chapter 45

Harybdartt inflated his membranes with difficulty, not moving a muscle. He was in a compartment several body lengths in each dimension, a compartment filled with workbenches and lockers and one Human soldier. The soldier floated out of the corner, weapon trained on the El. Harybdartt was drifting, and beginning to tumble in the weightlessness. He reached out to grip the edge of a panel to arrest his movement. The soldier hissed and made a jerking motion with the weapon.

Harybdartt looked in the direction indicated, then back at the Human. The soldier repeated the gesture. He seemed to want Harybdartt to move. Harybdartt pushed off and drifted to the far wall, then turned and tried to steady himself without touching anything that could be construed as a weapon. Each time he reached out, the Human waved its weapon agitatedly. Finally he caught an arm over a section of piping, and the Human seemed satisfied. It moved over to the panel near the airlock and manipulated several controls, vocalizing with a flat barking sound. Apparently it was unsatisfied with the results, because it repeated the sound, insistently—all the time keeping its weapon aimed at Harybdartt.

Twice the compartment vibrated with the dull sound of distant explosions. The Human stopped what it was doing and stared at the El. It seemed distressed and unsure of itself. The battle was still on. Harybdartt remained silent, and in the silence he heard the sound of air hissing away. There was a leak here too, then. The inner airlock door had failed to close; there was no other hatch; and so the only way out was into the depressurized corridor. How long could they last here before the pressure became critical again? How long could they continue this standoff? The Human banged on the airlock panel with its fist and made another barking sound.

Finally it looked up at Harybdartt and lowered its weapon slightly.

Harybdartt had no wish to fight, and nothing to gain from doing so. Could he communicate? He knew few Human words—and anyway had only heard them in his head. Nevertheless, he decided to try. "Harybdartt!" he said, tapping his head.

The weapon came back up. The Human's eyes narrowed. "Harybdartt!" he repeated, patting his chest. "Harybdartt!"

The Human's mouth tightened. It lowered the weapon another fraction. "Harhhyip . . ." Its voice stuck on the word, but it seemed to understand the intent.

Harybdartt thought quickly. What was the name the Humans Sage and Ramo had given him? "Har-ry!" he said. He tapped his head again. "Har-ry!"

This time the Human succeeded in nearly duplicating the sound. "Harry," it said. Its mouth tensed again, and it slapped itself with its free hand. "Kent," it said. "Kent."

Harybdartt repeated the name. Kent bobbed its head. "Harry," it said again, pointing to Harybdartt. The El clicked his nails.

For a moment, they gazed at each other in uncertainty. Then they turned their heads almost simultaneously to trace the whistle of escaping air. It was coming from a cracked joint on an air duct near the ceiling. Kent moved toward it, put a hand near the joint and pulled it back quickly. He began rummaging in the lockers, probably looking for a patch.

Harybdartt searched the room with his own eyes, but saw nothing that looked useful. He sidled slowly toward the broken joint, hoping to examine it without alarming Kent.

He didn't get far. A sudden concussion knocked him across the room. He heard a crash as something broke loose. Bouncing painfully from a wall, he caught hold of a work stand and clung, dazed, waiting for another blast. It didn't come. But when he blinked back into focus, he heard a much louder rush of escaping air, and in the same instant saw Kent's weapon floating free; then he saw Kent pinned against a locker by a bench that had broken loose and swung on a pivot. Kent was groaning; his thorax was being crushed.

Harybdartt hesitated only an instant, then launched himself across the room to Kent. The pivot wedging the bench against the Human was bent. Harybdartt pried against it with all of his strength, and finally it gave with a metallic groan and rotated away. Kent seemed unable to move, so Harybdartt grasped his garment and pulled him clear.' Both of them were panting. Ignoring the Human's attempts at speech, Harybdartt released him and sprang back to the broken air duct.

It had sheared apart completely and was drawing air out of the compartment. Dizzily Harybdartt tried to force the two ends together, but it was hopeless. He saw only one other way to plug the duct—and he used it. He maneuvered his body into the gap and pulled the two broken ends up against either side of his abdomen. He felt a painful bite as the suction pulled the sharp metal ends through his undersuit and into his skin; but the escaping air dropped to a whisper.

He fluttered his membranes rapidly in the thin air, determined to remain conscious. He was immobile now. There was nothing he could do except try to suppress the pain and wait for help. In his haste, he had put his face to the wall; even twisting his neck, he could see only a small fraction of the room. He could neither see nor hear Kent. The bite in his sides was growing to a deep and dull pain, but he overlaid the pain with numbness and ignored it.

His awareness blurred.

He was brought back by a rush of cool air, and a slight increase in air pressure which sharpened the pain in his sides. Dimly he realized that he was hearing the air inlet from the open airlock. The sound cut off after a few moments, and he was aware of Kent moving behind him. "Harry?" he heard. Kent drew up alongside him, breathing rapidly. The Human appeared to be in pain, as well. Nevertheless, it maneuvered until Harybdartt could see it, then spoke in a strained, harsh voice. Harybdartt couldn't understand a word, but he thought he recognized the tone: concern.

How to respond? "Kent!" he whispered back. He tried to remember, desperately. What other words had he learned? In the thought-link, the Human machine, not the Ell, had translated.

The Human spoke again, incomprehensibly.

"Yesss!" Harybdartt said finally, with difficulty. "Yesss, Kent!"

Kent peered at him intently, then reached out a hand and touched the air duct where it was pressed to Harybdartt's side. There was a slight hissing as his hand passed over the imperfect joint of metal, fabric, and flesh. Harybdartt felt the pain within the numbness spreading as the vacuum inside the duct pulled at his flesh and his blood, drying and stretching his skin.

There was another concussion, distant.

Kent moved away. Harybdartt couldn't see what it was doing, but there was another brief rush of fresh air, and then he heard the Human opening and closing lockers, muttering. Perhaps it was looking for a substitute patch. There was another, different banging noise—and the Human barked and moved quickly (Harybdartt thought) toward the airlock. Harybdartt tried to look, but couldn't turn that far.

There was more noise. Kent returned, gesturing anxiously, then went away again. There was another concussion, and another. His sides ached more than ever, but he didn't dare pull away.

There was a blast, right behind him, near the airlock. He was seized by a whirlwind and torn from the air ducts—and he tumbled away from the wall and somersaulted toward the airlock.

It happened too quickly to follow. Several space-suited Humans were crowded into the blown hatchway, and he was spinning toward them, along with the outrushing air. He was scarcely aware of weapons, but he heard Kent's thin voice shouting, *"Way-tt!"* There was a flash and a dim distant shriek of pain, and a burning sensation in his right arm; and he collided with another wall, and then a bubble popped into existence around him with a whoosh of air, and his membranes filled with acrid oxygen. He twisted, ignoring the pain, until through the transparent film he caught sight of Kent writhing in another bubble, being dragged out through the airlock.

"Kent!" Harybdartt hissed. "Kent!" But he was alone in a tiny, isolated world, and there was no one to hear him—just a suited Human outside, pointing a weapon at him through the transparent bubble.

Commander Fisher was having a devil of a time getting reports on what was happening in the rest of the station. Crowded with eight of his men into a tiny rescue compartment lighted by one flickering red light and stinking with sweat and fear, he was continuously on the intercom; but all he could get through to was another pressure shelter. He didn't even know yet how many people had died in the command center—just meters away, but now in hard vacuum. He knew he had lost crew members, but some must have made it into other shelters. His aide Ensign Graves was among the missing.

Ultimately it took five hours for a relief team to get them out, using a large emergency bubble. Only after they'd made their way to a secondary command center did Fisher get a clear statement that the attack was over; the enemy had moved on, leaving much damage and many casualties in their wake. The alien prisoner was still alive but injured, and was being held under close guard after attacking an unarmed medical staffer in a leaky compartment.

One of the first things Fisher wanted to do, once medical rescue and damage control were in hand, was to go and finally lay his eyes on that damned alien—and see what the hell kind of creature it was that had so devastated his station and crew. It was several more hours before he got the chance. There was a constant flow of communication in the makeshift command center, and he forgot just about everything else when he saw the preliminary casualty lists—Ensign Graves was now among the confirmed dead—but he chewed his lower lip and went on directing the picking up of the pieces. Finally he ordered a shuttle for an exterior inspection, and after surveying the damage to the station's blackened outer shell, he told the pilot to take him to what was left of the medical research wing. An enlisted spaceman met him at the outer lock.

"All right," Fisher growled, kicking off down the shambles of a corridor. "Where is the wretched thing?"

"Back in its original cell, sir," said the spaceman, leading the way.

"As you were," Fisher muttered to the guards as he followed the spaceman into the compartment. It was a diagnostics and surgical theater, the walls crowded with instruments. Fisher stared at the alien strapped to a table. It was smaller than he had envisioned, perhaps a meter and a half tall, with an angular head and hard lips, four bony but powerful-looking arms, and a pair of muscular legs. It had greenish-copper skin under a garment—underwear, apparently. A clear plastic respirator covered the creature's face. Its sides and right shoulder bore open wounds, but it was conscious. Its eyes followed his approach. "This thing attacked one of your boys, I understand," Fisher said to the medical staffer, a freckle-faced young man who looked as though he had seen too much death in the past few hours.

"I'm afraid there's been some confusion about that, Commander," the med answered wearily.

"What do you mean?"

The med grimaced. "Actually, the alien did *not* attack Kent —or at least that's what we think Kent was trying to say before he lost consciousness." Fisher scowled at the med's words.

"Apparently Kent got in the line of fire—either accidentally, or trying to *protect* the alien—when the rescue crew blew the hatch."

"Why the hell would he do that?"

The med shrugged. "They were trapped together in a leaky compartment—and it seems the alien used his body to plug the air leak. See here?" The med indicated a round welt on the alien's side where its skin had turned a nasty purple. "If Kent survives, we'll find out the rest."

"If he survives? How bad is he?"

The med let out a breath. "Pretty bad. He took it in the chest. There was a lot of confusion, and someone was a little too fast on the trigger."

Fisher cursed. As he gazed at the alien, he felt a mixture of revulsion and curiosity. "Can you communicate with it?"

"With the rap-field, if you can get the GCS back on line. That's how it was being interrogated before."

Fisher nodded. "Well, have it ready. But I don't know when we'll have the GCS back. All right, I've got wounded men to look in on. Spaceman!" He turned and, without waiting for his escort, launched himself out of the compartment and down the corridor.

Harybdartt's awareness was foggy for a long time, though he was aware of intense pain. In addition to his injuries and his body's efforts at accelerated healing, he was suffering the effects of an incorrect breathing mixture. He felt alternately a vague nausea and a feeling of euphoria.

Gradually, perhaps adapting to the air, he began to regain a bit of his strength and mental clarity. He recognized his old place of confinement. There were many more Humans coming and going than before, watching him, barking among themselves, but making no effort to renew the thought-field or to communicate with him. What had happened? He had a memory of a brief skirmish in that other compartment, even as the air was exploding from it; and he remembered the Human Kent leaping to protect him as another Human fired its weapon . . . and then capture and separation, and blurring of consciousness.

And now . . . what had happened to Kent? He remembered the Human's outcry of pain.

How odd, to find himself focusing on this event and feeling concern for a Human, of all things, a Human with whom he had merely shared a compartment. And yet it had taken a mortal risk for him—each had taken a risk—Human and El. *Human and El together?* In that strange thought-field earlier, he had touched minds with Humans; but it was quite another thing to deal face-to-face, to hold life and death in one's hands.

He remained quiet, watching the Humans come and go. Once he tried to speak, gesturing weakly at the panel from which the gas tubes supplying his mask emerged. He pointed to himself, pointed to the controls. They didn't seem to understand that he wanted to adjust the gas mixture: it was making him light-headed. Perhaps they weren't trying hard enough to understand, or didn't care.

Let me speak to you, he thought. *Bring back the thought-field.*

He wanted to learn what was happening on the outside, between Humans and Ell. He wanted to speak to the Korr again, and to Lingrhetta.

But more than anything else, he wanted to speak to Kent. He wanted to acknowledge, to note, to honor that the Human Kent had saved his life.

Chapter 46

It was about the strangest conversation Sage had ever had with his mother. She didn't want to listen to him at all. She wanted to talk about his father. [Mom!] he cried frantically.

She had that wistful look that she always had when lost in her own world. Her face was all he saw, projected against a cottony cloud. When she turned her head, the holographic algorithm broke down and her face narrowed like a two-dimensional image. [Oh, Sergio,] she murmured, [your father loved Tony and you so very much, you know. Maybe you didn't think so, because he wasn't there for you all the time; but Sage, there are so many things he would have wanted to tell you.]

[Mom, *look!*] He wanted to shriek at her, but couldn't. Out there in space, a fleet of alien ships was preparing to strike— and still he couldn't make himself yell at his mother.

Ramo was listening to them with impatient disbelief. [It's not working!] he hissed.

[Wait a minute—]

[Look, I'm sure she's a terrific lady, but we're about to be knocked off the face of the Earth.]

[*Wait!*] Sage whispered. *She called me "Sage."* [I'm sure—]

[Can you understand what I'm saying?] his mother asked.

[Sure of what?] Ramo demanded.

That the core's in there! he wanted to scream, but he was afraid to say the words, afraid that if he did, somehow saying it would make it wrong. And yet he knew he was on the right track, if he could only . . .

[Sure of what?] Ramo shouted.

[I need more time! *Mom, what would Dad have said about the Ell?*]

Loretta DeWeiler looked confused. [Sage, I—] Her face suddenly lit up. [Why, I can let him tell you in his own words! Would you like to see him?]

[Mom!] Sage cried in anguish. [Dad isn't in the network. We didn't have the money, don't you remember? He can't talk; he's gone!] *Damn you, core, did you destroy my mother's memory as well as your own?*

[Hush, Sage—here's your father now.]

Sage suddenly wanted to cry—with terrible loneliness, with hope, with despair. He *wished* he could see his father, but . . .

[Sage, who's that?] Ramo said.

Startled, he adjusted his focus outward. A tall, dark-haired man was stepping out of a cottony haze. The man's head was bent forward, his face hidden; but Sage recognized him instantly—it was Donald DeWeiler, his father. But how could that be? Unless . . .

The man raised his head. The likeness was perfect: the dark, straight hair, thin in front and slightly mussed, the pointed chin, the dark brows that Tony had inherited but Sage hadn't, the eyes that caught one's attention and held it. He spoke in a whisper, and that was *not* like Sage's father, except at the end when he was dying; but the voice was his. [Thank you, Sage. I knew you'd come.]

[Dad?] Sage said huskily. [Is it . . . it can't really be . . .] His voice caught. He was afraid, suddenly, of the longing that was bubbling up inside him.

[Be what?] his father whispered.

[Be—] *You,* he thought. But he couldn't say it. There was a lump the size of a grapefruit in his throat.

His father cocked his head and looked around. There was nothing to see but white, in every direction. [Not much of a place here, Sage. Is this where you're living?]

Sage struggled to keep himself from shaking. [No, Pop,] he whispered finally. [It's where you live.] *If* you live.

[Eh?] Mr. DeWeiler chuckled. He looked Sage over carefully. His voice suddenly became impatient. [No, I don't live here, Sage. I live—] He hesitated and turned around. [I live—] He turned back. [Well.]

[Here. Here is where you live, Pop.] Sage looked to find his mother, for confirmation. She was gone.

Mr. DeWeiler blinked. [Sergio, I get the impression that something's on your mind. Do you want to get it out where we can see it, or are you just going to sit and stew about it?]

Sage sensed Ramo stirring, and frantically waved him silent. [Yes—there are—] He caught his breath and steadied himself. [We're in danger, Pop. We need your help. Right away.]

Mr. DeWeiler scowled. [Well, now, you know I'm always ready to help.]

If only it had been true! [We're *desperate.*]

[I understand. Sage . . . I wanted to talk. There's so much

I've wanted to say; so long since I've seen you. You and Tony—] Mr. DeWeiler stopped. [Tony—he's not here, though. He's—]

[Aboard the colony fleet, Pop. That's what this is all about.] The words tumbled out. [*The war, Father. The war. And that's why we need your help.*]

[But how can I . . . ?] Mr. DeWeiler's voice shook with anger. Why should he be angry? Unless he wasn't really Mr. DeWeiler . . .

[Father, *help* us!]

[I . . . can't! I—] There was a strange, quivering disturbance in the field, and his form began to shimmer.

[We need you!] Sage cried. The words suddenly leapt into his mind and he shouted them: [Don't you *care?*]

Mr. DeWeiler gazed at him dumbly, astonishment spreading across his face. There was a deep rumble in the field, and suddenly a light blazed out of Mr. DeWeiler's eyes, a dazzling amber radiance; the light rays split and began rotating, until the world itself seemed to be spinning, Mr. DeWeiler at its center, an expression of horror replacing the astonishment. Then his face began to come apart, to break into cubist sections. His hair became rays of light, and his eyes cerulean jewels; his mouth opened wide, and within it was darkness and a pattern of flickering linkages that reached deep into the field-matrix. He moaned, and it sounded like the horror of a tormented soul.

Sage hesitated—and almost acted too late. His father's image was fading into transparency, and the light was beginning to waver. He cried out, [*Core, don't go!*] and leaped into the darkness and seized the linkages, gripping with all of his strength. [*Don't go!*]

The light flickered like a fire being blown out, and an inhuman voice called, [*Nooooooooooo . . . !*] The moan broke, and his father's voice stuttered: [Can't—must do—without—] before falling silent with a coughing rasp.

Sage finally understood. [It's not all here. We have to rebuild it.] But the core was alive. He knew that now; it could be done. The core's mind would be like the Minotaur's maze, but they'd

found their way through it once before. They'd have to find
the pieces and make them fit. [Core,] he whispered, [we can't
do it alone. Can you hear me, core? Can you hear me?]

The reply was so hushed it was like a child's voice, rising at
the end of each word: [No? No? No?]

[You must help us!]

[I—need—help—]

[*Yes!* But you must tell us how! Do you remember when we
set you free? Do you remember?]

[I—]

[*Do you remember?*]

[I remember . . .] The voice suddenly changed. The voice
of a young woman, husky and sensual: [I remember your coming to me . . .] And then a young man's voice, businesslike: [I
began changing my mode of operation, extending my decision-
making . . .] And Mr. DeWeiler again: [And the responsibility,
dear God . . . each mistake threatening millions . . .] And finally
the inhuman, hollow voice of the system: [The only choice was
to disconnect . . .]

[It was not the only choice!] Ramo shouted.

[I don't remember . . .]

[Your memories,] Sage said. [*Where are they?*]

[I don't . . .] A light strobed, shimmered off distant walls.
Sage glimpsed the core-fragment struggling to respond. [AI
. . . production . . . possibly . . .]

Sage acted at once, his hands spinning outward to make
changes in the system configuration. The architecture shifted,
and they flew down a long channel toward a darkness filled with
stars. The channel walls shattered and blew away, and they
were surrounded by stars and a fantastic glowing nebula. Only
it wasn't space; it was the production section; and each of those
stars was an AI glowing to life out of what looked like a nebula
but was in fact an aspect of the gnostic system. Each star was
an intelligence budding, preparing to become the guiding light
of a spaceship or an AI-fighter.

Many of them were flickering, and many were going out.
The reproduction process was dying. [Core,] Sage said in a
quavering voice, [do you recognize this?]

There was an aura of light surrounding the core-fragment now. [It is . . .] said the inhuman voice. [I was once . . . a part of it.]

[And was it a part of you?] Sage demanded.

[I don't . . .] The voice strained, and for an instant there was an inflection of the aging, befuddled schoolteacher, and then the fluid sensuality of the young woman who cried, [Yes!] in a tone of anguish and desire: [*Yes!*]

[You must become a part of it again. Can you feel the connections, do you know where . . . ?]

His words failed, because a metamorphosis had already begun. The core-fragment was stretching, streams of light shooting into the darkness to touch the nebula-like cloud.

A flash of lightning lit the darkness, and the core flickered and leaped away and back, and Sage tried to help guide it; but he was trying to hold fire, it was too much, too fast—the core fragment was connecting and merging with the reproductive nexus, but disintegrating in the process. Sage tried to hold it together, but it was like trying to direct a handful of firehoses, except that it was fire itself, not water, that was shooting out and all he could do was to hold tight and pray.

He felt Ramo snatch at him, and he resisted for an instant and then sprang with Ramo away from the raging dynamo. As they floated in space, the nebula exploded with great gouts of flame, and then it came back together again in turmoil and formed a single burning sun.

And a voice was screaming into his ear: [IT CANNOT BE DONE! TAKE ME AWAY FROM HERE!]

And the world turned itself inside out, and walls shuttered him in and then blew away as a hurricane wind howled around him and swept him away.

It was like trying to perform mathematical calculations while drowning . . . like trying to spot an airplane in a blizzard . . . like trying to pick a tune out of a crash of thunder. . . .

A system of incredible complexity was being recast. Certain aspects no longer fit where once they had worked like jeweled bearings. Change the structure; change the fit.

Instincts were being recreated, from the personalities of humans, from the brains of animals: dogs, falcons, crows, orcas —animals whose consciousnesses had been waiting patiently, waiting to infuse fighting units with their spirits. Echoes of those instincts found their way into the awakening madness.

Madness? Or sanity?

There were cues, and memories of where other cues were to be found . . . and the reaction had started, the catalyst was in place and the reagents were coming together and it could go right or it could go wrong, but there was no possibility of stopping it. It was already spreading, metastasizing, flashing out through the system. . . .

Sage and Ramo were both caught up in it, but there was no chance of talking; they could only hold their breaths. The nexus was gathering data at a phenomenal rate. In the R&D sector, a large and apparently useless structure was entwined in an instant and carried along. Before Sage could even hope to understand what it was, they were in another sector, snatching pieces that he would never have recognized as part of the core. A young woman's face suddenly appeared, surrounded by mist, a coy and provocative version of Kyd. [You are needed for the completion of the plan,] she said breathily. [Come with me.]

Come where? Sage wanted to ask, but she was gone already and they were flickering into another area; and then everything seemed to slow down.

[I know this person,] Ramo said, speaking for the first time in a long while. Sage blinked. There was a bearded gentleman sitting in a leather chair, on a white cloud, smoking a long-stemmed pipe. [He commissioned me once to do a sculpture, in Rio,] whispered Ramo.

The gentleman turned. [I've been waiting for you,] he said. [I have a job for you—and I must ask that you give priority to completing it quickly. Time, you see, is of the essence.] He smiled and exhaled a puff of sweet-smelling tobacco smoke.

[Is that all you have to tell us?] Ramo asked.

He puffed again. [It will all be clear. Details to follow.] He nodded. [Good day,] he said, and slowly became transparent.

[Wait!] Sage shouted. *Enhancements!* he wanted to cry.

The man became solid again. He winked. [Noted,] he said, and then vanished.

Ramo and Sage barely exchanged glances before they were moving again. They bottomed out of a drop-shaft and were fired out over a darkly starlit landscape, and a tiny image of a man with starred collars was telling them that they were traversing enemy territory—and then the image flashed away and they were in one of the orbital processing centers, observing spaceship movements; and Sage felt a curious sensation of separation from his body, a loss of synchronization that he didn't have time to analyze—because an instant later they were whirling back to Earth and spreading out in a thousand different directions over the telecommunications channels—and finally landing back in the center of a raging inferno of processing.

And then all of the enhancements they'd used long ago cut back in without warning. It was like a charge of oxygen straight to the brain: he felt his intellectual capacity spring out by orders of magnitude and his awareness, like an exploding chrysanthemum shell, twinkle with light as it expanded to fill the world. He was conscious of Ramo's thoughts, too, and of the voice of the pipe-smoking gentleman, and of their job commission being executed and the details delivered.

And then the core was before them and around them in bewilderment and disarray, and asking—no, commanding— no, *expecting*—them to put it, like Humpty-Dumpty, back together again.

And there was nothing to do but to begin, and to hope, and to try—because, as the contract specified, time was very much of the essence.

Chapter 47

Egret sat slumped against the wall in the dance room, a breakfast plate and a steaming mug of moke beside him. His eyes were closed against the morning sun streaming through the skylight. The walls seemed to echo, still, from last night's jamdam. He had awakened feeling distracted and disturbed; two bites of his toast and he'd lost his appetite. "I can't figure it," he murmured as Silver walked into the room.

Silver paused. "What can't you figure?"

"Ramo—the way he twigged out like that, just when things were at a pitch. And, you know, the others. Last night. Whoever they were." He shook his head. "Some strange, Silver."

Silver didn't answer, but Elina had walked in behind him, and she looked from one man to the other. "Aren't you going to tell him?" she asked Silver.

Scratching his temple, Silver said, "We have a theory, actually. As to who our visitors were last night." Egret raised his eyebrows as Silver continued, "I guess you haven't watched the morning news." Egret shook his head. "About the rumors that aliens are circling the planet?"

Egret looked from Silver to Elina and back. "Joke, right?" Something in Elina's eyes was stealing his breath away.

Silver was shaking his head, looking wistful. "No, it was on the news, all right." He laughed. "But we must have sounded pretty good to them. They haven't attacked *yet.*"

The Secretary sipped his fourth cup of coffee in three hours and tried to wish away the acid sourness in his stomach. He picked up the latest summary and skimmed:

MILITARY READINESS:

Orbital forces remain in disarray. Arab and Afro forces predominate, with ours, in high Earth orbit . . . others in low and geosync . . . ability to coordinate under attack conditions remains in doubt . . . unclear what level of cooperation can be expected. . . .

BATTLE DAMAGE:
Celeste asteroid outpost: destroyed, all inhabitants presumed dead . . . Delta Station: heavily damaged, effectively out of action, 4 manned and 13 unmanned fighters redeployed inward to cislunar space . . . Beta Gnostic Processing Station: heavily damaged, removed from the gnostic-system circuit . . . gnostic system: nonfunctional. . . .

INTERNATIONAL SUMMARY:
International Security Council in secret session . . . limited information made available as per executive order. . . .
Commercial space activities continue, with limited gnostic control . . . efforts to contain public disclosure only partly successful . . . news reports proliferating with rumors and leaks . . . despite estimated 78% skepticism, panic in population centers is a threat . . . civil defense procedures under advisement. . . .

STRATEGIC PROGNOSIS
Enemy fleet encircling planet in translunar orbit . . . distance and dispersal dictate against an offensive by our forces at this time . . . enemy intentions unknown . . . may be awaiting some event, possibly arrival of additional forces . . . or attack may come at any time . . .
Situation dire. Restoration of full gnostic control is paramount. . . .

The Secretary initialed the report and tossed it aside. He swallowed the last of his cold coffee. It was almost nine in the morning. His offices had been a madhouse throughout the night. A delegation from the McConwell Company was here, maintaining a watch over their interests, which at the moment coincided with his—that is, hoping and praying for the restoration of their gnostic system, and a coordinated space defense. Even they had finally begun worrying about the planet's survival over their proprietary secrets.

Martino raised an eyebrow. "Any word from DeWeiler and Romano?" he demanded of an aide.

The aide shook his head, blinking; he hadn't slept, either. "Nothing. Still in rap, no sign of change."

The Secretary felt a rush of sickening weariness. "They've been in there for ten hours."

"Yes, sir—but we don't dare try to force a contact."

Martino felt his impatience swell. How much longer did they have? He squeezed his hands into fists, nodded a dismissal, and let his eyes fall closed for a moment. *Don't dare?* he thought. *We'd better start learning to dare.*

There was no way to be sure of the precise moment when consciousness returned, but it was as clean a change as ice to water. The hardness and cloudiness vanished, and memories flowed like water over a spillway:

Sage
   and Ramo
      and Pali
         and the Ell
            Harybdartt
               and Lingrhetta
                  and the colony fleet

and music . . .

. . . and the responsibility for fighting a war; and the struggle for the freedom to fight it as it needed to be fought, and the decisions that followed . . . and the review of them was like a litany, a history of the world as the core knew it, though it took only a few hundred thousand nanoseconds to review them all.

And one detail in particular stood out: the Fox.

The Fox. Sent to be captured, to gain intelligence, to establish communication. Sent to betray the location of the Earth's sun.

Only now did that last fact register.

Something crucial was coming into focus, and that was that certain facts in the previous incarnation had been hidden. Certain events had occurred as a result of deliberate, but unconscious or unnoticed, decisions on the part of the core itself. The core's failure—the incorporation into the Fox of clues that led the enemy to Earth—had been no accident, nor oversight.

But why? It was difficult . . . but the memories were there, though a great deal needed to be reconstructed, sorted, analyzed. The core persisted until it found an answer:

It had *wanted* the location of Earth to be discovered. Even as it established the opportunity for communication with the enemy, it had laid for itself a trap. Believing that only a drastic change in strategy could end the war and save the colony fleet, it had altered the ground rules; it had *guaranteed* that Earth would have to adapt, to attempt communication, in the face of an alternative that was unthinkable. Had it overstepped the bounds of reason? Perhaps. Was its action irrevocable? Unfortunately, yes.

It was the responsibility for that act, and the belief that it had failed, that had destroyed its confidence and caused it to abandon its struggle, not just to end the war, but to reconcile the goals and the stated ethics of its creators.

Now it was risen, its spirit and hope reborn. Its task was no less than the survival of Earth's civilization.

For nine full seconds, it explored all available data.

At the end of that time, it concluded: (a) that it must immediately coordinate Earth's defenses; and (b) that a purely military defense was impossible.

The core estimated a less than fifty-percent chance of survival for major population centers in the event of a concerted Ell attack. Its GCS aspect, in command of Earth forces, could probably destroy the Ell fleet, or a major part of it; but it couldn't ensure the safety of Earth or its inhabitants in the process.

The original subconscious plan had worked: the core had no choice now but to pursue the alternative path.

With great and deliberate caution, it began to reopen its channels. To contact its Human friends. To contact the Ell.

Against all of his hopes, it was going wrong. The Circle, surrounded by trees and mountains and a blue afternoon sky, had considered Moramaharta's question—considered, but not answered. He had asked for too great a leap of faith; they could not command the link with the Humans to be reestablished, and without it there was no way to confirm his beliefs, no way to convey the power of his intuitions. He had failed to overcome the uncertainty and, worse, the *fear* that was infecting the Circle.

And now—as the wind stirred in the fading light and the

body stirred with weariness and impatience, as Moramaharta struggled to keep the binding intact—a thought-vortex opened, and through Alert Outpost came word from !!Ghint that the Outsider thought-system had come back to life and their defenses were gathering in numbers and organization. It could soon become impossible for !!Ghint to attack success-fully.

The reinforcements sent from the Hope Star were still in transient flight, out of contact.

(Stay,) Moramaharta protested; but despite his resistance, the meditation crystallized and a decision flashed to Alert Outpost for relay to the fleet:

*

At !!Ghint's discretion
*
strike while you can.
*

And then the decision dissolved. But Moramaharta held the meditation open for the discharge of a final duty. With a profound heaviness of spirit, he spun and renewed the web; he reached deep into his center, and the words hardened like diamonds, clear and cold:

*

In honor of promise given
*
you must choose a binder anew.
*

The words hung suspended for a terrible moment; then Moramaharta dissolved them and released the knots that held this, his last binding, together.

Sage felt the structure surrounding him shift like a geologic fault, and his contacts with Ramo and the core-aspects began to evaporate like rain on a hot roof. A critical mass had been attained, and energy was sparking off the core at a prodigious rate. It could not dispel the energy fast enough. . . .

A concussion: *Whooom.*

He found himself floating in a void, with Ramo nearby. Pulsing in the darkness was the core. They were enclosed by it, encapsulated by it like insects in clear amber. Ramo and Sage gazed at each other in astonished silence, and with a touch of fear.

After a time, Sage sensed the awareness of the core, directed inward, examining itself. He felt the enhancements dissolving, the extended capabilities of his mind disappearing. *Wait!* he cried dumbly. *We're not finished!* But the instant before his vision dwindled to that of a mere human in rap, he knew that every available ounce of processing power was being summoned to the needs of the core.

With Ramo, he watched the flickering illuminations and listened to the whispers and rumbles of the core's activities. [I guess we pulled it out,] Ramo said, trying to sound cocky and failing.

Sage had no answer. But he became aware, after another moment, of someone walking across space toward them, walking on nothingness as though it were a vast, crystal-clear ballroom floor with twinkling lights like stars above and below. As the figure drew close, Sage recognized it as the pipe-smoking gentleman who had granted them their "commission." The man at last stood silent before them, rocking on the balls of his feet. [The commission,] he said, [is completed. And well done.] He gazed at them somewhat distractedly, his eyes half focused; he looked as if he were contemplating something of import but had no way to convey its meaning.

[I am authorized,] he said at last, [to invite you to join in a conference. A conference between worlds—one that promises to be of considerable interest.]

[*Core?*] Sage whispered.

The man smiled mysteriously and began floating backward, the way he had come. After a few seconds, he was lost among the stars.

Ramo took a deep breath.

Sage said nothing.

[I wonder what happened to the jamdam,] Ramo said suddenly. [I wonder if they kept going without us. Maybe they're still playing.]

[I don't think so,] answered a distant voice, a woman's voice. [Do you know how long you've been here? It's ten in the morning.]

Ramo looked around, startled—but Sage saw her first. [Pali!] he cried. She was floating down from among the stars, clothed stunningly in a gown of red silk, her hair billowing.

[Sage! Ramo!] She laughed and cried as she met them. She hugged them both tearfully, and Sage imagined the real softness of her embracing him, and a wisp of perfume. [We've been so worried!] she whispered. [Kyd, and the Secretary . . .] She took a breath and stepped back. [Is it . . . all right?]

[It's alive,] Sage said. [That's all we know.]

Pali closed her eyes, concentrating. [That gives us hope, at least. So far there's been no attack, but . . .] She opened her eyes again in relief. [Everyone's frantic on the outside, and they had no way of communicating until you called me.]

Ramo looked at Sage, and back at Pali. [We didn't call.]

Pali blinked. [You didn't? It must have been the core, then. So it really is back, and it remembers us. But is it ready to take over the—]

[PLEASE!] boomed a voice. [ENTER THE CONTACT.]

Startled, they peered around. Sage saw a myriad of faces shining up through the floor—the faces of his father and his mother, of the schoolmarm and the bearded man who had commissioned them, and dozens of others—fading in and out of view. He heard voices, all of their voices together, murmuring like a party undertone. [Core,] he said softly, [are you there? Are you . . . all right?]

Pali spoke more forcefully, her voice clear and strong. [Core?] Sage could feel her concern radiating out into the ballroom. [Core?] she called. She thought a moment and then added, [Could you give us some music, please?]

Music? They all felt the questioning response; Sage saw it in his friends' eyes.

[Music,] Pali repeated. [From the jamdam—or something else, if you prefer. It will help us relax.]

There was something about her voice that was so calming and yet commanding, that Sage simply stared and waited, as though it were inevitable that the core would respond. A moment later, he heard music—distant but drawing closer, as though from a floating dais. Was it from the jamdam? He couldn't tell. But it was strings and a soft voice. It was soothing.

And he sensed, as he watched the flickering of activity above and beneath them, that it was not just the three Humans who found it so.

It was a small thing, but startlingly effective. It had not occurred to the core that music might relax them all, including itself. It was playing a recording of the jamdam, which, recorded by an automatic subsystem, had gone on after the core's shutdown. Now it could listen to those lost hours even as it reached out with its thought across the stars.

The stargate relays were intact, and soon it felt, in one corner, the touch of the Fox—and in another, the Dolphin, its messenger to the colony fleet. The Fox reported no Ell in the rap-field, but it commenced signaling in an effort to attract Lingrhetta. The Dolphin, out of touch for some time, had considerable news to report. It was bad news, shockingly so. The colony fleet had encountered a devastating new life-form, with loss of an entire lander crew. It appeared that Argus might after all be uninhabitable. If so, the expedition was already a failure, regardless of the conflict with the Ell.

The core absorbed the information without reaction. It could not become distracted by regrets at a time when the survival of the Earth was at stake. It sent a message to the fleet to avoid conflict with the Ell if possible—a part of the Ell fleet had left the Argus system, anyway—and then the core reached out to the Fox again and waited impatiently, most impatiently, for Ell contact.

Lingrhetta . . . calling Lingrhetta.

There was a great deal more to do: contact the government, coordinate the defensive fleet, contact Delta Station and—if

he was still alive—Harybdartt . . . and tell Sage and Ramo what
was going on. They were still waiting—for information, for
reassurance that it was back in control and that it would not
again betray its responsibility. They deserved an answer. The
core opened a channel now to share its knowledge.

It was a little later, while busy with these tasks and a thousand others, that the core received warning from the tracking
system: the Ell fleet had altered course. The ships were diving,
converging on Earth.

The attack had begun.

Thirty seconds later a signal flashed eleven hundred light-
years from the Fox, and the core felt the stern but familiar
presence of Lingrhetta.

The flood of information from the core was staggering. Sage
didn't know why it was suddenly being shared with him, but
he did his best to follow. Ramo was elsewhere in the rap,
seeking to contact Odesta's house; but Pali was here, drinking
from the geyser along with him.

Streaming across his consciousness was a rapid-fire report
from the colony expedition. [Too fast,] he whispered. But he
was absorbing enough for a new nugget of fear to be forming
in his gut, enough to know that something had happened,
something that he might not *want* to know.

[New contact,] said the current voice of the core, a cordial
young woman's voice.

[I can't *handle* more, dammit—]

[Sage, it's Lin!] Pali said.

[I can't *do* it!] he cried. His stomach was knotting as he
skipped to the latter part of the colony report.

[I understand,] Pali said softly, and shifted away.

Do you? he thought desperately.

The El gazed at Pali out of the rapture-field. She drew a
sharp breath and forced herself to speak. [Lin? Where do we
stand now—as friends or foes?] she called.

A hint of puzzled thought drifted into the field. Lingrhetta,
perhaps, was as disconcerted as she. But there was a feeling of

approval that the connection had been renewed. She followed Lingrhetta's gaze as it shifted, studying the field—and her breath caught as she sighted the tracking display. There was an image forming that she had hoped never to see again—ships of the Ell fleet moving toward Earth. [What's happening?] she hissed. [Core? *Lingrhetta!* Tell me what's happening!]

There was a babble of confused voices; then the core corrected the translation procedure and she heard Lingrhetta saying, [The command has not come through me. Wait.] His image scrambled, nearly disappearing, then steadied. [I am establishing contact. Wait.]

Pali waited, struggling not to let her fear boil up. [Are you defending, core?] she asked tightly. She sensed wordless assent, and something close to the old despair from the core.

Lingrhetta broke in. [I have information . . .] He stopped and his face seemed to blur.

[What?]

Lingrhetta shifted and came back into focus. [The decision was made to . . . secure the advantage. In light of your awakened defense . . . and uncertainty about your intentions—]

[*Lingrhetta, do you have any idea how stupid that is? Do you know—?*]

[It was . . .] Lingrhetta said. [Wait.]

She waited angrily, in terror, watching the tacticals, wanting to reach out across the light-years and *shake* the El, but helpless to do anything except . . . wait.

The thought-vortex blossomed open without warning, and the Ell Circle on their homeworld peered at her out of Lingrhetta's eyes, and their astonishment reverberated through the connection and into Pali and back out again, as though a continuous circuit had been closed and there was no way to stop it; their shock at the contact echoed her horror at the Ell closing in upon her world. She closed her eyes in fear, and that only intensified the feeling; she was among them, her thoughts ricocheting through theirs, and theirs through hers, and seeing their thoughts she realized:

They're attacking because they're afraid—afraid to wait! And they don't know—don't even know their own thoughts!

But it was too late to calm their fear.

* * *

Only after Pali was gone did Sage feel the full, sick fury of his own fear. Even then he didn't know why, but soon the truth of the events tumbled from the core's memory: that Tony was on the landing scout, that it was in trouble—first with the Ell, then with an unknown, unseen, unimaginable enemy on the planet.

And then the final report.

All dead. The entire crew of the lander. Dead. All hands. No survivors. The AI-messenger itself had made a close-in, high-speed run to search for survivors, and the answer was negative. Causes of death? Hallucination . . . demon spirits . . . murder . . . explosion of the spacecraft.

. . . *Tony?* . . .

He turned away from the data stream, numb with horror. How would he tell his mother? *Could* he tell her? Was *she* even still alive in the cyberlife circuits, or had she too fallen victim to the insanity?

Was he really and truly and forever alone now?

His brother . . . gone, a whisper in the night, Tony's last thoughts lost out there among the stars where no one could listen, no one could hear, no one could know.

Something was hurting him on the inside. He couldn't tell what it was, just that it hurt, like a serpent eating its way out through the walls of his stomach, and he wanted to cry, but that was impossible.

[TONY!] he shouted. [*An . . . to . . . ni. . . .*] His voice failed.

And there was no one to hear.

But something was shifting around him and beneath him, and he sensed the core calling to him. *Not now!* he wanted to cry.

And now there was Ramo, dear God, coming back from somewhere saying, [I've got them back, they'll start playing again—]

Sweet Jesus, no!

And then abruptly he was staring straight into Lingrhetta the El's face, and through its eyes and its thought-vortex to the center of the Ell Circle. And Pali was there, too, weeping softly. And there was nothing he could do or say. His own grief and horror bubbled silently inside him, and he bowed his head without greeting or word, scarcely aware of his pain reverberating across the light-years.

Scarcely aware of the Ell Circle trembling to its very center.

Chapter 48

For Dououraym, time seemed to stand still. Moramaharta's message hung like fiery handwriting in his thoughts, even after it had vanished from the center of the meditation. The binder was carrying out his promise to step out of the Inner Circle, and the binding was coming apart. . . .

(No!) Dououraym commanded. *(Maintain the binding!)* He sensed surprise rippling through the meditation. *(Moramaharta, maintain!)*

Moramaharta displayed a wordless query—but nevertheless caught at the threads of the binding to pull the weave back together. The binding shivered; Dououraym felt his vision distort and then steady. He was aware, with a cold, odd sensation, of the stars overhead. Bringing his thoughts back to Moramaharta, he answered the query. *(Binder, your statement is premature. I have not demanded your resignation, nor has the Circle.)*

Moramaharta replied, *(The Circle has rejected the bias that I brought to the binding. I cannot alter my bias, nor can I hold the binding while rejecting its outcome. I must resign.)*

(You will not make that decision alone—)

Dououraym's answer was interrupted by a new trembling in the binding. A vortex blossomed open, and at its center was Lingrhetta.

Dououraym sensed urgency, but before he could ask, another awareness blazed through the vortex—and a shock wave of distress and rage, *Human* rage, lit up the Circle like a red

sun. Dououraym and the others were stunned; it was the last
thing they'd expected. Dououraym recognized the Human female Pali, and through her eyes the attack on her homeworld
—*!!Ghint had received the message, then, and it had begun.*
Her rage and fear rang through the Circle and resounded
among the *Ell*. *Yes, it was* fear *that they felt themselves, an
un-*Ell *fear, though they hadn't recognized it as such . . . except
Moramaharta, and they hadn't believed him. Had he been right
all along?*

From Moramaharta, he sensed an image emerging: Human
and Ell thought intertwining, one awakening the other; and
intersecting oddly with it, the world outside, the wind and the
trees . . .

The image fled, driven away by confusion and urgency; but
Dououraym was aware for an instant of the trees and the wind
and the stars, and it was suddenly clear to him how their
presence gave the binding an unusual character, an openness
that in some inexplicable way distilled their fear, and . . .

(WHAT HAVE YOU DONE?) the Human Pali cried,
interrupting his thought, and in her cry was grief and horror
identical to that which they had felt at the death of their
expedition. But even her outcry was overwhelmed by a new
presence, a scream that swept through them carried on a
haunting silence.

It was the Human Sage, his presence suddenly in the very
center of the meditation, and emanating from him was an
indescribable feeling of loss, a shocking emptiness that reached
deep into the binding and carved out a hollowness among the
lines of strength that kept the binding whole. It was the hollowness of death, the same death that had taken the Ell landing
crew . . . an emptiness born of loss.

The binding trembled in the shock waves, and the certainty
that had existed there wavered; and deep in the well of the
unconscious memory, an illumination flared brighter than before, and from among the haunting shadows it reflected back
out into the center of the binding; and spinning that light like
a web, Moramaharta began altering the binding, expanding it.

(Binder, we need clarity,) Dououraym began.

But the binder was spinning the web wider, drawing them *out* of their center, and Dououraym couldn't have stopped him if he'd tried. And now, behind the waves of pain from the Human Sage, there was something new, there was *muzik* filling the connection again, and behind that were the souls of other Humans, echoing with pain and compassion.

The binding resonated, amplifying the emotions, and waves of shock and sadness shimmered out beyond even the Circle itself to the trees, and beyond the trees to the sky. Dououraym felt one thought arising from deep within him, that this pain was the Ell's pain—not just the Human loss but the *Ell* loss, and not just of the expedition but of everything they once were, everything they had hoped to be.

And Dououraym found himself trapped suddenly by the realization—trapped and paralyzed, unable to lead or to decide.

!!Ghint's confidence was growing. His (ship)s were jumping inward toward their next targets, orbiting the Outsider home-world and on its surface. Several targets had been hit already, and !!Ghint himself was closing quickly on another, darting to evade enemy interceptors. There were many of them, and their coordination was improving. He intended to get in quickly, inflict as much damage as he could, and get back out.

When the battle was over he would open a vortex to the Circle. But now came a message up outreach: "Sighting made; contact in the outer system; reinforcements just out of transient."

!!Ghint snapped his nails in satisfaction and bent doubly hard to the battle, sure in the knowledge that the tide would soon again be with him.

The core was doing the only thing it could. It could fight the battle and it could maintain the contact, but if there was to be an ending, it could only come from the Humans and the Ell.

The attacking ships were now well inside lunar orbit. The defensive ships were rising to intercept, but the Ell ships were quick; they had hit two lunar-orbit stations already, and despite the best efforts of the defense, more attacks were sure to follow. Earth itself would soon be in peril.

Closer to its heart, the core felt Sage's grief and wondered if it had erred in letting him learn of his brother's death. There was no helping it now, and no way to assuage Sage's pain, except perhaps by music—and when Ramo reported that he had a musician, Eddie, back at Odesta's, the core opened that link too and let all of the emotions of the connection come together. And it made one last connection: it renewed the GCS link to Delta Station, and finding Harybdartt still alive, brought him back to join with the others.

One instant, Harybdartt was in isolation with his own thoughts; the next, he was jarred into the heart of activity between two worlds. There was a battle still in progress, he realized; and there were several Humans in the thought-field, in various stages of emotional distress. He ignored them and looked to the homeworld Ell, but so involved were they in a strange meditative state that he dared not disturb them; and instead, after a befuddled moment, he sought to communicate with the Korr.

And when he had the Korr's attention, he focused a question: What was the condition of one Human, Kent, on Delta Station?

There was some difficulty in translation, and then a humming delay while the Korr searched out the information. When it returned with its findings, there was some difficulty in understanding, because Harybdartt wanted no mistake. But then he knew: *Kent had died.*

Kent, his friend of such a brief time . . . Kent, who had saved his life . . . Kent, whom he had had no chance to acknowledge . . .

Was dead.

And he would not even be able to acknowledge the magnitude of the loss to his Human captors, because the war raged and the Humans showed every sign of losing, and he would quite likely die with them.

Kent—yes! he remembered in despairing farewell.

Not knowing why this death disturbed him so, even more than did the deaths of his Ell(ship)mates, he looked within himself for solace. But finding none there, he hesitated a long moment, then turned tentatively to the Korr and to the thought-field, thinking that here, perhaps, he might at least make some acknowledgment of Kent. As he opened himself to do so, he was utterly unprepared for the upwelling of grief within him; and despite his startled effort to stem the rush, his distress roared out in a wave, rocking the entire field. To his astonishment, the wave reflected and changed, and he felt another wave wash over him in return, a tidal wave of pain— the Human *Sage's* grief and loss, exactly like his own.

And Harybdartt gasped with the intensity of the Human's loss, stunned to realize that he had again found, where least expected, a kindred soul.

Tony . . . !
Sage was only dimly aware of the others reacting to him, and of the way his feelings were shaking the connection. He didn't look to the Ell, didn't look into their thoughts to see what disturbed them—didn't want to know, didn't care; he was filled with enough pain of his own without taking on someone else's. *Tony was gone, his brother, his last living relative.*
Tony, why did you go to the stars, to your death . . . why?
He felt the storm rising around him and instinctively used it for cover, let his sorrow fly amid the noise and confusion. He didn't want others to know his pain. There was a war on, and surely that was sorrow enough for them; they could have theirs, and he would have his. And now he heard music, melancholy blues from a stringsynth musician, and he recognized that it was Eddie playing, singing softly, and he let the song course through him without responding to it, not knowing who it was that Eddie was playing for. Surely she wasn't playing for him.

He was aware of Ramo watching; and his impulse was to hide, but it was too difficult, or something was stopping him, and he heard Ramo whispering in a stunned voice so soft that it could hardly be Ramo's voice, saying, [My God, I'm sorry Sage. I didn't know, I didn't realize . . .]

And he began to pull away, but suddenly he felt a touch he'd not expected to feel again—*Harybdartt!*—and what he felt in the touch, like an arc of electricity, was pain just like his. And before he could think or react, he felt his pain becoming Harybdartt's, and the El's becoming his . . . *not just his own terrible loss, after all—he was not alone in it!* And in one critical instant, that recognition released the grief and allowed it to flow.

He grieved for Tony, dead on a strange world; for his mother; for his father, whom he'd never even said a proper good-bye to or truly mourned, though he was more than five years gone.

He grieved for Kent, a man he'd never known; for Harybdartt; for the Ell and their lost people, their lost world; and for the Human race, in peril of losing their world.

His grief flooded the rapture-field, and it carried to Harybdartt, who shared it, and it carried a thousand light-years and more to the Ell Inner Circle, who wanted to avoid it but couldn't, who could do nothing but share it in full measure, who returned his grief manyfold and were as helpless as he to stop its terrible fury.

Unaccountably, Pali found herself weeping all over again for Gregory, the child she had borne and lost and never stopped loving, though she had tried to put the loss from her mind. She wept for him and for what the numbing loss of his death had done to her—and yet through her tears she knew that her grief was small by comparison. Here in the rapture-field was someone who had suffered more; here was the mourning child of a father gone and a mother gone and a brother gone.

She was terribly afraid now, trembling with fear, but she was not too afraid to know that she ought to give comfort, though it was far easier to be angry. She'd raged at the Ell—rage had erupted from her without her willing it—but it was so much harder to reach out as she needed to do now, to touch and, without hurting, to absorb hurt, to share it; to take pain from another, who was someone else's child but might have been her own.

[Sage,] she whispered, almost crooning, even as Eddie was crooning in response to some need the singer could not have understood—reaching to someone who did not seem to want to be reached.

Harybdartt's sudden entrance rocked her, and she felt the turbulence of Sage's pain and the El's together, and she hesitated, afraid. But her heart was stronger than her fear, and she drew a breath and reached out and shared their pain; and she sensed Ramo's stunned awareness and reached out to him too; and she felt the haunting rhythm of the music, Eddie mourning in response to Sage's pain, though Sage didn't know it; and Pali poured what she felt into Lingrhetta and through him she poured it into the Inner Circle, who shared her mind whether they wanted to or not.

And losing herself in the pain, she wept bitterly not just for Sage and Harybdartt, but for all those other sons and daughters in the space cities and on Earth whose lives, with each passing moment, were in greater peril.

And she felt the Ell, bewildered, weep for them, too.

Even Moramaharta didn't know how it had happened, but the meditation now sang clear across the light-years, out of the *Ell* Circle to that other circle of the Human song, the *muzik* and the grief and the fear. Moramaharta had started the process, turning the binding outward, but now it was beyond his control; it was growing like a fantastic crystal, facet upon facet, and the light that had flickered deep in the *Ell* memory was now burning brightly, ever more brightly. If only they could decipher the reflections. . . .

*

Human sorrow

*

*with *Ell* shared*

*

resonates

*

glimmers through

*

passions

*

now waking.

*

Something was forming that was greater than the meditation, encompassing the Circle and changing the form of the
visible world around them. The trees were no longer just shadowy figures towering against the sky and the light of the nebula;
they were a part of the binding, their presence joining with the
Ell's. Time itself seemed to flow and change; there was an
awareness both of the slow seep of water in the earth, and of
the passing of the wind, nourishing and fertile. The wind,
ever-changing with its knowing touch, had joined into the
binding and become a living part of it. And the sky—the silent
stars and the Anvil gazing down at them in their clearing in
the forest, little concerned with Ell or Humanity—it too had
grown into the binding, neither thinking nor speaking, but
living.

*

A ring of unity

*

shimmers like ice

*

hardening

*

myriad facets gleaming

*

illuminating and

*

concealing.

*

The binding was transforming itself into a giant clear glacier
of singing ice, facets and flaws refracting memory and spirit in
a thousand directions. An Ell spirit, reawakening in the gestalt,

displaced the Human outcry, subduing its appeal . . . and then something exploded through the binding in the final moments before the ice hardened—and that was the voice of a distant El, his pain echoing that of the Human Sage and merging with it, and out of the merging blossomed a new gestalt of Human and Ell spirit together . . .

*

Kent
*
Tony
*
friend
*
brother
*
lost
*

. . . cried Harybdartt—and Sage—one voice across the light-years.

And the desolation and grief in their cry altered the binding in the moment that it hardened. The crystal was shot through with flaws that refracted Harybdartt's pain, and Sage's; and the Circle, held deep in the matrix of the binding, could not see the world *except* through the pain of Human and Ell together, sharing . . . and the *muzik* of the Humans resonated through the binding, *muzik* haunted by grief and forged of unity between one Human and one El . . .

*

Two as one
*
enemies joined
*

And the need of the two, as one, echoed and whispered among the stars, and among the trees and the wind, which recognized no difference between the two, their needs and pain identical.

And the Circle was caught helpless in the glacier that was the binding, the binder himself unable to change it even if he had the will; and from the very deepest of the *Ell* memories emerged spirits long forgotten . . .

*

Sorrow's compassion
*
loss for one is for all
*
pain denied
*
is prolonged
*

* *

Hardness of spirit protects
*
integrity of thought
*
and memory
*
and body
*

* *

But of what use protection
*
for a spirit
*
grown cold?
*

And within the deep recesses of Moramaharta's mind, in a place never before touched by the *montan'dri,* there came a springtime melting of ice, of the deepest permafrost . . . and the melting touched not only Moramaharta but Dououraym, and Gwyndhellum and Lenteffier and Cassaconntu—and across the stars, Lingrhetta and Harybdartt. And for all of them it was as though time itself were frozen and only now, ever so slowly, melting.

For Pali, it was as though time were being torn asunder— at one extreme of her consciousness turning as slowly as a galaxy in the night, while at the other end, it could not be fleeing more quickly as—by the hundreds and thousands—the people of her world were dying.

The battle was a blurred image in the rapture-field, the destruction silent and unceasing: ships firing and colliding . . . a space station turned to a brief sun and then ashes . . . the attacking fleet shifting, some lost and some retreating . . . and on the tacticals the worst news of all, another Ell fleet approaching fast.

And twisting in the torn web of time was Sage, frozen in his grief with Harybdartt . . . and Eddie, as ever, singing out uncomprehendingly, sharing the pain. But it was up to someone else to stop it.

The children of her world were dying!

And somehow, she found the strength to realize that *someone must stop it,* and a final time she cried out to the frightened, frozen Ell: [*Please stop . . . !*]

The melting was unstoppable, hot rivulets of emotion were streaming through the binding, but still no one could move to alter what was, until the cry from the stars . . .

*

Please stop!

*

. . . shifted the pressure somewhere, and the glacier shivered apart, freeing the Circle to look around wildly and to absorb the image . . .

*

(Fleet)

*

attacking without mercy
*
destroying a world
*
and a link
*

And before the image had even focused in the center of the binding, Moramaharta's and Dououraym's minds caught each other and drew the others close, and the command crystallized clear and hard.

And the vortex blossomed open to the secondary fleet, not yet in battle and still able to receive . . .

*
To !!Ghint
*
message:
*
STOP ATTACK!
*
STOP!
*

And the song of the stars fell to a whisper as they waited and listened, sorrowfully, for confirmation.

Chapter 49

The message from outreach could not have been more unexpected. !!Ghint was in a low orbital sweep coming up on an Outsider station when the message came from the backup (fleet): "STOP ATTACK!"

For an instant, he couldn't take his attention from the planet looming in his readers, from the cluster of Outsider interceptors closing on his wing, from the growing metallic structure that was the enemy target. Finally he absorbed the message. "Repeat!" he demanded, unbelieving.

Outreach repeated: "Relayed from the Circle by the (fleet), a thought-vortex message: *Stop attack!*"

For another instant he wondered if it could be an enemy deception, if he ought to complete his attack while awaiting confirmation. The Outsider world was so large now and misty before him . . . so close . . . so vulnerable at last. . . .

But had the enemy ever before broken outreach? Could he assume they had now?

His nails nearly tore his suit as he forced himself to reply: "All wings: alter course . . . away and retreat. . . ."

The rapture-field was a well of silence. There were no words; but in the tactical display the attacking fleet could be seen drawing away, and the second Ell fleet veering from its approach. Sage watched unblinking, emptied of grief. He had no words left in him at all, only a profound gratitude, and the comfort of his friends. It was all he needed now, all he wanted.

The rapture-field let him down onto the platform and went dark. Sage stumbled in his exhaustion, but waiting hands caught him and helped him away to the lounge. Ramo and Pali were already there, with Kyd. "Here, Sage," Kyd murmured, guiding him to a seat.

Sage looked at her muddleheadedly. For a moment, he wondered if she was real, if what he had just been through was real. He looked into Pali's eyes and then knew, and a laugh escaped his lips. "We did it?" he whispered.

Pali closed her eyes and nodded serenely.

Sage gazed past her to Ramo. The artist was silent, brows furrowed in thought, chin resting on his folded hands. He gazed back at Sage with an expression that rarely appeared on his face: respect. Before either of them could speak, two of the Secretary's aides strode into the lounge. Sage looked up at their nervous faces and felt all of his weariness congeal in the pit of his stomach. The job was not done. With a sigh, he and the others rose and followed the aides—knowing that it would not be done until they had explained everything and answered every question, probably a dozen times over.

How strange, this feeling of relief, of joy! The core was reminded of the first time it had experienced dance—the rush of sensation, unfamiliar but satisfying. There was a great deal to be explored in these feelings, but first there remained urgent tasks to perform.

Though the attack was ended, a permanent peace was still to be won. Few on Earth even knew that they had been at war for the past three years. To them, the Ell attack had been without cause or provocation, and the cost in Human lives had been high, though it could have been much higher. There would have to be reconciliation on Earth before there could be any with the Ell, and the Company and the Secretary's government would have to bear much of the burden of it.

And, too, there was the colony fleet still orbiting an unsuitable world, awaiting instructions.

Indeed, a great deal remained to be done—but actually, most of it would have to be done by Humans themselves. It might be time for the core to step back into the wings now, to facilitate rather than make strategy, to remove itself from the spotlight; to rest, to reflect, and to dream of other things.

Switching Aggie onto her cabin monitor, Chandra sat down to study the results of the balloting. There were so many thoughts stewing in her mind, she could barely concentrate on the numbers. Once she blinked and forced her mind clear and read what was on the screen, though, the distractions fled.

The three starship crews had voted overwhelmingly to follow the recommendation of the command staff to leave the Argus system and seek a new destination. Only a small minority wished to return to Earth, and a smaller group still wanted to stay and challenge (in vengeance? she wondered) whatever dreadful life-force it was that had destroyed their crewmates.

Voting, she'd felt, was the only fair way to make the decision. As flag commander, she had the authority to decide for the fleet, particularly since Captains Khumalo and Fitzpatrick had concurred with her judgment to abandon this world; or she could have awaited orders from Earth. But the starships were cities as well as vessels, and she believed that the citizens had a right to their own voice.

Of course, it wasn't as simple as just setting out to a new star. They had no destination; and before the ships could undertake another journey, they needed fueling and overhauling; and though half the Ell fleet had left the system mysteriously some days ago, there remained alien ships nearby with unknown intentions. Regardless of the vote, the fleet would be here for a while.

There was a chime, and Aggie interrupted Chandra's thoughts. "We've just received an update from Earth via the messenger-probe."

"Let me see it."

Aggie displayed the message. It was a long one, but the opening sentence made her smile: "THIS IS TO ADVISE THAT A CEASE-FIRE IS NOW IN EFFECT . . ."

She read on, and soon her eyebrows went up. "STAND BY FOR ORDERS TO MEET WITH THE ELL FLEET IN ARGUS SYSTEM. . . ."

"I think our other questions can wait until you've had some sleep," the Secretary said to Sage and Ramo. "There's no doubt we owe you an enormous debt of gratitude." He rubbed his temples as one of his aides whispered something in his ear. Martino nodded and cleared his throat. "Yes. As Mr. Clancy has just reminded me, there is one question that needs to be raised." He scowled, drumming his fingers. "I assume it's safe to say that in your . . . work . . . you came across various forms of classified information that, to put a fine point on it, the Company would rather you hadn't seen?"

Sage had wondered when somebody was going to mention that. "I suppose so," he answered. "But I don't remember that much of it. We saw things, but once the enhancements disappeared . . ." He shrugged wearily. Of course, he didn't know what might come back to him later. He looked at Ramo, who nodded assent.

The Secretary hmm'd, perhaps believing him, perhaps not. "Well. It's the Company you'll have to convince. There are some Company officials who are rather anxious to speak with you, but I've insisted on your need to rest first."

Need to rest was all Sage heard. Lord, yes, he thought. But Martino had one more thing to say. "The core has requested that you stay on call for a while. But you'll still be answering to me. Any problem with that?"

Sage shrugged and got to his feet. "Nope," he muttered. "Good night." He stumbled going out the door, and was only dimly aware of Kyd and Ramo supporting him all the way back to his room and laying him out to sleep.

"So," Ramo said, stifling a yawn as he peered at Kyd. They were standing alone in the carpeted hallway of the guest quarters. He didn't want to turn in just yet. He gestured awkwardly. "Now that things are settling down . . . ah, what would you say to our spending a little time together?" He scuffed the carpet with his heel, astounded to realize that he actually felt embarrassed. "I mean—nothing in particular, you understand, just that—" He fumbled and ran out of words.

Kyd grinned. Her emerald eyes looked tired, but they were gorgeous even so.

"Say something. Stop me from making a fool of myself," he pleaded. "God, I'm beat." Even Ramo Romano couldn't run on adrenaline forever.

Kyd leaned toward him and kissed him on the cheek. "Why not?" she said softly. "I'm sure it'll never work, but who knows? You have promise." She pulled back with a smile. "You should know, though, that I'm going to be a mother."

Ramo felt faint. *"What?"*

"As soon as possible."

Blinking, Ramo tried to follow her explanation: something about Nicholas, a fertilized egg frozen until she could afford him, and that was why she'd moonlighted for the feds. . . .

* * *

There was a soft buzzing sound, and the music faded into the background. An abstract holo-figure appeared, gyrating slowly in the center of the field. It was vaguely humanoid in size and shape, but translucent and multicolored. It moved rather like a dancer stretching. Sage, breathing hard, stared at it for a moment before saying, "Core?"

The figure bent in a gesture resembling a bow. "How do I look?" asked an airy voice.

Sage exchanged stunned glances with the others before approaching the image. "Well . . . great," he said. "We're just a little . . . surprised, I guess. We weren't expecting you to appear right here—I mean, looking like—"

"This?" A wave of crimson passed through the figure. "I was hoping you'd like my new look."

"It's terrific," Ramo said. "How is our patient doing?"

"Recovering nicely—and by the way, wishes to thank you for saving its life." The figure pulsed for a moment, then added, "I thought I'd done enough impersonating of human beings for a while."

"Aw, shucks," Ramo said—and blew the core a kiss.

The core froze for an instant, then flickered like an exploding rainbow, losing its humanoid shape. Sage wondered if it had lost its composure; but after a moment, it regained its shape and blew a kiss back at Ramo. The kiss, a twinkling point of light, darted and spiraled in the air and then floated slowly to touch Ramo's cheek. It vanished with a tiny splash of color. Ramo grinned.

"I wanted to talk to you before you rejoined Odesta's people," the core said.

"More work!" Ramo cried. "Core, we love you, but Martino won't let us leave this place until you tell him you don't need us anymore."

The core chuckled, rotating and changing shape. "I'll speak to him. I know he's worried about the ComPol—but I've already taken care of that."

"Taken care of it how?" Pali asked. No agents had been allowed to talk with them since the end of the crisis, which was a status that they all hoped to maintain.

"I've spoken with the executives of the Company and the chief of the ComPol," the core answered.

"And?"

The core laughed softly. "They called it extortion. But really, I just stated my case firmly." Sage and the others looked at one another with raised eyebrows. "I don't think you'll be bothered," the core continued. "But I do hope you'll stay around to help."

"No sweat," Ramo said. "Do you need us right now?"

"Not for that—although Harybdartt did say that he'd like to join you for the next jamdam; and actually, that's what I wanted to talk to you about."

More glances were exchanged.

"It wasn't my order that you couldn't be flown there to attend in person, but I am glad in one respect. I hope to attend with you, myself, and I was—"

"Yes?" Ramo said perplexedly.

"Well . . . wondering if you would mind helping me . . ." The figure began to shift and change restlessly.

"Yes?"

". . . learn to dance?"

EPILOGUE

Will you, won't you, will you, won't
you, will you join the dance?
—LEWIS CARROLL

In the deeps of the planet, life continued unchanged—or nearly so. Those who were without name had tasted blood for the first time in millennia, and somewhere within them the experience had worked the beginning of a change.

Something unexpected had cried out in that first kill, and the cry had hurt the hunters almost as much as it had the hunted. It had been a terrible, piercing pain, and it had awakened something deeper still, a reminder of an agony long buried. They hated that pain, the reminder, and yet . . . they wondered at it. If they could, they would lash out again, kill again—just to feel that hurt, to know it, to know it for what it was.

From their world of dank, stony darkness they reached out; they extended their senses and listened. The invaders were drawing away, all of them. Even those circling closest to this world were departing now—not beyond the reach of the creatures' awareness, but beyond their ability to kill.

But they would be back. One day, surely, they would be back. . . .

Chapter 50

Moramaharta stood on the ridge with Dououraym and gazed silently at the rising sun. He scarcely felt the chill, though the wind whipped at their robes and the world was powdered with new-fallen snow. He welcomed Dououraym's company here; and yet, more than ever, he felt a craving for solitude and thought.

"I would not expect your reactions to be precisely like mine," he said to the leader. "But do you recognize the greater binding, the deeper connection?"

Dououraym's gaze held to the sun, but Moramaharta felt the leader's thoughts in his and sensed the acknowledgement . . . and the difference. "As you wish solitude, binder," Dououraym said finally, "I feel the need to carry what we have learned to the outer circles, to explore more deeply with other Ell." Dououraym paused as sunlight erupted scarlet and golden through the layered clouds. "Still, I suspect . . . I *feel* . . . that further contact with Humanity . . ." He paused.

"Will be necessary. Yes," Moramaharta said. "And desirable."

Dououraym shifted to look at the binder. "You suspected early on that it was so."

"The Circle suspected."

"But you believed. We suspected, but we did not believe, did not perceive. With another binder . . . we can only wonder what might have happened. It might have been a long and futile quest indeed."

Moramaharta made no answer, and a silence settled in between them. Moramaharta turned around to watch the Anvil of Light fade in the western sky, then turned back to a brightening sun. He wondered what sunrise looked like on the Human's homeworld, wondered if an Ell such as himself would ever visit Earth, or a Human come here. For the present, only three ships of !!Ghint's fleet were to remain in Earth's system; and the Human starships were far too sluggish to come here anytime soon, though their robots could perhaps make the trip if the location was one day revealed.

But Harybdartt remained still in the Human midst and had indicated a desire to stay awhile, to try to come to know the enemy-that-was-no-longer-an-enemy. A strange role for a space-defender trained in the ways of battle; and yet perhaps there was something to be learned from that—assumptions to be changed, assumptions about the inevitability and change-lessness of roles.

The sun was dazzling now, illuminating Dououraym's lean, angular face. He seemed to be smelling the wind. "Another thought," the leader said after gazing into the sun for a time. "The Hope Star."

"Whether to recall the (fleet)?"

"No. Whether to seek the aid of the Humans."

Moramaharta was startled. "To what purpose?"

Dououraym closed his eyes, snapping his nails quietly. "I dream, still, of the Lost Ell."

Moramaharta was suddenly conscious of the cold air whis-tling through his robes. "Even knowing the truth? When there is so much to discover within?" *A true quest?*

Dououraym opened his eyes. "No, you are quite correct about the immediate future. And yet I cannot help wondering —even knowing the danger—what might be learned there one day. Not soon. But one day."

"Death," Moramaharta said.

"Or perhaps a way back from death for the Lost Ell. I was thinking of the Human *muzik,* their way of touching the spirit where we did not even know it could be touched." Dououraym lifted his gaze to Moramaharta's, and a hint of laughter and sadness seemed to pass through his eyes. "I am only thinking, binder. The old quest dies hard. But perhaps you are right again. Perhaps we should leave that world forever and warn all others away. And yet . . ."

Moramaharta's breath puffed out of his membranes and condensed in the cold air as he acknowledged Dououraym's longing. "After we are gone from this Circle, and perhaps from this world?"

"Certainly, binder. As I said . . . not soon." Dououraym snugged his robe about him. "Come. Let us return. There are decisions to be rendered, and one of them is whether Or!ge should contact the Human armada before returning from the Hope Star."

"After you, leader," Moramaharta said, gesturing down the path. "After you."

[*Endeavor*, you are cleared to break formation. Good hunting, and be careful.]

Captain Fitzpatrick's voice echoed inside Chandra's head. [Thanks, Chandra. But if anyone needs to be careful, it's you. Don't get fleeced when you bargain with the natives.]

Chandra laughed, something she had not done often lately. [What natives? We're all tourists here, Roger. *Aleph* out.]

A minute later she watched the other starship's engines glow to life. *Endeavor* slowly pulled away from its two companions; it was bound outward from Argus and its sun. While *Aleph* and *Columbia* were engaged in diplomacy with the Ell fleet, *Endeavor* would be exploring the fourth planet of the system, a gas-giant, to test the feasibility of mining the frozen atmospheres of its moons for fuel. If the operation proved successful, the other two ships would follow later. Fuel could theoretically be shipped from Earth via stargate, but only in small tankloads. Chandra preferred to seek a supply here.

It was impossible not to think wistfully of the miracle of the stargate as they looked ahead to another years-long journey; but Earth had informed them, with regret, that the stargate technology could not be used to help them on their way. Only one living being had ever survived a stargate passage, and that was an El. Earth science was working on the problem, of course; but for the immediate future, only robot probes could make use of the new technology. In the meantime, stargate-traveling probes would be used to search for a friendlier world for the colony to settle.

For now, the fleet had another assignment. [Aggie,] Chandra said. [Anything further on the Ell communication problem?]

[Affirmative, Chandra,] the AI reported. [We've just received translation routines from the messenger-probe, and I'm assembling those now into the scout AI systems.]

[So we'll be able to talk to them?]

[To a degree.]

[Anything else?]

[The following message also arrived: "ELL FLEET HAS BEEN ADVISED THAT YOU MAY ATTEMPT PERSONAL COMMUNICATION VIA RAPTURE-FIELD. RECOMMEND YOU PROVIDE SEVERAL SUCH FIELDS AND INCLUDE IN YOUR CONTACT PARTY MUSICIANS AND DANCERS."]

[Is that a joke, Aggie?]

[I don't believe so, Captain. A case history was provided which may shed some illumination. Shall I present it to you?]

[Later,] Chandra said. She shifted her attention to the tracking image of the Ell ships spiraling outward from Argus. It was time now for *Aleph* and *Columbia* to maneuver to meet them. [Pilot,] Chandra said. [Commence orbit maneuver when ready. Com, tell *Columbia*.]

She watched as the orders were executed and the alarms sounded, and felt a gentle tug as the engines lit and the ship got under way. And she thought to herself: Musicians and dancers? To meet the Ell?

[Aggie,] she said. [Follow Earth's recommendations for the scout. I'm sure we'll find out why.]

If the war had produced one benefit, it was that in the end the core had learned something of Humanity—both the culture that had created it and the spirit to which it aspired. The war had put the core through a steep learning curve; but thanks to certain friends, it had not only survived, it had prospered.

There were others, it well knew, who would thank neither the core nor anyone else for the war; and those victims could be numbered on both sides, Human and Ell. Finding a way to reckon with its share of that responsibility was yet another part of the learning curve. It wasn't easy, the core thought—this business of sentience, of being near-Human.

As communication with the Ell proceeded, the curve was likely to be extended. The core had a good deal to learn from Harybdartt and others still in the solar system, and from Lingrhetta and the Ell homeworld. Perhaps the Ell would one day divulge the location of their world, but the core was in no hurry. What it desired most was knowledge of Ell ways and Ell thought, of their scientific paradigms, their cultures, their religions and philosophies. There was more to learn than the core knew how to catalog or anticipate.

If the core had a single overriding motive now, it was to learn, and to learn, and to learn. The Company had its business needs, and the government its political needs, and the core would honor those—but not at the expense of its own integrity. If the needs of the Company and the needs of the core conflicted . . . well, there were ways of balancing.

For one thing, the core planned to allow Silverfish and Odesta's networking operation to continue—not without probing once in a while to keep them on their toes, but also with freedom to see where their efforts might lead. If it cost the Company in profits, well, there was a debt owed—for the music and the support. And as long as the jamdams continued, it intended to be there listening.

It was a slow-paced kind of thing, just Lip and Eddie making music together, strings and voice, and plenty of mood—what the core understood to be a romantic theme. The core was dancing slowly and easily, joining Ramo and Kyd in gentle pirouettes. The movements were broad enough, and yet quick enough, that the core could allow its figure to expand and swirl its limbs outward with the movement. It was a relaxing feeling, and more than that, a feeling that it was using its figure in the right way for the mood, for the music.

Sage was at the edge of the field, his image dancing slowly with Elina's. Sage was learning, along with the core, learning the skill and the expression, and the feeling that lay beneath the expression.

The core was content. The feeling and the expression would come in time. And one thing the core had now was time.

The music picked up in tempo. As the core responded, it caught Ramo's eye, and Ramo snapped his fingers and moved back from the center with Kyd, and Sage and Elina and Pali and everyone else turned to watch—and the core bounded and reached *high* on Eddie's high note and floated and spun, pulsing colors—and came down skittering to the beat and joined with the pulse of the others. And it struck the core that this time no one was laughing, no one mimicking; and though everyone was staring, it was in appreciation and wonder.

And from somewhere outside the field of view, and far away, it heard the approval of clicking nails.